SILENT
AS THE GRAVE

ALSO BY ZOE AARSEN

Light as a Feather
Cold as Marble

SILENT
AS THE GRAVE

BY ZOE AARSEN

SIMON PULSE
NEW YORK   LONDON   TORONTO   SYDNEY   NEW DELHI

SIMON PULSE
An imprint of Simon & Schuster Children's Publishing Division
1230 Avenue of the Americas, New York, New York 10020
First Simon Pulse edition September 2020
Text copyright © 2020 by Zoe Aarsen
The author is represented by Wattpad.
Cover illustration copyright © 2020 by Avery Muether
All rights reserved, including the right of reproduction in whole or in part in any form.
SIMON PULSE and colophon are registered trademarks of Simon & Schuster, Inc.
For information about special discounts for bulk purchases, please contact
Simon & Schuster Special Sales at 1-866-506-1949 or business@simonandschuster.com.
The Simon & Schuster Speakers Bureau can bring authors to your live event.
For more information or to book an event contact the Simon & Schuster Speakers Bureau
at 1-866-248-3049 or visit our website at www.simonspeakers.com.
Cover designed by Laura Eckes
Interior designed by Mike Rosamilia
The text of this book was set in Adobe Garamond Pro.
Manufactured in the United States of America
2 4 6 8 10 9 7 5 3 1
Library of Congress Cataloging-in-Publication Data
Names: Aarsen, Zoe, author.
Title: Silent as the grave / by Zoe Aarsen.
Description: First Simon Pulse paperback edition. | New York : Simon Pulse, 2020. |
Series: [Light as a feather ; 3] | Summary: "McKenna has managed to rid Violet of the curse claiming
the lives of so many in Willow, Wisconsin, but evil still plagues the town. McKenna's friend Mischa now
carries the curse, and when it comes for her family, she pledges revenge on those she deems responsible
for their deaths . . . including McKenna and everyone she holds dear"—Provided by publisher.
Identifiers: LCCN 2020020698 (print) | LCCN 2020020699 (eBook) | ISBN 9781534444348
(hardcover) | ISBN 9781534444331 (paperback) | ISBN 9781534444355 (eBook)
Classification: LCC PZ7.1.A145 Sil 2020 (print) | LCC PZ7.1.A145 (eBook) | DDC [Fic]—dc23
LC record available at https://lccn.loc.gov/2020020698
LC ebook record available at https://lccn.loc.gov/2020020699

FOR DEBORAH WOLF

CHAPTER 1

IT WAS HOT IN TAMPA, EVEN IN APRIL.

No one else seemed to notice the heat, but every morning when I put on shorts and a T-shirt for school, it struck me as odd. If I were at home in Willow, I'd still be wearing sweaters at that time of year. Possibly even a winter coat. Whenever my thoughts drifted toward life back in Wisconsin, my throat grew tight, and I had to blink away tears. Being a new student with no friends in an unfamiliar town wasn't at all how I'd imagined my junior year of high school back in September. Although I did my best to hide my disappointment about my circumstances, I walked around Florida feeling like an anvil in my chest was weighing me down.

So it was better for everyone—mostly me—not to think about things happening outside of the neighborhood where I'd been sent to live with my dad and his wife. And it was *definitely* for the best that I not allow myself to get caught up in imaginary scenarios about what might be unfolding in my hometown. There wasn't much I could do about it, and the little I could do, I'd already done.

Aside from my constant discomfort from the unrelenting humidity, I'd become accustomed enough to my routine in Florida

1

that sometimes—just for a minute or two—I'd forget everything that had led me there. I'd be focused on trying to determine the value of a cosine, or join in on a discussion in my Federal Government class and forget all about Olivia Richmond's birthday party back in September. The game, Violet, all of the death—everything would drop from my thoughts as if it had never happened.

But then, with a jolt, it would come back to me. A familiar sensation of dread would rush in, and my heart would ache at the thought of how much I'd left behind. My mom. Our little house on Martha Road. The friends I'd known since I was born. Trey . . . When I thought about how much time had passed since I'd last seen him, and how much more would pass before I'd see him again, it felt like a knife slicing through my heart. My daily existence was like having a nightmare about knowing I was supposed to be somewhere else, doing urgent other things, except I was awake.

Dad and his wife, Rhonda, kept encouraging me to make new friends and "create a life for myself." But I had to admit, I wasn't trying very hard at that. I was eager to get back to the life I'd left behind, even though in a few small ways, I was clinging to fragments of it as best I could. One of the ways in which I was desperately hanging on was by FaceTiming with Henry Richmond every morning.

"So, what is it that you do at your job?" he asked. He was standing out on the small balcony of his studio, and I could see the sparkling teal waves of the Mediterranean behind him. Henry had been teaching private tennis lessons as one of the staff instructors at Château du Mouton d'Or on France's Cote d'Azur since February.

"Whatever they ask me to do," I replied. "I mean, I've only worked there a week, so I'm still kind of learning."

The last time I saw him in Wisconsin, I didn't expect to see or hear from him again. But he'd surprised me by calling during my first week in Florida. His lunch break just happened to coincide with my morning alarm clock setting. Even after weeks of this routine, I hadn't gotten over how simultaneously comforting and weird it was to be able to see his face in real time from five thousand miles away. Mom and I FaceTimed often, but seeing Henry in France was a million times more magical. Even though he wasn't physically *in* Willow, he knew that all of the traumatic, paranormal things I'd experienced over the better part of the last year had been *real*. Since I couldn't talk freely with Trey on the phone, and Mischa didn't remember the details of how we'd broken the curse on Violet in January, Henry was the only person with whom I could regularly communicate who truly understood the complexity of my life.

And although he never said so, I think he felt the same way about me. It wasn't like he could tell his coworkers at the hotel that he'd spent his winter break chasing a bunch of high schoolers around Michigan to avenge the death of his sister. Secrets were burdens, and secrets like the ones we kept were walls that separated us from people who would never, ever understand the things we'd witnessed.

"What kind of things?" Henry pressed. "You said you're working in a assisted living facility, and you're in Florida. So are you yelling at people for not wearing enough sunscreen at the pool? Organizing shuffleboard tournaments?"

"No, it's not like that," I said with a smile. "I bring the patients their mail, sometimes help them open it and read it. I clean up around their rooms, bring them dinner. Mostly it's just . . ." I paused, not wanting my job to sound as sad as it sometimes was. There was one resident, Ruth, who rarely said more than five words a day to me, but she never failed to whip out a deck of cards and challenge me to a quick game of War when I stopped by her room. At work, I was simply known as the new girl. No one at the assisted living facility thought of me as a troublemaker with mental problems, which was unfortunately my reputation back at home in Wisconsin. It was enormously satisfying to make such a big difference in people's lives with small gestures like remembering who liked tapioca pudding and who needed to be reminded when *Jeopardy!* came on, especially after I'd felt like such a colossal failure for months while trying to figure out how to save Mischa from becoming Violet's next victim. "It feels nice to do kind things for people who appreciate it."

I'd been begging to be allowed to take a part-time job since arriving in Florida, wanting my own source of income and a reason to get out of my dad's condo after school for a few hours a day. It had been tough convincing my dad that I could keep up with my schoolwork *and* hold down a job. But he'd caved when I was offered a part-time position at Oscawana Pavilion Assisted Living Facility. I guess he figured I couldn't get into much trouble surrounded by senior citizens. There was no way he ever would have let me work at Shake Shack or Starbucks with people my own age.

"Do you have to wear a uniform?" Henry asked. His uniform at the hotel was a light blue polo shirt and a pair of white shorts. I frequently teased him that it made him look like he'd just stepped out of a chewing gum magazine ad from the 1980s. The truth was that he'd gotten very tan in the last few weeks, and he looked so hot that I was sure he was receiving plenty of attention. Something about the probability of women in France noticing Henry made me anxious, although I knew I shouldn't have cared about his romantic endeavors. I would have forfeited my morning chats with Henry in a heartbeat if it had been an option to instead talk to Trey every day. But I still sensed that I might have felt more than a twinge of jealousy if the morning conversations were to stop because Henry had found a girlfriend.

"Not really a uniform. Just pink scrubs. The nurses wear blue ones."

"Scrubs, huh? Send me a picture."

Back in February, I would have blushed, but we joke-flirted back and forth with such frequency now that it didn't even occur to me to be bashful. "Why do you need a picture? You know what I look like. You're looking at me right now."

"Yeah," he said, "but it's not like I can see you. You're practically in the dark."

He wasn't exaggerating; I was still in bed and hadn't pulled the curtains open yet. "That's because I'm wearing pajamas and my hair's a mess."

"You're gonna be late for school," he said, raising an eyebrow at me.

"Maybe."

Dad would never let that happen. It was quite clear to me that he and Mom were in some kind of silent competition about who was the more responsible parent. I'd gotten into a ton of trouble twice on Mom's watch back in Wisconsin, and even though that wasn't a reflection on the quality of her parenting at all, it fueled some kind of weird obsession of Dad's to do a better job. If I wasn't at the breakfast table downstairs within the next eighteen minutes, I could expect a knock on my bedroom door.

"I've gotta get back outside," Henry said. "I've got a doubles match with a countess."

"Sounds fancy," I teased.

"Oh, it is."

We said good-bye, and I wondered momentarily if the countess was beautiful. I didn't want to think too much about it, but I was curious about why Henry made a point of checking in with me every day instead of walking down to the beach to eat lunch with his coworkers. Curious, but grateful for it. Our past had bound us in a way that was stronger than friendship. Our check-ins meant more to me than I suspected he knew; the few times he'd been a little late calling me, my heart had sunk at the possibility of him having moved on, found something—or someone—else to fill his time.

As always, as soon as I ended my chat with Henry, I wondered what Trey was doing at that very moment. Although I would have loved being able to FaceTime with him instead of writing letters, seeing him on a screen and talking to him might have just broken my heart. There was no way we would see each other again until July at the soonest, when he would turn eighteen and be released from Northern Reserve. Although Henry and I sometimes flirted with each other, it was always in a spirit of silliness. We never came near crossing any lines—not the way he had the night we were alone in his parents' basement and almost kissed. I reassured myself that my dependency on him was because he'd taken on a brotherly role in my life, and not because I was in denial about having feelings for him.

I groaned, stretched, and climbed out of bed. Dad probably wouldn't have been thrilled to know that I began every day by chatting with a friend from home since I'd failed to report having made any new friends in Tampa. Of course, he was right; I wasn't making my semester there any easier by keeping to myself. But I had my reasons for not socially investing myself at my new school. First, I'd lived my entire life up until that point in a tiny town with just over four thousand residents, where I'd been acquainted with everyone and had never had to make new friends. Second, I'd just endured a pretty traumatic experience over the last five months, and I couldn't discuss it with anyone. Not a single person, and especially not Ms. Hernández, the school counselor who I was required to spend my study hall with and who asked me relentless questions that I refused to answer about Violet, Trey, and all the trouble I'd gotten into at home.

The thing was, I viewed my life in Tampa as temporary. I didn't want to settle in and get comfortable—not when I expected Trey would be released in July. I wasn't sure what the future held for us, but finding a way to never be separated from him again superseded everything else.

And then . . . there was the matter of Mischa.

I didn't want to get too comfortable in my new life at all, because of the frail balance on which it hung from a promise she'd made.

I never had the pleasure of hitting snooze on my alarm—even for ten minutes—because I had to cast my protection spell before I left for school. It was a spell given to me by Kirsten, the witch we'd met at the occult bookstore in Chicago. The incantation, meant to protect Mischa and her family members, had to be performed every day, at the same time.

Every single morning, in a clockwise direction, I carefully sprinkled salt around the four white candles on my nightstand in the shape of circle, making four complete circles—for Mischa, her sister, and both of their parents. As I lit each of the four candles, I whispered, "With this candle, I focus my intent and protect Mischa from all that would harm. With this candle, I focus my intent and protect Amanda from all that would harm." And onward, until I'd protected all four members of the Portnoy family.

There were mornings, like that one, when I was cutting it close on time and rushed through the whispering part. But the thought of getting lazy about the amount of intent I applied terrified me. Ever since Mischa had e-mailed me back at the beginning of February talking about her newly discovered powers with tarot cards, I'd been terrified that the evil spirits who had originally tormented Violet until she delivered souls to them had refocused their attention on Mischa.

Violet had told me that when she'd refused to take orders from those spirits at first, they'd threatened her mother's life. I knew that Mischa was strong-willed and that I could count on her to resist their threats, but I also knew that Mischa was a survivor. She was the most determined person I'd ever met. If she were made to feel like she had no choice but to deliver souls or have terrible things happen to her family, Mischa would do whatever it took to protect herself and her loved ones.

In that way, she was even scarier than Violet. In my experience, Violet was selfish and manipulative. But Mischa was fearless, physically strong, and stubborn. I didn't want to have to find out what it might be like to challenge her.

Luckily, two new moons had passed since we'd lifted the curse from Violet, and I hadn't heard any news out of Willow, Wisconsin, about tragic or unexpected deaths yet. Which suggested to me that my protection spell routine was working, and that Mischa had been keeping her promise about staying away from tarot. She'd sworn that she'd never actually given a full reading to anyone after discovering her uncanny ability to always pull the Tower card out of the deck, and I reluctantly believed her.

I blew out my candles, swept the salt into the trash can per Kirsten's instructions, and got dressed, hoping—as I did every day— that I'd just safeguarded the lives of Mischa, Amanda, Elena, and Adam Portnoy for the next twenty-four hours.

"Just in time for the last cup of coffee," Dad said when I finally stepped into the kitchen. He poured the last of the pot into a mug for me as I grabbed a banana off the counter. He was dressed for work, although to anyone other than me and Rhonda, it might have been hard to tell. Dad's work outfits were T-shirts or polos with USF Bulls logos on them instead of just plain T-shirts or polos, and khaki shorts instead of his usual running shorts. He was a professor in the psychiatry and neurosciences department at the University of South Florida's medical school, and from the handful of times I'd accompanied him to campus, his super-casual attire was not uncommon among faculty.

"Don't forget. I won't be home until seven thirty tonight," I reminded him.

"I didn't forget. Text Rhonda when you're ready for a ride home and she'll pick you up," he told me.

I quickly replied, "I can take the bus." A huge part of why I'd wanted to get a job was to gain some independence. Since moving down to Florida, I felt like I was always being watched. Even when I disappeared to the gym in my dad's condominium complex at night after dinner, Rhonda often joined me. She insisted that it was to fire up her metabolism, but I knew the real reason: She and Dad were terrified that I was going to vanish the first chance I got.

"She'll pass by there on the way home from the hospital anyway," he informed me. "Who were you talking to this morning?"

I gulped down some coffee to hide my surprise at his question. Whenever I was chatting with Henry, I tried to keep my voice down so that Dad and Rhonda couldn't hear me because the walls in their condo were thin. "Just a friend from home," I answered honestly.

"When it's six o'clock here, it's five o'clock in Wisconsin," he reminded me, as if I wasn't aware of the time difference. "Kinda early to be talking to someone back at home."

"He's not in Wisconsin," I clarified. "Sometimes I talk to Olivia's brother. He's taking the semester off from school to teach tennis in France." There was no point in lying. I'd only been allowed to have a phone again because both my mom and dad had access to everything, including passwords to all of my accounts. If he wanted to know who I was speaking with every morning, it wouldn't take him long to find out. Henry, Mischa, and even Cheryl knew better than to ever put anything in writing that they wouldn't want my parents to read.

Dad crossed his arms over his chest as he swished coffee around in the mug he held. "Hmm. That Richmond kid, huh? The one who was at the ski lodge with you?"

I hurriedly clarified (not for the first time) that Henry had *not* been at the ski lodge *with* me and Trey, which was the story we'd all been telling for months, and I dashed out the back door to begin my walk to school. Since the end of January, I'd been evading questions

10

from both of my parents about why I'd escaped from the boarding school where I'd been sent in the fall, and how Trey and I had ended up in Michigan to meet up with our former classmates during their ski trip. There was no way I could tell them any of it without sounding like a maniac—that we had to stop Violet before a bunch of people whose deaths she'd predicted were expected to die. I guess I just had to accept that no matter how much time passed, my dad was never going to let it go.

It was barely six thirty in the morning when I reached our corner, and the humidity was already at 70 percent.

My high school in Tampa was a lot larger than Willow High School, with nearly three times as many students. You might think it would be hard to avoid making friends while surrounded by so many people, but I was finding it easy to go unnoticed. Teachers didn't make a big deal on my first day about introducing me. My chemistry partner, Alianne, was nice enough, correctly read my disengaged vibe, and politely ignored me in the cafeteria at lunchtime. No one encouraged me to join clubs or sports teams.

During study hall, I took my usual seat on the red couch in Ms. Hernández's office and we went through our routine, which, at this point, going into my tenth week at Hyde Park High, was becoming rote.

"How are things with your stepmother?" she asked.

"Fine," I replied. I'd made the mistake during my first social work session at school of describing Rhonda as very young and pretty, and had mistakenly given Ms. Hernández the notion that all of my erratic behavior since the fall could be explained by some kind of issue I had with her.

"Has she laid off on the prom pressure?"

"Yes," I said. "For now." Rhonda had read in an e-mail sent out to parents by the principal's office that junior prom would be held in mid-May, and she'd immediately suggested that we go shopping for a dress. It broke my heart a little to tell her that I had no interest in going to a dance in Hyde Park with a bunch of people I barely knew. Even though she wasn't old enough to be my mom, she was really trying hard to fill the role, or at least qualify as world's coolest stepmom.

"What about the boyfriend? How's he doing?" Ms. Hernández asked. She never failed to ask me about Trey during every single one of our sessions, even though I'd never mentioned him.

"As well as can be expected," I replied. The bitter reality was that I didn't know how Trey really was. The one phone call per week I was allowed to have with him was monitored by the administration at his military-style school. Weekly, he told me in a cool, emotionless voice not to worry about him, because everything there was great. This made me suspect that things were far from "great," but there was nothing either of us could do about that until he turned eighteen and was free to leave.

Investing as little energy as possible, I moved through the rest of my classes that day. A surge of joy rose within my chest when the final bell rang. As I stuffed my bag at my locker, I tried to ignore people around me talking about either band practice or a concert that night at the Amalie Arena. Back at the start of the school year in Willow, I'd had a packed calendar too. But there was no point in lamenting the time when I'd been involved in student government and been excited about things like yearbook committee and live music. Those days were over.

Oscawana Pavilion Assisted Living Facility was only about six-teen blocks away from my high school, but it was hot enough when school let out that I'd show up drenched in perspiration if I didn't just wait for the bus. So I popped my earbuds in my ears and tried to remain patient. I was starting to feel anxious and felt the urge to walk to the next stop, assuming I could beat the bus, but I knew I'd never make it in time.

By the time the bus arrived, my scalp had broken out into a rush of tingles. I knew that this was Jennie's way of wanting to initiate contact with me, and since I'd been home in Willow over Christmas break, the tingles had become an increasingly frequent sensation. As always, the physical sensation of being lightly jabbed by needles was accompanied by a potent mixture of emotions that never failed to nauseate me a little. The thrill of being contacted by my twin sister swirled around with panic that I was either going insane—or veer-ing off into a strange lifestyle of having paranormal powers that was going to result in my being considered a total freak by other people.

Even though I'd been finding all sorts of new ways to receive her messages (with varying degrees of effectiveness), Jennie had a way of reaching out to me at moments when it was extremely incon-venient for me to try to respond. Like when I was hanging on for dear life to a pole on a crowded bus. I'd run out of patience for the pendulum; asking Jennie yes-and-no questions could be extremely time-consuming, and I couldn't exactly whip it out in public places.

I did my best to try to ignore the tingles. Whatever it was that Jennie was trying to communicate didn't matter; I had to be at work in fifteen minutes to clock in.

The moment I stepped into the assisted living facility, I was grateful for its excessive air-conditioning. I passed through the lobby, where an elderly man was playing the grand piano for the amusement of several women, some of whom were playing mah-jongg. The lobby had several enormous fish tanks, which were among my favorite things about working there. I tended to take my fifteen-minute break in the lobby just to stare at the fish.

On my way to the bathroom to change into my scrubs, I was greeted by Luis, my manager. "Slight change to your rounds today, honey," he said. I might have taken offense to my boss calling me "honey" except that Luis referred to everyone as "honey." He was an overweight gay man in his forties who seemed to have gotten to know every single resident in the home personally, which endeared him to me. "We've got a new resident in the Daytona wing. Her name is Mrs. Robinson. If she hasn't already placed a dinner order with the kitchen by the time you check in on her, could you walk her through the process?"

The assisted living facility had three floors, and there were four corridors on each of them. My rounds included the east corridor on each floor, each of which had six resident rooms along it. It might not seem like checking in on eighteen senior citizens would take me four whole hours, but every day, it did. I was almost at the end of my shift—the sun had already started setting—by the time I had my first encounter with Mrs. Cherie Robinson, Oscawana's newest resident.

When I knocked on the door to her room, I heard a raspy voice call out, "Come in!"

A thin, frail Black woman sat in the upholstered chair in the corner of the room. Her walker was set beside the chair, and as I entered the room she didn't turn away from her television set, which was tuned in to the local news. "Hi, Mrs. Robinson. I'm McKenna, your evening aide."

"I know," she told me without looking at me. "The nurse told me somebody would come by to help me order dinner. They left a menu around here, but I can't read a damn thing on it."

"I can help you with that," I said cheerfully. Many of the residents had difficulty with farsightedness, but within a few days at Oscawana they usually realized that the cafeteria options didn't change much from day to day, so being able to read the menu wasn't that important. My eyes scanned the room for where the nurse might have left the menu.

As I walked over to the kitchenette counter to retrieve it, Mrs. Robinson asked me, "Aren't you going to introduce your friend?"

Startled, because I hadn't notice anyone enter the room behind me, I looked over my shoulder and didn't see anyone. "I'm sorry. There's no one else here with me," I told her.

"Sure there is. She's right next to you," Mrs. Robinson insisted.

My scalp broke out into a raging storm of pins and needles. It was then, as I stood at the table and took a closer look at the elderly woman where she sat in front of her television, that I noticed the milky white cataracts covering her eyes. Mrs. Robinson was completely blind.

CHAPTER 2

"YOU SEE SOMEONE NEXT TO ME?" I ASKED SOFTLY as I took a step closer to Mrs. Robinson.

She scowled at me playfully. Her white hair had been cut very short, and she wore heavy turquoise earrings that pulled her earlobes downward. "I can't see much of anything. Can barely see *you*. But I can tell she's here. Shame on you if you're ignoring her, because she seems to be quite attached to you."

My scalp was tingling again, and it felt as if my heart was beating loudly enough for Mrs. Robinson to hear it. I sank down into one of the chairs at the table, fully aware that I was cutting it close to the end of my shift and I might be in trouble if I clocked out a few minutes after seven. Naturally, I assumed that this woman was somehow able to sense Jennie's presence even though I couldn't, which thoroughly freaked me out.

"I had a twin sister," I said, but my voice emerged from my throat as more of a hoarse whisper than I intended. "But she died almost eight years ago."

Mrs. Robinson made a grumpy noise, kind of an *umph*, and I couldn't tell if it was an acknowledgment or dismissal of what I'd just

16

told her. After a long pause, she said, "Where I come from, we'd call her *an invisible*. They're all around us, but you're lucky. You have one all to yourself."

She had pronounced "invisible" with such a strong French accent that at first I hadn't understood the word she'd said. I didn't know how to reply. At Dad's, we didn't talk about the fire, or about Jennie. Not ever. I was sure Rhonda knew what had happened, but it was like an unspoken rule that it was a forbidden topic of conversation in Florida. I was completely baffled by how this woman I'd never met before seemed to have known the most important thing about my childhood before I'd even entered her suite.

I asked, "Where do you come from?"

"Born and raised in Louisiana. My daughter brought me here to Florida five years ago, after I had a stroke. She said she couldn't trust me to live alone anymore."

"Your daughter lives in Tampa?" I asked, not wanting to press too hard with my questions in case Mrs. Robinson was upset about having been "dumped" in the assisted living facility, as several of our residents were.

"Oh, yes. She's a big star over here. She does the weather report on Channel Eight," Mrs. Robinson informed me with pride. "I was staying with her and her husband for a while, but I just can't take the stairs in their house. I've got bad knees and bad hips. Arthritis. And the humidity doesn't help."

"Well, we're glad to have you here," I assured her. "We should put in your dinner order. It's almost seven."

Ignoring me, or perhaps just eager to get back onto the topic of invisibles now that she'd found someone she assumed qualified as an appropriate audience, Mrs. Robinson told me, "My daughter doesn't like when I talk about voodoo. Especially around here. She says people who aren't from the bayou don't want to hear about *loa* and *mystères*. She thinks that kind of talk scares you city folk. But then you show up in my suite with an angry invisible following you!" She chuckled. It hadn't escaped my attention that she'd referred to Jennie as "angry." "Just goes to show, voodoo's everywhere. It's the way the universe works, *ma chèrie*."

Before moving to Florida, I'd never been farther south than Chicago, so I knew very little about bayous or the practice of voodoo. When Kirsten had told me over the winter that I had paranormal abilities, I'd been more alarmed than delighted, and it had taken a while for me to adjust to the idea that my abilities might give me leverage in combating the evil spirits that were issuing orders to Violet. But Mrs. Robinson's awareness of Jennie's presence piqued my interest, even though I wasn't convinced that I wanted to formally develop my connection to the "other side." As much as I longed for my life to be restored to normalcy, Jennie was still reaching out with regularity, and the spell I had to cast every morning to safeguard the Portnoys was a source of stress. Perhaps this Oscawana Pavilion resident could teach me how to communicate with Jennie and find out what she so urgently wanted, as well as aid me in finding a way to break the curse on Mischa without jeopardizing anyone else's safety.

"Okay," I sighed, hoping Luis would be able to correct my time card when I made my way down to the first floor. I didn't want to get in trouble my second week on the job for incurring overtime without getting approval first. And after so many months of chasing Violet in maddening circles, I didn't want to get my hopes up too high that this woman would be able to provide me with actionable answers. "I surrender. Tell me more about this invisible and why she's angry at me."

Mrs. Robinson leaned back in her chair, smiling, and pressed her hands together. "She's not angry at *you*. She's trying to talk to you, and you won't listen!"

"I *am* listening," I insisted. "I don't know how to hear her. Sometimes I ask her questions with a pendulum, but she doesn't always answer. Do you know what she's trying to tell me?"

Mrs. Robinson grew serious and hesitated long enough to make me uncomfortable before speaking again. "You're in a whole lot of trouble. I probably shouldn't even have the likes of you around here, but this life for me is almost over, anyway. Your invisible—your sister, you say? She's stuck underwater in the dark place because she's worried about you."

My blood was running cold. I had no idea what she meant by *the dark place*, but I didn't like the sound of it, or of Jennie being there.

"Now, I can't understand what she's trying to communicate because that message is for you and not me. But you've got *loa* all around you, and she's protecting you from them. You did something to upset them, and whatever it was . . ." She trailed off and closed her eyes, shaking her head as if whatever I'd done was too terrible to put into words.

Afraid, I asked, "What are *loa*?"

"They're the spirits, *ma chèrie*. They bring us messages from the Bondye, but they need to be fed in order to stay strong enough to manage their business," she explained.

I didn't want to ask what the *loa* liked to be fed, or what kind of business they managed. I had a bad hunch where this conversation was headed. "What do they eat?"

Mrs. Robinson pressed her lips together as if trying to decide whether or not to answer me honestly. "They feed on life."

Life. Of course. This conversation was getting to be too much for me. I couldn't go down this road again. I had found a decent balance, with the protection spell, and I couldn't risk that.

"Mrs. Robinson? My shift ended ten minutes ago, and I'm going to get in trouble with my boss," I interrupted her as she went on about *loa*. The sun had completely set during the few minutes that had passed since I'd entered her suite, and I rose from my seat to turn on the overhead lights in the room. "We need to get your dinner order in, or you might have to actually go down to the cafeteria if you want to eat."

She was adamant that she didn't want to socialize that night, so I called down to the cafeteria and placed her order for a bowl of chicken soup and a side of mashed potatoes. I felt my phone buzz in the breast pocket of my shirt and didn't have to check it to know that it was Rhonda, texting me to see if I was ready for her to pick me up. But despite everything, I couldn't make myself step out of the room.

I knew—after everything I had already done and all of the warnings I'd been given by Judge Roberts—that the smart thing to do would have been to bid Mrs. Robinson a good night and leave—go back to Dad and Rhonda's without giving Mrs. Robinson's observations another thought.

But my scalp was still tingling as if I'd rubbed peppermint oil on it. Jennie wanted to communicate.

"Can you teach me how to talk to her? My sister?" I asked. I may have been doomed to light candles for the Portnoys for the rest of my life, and I wasn't interested in receiving messages from dead people like a reality TV ghost whisperer. But I couldn't resist the possibility of strengthening my connection to Jennie. Finding a way to communicate effectively with her would have been for me like anyone else having the ability to hop into a time machine and revisit the happiest day of their life. "You're right. I *am* in trouble. I mean, I thought I was out of it, but I might not be."

Mrs. Robinson told me, "I can try. But first, is there any salt around here?"

Each of the suites had a tiny kitchenette: two cabinets, a sink, and a small fridge, and I was pleased to find brand-new, sealed salt and pepper shakers in the cabinet over the sink.

"Good girl," Mrs. Robinson said when I told her she was in luck. "Shake salt along the perimeter of this room. Right where the wall meets the floor. And do a little extra around the doorway."

As I did what she asked, I felt like a total weirdo. I went somewhat easy on the amount of salt I shook because I didn't want to attract bugs, even though housekeeping would probably vacuum up all of it within the next two days. Despite salt being mostly harmless, I knew I would probably be fired in a heartbeat if Luis were to find out. I wondered why Mrs. Robinson's daughter hadn't sprinkled the salt for her when they'd moved her in earlier that day if it was a priority. Probably because dumping an entire shaker of salt into carpeting was ridiculous.

"The salt keeps the evil out," Mrs. Robinson called to me as I emptied out the rest of the shaker near the door.

"Okay," I announced. "You're all salted up."

"Good. Good," Mrs. Robinson told me, and "Now. When you come back, bring me some filtered water and essential oils—orange, lavender, and clove. And fennel! Don't forget the fennel. And red brick dust."

"Um, I don't know where to get that," I admitted, reluctant to disappoint her but knowing better than to commit myself to something insane, like smashing bricks into dust on my night off. She clearly wasn't going to teach me what I wanted to learn until I fetched the items on her wish list, which was frustrating. But I couldn't blame Mrs. Robinson for taking advantage of the situation. In the eight long years since Jennie had died, I'd only been able to communicate clearly with her once beyond simple yes-and-no answers to questions, and that had been at Christmastime, when she'd appeared in the form of a ghost that was rumored to roam along a highway during snowstorms. Having to wait another two days shouldn't have felt like as much of a punishment as it did.

"Then eggshells. You can peel them off boiled eggs if you have to. Just bring me eggshells, as many as you can," she said. "And sprinkle some salt and pepper in your shoes before you go to the store. Don't want you handling my business with evil following you around."

I have to admit, I began to wonder about the validity of her advice when she issued the order about the salt and pepper in the shoes, and I vowed to Google the authenticity of that as an actual voodoo practice later on. "I don't work on Tuesdays. But I'll bring it all on Wednesday."

I didn't know what Mrs. Robinson had in store for me, but I was lost in thought on the ride home with Rhonda. It was troubling to think that the *loa*, or Violet's evil spirits, were mad at me, specifically, and surrounding me. Nothing ghostly had ever happened in my bedroom in Florida, and I'd never sensed any strange presences around me either. My heart was fluttering at the prospect of learning a better way to exchange information with Jennie. But icy terror was tickling at the tips of my fingers and toes at the possibility that Mrs. Robinson's guidance might broaden my knowledge about the curse that was now on Mischa. As much as I was hopeful about finding a better way to protect Mischa, I genuinely dreaded the prospect of getting pulled back into the death trap that Violet had sprung on me and my friends back in September.

"Have a good day at school?" Rhonda asked.

"It was fine," I said. "I have a ton of calculus homework."

Behind the wheel, she shook her head. "Calculus. I didn't even take precalculus until senior year. You've got a head for math. When I was your age, I just did not have the patience."

Rather than asking her what her interests at my age were, which I knew she was hoping I would, I let the conversation die off. I was preoccupied with thoughts of whether or not Violet's spirits had the ability to take their aggressions out on me if they thought I was tampering with Mischa's obligations to them. It had certainly seemed like they'd been able to manipulate elements in the real world in the past to try to prevent me from making progress toward breaking the curse on Violet. They'd managed to drop an enormous icicle on Henry's windshield back in January, shattering it. I suspected they'd caused my mom and Mrs. Portnoy to get into a fender bender over the winter too. The spirits' power in our world seemed to require an enormous amount of energy on their part, which meant that the actions they were able to manifest were spur-of-the-moment and delivered in quick bursts. Even if they were fastidious planners, they seemed incapable of hatching elaborate plots, which was a small comfort. But now that I was dwelling on it, I'd been in Florida for two and a half months without experiencing any moments of dread or terror, which seemed suspicious.

Maybe they were waiting for me to get good and distracted before they made their move, so they'd catch me off guard. It was a lucky thing that Mrs. Robinson had stepped into my life to remind me that the danger was ever-present. Or *was* it? It had been weeks since I'd gone down a mental rabbit hole of paranoia like this, wondering if I was fearing the right things and if I had anything truly to fear at all.

We were about halfway through eating dinner before I sensed the awkward tension between Rhonda and Dad. I had just swallowed a large gulp of water when I realized that they were both eating in silence, and Dad occasionally glanced over at me with a stern look. My stomach sank. I had been trying to follow orders, be helpful around the house, and not be a nuisance. Living with them was a privilege, and I was desperate to avoid being sent back to the Sheridan School for Girls.

"Is everything okay?" I dared to ask.

"Fine," Rhonda said curtly, making it clear that she was lying. I liked Rhonda, but she could be passive-aggressive.

"You guys are being really quiet," I said, convinced that in one way or another, they were fighting, and the reason for their fight had something to do with me.

After dinner, I loaded the dishwasher without being asked. Dad went straight to the living room to watch one of the crime shows he loved. Instead of walking over to the gym, Rhonda went upstairs to the bedroom she and Dad shared. I genuinely hoped that I hadn't inadvertently offended her on our drive back from the assisted living facility. Later, while I was trying to do homework, my phone buzzed with incoming messages. When I finally took a break from what little progress I was making and took a look at my Instagram account, I saw that the messages were from Mischa. She was freaking out, claiming that weird things had started happening with increasing frequency, and she was pretty sure something *very* bad was imminent. Before I even read the fourth message in the string of short, urgent notes she'd sent, I tapped the contacts on my phone to call her. Hearing from her on the same day as having Mrs. Robinson tell me I was surrounded by angry *loa* was enough to completely shake me.

"Why are you *calling me*?" she asked.

"Because I don't want to text about this stuff! You *know* my parents spy on my social media accounts!" I exclaimed. "What is going on? You haven't touched any tarot cards, have you?"

"No! God! I said I wouldn't, and I haven't," she insisted. With an uncharacteristic trembling in her voice, Mischa continued, "But listen. They're mad at me for not listening. I don't know how much longer I can keep resisting this." She kind of sounded like she was hiding in a closet from a home invader, terrified of being overheard.

"What's been happening?" I asked, trying to keep my voice low.

"Well, two new moons have passed since January, when I went missing, right? And no one died in January, so technically they didn't get what they wanted from Violet before *that* new moon either. So I'm three behind."

"No," I argued. "*You're* not behind. This was Violet's problem, not yours." Since January, whenever I'd touched base with Mischa, I had made a point of adamantly insisting that she not take responsibility for any part of the situation. Accepting responsibility was like taking ownership, and it seemed dangerous to me for Mischa to mentally acknowledge any of the burden of killing.

Mischa groaned. "Whatever! I keep seeing *threes*. Everywhere I look! And I'm not being paranoid, okay? Last night, the alarm on my phone went off at three thirty-three a.m. And at lunchtime today? I bought an iced tea and carrot sticks in the cafeteria? Three dollars and thirty-three cents. And that's just *today*. For the last few weeks? Every morning when we leave for school, Amanda has to start the car three times. *Three*. It always works on the third try."

I listened without interrupting, mostly because I didn't know what to tell her to convince her to continue resisting. She was in a sickeningly awful predicament. It was one thing to fear for your safety. It was quite another to intentionally *kill* another person.

"Look," I said when it seemed like her rant was over. "I know you're not being paranoid. If anyone on Earth is going to believe that these things aren't just coincidences, it's me."

"So what am I supposed to do? I don't think I can keep ignoring this!"

I had never told Mischa what Violet had relayed to me about her early experiences with the curse after she had inherited it from her grandmother. Telling Mischa that the spirits had electrocuted Violet's mom and nearly killed her when Violet was refusing them seemed like a surefire way to make Mischa whip out a deck of tarot cards and give some unsuspecting kid a death prediction as soon as possible. It made me feel terrible keeping that from her since I had every reason to believe—even though I didn't want to think about it—that eventually the spirits would pursue Mischa's family if they didn't get what they wanted.

"I'm working on this thing every day. I'm so close to finding a way to get it off you. I swear," I assured her. This was wholly untrue because I'd been focused on keeping a low profile in Florida and had been naïvely hoping that things in Wisconsin were under control. But I did feel slightly better about lying to her regarding the status of my progress, because meeting Mrs. Robinson was *something*.

"Well, work faster! I'm honestly, like, scared. And this is super messed up because I qualified last weekend at the state championships to advance to the Region Four meet in three weeks—which is *amazing* considering that I missed two invitational meets and who knows how much practice in January. But instead of throwing myself one hundred percent into training, I'm freaking out about stupid evil spirits! I mean, do you understand how ridiculous this is? I have a real shot at qualifying for the *Olympic team*, and I'm worried about potentially having to *kill people*!"

"Just . . ." I struggled to find convincing enough words to encourage her to keep resisting. I had no reason to believe that Mrs. Robinson's knowledge of voodoo would be of any assistance at all in Mischa's situation. We hadn't even *talked* about Mischa. "Don't predict any deaths, okay? We both know how that ends."

"How much longer?" Mischa demanded. "How am I supposed to believe that you're getting anywhere? Every time you've said you've known what we have to do, you've made things worse!"

My breath caught in my throat. She'd forgotten that I could have easily turned a blind eye after both Olivia and Candace died in the fall. After all, Jennie had protected me from the curse that Violet had issued to them, as well as to Mischa. It was only because I'd wanted so desperately to be part of their close-knit circle—even after Mischa was all that remained of it—that I'd dedicated myself to trying to stop Violet. Maybe I'd been trying to save Mischa because I *hadn't* been able to save Jennie from the fire that had burned down our house when we were eight. But the fact remained that since the fall, I'd wrecked my life—and Trey's—in service to Mischa, and I'd not been under any obligation to do so.

Before I could utter a word, I heard Mischa sob over the phone. "I'm sorry. I know this isn't your fault, and you're the only person I can count on. I'm just scared," she said through her tears.

"I know. And I *am* trying. I *will* figure this out," I promised.

I ended our call feeling like my heart was as heavy as a brick. It was so easy down here in Florida to simply not think too seriously about what was happening back in Willow. All I really wanted to think about was Trey being released from Northern. If I were to insert myself back into the workings of this curse, I'd be risking any kind of future with him. Or any kind of future at all in which my parents didn't disown me.

After finishing my homework, I changed into my pajamas, and when I stepped into the hallway to brush my teeth in the bathroom, I could hear Dad and Rhonda talking downstairs in hushed voices. Whatever they were discussing, it sounded serious, and my stomach clenched at the likelihood that it had something to do with *me*.

The next morning I kept my chat with Henry brief because I didn't want to skimp on the candle protection spell.

"Are you trying to get rid of me?" he teased.

Perhaps it was his tone, or maybe just because I was still on high alert after my conversation with Mischa, but it occurred to me that because Henry was someone whom both Mischa and I cared about, I may have been putting him in danger by not informing him about Mischa's predicament. He'd been so happy back in January when we believed we'd broken the curse that I feared he might get mad at *me* if I admitted we hadn't been so successful, after all. And I couldn't stand the thought of Henry being mad at me. Without intending to fill him in on all the details, I said in the calmest voice I could muster, "There are some things going on in Willow that make me and Mischa suspect we're not completely out of the woods with this Violet thing."

"What? Are you kidding?"

"Didn't want to freak you out," I told him. Trying to make it sound like not a big deal, I told him about the candles Kirsten had instructed me to burn every morning.

I must have failed in making the entire situation seem like nothing but a precaution, because Henry's response was an explosion of fury. "How long have you known that we didn't break the curse? Why didn't you tell me sooner? I'm going to fly home tomorrow and wring that little witch's neck!"

It took me a few minutes to calm him down, and I had to swear up and down that I was sure Violet didn't have any power over the situation anymore. Perhaps it was a little bit of a lie to tell him that I was still figuring out what had happened, but I was honest enough to tell him that I thought there was the tiniest possibility that the curse had shifted to Mischa. I was still nervous he was going to hop on a flight to Wisconsin, but I had to get off the phone so that I could light my candles.

I set up my candles, poured my salt, lit the wicks, and uttered my chant with total sincerity, sensing that it had never been more important to complete the spell with attention to detail. Once at school, I endured my classes in a distracted daze. I kept reminding myself that technically nothing had changed since the day before. Mischa and I were in the same situation we had been in since January, only perhaps with slightly higher stakes because three new moons had passed. There was no reason for me to feel like I was walking along the edge of a cliff. Everything was still under control. But by the time the bell rang to signal the end of chemistry, my last class of the day, I had already thrown my bag of books over my shoulder and rocketed out of my seat, eager to put all of my focus back into getting the curse off of Mischa. Even though it made me feel like a complete nut, I'd sprinkled paper packets of salt and pepper from the cafeteria into my Vans in the bathroom after lunch.

Instead of walking directly home, I detoured to the natural foods store and bought a dozen eggs, all of the essential oils, and the fennel that Mrs. Robinson had specified. The haul was expensive, and I blew half of my first weekly paycheck from my job, but I didn't mind. My conversation with Mischa had made me anxious enough to consider hopping on the bus to pay Mrs. Robinson a friendly visit even though I wasn't on the work schedule. However, Tuesday nights were when I was scheduled to speak with Trey. If there was any part of my weekly routine that I would never jeopardize, it was that phone call.

When I got home, I was surprised to find the house empty. It was rare that I arrived back at the condo earlier than Dad, and even though I never minded being home alone in Wisconsin, in Florida I felt kind of like a trespasser on someone else's property. To busy myself and do something unexpectedly nice, I started dinner. I'd just set a tray of chicken in the oven to bake when I heard the growl of the automatic garage door opening.

"Hey there," Dad greeted me as he entered the kitchen. He was still wearing his USF baseball cap in the house, a habit that drove Rhonda nuts. "What's all this?"

"Just trying to be helpful," I said. "I wanted to fix a salad, but the rest of the kale in the fridge was kind of gross."

Dad leaned against the counter and crossed his arms over his chest. "Listen, tiger. We need to have a little talk." For a second, I thought he was going to tell me what was going on between him and Rhonda, and I prayed once again that whatever it was, it hadn't been inspired by anything I'd done. But then I heard the garage door lifting again, which meant that Rhonda was home.

"Sure, Dad."

Perhaps because Rhonda was about to enter the house from the garage at any second, he told me, "After dinner."

Now I had a real reason to be paranoid. Rhonda gave me a weak smile as I set the table, and our conversation throughout dinner was shallow. Dad bored us with a description of politics going on in the surgery department at the school where he worked. By the time Rhonda excused herself and cleared her plate, I was certain that the barely perceptible hostility between them definitely must have had something to do with me. Rhonda had avoided making eye contact with me the entire time we'd been seated at the table.

Finally, while still picking at his Brussels sprouts, Dad told me, "You left a candle lit in your bedroom this morning when you left for school."

It felt as if blood had frozen in my veins. Was it possible that I'd left my candles out? I was always careful about setting them back in the top drawer of my nightstand after I blew them out. My thoughts raced back to the state of mind I'd been in earlier that morning. I'd been much more focused than I usually was. I'd ended my call with Henry to chant the spell without distractions. I could specifically remember blowing out the candles and setting them back in the top drawer of my nightstand. There was no way I'd left the house with a candle burning.

"Are you sure? I didn't have any candles lit last night," I said, trying to act surprised.

Dad shifted his posture uncomfortably as if he really did not want to be having this conversation. "Rhonda found it. She said there was a weird setup of candles in a pentagram on your nightstand with a circle of salt around it?"

Iciness crept into my fingers and hands. This was a message, a warning. The spirits knew where I was. They wanted me to believe that they could hurt my father or his wife whenever they wanted.

"Dad." There was no point in pretending like I didn't know anything about the candles or the salt. Insinuating that Rhonda was a liar was not going to work in my favor. "That's really freaky. Sometimes I light candles, but I would never arrange them in a pentagram. I thought I blew them out this morning before school. I'll be more careful in the future."

Dad folded his hands together and looked directly at me to make it clear that he meant business. "No more candles. I don't want any open flames in this house."

This was a reasonable request, I knew. Especially after he and I had lost so much because of fire. But those candles, that ritual—they were the only way I had of protecting Mischa. I was about to object when he silenced me with a wave of his hand. "I mean it. Rhonda was very upset this morning, and I thought all of this nonsense with witchcraft and devil games was over."

I was just going to have to agree and figure out a more discreet way of conducting the candle ritual moving forward. Arguing would be futile, and if Violet's spirits were meddling with candles and lighters in my bedroom when I wasn't home, then it was probably for the best that I kept those materials somewhere outside.

"Okay. Sure, Dad," I said. As much as I never wanted to return to the Sheridan School for Girls or any type of boarding school like it, the idea of being considered a burden on my dad's marriage was even more upsetting to me. "Has Rhonda been acting kind of strangely lately because of me? Don't tell me everything's fine. I can tell there's something going on with you guys, and if it's not cool for me to be here, Mom's attorney can talk to the judge in Shawano County and figure out another—"

"Rhonda's pregnant," Dad said at a barely audible volume. He cleared his throat and took a sip of water as if even saying the words made him uncomfortable.

"Oh." I was as stunned as if I'd almost been hit by a car. It had never occurred to me that Dad and Rhonda would want to have kids together. The possibility of having a half brother or sister had never even crossed my mind. Rhonda was considerably younger than Dad, but I had always kind of figured that Dad was done with kids, in general. He wasn't even the kind of guy who liked to joke around with coworkers' little ones at picnics.

"And she's having some complications," he added. "That's not a great sign, so early on."

"I didn't know," I said, my face turning red. This conversation had suddenly gone in a much different direction than I'd anticipated. "That's big news. Great news. I mean, not the complications, but I—you know. Didn't know that you guys were even—" I cut myself off. Talking to my dad about something that even loosely bordered on his sex life was just too gross to continue.

"We've always kept things kind of open-ended on the topic of kids. Rhonda didn't seem too keen on the idea of changing diapers in the middle of the night until . . . Well, opinions change when different circumstances present themselves," Dad said, sounding tired. "But right now, it's important that she not be under any additional stress."

I held my breath for a moment, waiting for him to specify that stress being caused by *me*. But instead, he said, "Please don't mention to her that we spoke."

CHAPTER 3

AFTER CLEARING THE TABLE, I BOILED EGGS that I'd have to peel in the morning for Mrs. Robinson and placed them in the fridge. As I climbed the stairs to my bedroom on the second floor to be ready when Trey called, my thoughts were racing. A little half brother or sister? Butterflies swirled around my stomach at the thought of having a tiny sibling around. Of course, my mom might have been upset by the news, but I was getting the sense that her relationship with Glenn was more serious than she was letting on, so perhaps she might not have minded too much if Dad were to have another kid.

And then darkness crept into my thoughts: If Violet's spirits were able to jeopardize my mom's safety and lure poor Stephani deMilo out onto thin ice, what chance did a defenseless infant stand against them? Caring about another person only made me more vulnerable. Just when I thought that breaking the curse couldn't seem less possible, the stakes were unfairly raised on me again.

I stepped into my bedroom, wondering how I might explain any of this to Trey, when I noticed the top drawer of my nightstand had been left open by an inch. I dashed around the foot of my bed to peer inside. My fears were confirmed: the candles, candle holders, salt, and lighter were gone. Rhonda must have thrown them out, and the realization made my heart beat wildly. This would not have been a big deal except that the sun had set. There was nowhere within walking distance where I could buy replacements for any of those items before I had to perform the protection spell again in the morning.

Panicking, I texted Kirsten to ask if she might be able to light the candles in Chicago on my behalf in the morning. Even if she agreed, that still would have been a disruption in the routine, which was troubling. But I had to try.

She hadn't texted back yet when my phone rang at seven thirty with Trey's call. Although I really hadn't wanted to upset Trey with news about Violet or the curse while he was stuck at Northern Reserve, I now felt compelled to at least make him aware that it wasn't over—if only for his own safety.

"Hey," Trey said once the operator at Northern Reserve had patched through his call to my cell phone. As always, even under the most awful circumstances, the sound of his voice sent a thrill through me. Connecting with him, hearing his breath on the other end of the phone, knowing just for a few minutes exactly where he was and what he was doing, calmed my nerves even as my pulse quickened. It wasn't as if contact with Trey made me forget about the danger that Mischa was in, that we were *all* in. Rather, he reset my belief that one day the nightmare that Violet had unleashed upon us would end. Deep in my bones, I felt that Trey and I belonged together. Knowing that he was mine and I was his reaffirmed my belief that there was order in the world; despite all of the chaos we had yet to conquer, our bond was real, and nothing could tear us apart.

"Hey," I replied. Subtly updating him about Mischa and her fear of the number three, Mrs. Robinson, and candles in my bedroom lighting themselves on fire was going to be tricky. Since I knew a monitor was listening on the Northern side of the call, I had to choose my words carefully. I assumed from my own experience at Sheridan that the guards at Northern probably only half listened, and most likely had a list of keywords based on Trey's case history for which they were supposed to keep their ears peeled. So I had to do my best to avoid saying words like "violet," "curse," "death," and "revenge."

"How are things in sunny Florida?" he asked. "Have you found a date to prom yet?"

"Ha." From what I'd gathered, prom was a really big deal at Hyde Park High School, even bigger than it had been in Willow. I'd made the mistake of mentioning the chosen theme, Moulin Rouge, to Trey on our last call. I had guessed correctly that he'd find the idea of teenagers in suburban Florida dressing up like turn-of-the-century Parisian courtesans to be amusing. If Olivia had simply not invited Violet to her birthday party back in September and set a horrific chain of events into motion, I probably would have been very excited about prom. I had to believe that one way or another, Trey and I still would have fallen in love that year, and I'd be begging him to humor me by renting a tux. As a tenth grader, I'd imagined going all out for prom with a full-length gown and gloves. But there was no way I'd even consider going to the dance in Tampa with anyone besides Trey. Prom was just one more part of the normal high school experience I'd have to forfeit, and resenting it would prevent me from remaining focused. "Haven't been looking for one, to be honest."

"I'd assume you wouldn't have to look too hard, being the mysterious new girl in town," Trey teased. His voice sounded different, and I realized it was because I could hear an unfamiliar echo. "You're probably way more of a source of intrigue than you realize."

I asked, "Where are you? It sounds like there's an echo."

He hesitated before replying. "The infirmary. It's a big room with a lot of tile."

I was lying on my stomach across my bed, but at Trey's mention of *infirmary*, I rolled over and sat upright in alarm. "Um, are you going to tell me why you're there?" I asked, instantly worried.

He hummed, "Uhhhh," for a prolonged moment as if he wasn't sure whether or not it was safe to say. "Just not feeling well. They quarantine you here at the first sign of the sniffles—or any other kind of trouble."

The melodious tone his voice had taken on insinuated that this wasn't the whole truth. Trey was usually being sarcastic, and he normally spoke with a cool, detached delivery. But he shifted into a more vibrant, singsong voice when he was hinting there was something he couldn't tell me. Something was going on at Northern, something he couldn't describe over the phone, which made me even more worried. Automatically I wondered if he'd gotten into a fight or was more ill than he was telling me. Not being able to ask outright killed me. I just needed to know he was okay.

"Oh, really," I replied flatly to suggest that I got the message that something else was happening. "I wonder where you might have picked up a case of the sniffles."

"How about you? Have you been feeling blue?" he asked.

I waited a beat before responding. We often used "blue" and

"purple" to refer to Violet, and I was tempted to reply that I had indeed been feeling a little blue. But knowing that Trey—one way or another—had landed himself in need of some kind of medical care made me a lot less eager to burden him with an update about evil happenings back in Willow. Nothing frustrated Trey more than being closely handled by authority figures, so if this infirmary business had anything to do with that, he was probably already in a volatile state of mind. The last thing I wanted to do was tell him something that might serve as a catalyst for him to mouth off to a guard or lash out at a fellow student.

For a second, I considered telling him about Dad and Rhonda's big news, but even that seemed too personal to share on a monitored phone call. "All good," I lied.

After we said our good-byes for the week, a lump formed in my throat. Something was wrong, I was sure of it, and there was no way for him to communicate what it was.

Even though I knew that tinkering around with my pendulum while I felt like Mischa and I were in danger wasn't a great idea, I couldn't resist the urge. By nothing short of a miracle, it had still been in my pillowcase atop my bed when Mom and I had driven up to Sheridan in February to collect the handful of belongings I'd left behind there.

I snuck downstairs to the kitchen carrying my last stick of palo santo, lit it with a safety match from the box that Dad kept over the sink, and carefully carried it back up to my room, cupping the glowing end of it with my hand to avoid setting off any smoke detectors. The small stick of soft wood burned for only a few seconds before the ember died off. But the scent of it in my room made me feel a little more secure about withdrawing my pendulum from my sock drawer, where I kept it hidden.

"Pendulum," I asked. "Is Trey in trouble?"

Yes.

"Does the trouble he's in have something to do with Violet?"

The pendulum rotated clockwise twice—yes—but then wobbled and dangled from my fingers without moving in any particular direction. "Does that mean . . . maybe?" I asked in confusion.

Yes.

Great. Frustrated, I sighed. I was going to have to insist that Mrs. Robinson teach me how to reach out to Jennie the next day. Maybe even explain to her why it was so urgent. Mischa and I couldn't afford to be taking actions based on assumptions any longer, and if Trey was in serious jeopardy, then I needed detailed guidance. Getting real answers out of the pendulum took too long, and I could never be sure if *yes* or *no* was the complete answer to my question, or just a response to part of it.

As far as I could tell, since arriving in Florida I'd only been receiving messages from Jennie rather than being able to effectively transfer any information back. Our communication was completely one-sided. Although Olivia's spirit seemed to have been able to master communicating with me by manipulating physical objects like my music boxes, Jennie's spirit had an easier time with electrical devices. Early in March, when I'd set my earbuds in my ears as I began my walk to school, I'd heard a voice I knew was Jennie's before I'd even tapped my phone to start playing music. She'd been repeating a three-syllable word over and over again. At first it had sounded like "tomato," but it was quickly drowned out by a noise that sounded like high winds, the kind that knock the breath right out of your lungs and whip your hair around your face. Wisconsin storm season wind, the kind I'd never yet experienced in Florida—the kind that used to drive Moxie to hide under the bed and whimper. Almost a week ago, I'd left my laptop open to a blank page in Microsoft Word while doing homework late at night, and I'd come back from refilling my water bottle to find that she'd managed to type characters that formed a shape on the page like this:

—
\ /

At first I'd thought she was warning me about a "V." *Violet.* Being certain that Jennie was trying to caution me about something but having to guess what it might be felt like scratching off a lottery ticket to find all winning numbers until reaching the last one and realizing I hadn't won anything at all. Like being hit with a one-two punch of hope and defeat. Upon seeing the characters on my screen last Wednesday night, I asked the pendulum to confirm my shot-in-the-dark suspicion that Jennie was trying to warn me about a tornado, and the pendulum had said *Yes.* From there, the messages became muddled, and no matter how I phrased my question about who was in danger because of a tornado, the answer was always *yes, yes, yes.*

But it was early April. Tornado season didn't truly begin in Wisconsin until summer.

I checked the local weather in Wisconsin every morning on my phone, and never once in the last six days since the weird typing incident had unseasonable storms been mentioned in the forecast.

By midnight, when I knew I had to at least try to sleep, Kirsten still hadn't replied to my text. I was panicking. A thorough scouring of social media with what little information I knew about her turned up nothing. The only account that I came across that I suspected might be hers was on Instagram, and it was private. I tossed and turned, knowing that it wasn't fair to be furious since Kirsten was basically a stranger who didn't owe me anything. But still, I didn't want to think about what might happen the next day if too many hours passed before one of us was able to perform the candle ritual again.

In the morning, I slept through my alarm but was relieved to see that Kirsten had texted me back at around four a.m. She promised to light the candles and chant the words of protection for Mischa and her family as soon as she arrived at the bookstore that morning, but urged me to buy more supplies as soon as possible. I can't promise that my version will be as effective as yours, she texted me, reiterating her belief that somehow I had more control over witchcraft than she did.

I fired off a text message to Henry apologizing for missing his FaceTime request, showered, and quickly peeled the eggs I'd boiled the night before. I placed the broken shells in a Ziploc bag, slipped that into my tote bag along with the other items I'd bought for Mrs. Robinson, and dashed off to school.

Throughout the day, a powerful feeling of impending doom followed me around like a shadow. I attributed it to my most recent conversations with Mischa and Trey, but this felt different than just a general sense of looming danger. This felt much more urgent, much more targeted at . . . me. By lunchtime, as I tucked myself away at the end of the table where I always ate alone outside, I had started to get the sensation that I was playing hide-and-go-seek with someone, or something, and they were getting closer to finding me.

Ms. Hernández stared at me patiently during our weekly appointment from her seat across from mine. I'd already told her—probably unconvincingly—that there wasn't much going on in my life. "Really? *Nothing?* How's Trey?"

"Fine."

"You seem awfully quiet today. But I can see the wheels turning in your head. You look like you've chewed through your lower lip too. You can trust me, McKenna. If there's something going on, I'm here to listen."

I forced a smile, imagining a world where I could unload all of my normal teenage problems on her. This wasn't it. "Nope. Everything's, you know. The usual."

During chemistry, my lab partner kept shooting me dirty looks as I checked my phone every ten seconds or so. I was certain that I was going to receive a text from Mischa, Kirsten, or my mom, informing me that some kind of tragedy had occurred.

As I waited for the bus, I gave in and texted Mischa. It was still only lunchtime in Wisconsin, so I figured she'd reply quickly since there was no way she'd already be at the gym for practice. What's up? I wrote, not wanting to let on that I was more worried than usual. It was better that she had no clue about the candles and my failure to light them that morning.

The bus was later than it had ever been before, and Mischa didn't reply. As a distraction, I popped my earbuds in my ears and was scrolling through my apps on my phone in search of Spotify when I heard high-pitched static. Even though I wasn't listening to any audio, I tapped my volume + button several times until the static was loud enough to hurt my ears, and then I heard it: that wind sound again. Wisconsin storm wind—with an earsplitting, high-pitched whistle at the top and the threat of destruction roaring at lower octaves.

"What the . . . ," I mumbled. "Okay, okay. I'm on it." My heart beat wildly; *something* was happening—if it was a tornado touching down in Willow at that very moment, I had no immediate way of finding out. My brain short-circuited for a second as I tried to decide what to do first: text Mom, or check the weather? My fingertip made the decision for me. I tapped my phone to check the weather in Willow. Nothing strange. Gray skies, 60 percent chance of rain at that hour.

Feeling my chest tighten as my breath hastened, I checked local news in Wisconsin, scrolling furiously. My eyes scanned over headlines in search of something—*anything*—absolutely positive that I'd see a shocking breaking story. The Brewers had won the game the night before against the Reds. The State Assembly was preparing to vote about moving a bunch of coal piles in downtown Green Bay. A new medical facility had been opened in Kaukauna. The bus pulled up to the curb, and I boarded it, so distracted that I knocked shoulders with a guy carrying a skateboard as he passed me to exit.

"Watch it," he snapped at me.

I mumbled an apology over my shoulder as the doors closed behind me, flashed the driver my fare card, and sank into the closest available seat. As the bus merged into traffic and my heart rate returned to normal, I gave up, clicking my screen off. I couldn't find proof of anything out of the ordinary happening in Willow, and I was relieved that I hadn't texted Mom and freaked her out.

And yet the weird feeling persisted.

Once at the assisted living facility, I said hi to my manager, Luis, changed into my uniform, and hurried through my schedule of visiting patients. I was saving Mrs. Robinson for last, but I also wanted to make sure I had enough time remaining at the end of my shift to receive a proper lesson from her about reaching out to Jennie.

And, of course, because that was my plan, every possible thing went wrong on my rounds. Mrs. Schwartz on the second floor—who walked painstakingly slowly with a walker—wanted me to escort her down to the dining room, and she insisted on stopping in the open doorways of all her girlfriends to chat. Mr. Torres asked me to open his mail and read a letter to him from his daughter in Puerto Rico, and I struggled to phonetically sound out words I didn't recognize from Spanish class. Then Mrs. Jacobson insisted that the dinner she'd received hadn't been what she'd ordered, and the head of kitchen services angrily told me that she had been pulling this stunt almost every night, and I had to sort that out to make sure she ate something before the kitchen closed.

Finally, with only eight minutes to spare before I had to clock out, I arrived at Mrs. Robinson's room. "Did you bring the oils and the eggshells?" she demanded the moment I stepped through her doorway.

"I did. But I have to run down to my locker to get them, and clock out. Do you mind waiting a few minutes for me to come back upstairs?"

Hanging out with a patient on my own time after a shift may very well have been a violation of one of the terms of my employment, so

I just smiled at Luis in the elevator as I rode back up to the third floor and told him I'd left something behind in Mrs. Robinson's room. A fresh crop of zinging tingles broke out across my scalp, and I attributed them to Jennie's awareness that I was on the brink of figuring out how to hear her more clearly. Hope swelled in my chest at the thought that within the next few minutes I might finally be able to ask her what was going on, what I needed to prepare myself for. But naturally, that hope coincided with fear that Mrs. Robinson might be a quack, and that her advice might just be another dead end.

I knocked twice on Mrs. Robinson's door before entering, and she greeted me with, "Took your time, didn't you?"

Her television was on at a low volume, and she sat in a chair in front of it, her cataract-covered eyes fixed on its screen as if she could see it. "How did you know it was me?" I asked. "Both just now and when I came up a few minutes ago?"

She toyed with the amulet she wore around her neck. "I could hear you! Well, not you, but *them*. The *loa* that follow you around. They're worked up about something tonight. That's for sure." She then repeated for emphasis, "That's . . . for sure."

My scalp was burning; the tingles were making their way down toward my ears. I set the bottles of essential oil on the coffee table and twisted off the cap of the orange oil so that she could take a whiff. "Mrs. Robinson, I really hope you can tell me how to communicate with my sister in the dark place, because . . ." I paused to take a breath. "Because I think whatever she's trying to tell me is urgent."

The elderly woman instructed me to heat a cup of water to a boil and then place three drops of each of the three essential oils into it so that we could spray Florida water around the room. I had to improvise a little by heating the water in a microwave and then flicking our mixture around with my fingertips because I hadn't brought a spray bottle with me. Mrs. Robinson also requested that I reinforce the layer of salt around the perimeter of her room with the eggshells. I didn't have the heart to tell her that what I'd set down on Monday had been vacuumed up, and I scattered the eggshells sparingly. Housekeeping would definitely have something to say about finding eggshells mashed into the carpeting.

With all of that done, I sat down across from Mrs. Robinson, and waited for her to speak.

"All right. Now," Mrs. Robinson said, "if you're sure your sister keeps trying to send you messages, then what you need to do is listen harder!" She ended with a yell, as if the solution should have been plainly obvious to me.

Defensively, I insisted, "But I *do* listen! Even on the way here, I thought I heard her on my earbuds—like, these little headphones that you put inside your ears to listen to music," I clarified. "It just sounds like loud wind. A very *specific* kind of wind. If she's saying words, I can't hear them."

"Well, then. If you think she's saying words you can't hear, you're not listening to the right station!" she exclaimed, as if my trying to tune in to messages from the afterlife were a joke.

"I don't understand. She's not a radio broadcast."

"But she *is*! If that's how she's trying to reach you, she's manipulating radio waves. I bet if you tune in to the right frequency, you'll be able to hear her just fine," Mrs. Robinson said with a big smile.

I held back a frustrated sigh. Mrs. Robinson probably assumed that most people had radios available to them. "I don't even think

47

we *own* a radio. I mean, maybe my dad has one for emergencies?" There was a radio in Dad's car, of course, but I didn't know when I'd be allowed to apply for a driver's license again. And of course, he only listened to his favorite talk shows on satellite radio.

Just as it occurred to me that I might be able to use an app on my phone to listen to local radio stations, two things happened.

First, behind me on the television, I heard a newscaster with a rich baritone voice making an announcement in a teaser for the nightly news. "Deadly tornados touch down in Wisconsin this afternoon. Tune in at eleven for the latest."

And my phone buzzed with an incoming text.

CHERYL 7:18 P.M.
Have you heard about Mischa? Call me asap.

CHAPTER 4

IT WAS IMPORTANT TO REMEMBER, MRS. ROBINSON told me, that Jennie was no longer on the physical plane. Spirits could pick up information from the living world from their side of things, but they didn't exist or communicate the same way the living did. So although Jennie may have been able to manipulate radio waves and recognize me by my spirit, she may have lacked the finesse to make it clear that she was warning me about a *tornado*.

Of course, I'd guessed early on that's what she had been implying. It had just seemed pretty far-fetched that she was suggesting an actual tornado was going to touch down in Willow. Tornados in our part of Wisconsin weren't unheard-of, but rarely until after May, when the temperature began to rise for summer. The only other tornado to ever touch down in Willow that I knew of had done so when my dad was in high school; it had torn the roof off the old high school gym. And that had been thirty-five years ago.

When I stepped into the hallway outside Mrs. Robinson's room to call Cheryl, she told me that power lines and cell phone towers had been torn down all over town, which was why I hadn't heard the news until two hours after the devastation had occurred.

No one in Willow had been able to use their phone until service was restored. And our town was so small that it would have taken a lot more than a powerful tornado to create a national buzz on social media.

The big news was that Timber Creek, the gated community where the Portnoys lived, had been where the first and largest of the three tornados had touched down.

"Mischa's house was flattened," Cheryl informed me in a strangely calm voice. She didn't know anything about our failure to fully break the curse. I'd spared her having to feel any sense of responsibility about that since she'd been so eager to help us infiltrate Violet's New Year's party, and had played a key role in us getting Violet to participate in a second round of the game in Michigan. She still saw Violet every day at school, and it seemed unfair to put the burden of knowing there was unfinished business on her. "That's what I heard, anyway. But . . . McKenna? My mom's friend from work lives across the street from the Portnoys, and she said that Amanda's . . . hurt. Like, badly. It doesn't . . . look good."

Amanda, Mischa's sister, aspiring Olympic gymnast—on the brink of death. Amanda, the most popular girl in the senior class at Willow High School, who was always with her boyfriend, Brian. She was only eighteen.

My mouth went so dry that I coughed when I tried to swallow. Out of all the streets in Willow, out of all the families I knew in town . . . the tornado had flattened *Mischa's* house. *Her* sister had been injured—and on the day when I hadn't been able to perform the protection spell. Suddenly dizzy, I leaned against the cool wall and pressed the back of my left hand against my forehead. I felt like I was dreaming, like what Cheryl was telling me couldn't possibly be true. It was too horrible to believe.

An unfamiliar throbbing sensation began at the back of my head.

"She must have just gotten home after school. When the tornado hit, it just tore right through the house. There's nothing left but a pile of bricks. And her body was thrown into my mom's friend's front yard. I mean, this is awful, but my mom's friend said she was out there for over an hour, just, like clinging to life. Ambulances couldn't get through because there are so many power lines down in the streets."

I couldn't feel my legs or feet. It truly felt as if clocks had stopped ticking, and I was standing in a hallway under fluorescent lights in another dimension. The pulsing in my head grew stronger, making it feel as if my brain was beating like a heart, pressing painfully against the inside of my skull. Without even feeling my knees bend, I slid down the wall until I found myself squatting on the floor. A cheerful aide wearing scrubs passed me and smiled, but looked away quickly when she saw the aghast expression on my face.

"Are you there?" Cheryl asked after a prolonged moment of silence.

I hoarsely choked out, "Yes."

"I don't know if this is true or not, but my mom's friend said she thinks Amanda's spine snapped. She was afraid to move her."

A broken back. That would probably mean paralysis.

"There's more," Cheryl said.

Somehow, I had known the moment my head turned toward the TV at the sound of the newscaster's voice that there would be.

"The second tornado touched down across town. It hit Mischa's dad's car dealership."

I summoned a memory of Portnoy Luxury Automobiles to my mind. I'd never actually gone inside or looked at a car there, but I'd probably driven past it a thousand times in my lifetime. It was on the far side of town on the way to Ortonville, the more upscale part of town, closer to the subdivisions of Sherwood Hills, where Candace had lived, and Timber Creek.

I barely felt my mouth form the words. "Is her dad okay?"

There's no reason to assume he's dead, I told myself. *He might have been working in Green Bay or Sheboygan today.*

"I don't know. All I heard was that there are cars everywhere."

That was two tornados. Two members of the Portnoy family. As if on cue, Cheryl continued slowly, knowing how much the news she was delivering would tear a hole in my heart. "And the third tornado touched down on State Street, not far from Mischa's mom's real estate office."

I waited. "And?"

"It ripped up the asphalt, messed up buildings and cars along one side of the street. And the other side of the street looks fine, like nothing happened."

Don't leap to conclusions, I ordered myself. Mischa's mother was a real estate agent. She rarely had reason to be in the office since she was often showing houses to prospective buyers around town. But deep down, I knew it was too coincidental. In the past, when the evil spirits had demonstrated their ability to interfere with matter and energy in our world, I'd always interpreted their actions as threats. This time, they'd called my bluff. They'd shown me—and Mischa— what they were capable of doing.

"Do you think Violet has anything to do with it?" Cheryl asked. "She's been missing at school a lot this spring. I mean, not that I've been paying much attention. But she's in US History and calculus with me, and she was out for almost two weeks straight in February."

"I don't know," I replied. "I don't think so." Surely the tornados had to do with the curse that had originally been on Violet, but I didn't have any reason to believe that she had involvement in its cycle anymore. The spirits had moved on and were focused on Mischa. Even though I hadn't heard about Violet missing school, I was too stunned by everything Cheryl had just told me to consider what that might mean while we were still on the phone.

The pain in my head was unbearable when I asked Cheryl to call me if she heard any news. One, two, three. Mischa had been right. Violet's spirits had collected on their debt, *three times*, just like they'd been threatening they would.

I tapped Mischa's name in my contacts list with every intention of reaching out to her, but couldn't think of any words to type. There was a possibility that Mischa didn't know anything about Amanda yet because she had been at the gym in Ortonville the whole time. I didn't want to take the chance of being the one to break that news.

So I tapped the audio button and listened to her phone ring, expecting that she wasn't going to pick up. In a voice that didn't even sound like mine, I left a blunt voice mail telling Mischa to call me. I already knew she wouldn't.

I wandered back into Mrs. Robinson's room in a daze. Mrs. Robinson didn't ask me what had happened. Even though she couldn't see the despair on my face, she was able to deduce that whatever news I'd just been given on the phone had been bad. "Hand me that book up there on that shelf," she told me, pointing up to the top of the credenza to the right of her TV. When I walked over, I found a row of corny bodice-ripper romance novels, and she clarified, "The Bible."

I found a dog-eared paperback King James Bible at the end of the shelf, and handed it to her. She blindly thumbed through the pages, into which she had crammed all sorts of folded notes, bookmarks, and old photos. From a page near the middle of the book, she withdrew a small leather pouch that had been flattened during its time in the Bible to look more like an envelope. She gestured at me to take it from her.

"This is a gris-gris," she informed me. "You take this home, put it on a cord, and wear it around your neck. Find something that belonged to your sister and place it inside—it can just be a tiny bit of something, a scrap of fabric, a little photo, whatever you've got—and this will protect you. Do you understand?"

The gris-gris looked pretty old and, honestly, gross, like perhaps someone else had worn it for a long time. If I hadn't just heard that my worst fear had come true, I would have only humored Mrs. Robinson and tossed it in a dresser drawer when I got home. But instead, I held it in my palm as if it was precious.

"And you need protection. Because these *loa* that follow you around? They're happy right now. They're celebrating. If you could hear them like I do, you'd know. They're saying *we told you so.*"

They sure had told me so.

"How can I hear and see them like you do?" I asked.

Mrs. Robinson laughed at me. "Well, you can't! It's taken me eighty long years of trying! But I'll tell you what you *can* do."

I leaned forward, desperate for any guidance she could give me. "You take a pinch of salt and throw it in the air to the east. . . ."

I listened intently, even though I was skeptical about the magical power of common table salt. But I was upset enough by the news from Willow to consider anything that might offer protection.

"When it hits the ground, if it looks different from just regular old salt, then you've got something bad on your tail."

I thanked Mrs. Robinson for her guidance, and assured her that I'd be back the following afternoon. Once back in the hallway, I texted Mom with numb fingers. She wrote back within seconds, assuring me that she was fine. The tornado hadn't touched down anywhere near Martha Road, although it had done some damage in Glenn's neighborhood. I should have called her, but in my gut it felt safer to avoid making that much more of a connection. She was safe—for now. Mischa's family had been punished and not mine . . . but what if my family was next if I kept trying to help Mischa? As I clocked out for the night, I felt cold, and my limbs seemed to be moving too slowly, like in a nightmare when you're running away from something scary and your legs just pinwheel like you're in water.

It had been foolish of me to play along with Violet's game back in September, but I'd known all along that my friends' subsequent deaths hadn't really been my fault. *This*, however, was. If Amanda Portnoy didn't survive, or if Mischa's parents had died during the tornado, those deaths were on *me*. I was the one who'd begged Mischa not to follow the spirits' orders. Not even twenty-four hours had passed since Mischa had called to tell me that she was scared of *exactly this*. I *could* have sneaked out of the house the night before to buy more candles, but had chosen to talk to Trey instead. Three new moons had passed since the night the curse had jumped from Violet to Mischa—over three months, and in all that time, I *hadn't* made any real effort to figure out how to help Mischa.

I'd let the distance between Florida and Wisconsin convince me it was safe to wait.

But maybe Mischa's mom and dad were injured or rattled, but fine. Maybe Amanda could still make a full recovery if Mischa issued three more death sentences before the new moon. This could all have been just a stern warning.

The powerful wave of nausea in my stomach said otherwise, though, and I feared that we'd run out of warnings. This was real, as real as the accident into which Trey and Olivia had gotten, as real as Candace drowning in the Pacific.

Dad must have heard the news about Willow, because he texted me from the parking lot of the assisted living facility to let me know that he had come to pick me up instead of Rhonda. It was raining when I stepped outside Oscawana Pavilion, and I felt my temper surge as I hesitated under the awning over sliding front doors. I was angry at Dad for having driven over in the rain. Angry that we had to ride home together on slick roads. Angry at myself for putting everyone I knew in danger—again.

"You've probably heard," he greeted me as I climbed into the front seat. He sounded grim, which was rare for him.

"Mom's fine. Nothing happened on our street," I replied stonily.

Before pulling away from the curb, he said, "You've gotta remember, McKenna . . . extreme weather systems have nothing to do with ghosts or spirits or occult games."

"I know, Dad," I replied because I had to, although he really had no idea what he was talking about. On one hand, he was right. Bad things happened everywhere, to a lot of innocent people. But surely by now—after Olivia's accident, and the meningitis outbreak that had almost killed my classmate Tracy Hartford, Stephani deMilo's tragic "suicide," and the avalanche that had endangered every eleventh grader from Willow High School on the ski trip in January—he realized that something was very suspiciously wrong in our town.

The trouble in Willow, Wisconsin, was painfully obvious to anyone whose mind was open to the possibility of paranormal interference with the regular world. Kirsten texted me before Dad and I even got home asking simply, WTF? She didn't need any convincing.

I didn't write back. I couldn't. My whole chest ached with heaviness because Mischa still hadn't replied, which meant either she was completely—and understandably—emotionally devastated, or furious.

With *me*.

Mom had tried calling me twice by ten p.m., and knowing that it probably seemed unforgivably rude that I hadn't answered, I called her back. Our house was completely unscathed, but a tree had fallen over on Glenn's property and wrecked his roof as well as one of his walls. He'd be staying with her at our place for a while. She hadn't heard any news about the Portnoys, but that wasn't surprising. Mom didn't socialize much around town, and said she hadn't ventured past the corner to check out the damage since getting home from campus earlier that day. In futility, she urged me not to worry as we said good-byes, and tried to assure me that the fire department was taking care of "everything." Figuring that following Mrs. Robinson's wacky instructions couldn't hurt, I still felt a little self-conscious as I strung an old shoelace through the hole punched in the gris-gris so that I could tie it around my neck. She'd told me to put something inside of it that had belonged to Jennie, which was easier said than done since I was at Dad's and not in Willow, where Jennie's few remaining possessions were stored in Mom's garage. But then I remembered that I had an old school photo with me in Florida, tucked into a page in a photo album with all of the Polaroids I'd taken in middle school. It was one of two wallet-size school portraits I had of her, first grade and second grade.

I snapped a picture of it with my phone before I cut the original photo to fit inside the leather pouch.

All night, I kept one eye on the WBAY-TV website for local news from the Green Bay area while testing out various radio apps on my phone, trying to find a signal that would allow me to hear Jennie's voice. Ever since Trey had read *Requests from the Dead* in the fall and had assured me that it was difficult for spirits on the "other side" to manipulate objects in our world, I'd trusted that they were limited in their ability to make good on their threats. Perhaps their stronghold in our realm was increasing now that they'd made the leap from Violet to Mischa, or they'd always been stronger than I'd realized. I fell asleep wondering if causing three tornados and nearly killing Amanda Portnoy was just a modest sneak preview of their capabilities.

Henry—thousands of miles away in France—had the full scoop by the time his FaceTime request woke me up in the morning. The buzzing of my phone woke me up, and I tapped its screen to speak with him before realizing that my hair was completely askew, and I had weird crease marks on my face from my pillowcase.

"Hey," I said, wiping my eyes with the back of my hand. "You heard about the tornados?"

He wasn't wearing his preppy pastel tennis outfit for work. "Both of Mischa's parents," he said without emotion. "Dead. Totally random—they were on opposite sides of town when the storm hit. And Amanda's on life support. Rumor has it she won't live until the end of the day. If she dies, then that's only three casualties in a town with a population of almost five thousand people."

I fell back on my pillow, feeling like I'd been punched in the solar plexus. "How did you find out? Did your parents hear that?" If there was any possible chance that this was an unconfirmed rumor, I needed to know.

"No," Henry said glumly. "Chris Stephens is a volunteer fire-fighter in town now."

The name was familiar, although I couldn't remember what Chris looked like. He'd graduated the year I was a freshman, and he'd been on the tennis team with Henry—that much, I remembered. It was easy to retain at least a vague memory of kids in other classes when your high school only had about four hundred students, total.

Henry continued, "He texted me last night and said it was surreal having to put Amanda's body on a stretcher. He was her orientation buddy on her first day of high school. He said he cried all the way to the hospital to drop her off. Even if she survives, he said her spinal injury is pretty severe. She'll never walk again."

A chill ran through me despite the fact that it was hot in my room. I watched the ceiling fan overhead turn in lazy circles. The time had arrived when I had no choice but to tell Henry the truth about what had been happening since January. He was in danger; we all were, and so were our families. "She knew this was going to happen. Mischa. Ever since we went to Michigan and played the game with Violet again, she's been getting weird signals. We think the curse was passed to her when we took it off Violet because it skipped her when it was her turn. Mischa was supposed to die before the end of November. And then Stephani died before the end of December. Maybe Violet killed someone else in November, but I think she was planning on catching up on however many souls she was behind with her big ski trip stunt in January."

Henry shook his head, and when he spoke, he sounded angry. "Why didn't you tell me, McKenna? I'm out here prancing around on a tennis court like—like—an idiot—and all these months, Mischa's been in danger?"

"I told you about the candles. We thought we had it under control," I admitted.

"Well, now Mischa's parents are dead, and Amanda could die at any second. And I'll tell you what else," he said. His eyes had gone steely in a way I'd never seen them look before. "I'm flying home to Wisconsin today to deal with this once and for all. This has to end."

I saw his hand reach for his phone screen as if he was about to tap to end our call, and I shouted, "Wait! Henry!"

But he was gone.

Deal with this once and for all? What could he have meant by that? I desperately hoped that he didn't think that hurting or even *killing* Mischa—or even Violet—would end things.

And a second later, Dad knocked on my door. "You up in there? Coffee's ready."

I knew better than to play sick or plead my case for staying home. There was no way Dad would have sympathy on me because of bad weather back in Wisconsin. Not even for the tragic death of a friend's parents. So I threw on clothes and tied the gris-gris from Mrs. Robinson around my neck. As I locked the door behind me to begin my walk to school, I realized I had completely forgotten to do all of my homework.

It was still raining. I pulled the hood of my raincoat over my head and hunched my shoulders, beginning my walk to school at a faster-than-usual clip. I wouldn't have considered myself to be much of a daydreamer before Violet Simmons entered my life, but in the months since I'd moved to Tampa, I'd become a full-time space cadet, always lost in a deep spiral of what-ifs. It was probably for the best that I wasn't allowed to drive anymore. That morning I was dazed by imagined scenarios about what might happen if Henry actually did try to take out Violet when he arrived in Willow.

When I reached the first intersection on my path, with a strip mall of small businesses on one corner and the freeway overpass ahead, I stopped to wait for the light. But as the light turned green for me to cross the street, I stepped off the curb, and an oncoming SUV just a few feet in front of me attempted to roll to a stop through an enormous puddle and hydroplaned.

The back end of it whirled unexpectedly toward me faster than I could make sense of what was happening. Move! my brain commanded my body. But I stood there, paralyzed with fear, until suddenly I was slammed against the pavement.

"Are you okay?"

My entire body hurt. It took a second for me to realize that I was still alive—and lying on my side, looking into the treads on the rear wheels of the SUV that had almost just hit me. My heart pounded in my ears. A kid I recognized from school was climbing off of me; he'd knocked me out of the SUV's path a fraction of a second before it would have hit me.

Shaking, I got to my feet, noticing that my jeans were soaked from the puddle into which I'd fallen. "Yeah. Wow. Thank you," I sputtered. "I don't know what came over me. I couldn't move."

The middle-aged female driver, frantic, hopped out of the driver's seat and dashed toward us, apologizing profusely as other cars slowed down to see if we were all right. Her children, inside the SUV, were screaming at the tops of their lungs. In a daze, I noticed the street signs on the corner where I'd nearly just died—South Willow Avenue and West Platt Street.

I broke into a cold sweat under my raincoat despite the humid morning as I shook off everyone's help. Fear took over, and—practically disassociating—I ran the rest of the way to school. Once inside the building, I was able to pull myself together enough to look normal, but my hand still shook as I twisted the combination code to my locker. Because that was a warning. . . .

Violet's spirits had the upper hand now. Mischa was going to obey all of their orders . . . and this time, they were going to do everything they possibly could to stop me from interfering.

Including killing me.

Now I understood that Mrs. Robinson had given me the gris-gris because she'd known—and maybe hadn't wanted to tell me for fear of scaring me—that I was in imminent danger.

I still had moments before the homeroom bell, so I went straight to the cafeteria. I breezed right past the cereal bar and coffee station, and I grabbed a handful of salt packets from the condiments counter. Knowing that there wouldn't be many people in the outdoor eating area at that hour, I stepped through the double doors and used the compass on my phone to figure out which way was east.

Then I tore open two of the tiny salt packets, poured them into my hand, and threw the salt in the air. A girl sitting at a nearby table with huge headphones over her ears looked up at me in annoyed curiosity. But I ignored her, and instead looked down at the pavement where the salt had landed.

And I involuntarily gasped.

The salt had turned red.

According to Mrs. Robinson, this meant something was "on my tail." Presumably . . . something bad.

Throughout the school day, I completely ignored my teachers and scanned the dials on all of the radio apps I'd installed on my phone with my earbuds mashed securely into my ears. I refreshed the *Willow Gazette* website every minute or so hoping for updates, and worked myself into a state of outrage by lunchtime that news coverage about the damage in town was so vague. I figured that Henry wouldn't arrive back in Willow until around noon the next day with all of the connections he'd have to make, and not only did I need to figure how to get myself back to Wisconsin before he could hurt Violet, but I also needed more than ever to open some kind of a communication channel with Jennie. Without her direction, I had absolutely no idea what to do.

In calculus, my second-to-last class of the day, I found myself face-to-face with the guy who'd saved me that morning. "Hey. That was wild this morning," he said as he sat down at the desk next to mine.

I agreed. "Yeah." I was lost in thought about how I was going to get back to Willow, but he had no idea what a huge risk he'd taken by trying to save my life. So I added, "Thank you again. Really."

"I'm Ernesto," the guy said. He was a head taller than me, with broad shoulders, glasses, and an earring in one ear.

"McKenna," I said.

"You're from Wisconsin, right?" he asked.

I felt a blush creep into my cheeks. I didn't think anyone at Hyde Park High knew anything about me, at all. "Uh, yeah."

Ernesto smiled, pleased with himself. "Knew it! I recognized you from the news! When you showed up in this class, I was like, *It's that girl!*"

Great. All this time, I'd thought I'd been a low-key, under-the-radar new kid who no one cared to meet, which had been fine with me. Ernesto was making it sound like everyone knew my story and had been gossiping about me since February. "There's more to the story than what you saw on the news," I muttered.

"All right, everyone!" Mrs. Orian, our teacher, said as she entered the classroom and pulled the door closed behind her. "Let's take out last night's homework."

Just as I was digging out the worksheet I'd started in study hall the day before but failed to finish at home, I received a text message that almost made me jump up from my desk in shock.

VIOLET 12:53 P.M.

Call me. We need to talk.

Mrs. Orian scowled at me. "Miss Brady. Care to share with us?"

All eyes in the classroom were on me. I hadn't realized that I'd gasped so loudly when I'd seen Violet's name pop up on my phone. I collected my backpack and stepped away from my desk. "I have to, uh . . . bathroom."

I rushed out of the classroom to a chorus of snide remarks and giggles. Once in the cool hallway, I jogged toward the double doors that led to the side courtyard, where I would be able to talk on the phone with some privacy.

Violet didn't even greet me when she answered her phone. "Thanks for calling. I didn't think you would—"

"Have you heard from Mischa?" I interrupted her.

"No, of course not!" Violet replied. "I'm the last person she'd ever contact. Every time I run into her around town, she's still pissed off at me. She doesn't seem to have any idea that you guys made me play the game again, or that none of what happened in the fall was really my fault!"

I resisted the urge to argue with her. Two of my friends were dead, and Tracy Hartford had lost most of her hearing during her bout with meningitis over the winter. But reminding Violet that all of those things were, indeed, kind of her fault, wasn't going to get me far. I was very aware that I might need Violet's help to keep Mischa from giving in to the spirits—especially since there was no way Trey was going to be able to get a leave from Northern Reserve approved any time soon.

"Yeah, we didn't tell her about any of that," I said. "It's complicated. Better that she not remember anything from January."

"Listen," Violet said. "The curse clearly jumped from me to her. I mean, there's just no other explanation." She didn't have to mention the tornados for me to know what she was referring to.

"You told me that when you first inherited the curse from your grandmother, you tried to ignore the spirits when they demanded souls," I said. "And they threatened to kill your mom? Well, Mischa's been getting weird messages about the number *three*. And now both of her parents are dead, and Amanda's probably going to die soon too."

The line fell silent. "Well, at least she's caught up now."

"Are you kidding me, Violet?" Her casual attitude about death never failed to blow my mind every time it surfaced.

"I'm not making light of it, okay? It's awful! I feel so shitty! I'm just saying, there wasn't anything she could do to stop it. At least the worst is over now. Plus, my life isn't all that great now that the curse isn't on me anymore, but that's irrelevant."

I ignored Violet's defeatist attitude, refusing to believe there was nothing we could do. We hadn't broken the curse, but we'd changed the circumstances, and that made me believe more than ever that it was possible to end this. But dealing with a murderous version of Mischa was more than I could handle on my own. "Do you have any idea how bad this is? Mischa was ignoring the spirits because I begged her to. Now she's probably furious! She's going to come after *me*. She's going to come after *you*!" I hissed.

"I know, I know! That's why I texted you! The next new moon is on April twenty-second. Maybe we can figure out how to end this before then."

I felt, once again, as if I was going to start crying. "How?! I'm all the way in Florida! And I thought we'd already ended it!" Kirsten had told me shortly after our adventure in Michigan that she believed the original spell that Violet's grandmother had cast to help Violet's mother with fertility had mixed with another spell or curse. "Spell interference" was what she'd called it. But we were back at the starting line in terms of solving the dual mysteries of exactly what was happening and how to undo it.

"You need to get back to Wisconsin. I'm not dealing with Mischa alone. She won't even talk to me, so it would be impossible. And it's only going to be harder if she's sent away now that her parents are dead."

Violet told me that she'd heard Mischa had spent the night at Matt's house, but we agreed it was unlikely that she would be allowed to live with her boyfriend for long. I knew Mischa had at least one living uncle, her uncle Roger, but he lived in northern Wisconsin.

"There's a memorial for Mr. and Mrs. Portnoy on Sunday, and their funeral is on Monday," Violet told me. "They can't really sit shiva because the house is totally destroyed, so they're just having people pay respects at Gundarsson's. Tell your parents that you need to be here for that."

My stomach twisted into a knot. "It's not as easy as just hopping on a plane. Even if my parents are open to the idea of my coming back to Willow to support Mischa, a flight on short notice is going to be expensive. My parents aren't like yours. They can't just drop hundreds of dollars on a whim."

"Whatever! I'll pay for your flight. Just get their permission, and tell me whether you can fly tonight or tomorrow."

I took that in for a moment. Wisconsin. Suddenly, it seemed very real that I'd be home again within the next twenty-four hours.

"Oh!" I exclaimed, almost forgetting. This wasn't going to be good. "One more thing. Henry Richmond is on his way back to Wisconsin right now. And . . . um, he wants to murder you."

"What?!" she exclaimed.

"I just wanted to warn you. He may have gotten it into his head that killing you will break the cycle. So I guess if you see him . . ." I trailed off, not wanting to explicitly tell her to call the police.

"Great," Violet muttered. "Remind him that we have a private security service, and my dad keeps guns in the house." She ended the call before I could reply.

Since I'd taken my backpack with me when I'd left the classroom, I hung out in the courtyard rather than returning to class. Violet's mention of *guns* had made my heart start racing again; we were all in enough danger without lethal weapons as part of the equation. The enormity of the possibility that my life in Florida—and maybe my life in general—might have been coming to an end cemented me in place. I felt, not for the first time since September, an anxious churn in my stomach like I was waiting in line to board a roller coaster. I was excited because there was nowhere in the world I would have rather been than Willow. But I was equally terrified of what would happen once I arrived.

Moments before the bell rang, my phone buzzed with another

incoming text. I assumed that it was from Violet, but when I looked at it, my heart leapt into my throat.

MISCHA 1:13 P.M.

I should never have listened to you. This is your fault, and I'm going to make you pay.

CHAPTER 5

IBOARDED THE BUS BOUND FOR WORK AFTER school, fully aware that it was kind of insane to be going to work for my shift when it was imperative that I get on a plane to Wisconsin immediately. While waiting for the bus to arrive, I'd been mentally rehearsing ways in which I could ask, but the disappointment I anticipated hearing in my mom's voice was not making me feel good.

However, just as I was swiping my bus pass, I heard a distinct noise come through across my earbuds over the static. "Remind her. Just remind her."

I practically ran down the aisle of the bus to throw myself into a seat and check my radio app. It was tuned in to AM 1350, and I tapped the up button a few times to bring it to 1354, at which the static subsided. I angled the microphone on my phone toward my mouth. "Jennie? Can you hear me?" And then, just to seem like I was talking to a living, breathing friend and not the ghost of my dead sister, I added for the benefit of those sitting around me, "I just got on the bus."

"Yes." Her reply was loud and clear. My heart skipped a beat. I was both overjoyed and frightened at the same time—relieved to have finally made contact but also thoroughly freaked out to be having a conversation with a dead person in the "dark place" while riding the number fourteen bus. When I'd been able to talk to her back in January through the form of a ghost she'd taken, everything she'd said had been stiff and formal, and it had seemed like she hadn't really been able to hear me clearly. So I wasn't sure of what to expect. "I can hear you."

I stared into the floral print of the scarf wrapped around the hair of the woman sitting in front of me, wondering if this was real or if I had finally completely lost it. I guessed I just had to believe. "Did you hear about what happened in Willow?"

"I *told* you that would happen," Jennie told me. Her voice didn't sound the way I remembered it. It was lower in pitch, and hearing it made me recoil the same way that hearing my own voice in videos did.

"Is this a good way to reach you?" I asked, automatically fearful that I might not have the presence of mind to ask her every question for which I needed answers at that very moment. The thought of our connection being broken also made me frantic; in a way, I resented having to use this precious line of communication to solve a problem instead of grow closer to the sister I'd unfairly lost so long ago. "Like, whenever I want to talk to you?"

"I'm always here," she replied.

Thinking about how Mrs. Robinson had described Jennie as being "stuck in a dark place," with all my heart I wanted to ask my twin if she was at peace in the afterlife. If she was safe, if she was intentionally lingering in an unpleasant state of being for my benefit so that she could contact me this way. But deep down, I suspected

71

that was the case. And if she had been avoiding eternal peace—or , heaven, or whatever awaited us after death—for the purpose of being able to help me now, then I couldn't waste time with my own selfish emotional needs. So I launched directly into questions about Mischa. "If you knew that tornados were going to hit Wisconsin, can you tell me how to break the"—paranoid, I looked around and dropped the volume of my voice—"curse on Mischa?"

"First, you have to get there. Remind Mom about my funeral," Jennie told me.

I thought back to that day. I had very few memories of it, as I'd been little. I suspect my parents had given me a sedative from my pediatrician. I know that I didn't wear black because I didn't own anything black at the age of eight, and I remember my mother arguing with my aunt Jean about how inappropriate it was for children to wear dark colors. "What about it?" I asked.

"Elena and Adam Portnoy were there. Elena brought dinner to the house six times after the fire," Jennie told me.

Hearing this sparked a vivid memory of the doorbell ringing at our new house, or rather, the house Mom lived in today, the house on Martha Road we'd bought after our one on the corner burned down. We'd stayed with my grandparents in Minnesota for a few weeks immediately following the fire before the new house had suddenly gone on the market, and Mom had insisted on snatching it up, even though Dad thought it was kind of unhealthy.

Jennie was right. For the first few weeks of the school year that fall after we'd returned to Willow, moms in the neighborhood took turns showing up on our front porch every night with casserole dishes, often still hot from the ovens in their homes. Of course Elena

Portnoy would have been one of those moms. She may have even been the realtor from whom Mom and Dad had bought our house.

"Good point," I told Jennie. "She'll feel guilty if I'm not at the funeral if I remind her about that." Mom was not one to care much about social standards, but I knew she held dearly every memory she had of Jennie and people in town who'd checked in on us back in those bad days.

I noticed then that my scalp was tingling so severely that I also had goosebumps up and down my arms. The bus was air-conditioned but humid, so I assumed my physical reaction was to Jennie's presence rather than the temperature around me. "Is Amanda going to die?" I whispered, dreading the answer.

"Yes. Unless . . ."

I sat up straighter in my seat.

"Someone else takes her place in line. That's always how it works. A life for a life. An even trade."

Of course. Amanda was the compromise. The spirits had left her clinging to life by a thread as a means of pulling Mischa's puppet strings. They knew that there was no one in life for whom she'd be willing to kill other than Amanda. If they'd just let Amanda die quickly, they'd have no leverage over her anymore. This was their way of blackmailing her.

"Is Mischa mad at me?"

"Very mad," Jennie confirmed. "She blames you. For everything."

Great.

Jennie went on to tell me that I could trust Violet this time, and it would be foolish of me not to. Since the curse was no longer on her, it was as if she wasn't even on their radar anymore. And Jennie seemed to think there was something else, something unrelated to Mischa, for which I'd require Violet's assistance.

"It's the house," Jennie said, sounding confused. "It's unclear. It just has to do with that house."

The bus was pulling up to my stop, and as if she somehow knew that, Jennie said, "We can talk more later."

She'd said she was "always here," but that wasn't true. I'd been listening for her voice for weeks, and I had never heard her this clearly before. "This radio station? Always?" I asked.

"Always," she assured me.

By the time I passed through the front doors of the assisted living facility, I was bursting at the seams to tell Mrs. Robinson that I'd been able to reach Jennie and actually talk to her. I was so excited that, after changing into my scrubs, I clocked in and raced up the stairs (better to avoid elevators after that morning's close call with the SUV, I figured) to the third floor before starting my schedule. But when I reached her room, I heard an unfamiliar voice coming from inside.

". . . in bed before eleven every night, you hear me? No more of these late-night movies."

I knocked lightly on the door and cracked it open to find a beautiful woman sitting on the love seat in Mrs. Robinson's room. She raised her head when I said, "Excuse me. Just checking to see if Mrs. Robinson's ready to submit her dinner order."

"You must be the one indulging my mother in all of her voodoo nonsense," the woman snapped at me. When she stood, I saw that she wore an impressive business suit. Mrs. Robinson had said her daughter was a local newscaster, and I deduced that this was her.

"I, uh . . ." I didn't know what to say.

"You leave her be! She's just doing her job. She's the nicest person around this joint," Mrs. Robinson defended me.

But Mrs. Robinson's daughter walked over to where I stood in the doorway. "My mother had a stroke five years ago, and she's been struggling with neurological issues ever since. All of this voodoo stuff is bad for her health, okay? I don't want to find any more eggshells scattered around this room—or matches or candles or essential oil or powders—or I'm going to talk to your manager."

I nodded, stunned. Just as I was about to excuse myself, Mrs. Robinson called out happily, "So, you got through to her! Your sister! They aren't happy about that. No, they aren't."

With a weak smile, I excused myself and took the steps back down to the first floor to begin my daily duties. Well, this was a frustrating turn of events. I had been counting on being able to ask Mrs. Robinson questions about how we might be able to use voodoo to banish the spirits harassing Mischa. As much as I was excited about having made contact with Jennie, the directions she'd given me on Christmas Eve had only made the curse jump from Violet to Mischa. I needed all the help I could get.

I couldn't afford to botch an attempt to break the curse a second time.

On my ten-minute break, I called Mom. At first she flat-out refused to consider the possibility of my returning to Wisconsin before June, which was when the judge had approved me for a one-week visit at home. I reasoned that my spring break in Tampa was the following week, so I'd only miss one day of school—even if I stayed in Wisconsin through the weekend and attended the funeral on

Monday. But Jennie was right; Mom only relented when I reminded her that Mrs. Portnoy had once been there for us.

"Mischa's totally alone, Mom," I reminded her. "Everyone's been telling me that the doctors don't think Amanda's going to pull through." Mom didn't need to know that Mischa was ignoring my calls and texts, and probably architecting my violent death at that very moment.

Mom sighed, and I could practically hear her changing her mind over the phone. "I don't think I can swing it, McKenna. Would you mind asking your dad to pitch in for the flight? Last-minute airfare from Tampa's going to cost twice what it usually does, plus it's Easter weekend. There may not even be any tickets left."

"I can cover the plane ticket," I lied, suspecting it would be best not to mention that Violet Simmons had anything to do with my plan to return home for the weekend. "I have a job, remember?"

"Ask your father," Mom said sternly, making it clear that she wasn't looking for a reason to talk to him—and that I'd need his permission. Luckily for both of us, Dad tended to leave matters related to custody of me up to Mom as long as they were within the legal terms of the judge's ruling on my case. If I told him she'd already given me her approval, he wouldn't fight me on leaving Florida for a few days. And he was just as eager to avoid conversations with her as she was reluctant to communicate with him.

I texted Violet before heading back inside and she replied almost instantly, saying she'd text me flight info. At six forty-five, when I returned to Mrs. Robinson's room, I was dismayed to find the door locked. She and her daughter must have gone down to the dining hall together. This was a bummer. Not only was I prevented from requesting her advice, but I also wasn't able to tell her I'd miss the next few days at work.

My manager wasn't thrilled to hear that I was asking for time off so soon after beginning work. "The residents like you, McKenna, but this is only your second week with us. I can't guarantee that your job will be open when you get back," Luis told me. "I mean, this weekend is Easter. How am I supposed to find someone to fill your shifts?"

I swallowed hard, regretful that I was jeopardizing the one thing about life in Tampa that I genuinely enjoyed. But saving Mischa was my priority. It was imperative that I get back to Willow and deal with her before she started issuing death sentences. There was no option in the matter, especially if there was even the tiniest glimmer of a chance that we could save Amanda's life.

Rhonda was listening to rap when she picked me up at the end of my shift, which reminded me of how much cooler she was than Dad.

"So. Wisconsin, huh?" she asked as we pulled out of the lot. Violet hadn't wasted any time in booking my flight, which of course made me paranoid about her eagerness to have me back in town. She must have been really afraid that Mischa—or Henry—was going to hurt her.

"Yes," I said while buckling my seat belt.

"You know, your dad's feelings would be really hurt if you got into any more trouble while you're there. I know he's been very cool about you coming to stay with us, and I don't want you to feel unwelcome—we're both glad to have you here—but he trusts you, McKenna. You promised him there wouldn't be more problems, and I'm counting on you. I mean, you don't owe me anything, obviously. But I like to think that we're, like . . . friends?"

We'd stopped at a red light, and I stared out my window at a busy taco restaurant where people were eating outside on the patio. "I know," I said quietly. I couldn't promise that there wouldn't be any more trouble, but the thought of getting hurt, getting *killed*—doing anything more to upset and disappoint my parents—did weigh heavily on my heart. "I'll be back on Tuesday."

Dad was—not surprisingly—distant and quiet when we got home. Throughout dinner, he only seemed to want to talk about the cost of property damage in Willow due to the tornados, as if it were of any real interest to him when he hadn't set foot in the town since my eighth-grade graduation ceremony. As I expected, when I announced that I needed a ride to the airport in the morning, he simply asked if Mom had given me permission to fly back to Wisconsin.

I set my alarm for five a.m. and climbed into bed. Already knowing that my night would be sleepless, I pressed my earbuds into my ears. "So," I said. "The house."

As I'd hoped, Jennie's response came through immediately. I felt a little burst of joy at the sound of her voice again, now reassured that I actually *would* be able to communicate with her whenever I wanted. But her words were as vague as everything else she'd told me so far. "That's part of it, but not all of it. And it's not the whole house. I don't know how to explain it, but what I see is *half* of the house. I don't know what that means."

Violet hadn't told me that she'd booked me a first-class ticket, and it was a nice surprise when I checked in for my flight at six thirty the next morning after Dad dropped me off at the airport.

I'd arrived with almost an hour to spare, which gave me plenty of time to browse magazines, as well as low-key freak out about the situation awaiting me in Willow. As I stood in line to pay at Hudson News, Johnny Cash's lyrics, "I fell into a burning ring of fire," drifted over the sound system. It struck me as an odd song to hear at that hour of the morning, but then again, it was a strange time of day to be buying Twizzlers and a paperback.

"Ladies and gentlemen, this is a sold-out flight, so we ask that if you're unable to stow your luggage in an overhead compartment, please allow one of our flight attendants to assist you with checking your baggage."

Outside the large windows at the gate, the sky was blanketed by gloomy clouds. I quickly checked the weather on my phone: thunderstorms. Great. I'd been so anxious about getting my parents to agree to this trip that I hadn't factored in the element about my own life being in danger, and spending over three hours on two different planes during inclement weather definitely put me at risk.

After settling into my seat in first class, I popped in my earbuds and listened for Jennie over the flight attendant's preflight speech.

"Any ideas on what I'm going to have to do to get this thing off of Mischa?" I asked in a low voice, hoping that the guy in the suit sitting next to me would assume I was on a regular phone call. Now that I would be landing in Wisconsin in a few hours, I had to deal with the fact that I might find myself facing Mischa as soon as the next morning, and I had no plan whatsoever.

Jennie hesitated. "I can't see into the future. I can't tell you how this will end."

"What about when you showed me all that stuff about Violet?" I asked. "In the future? With the doctor?" Back in January, when we'd confronted Violet in Michigan on the ski trip she'd organized and forced her into playing a game of Light as a Feather, Stiff as a Board, Jennie had shown me how Violet would die one day.

"That was different. Hard to explain. Someone else was showing me, and I was letting you watch."

I honestly didn't want to know enough about life after death to ask her to elaborate on what she meant by that. "Any kind of guidance at all would be helpful. Like . . ." I side-eyed my seatmate to make sure he wasn't listening too closely. He appeared to be deeply engrossed in a book. "What if Mischa dies while it's on her? Wouldn't that just make the curse jump to someone else?" I wasn't suggesting that we would *kill* Mischa. The thought of Mischa dying under *any* circumstances made my stomach turn. I hadn't really known Olivia and Candace all that well when they'd died in the fall, if I was being honest. But I'd become much closer with Mischa over the last few months. If she died, I would be devastated; I couldn't even allow myself to imagine what that might be like.

However, even after being trapped in this horrific loop of predictions and death since September, I still didn't fully understand how anyone could ever appease the spirits of Violet's five dead sisters.

"Yes," Jennie sounded like she was uncertain. "I think it would transfer to whoever killed her. It's like an electrical charge. It will always jump to whoever's closest."

"Well, that's no good," I muttered, hoping for everyone's benefit that Henry had abandoned that line of thinking. I didn't want to think about the curse transferring to *him*.

The flight attendant passing my row while conducting the preflight check gave me a cold smile and said, "Please turn off any electronic devices."

I nodded and tapped my phone as if ending my call, but Jennie continued talking. "It's inside of Mischa now, just like it was inside of Violet. You have to get it to come out of her in order to get rid of it."

Inside of her. Like demonic possession? I anxiously waited until we reached our cruising altitude, high above the green patchwork of Georgia, to ask more questions. "Do you mean we have to perform, like . . . an exorcism?"

"I don't know everything," Jennie admitted. "There are five spirits. They work together, and they're powerful. You might not be able to demand that they leave Mischa's soul. You might have to lure them out."

Lure them out . . . A nasty shiver ran through my body and left a stale taste in my mouth. A formal exorcism was scary enough. But luring sounded like something different. Luring would require *bait*. The only time I'd ever seen them, or what I had assumed to be them, was in Michigan when Jennie had predicted Violet's death. They'd looked blurry, like they were figures in an oil painting that had been smeared. Or like a field of energy in the *form* of a person, suggesting the presence of someone without anyone actually occupying space. Kind of like a reflection in a dirty mirror. It was hard to imagine those five things being inside of Mischa, if that was actually how they always looked, and even harder to imagine what they might be capable of doing *outside* of her.

"And if we find a way to lure them out, then what happens to Mischa?" I asked.

"I don't know," Jennie replied.

In Chicago, I guzzled a large coffee during my layover. Johnny Cash's "Ring of Fire" was playing on the sound system again, and I momentarily marveled at the weirdness of hearing that song twice in one day.

I really wished I had a way of getting in touch with Mrs. Robinson back in Florida. I considered calling the Oscawana Pavilion front desk and asking to be put through to her room, but I knew that could result in serious drama if Mrs. Robinson's daughter was screening her mother's calls.

When the flight attendant tapped on the microphone at the gate service desk to announce boarding for the flight to Green Bay, I stood and stretched. There was no first class on this flight, but I was in the first boarding group. I stepped into the short line behind a woman with a severe haircut and a phone pressed to her ear, my boarding pass in hand.

But then, from behind me, I heard my name called.

"McKenna."

I turned around and froze before my mind registered what my eyes were seeing. Because twenty feet behind me stood Trey Emory.

CHAPTER 6

"WHAT ARE YOU DOING HERE?" I ASKED AS MY face broke into a wide smile. I stepped out of line and impulsively threw my arms around Trey's neck. As I squeezed him and tilted my head back to kiss him, my heart swelled with joy. I was so caught up in the thrill of unexpectedly seeing him that only when he pressed his lips against mine did I realize that this was all wrong. What was Trey doing at the airport in Chicago? He was supposed to be at his boarding school. In an instant, my excitement turned to ice-cold dread.

"I was on my way to Florida to find *you*," Trey said. He wasn't smiling about the irony of the two of us running into each other by happenstance at O'Hare airport. The grave expression on his face deepened my fear about his reason for not being at Northern Reserve Academy at that very moment.

"What are you talking about?" I asked. "How are you even here right now?" He looked terrible. He was pale and seemed to have lost even more weight than when I'd last seen him in January. A fading green-and-yellow bruise encircled his right eye. He wore a heavy black winter coat that I didn't recognize, which served as a reminder that it was still cold in the Midwest. I took his hands in mine and stared down at his familiar fingers, at the slim, slightly raised pale scar across his left palm. "Why? How?"

Trey looked around suspiciously, and his eyes lingered on an airport security guard standing outside the Hudson News convenience market. "It's a long story. Why are *you* here?"

The line of passengers waiting to board my flight advanced. The flight attendant announced, "Now boarding passengers for Flight 4632 to Green Bay in Group B. Seating all passengers in Group B."

"I'm going home," I stated the obvious. "You know there was a tornado, right? Two days ago?"

"I saw it on the news."

"Two people in Willow died," I told him cautiously, knowing that he didn't have access to the Internet at Northern Reserve and usually didn't talk to his mom and brother on the phone until the weekend. If he'd heard about the Portnoy family somehow, he probably would have already guessed—based on how I'd hinted on our weekly call that trouble was brewing—that the evil spirits behind the curse were somehow involved with the weather in our hometown. But when he remained silent, waiting for me to continue, my heart sank. I was going to have to be the bearer of bad news. "It was Mischa's mom and dad. And her sister has a spinal cord injury. From what I've heard, her chances aren't good."

Before saying a word, Trey shook his head. "No way."

"Way," I confirmed. I went on to quickly give him a recap of the last two and a half months with details that I couldn't share on our monitored phone calls—about how Mischa had been resisting the spirits' orders to predict deaths.

As I backtracked in the story and told him about how Violet had visited me in Willow before I moved down to Tampa, I noticed him balling his hands into fists at his sides.

The flight attendant announced into the microphone, "Now boarding all passengers in Group C. If you are in Group C, you are now welcome to board."

I winced, knowing that there wasn't enough time remaining for us to keep talking. "I can't miss this flight," I said. "Henry's on his way back to Wisconsin from France, and I'm afraid he's going to try to hurt Violet. Or worse. And I have to stop Mischa from doing something stupid to try to save Amanda's life."

"Oh. Right," he said, as if realizing for the first time that I really needed to get on my plane.

"Can you come with me? To Wisconsin?" I asked. I couldn't leave him, but I couldn't not go back to Willow.

He looked regretfully down at the boarding pass in his hands. "I don't know if they'll let me switch this for another flight. I think I might need a credit card to pay a change fee."

The line of passengers boarding my flight was dwindling. I didn't know what to do.

"Can you give me your phone?" Trey asked. "I just need a way to get online and pay the change fee without having the actual credit card like, physically in my hand. I can get myself on the next flight to Green Bay and give you your phone back tonight."

I was about to hand it over when I thought about Jennie and how long it had taken me to find her. If Trey took my phone and then *didn't* make his way to Wisconsin, I wondered if I'd be able to hear her again. "What if . . . what if I text Violet and ask her to book a flight for you?"

Something surprising—outrage, maybe—registered on his face, and I realized I'd made a huge mistake by even offering this suggestion. "No," he said emphatically. "No Violet. If I'm going to follow you to Wisconsin, she can't know I'm there."

"Okay, fine," I said. "No Violet. Bad idea." The last passenger for my flight was having his boarding pass scanned. I'd arrived—unexpectedly—at a moment I'd been dreading. I loved him, but did I trust Trey? Enough to give him my phone, my access to Jennie? Potentially my only weapon against the spirits tormenting Mischa? I could understand, based on Trey's last interaction with Violet in the woods in Michigan, why he would be reluctant to involve her. But his reaction was surprisingly volatile.

I wondered if somehow *she* had something to do with why he wasn't at Northern.

Trying hard to look like my heart wasn't breaking, I handed Trey my phone. He was, after all, someone I'd known my whole life. He'd known Jennie too. If there was anyone in the world I should have been able to trust with my line of communication with her, it was him. "I really need this back, and I can't explain why right now."

Trey nodded. "I'll just use it to change my flight online from here. I swear. I mean, I can't go anywhere. I'll never make it through security a second time. You'll have it back tonight."

I leaned forward and give him a peck on the lips before dashing over to the flight attendants' desk. I shoved my boarding pass at the flight attendant, who scanned it, and I took one last look at Trey over my shoulder.

"What's your PIN?" he called out to me.

"One zero zero nine," I called in reply. As I walked down the passenger boarding bridge, I wondered if Trey would recognize the numbers. October ninth, ten-nine. The date of the fire that burned down our house on the corner.

By the time I buckled myself into my seat, I was already regretting what I'd done. My stomach churned from anxiety throughout the entire hour of my flight. Without my phone, it would be difficult to reach Henry, I couldn't talk to Jennie, and I wouldn't have any way of tracking down Mischa. And Trey would be able to look through anything on my phone . . . including my call log, which was full of no one but Henry.

The fact that he'd busted out of Northern troubled me, as did his claim that he'd been in the infirmary there on Tuesday night, when we'd last spoken on the phone. How on earth had he been able to get himself to Chicago—especially if administrators at Northern were probably searching for him?

When I landed, I found Mom waiting for me at the baggage claim. "Did you want to stop for lunch?" Mom asked. "I texted you, but you didn't reply."

After the way I'd begged my parents to allow me to have a phone again after I moved to Tampa, there was no way Mom would ever believe I'd left my phone behind in Florida. But I hadn't expected that my missing phone would be an issue almost immediately after I landed in Wisconsin. So I lied. "I think I packed it into my bag."

"Well, I hope it turns up when we get to the house," Mom told me. She studied me hard for a moment before she raised an eyebrow at me and continued, "Mary Jane stopped by last night to tell me that Trey's gone missing from his school. She asked me to let her know if you hear from him."

My stomach iced over, and I prayed that my face wasn't revealing anything. "Oh. Wow. I just spoke with him on Tuesday night. He said he was in the infirmary, but didn't say anything about leaving Northern. How could he have gone missing?" I let some of the real anxiety I was feeling play out on my face, hoping Mom would take it as concern for him.

Mom met my gaze for just a fraction of a second, and the doubt I saw in her eyes felt like a little stab in my side. "I think he'd be smarter than to contact you and put you in a difficult position. But I hope that when you find your phone, you'll tell me if he's reached out to you."

"Mom, I really think my phone's in my bag," I insisted, trying to steady my voice so that she wouldn't think I was trying to start an argument with her. "I thought I had it with me on the way to the airport, but I may have even left it at Dad's because it was so early in the morning when we left the house. You can search my stuff if you want."

We stepped outside the sliding doors of the airport, and Mom looked straight ahead as we continued on to the parking lot. "I don't want to search your stuff. I want to be able to trust you."

I let the conversation drop, even though knowing that my mom believed I was lying about my phone made me feel awful. On the ride back to town, I imagined scenarios in which Trey was apprehended by authorities with my phone in his possession, and tried to think up lies to have ready in case I needed to explain to my Mom how *that* may have occurred.

Twenty minutes later, when we reached the outskirts of Willow, I saw the first evidence of the tornados that had touched down. The way they'd inflicted damage in focused areas was eerie. On some blocks, trees had been uprooted and cars had been flipped along one side of the street, while everything on the opposite side looked perfectly normal. Mom insisted on driving me past Glenn's house so that I could see the tree that had smashed through his living room. I got the sense as we slowed down in front of his address that this was Mom's not-so-subtle way of reminding me before we arrived home that Glenn was crashing there, and would be for a while until his house had been repaired.

We turned at the corner of Martha Road and drove past the familiar houses of my street. This was the first time I'd ever traveled down our block without feeling an instant sense of security, a reassurance that I was safer simply by being home. My throat tightened; I wasn't sure if tears were threatening to form because I felt even more endangered by being back there, or because Martha Road was no longer truly my home. Since moving to Florida, I'd focused every spare ounce of my energy on yearning to be back there, and now I had to admit that it seemed unlikely that I'd ever actually live on that street again.

It was a gloomy, overcast day, and the dead, yellowed lawns of our neighbors made our street look as if winter had simply exhausted it. I noticed as we pulled into our garage that the FOR SALE sign was still standing on the Emorys' front yard. It was a relief but not a shock that they hadn't found a buyer yet, since Willow wasn't exactly a real estate hot spot. But the sign served as a reminder that Mrs. Emory was being sued for an enormous sum of money by the Simmons family for the actions she'd taken as a college student. Trey and I hadn't discussed the status of that lawsuit in any of our phone conversations since January.

What Mom hadn't told me earlier in the week when we'd touched base was that Glenn's two dogs and ancient cat were also staying at our house until his house was livable again. "Luckily, so far everyone's getting along," Mom told me as Glenn's dogs circled me, tails wagging, the moment I stepped inside the house. Maude, my mom's puppy, certainly seemed to be happy about the company.

As the afternoon passed, I wondered where Trey was—if he had gotten a ticket, if he had successfully got on a plane without being noticed. The uncertainty was torture.

And I felt lost without my phone. It was possible that Violet was texting me to see if I was home yet, and her house was much too far from mine for me to even consider walking. Matt Galanis, Mischa's boyfriend—with whom she was most likely staying—lived pretty far from us but within walking distance. I was putting Maude on her leash with the intention of strolling over to his house to see if Mischa was there when our landline rang. I heard Mom answer it in the kitchen. And then, "McKenna? You've got a call."

"Who is it?" I asked. No one *ever* called our landline except my grandparents and telemarketers fund-raising for charities.

"It's Cheryl," Mom said.

Out of everyone I knew, Cheryl was my only friend who would have even known my home phone number from back in the days before we all had cell phones. Maybe she'd been trying to reach me on my cell and Trey had told her that I was back in town, and that he had my phone? Cheryl was the only one of my female friends who Trey truly liked, so it was possible—though unlikely—that he would have replied to her. He hadn't hesitated to do whatever I asked of him in an effort to save Mischa's life, but I got the sense that he thought she was shallow and pretentious. I took the phone from my mom and pressed it to my ear. "Hello?"

"McKenna, it's Violet." Her voice was trembling and high-pitched. "I need you to come over to my house *right now*."

My heart immediately started to pound. I side-eyed my mom, who was making a pot of coffee. I had to sound casual. "Uh . . . what's going on?" There was no way my mom was going to agree to drive me over to the Simmons house. Technically, Violet still had a restraining order against me. But something had to be very wrong, and I fervently hoped Henry didn't have anything to do with it.

On the other end of the line, I heard another voice in the background before Violet replied, "Amanda Portnoy's doctors are saying that she's not showing any signs of improvement, and Mischa's here. Just come as fast as you can."

Mischa? At Violet's house? "Are you safe?" I asked.

There was a long pause before Violet said, "No. Just hurry."

Click.

My chest ached as if the wind had been knocked out of me. The only reason I could think of for Mischa being at Violet's house was if she'd decided to kill Violet—either in an attempt to rid herself of the curse, or to punish Violet for having started all of this in the first place. As extreme as it may have been to imagine Mischa showing up at Violet's house in a murderous rage, I knew that's what Henry had been thinking too—and Mischa had just as valid a reason.

"I'm going for a walk," I announced in a tiny voice. My mom said something in response about the cold, but I was already on my way into the living room to put on shoes. Maude whimpered at the front door when I set her leash back on its hook on the wall. I couldn't put her at risk.

Outside, I jogged toward the only destination that came to mind: the Richmonds' house.

My stomach sank when I rounded the corner of Cabot Drive and didn't see Henry's truck in the driveway. I didn't know for sure if he'd even made good on his threat to fly home to Wisconsin. But I dashed up the front steps anyway and jammed on the doorbell, winded and frightened that Mischa had already done something irreversible in the fifteen minutes it had taken me to get there.

It felt like an eternity passed before I heard the lock on the door twist from the other side. When the door opened and I saw Henry standing there in his boxer shorts and a T-shirt, hair rumpled, I almost cried in relief. "You're here!"

"What are you doing here?" he asked as he opened the screen door and stepped out onto the stoop. "I thought you were in Florida until the summer."

"I'm here for Mischa's parents' funeral," I said. I couldn't get into everything until I was sure no one could hear us. "I'm sorry to come over here unannounced like this, but I need a ride to Violet's house. It's urgent."

Anger simmered in Henry's eyes at the mere mention of Violet's name. "Are you serious?"

"Mischa's over there, and Violet called me in a panic. Mischa might be about to do something crazy."

"I texted you an hour ago, and you didn't write back," he said. "I thought you were mad at me."

"I'm not mad. I lost my phone," I told him, wondering what

Trey must have thought when he'd seen that text come through from Henry. I'd deal with that guilt later.

Henry calmly ran his hand through his hair and studied me. For a second, my heart flooded with fear that he might tell me that perhaps we should step back and let Mischa do whatever was on her mind. But then he said, "Okay."

Henry pulled on a pair of jeans, and we hopped into his truck. It felt as if we were driving across town in slow motion even though the peek I stole at Henry's speedometer revealed that he was driving way over the speed limit. When we arrived at the Simmonses' property, Henry idled in front of the gate across the private drive leading to Violet's house. He lowered the driver-side window and pressed the button on the video security panel to announce our arrival.

But no one responded. We didn't hear a crackle over the intercom signaling that anyone inside the house had activated the system to greet us or open the gate so that we could enter.

"Maybe we're too late," I whispered, gazing through the windshield and past the iron stakes of the fence at the peaks of Violet's mansion in the distance.

Henry shook his head. "We need to get in there. We'll have to climb over the wall."

My entire body felt like blocks of ice. "I'll need a stool or something to stand on. It's too high." I already knew from experience that the wall couldn't be easily scaled. Violet's grandparents had put quite a bit of thought into keeping intruders off their property. "And there are chunks of glass embedded in the cement along the top. We'll have to put down a blanket or something, or we'll both end up needing stitches."

"We can use my coat, and I'll lift you," he said as he threw the truck into reverse. Just as he was cranking his steering wheel to pull back out onto the rural highway so that we could drive to a point at which the wall was lower than it was near the gate, the gate creaked as it opened inward.

"Look! She let us in!" I exclaimed—although I didn't know if it was Violet or Mischa who had opened the gate from inside the house.

Henry slammed on the gas and we barreled down the private drive, under the canopy of tall trees that had made me feel as if I were entering another world the first time I'd visited this place. When we reached the fountain and roundabout parking area in front of the house, Henry parked haphazardly and we both leapt out of the truck in unison. I took notice of a dark green Mini Cooper parked next to the fountain and assumed it was Violet's; she'd recently turned seventeen, and it was easy to believe her parents would buy her a brand-new car.

"Do you think she's going to answer the door?" Henry asked as we ran up the steps.

"I don't know," I said. "Maybe we should get inside another way." I grabbed the handle and pushed down the lever to see if the door would open, very afraid of what we were about to walk into, but the door was locked. My finger hesitated before I pressed the doorbell. There was a possibility that Mischa had killed Violet, and we were going to cross the threshold into a crime scene. In that scenario, there was also a possibility that Mischa was planning on killing the two of us the moment we stepped inside too. I was sure Violet's house had a heavy video surveillance system. It was a possibility that either she or Mischa was already watching us standing there on the doorstep as we deliberated what to do.

Just then, Henry startled. I followed his eyes to the big living room picture window on our left. We both saw just a flash of the curtains moving, and a quick glimpse of Mischa watching us before she vanished from view.

I unleashed my fists on the front door and pounded with all my might. "Mischa, let us in! Open this door!"

But when the door didn't open within the next few seconds, Henry and I realized in unison that we were going to have to somehow break in.

"The sunroom doors," I said. "Around the back."

Without waiting for him to reply, I dashed down the stairs, intending to sprint around the side of the house, but then stopped so fast in my tracks when I heard the door behind me creak open that I almost fell over.

"Inside." It was Mischa who had answered the door, and she was positioned strangely, her body contorted inside the house so as to poke only her head through the doorway as she leaned back to greet us.

"Stay behind me," Henry commanded in a low whisper as I reached him on my ascent back up the stairs.

When we stepped into the Simmonses' foyer, we saw why Mischa had opened the door at such an odd angle. She held Violet in a headlock and had her hunched over in a way that prevented her from making eye contact with Henry and me.

A bolt of terror shot through me. I wouldn't consider my emotional maturity adequate for the task of negotiating the release of a hostage, and I was not prepared to watch Violet—or anyone else— die. There was truly no telling what Mischa might do, and what it would mean for all of us if she decided to snap Violet's neck and make us witnesses to a violent murder. She had extraordinary upper-body strength for a young woman our age; she specialized in floor routine and the parallel bars in competitions.

"No phones," Mischa growled at us through gritted teeth.

"Just do what she says," Violet instructed us. "There are knives in the kitchen, and she isn't playing around."

"Mischa, come on. This is ludicrous," Henry, ever the peace-maker, said in a calm voice.

Mischa fired back hatefully, "My sister's in a coma. Every hour that passes, she suffers more brain damage. I don't think this is ludicrous."

My heart ached for Mischa. Jennie and I had shared a bond so special before her death that I was, even then, eight years later, desperate to restore it in any way I could. Mischa and Amanda weren't twins, but shared a similar bond. They were sisters, but they were best friends, too. I couldn't imagine how Mischa would ever navigate the loss of her parents if she also lost Amanda.

Henry gently continued, "I know it doesn't seem like it, but we're all on the same side, here."

Mischa shook her head. She was wearing an oversize T-shirt over leggings, and looked like she hadn't showered or brushed her hair in days—which may very well have been the case. "Violet's not on our side! She started this—and I figured out how to end it. We need to play the game again!"

I took a step back in fear and reached for the gris-gris I wore around my neck to be sure it was still there. I'd never seen Mischa look so disheveled and enraged before. Her state was understandable considering everything that had happened, but it was still jarring to see someone—a friend—who was usually so together look so completely . . . monstrous. "It won't work, Mischa. We *did* play the game again, in January with Violet while you were missing. All it did was lift the curse off her and put it on you because it had skipped you."

"I *know that*! Don't you think I *know*? You're not listening!" she insisted. "We'll play the game, and I'll predict Violet's death so that the curse moves back to her, and then she'll have to kill herself— *while* it's on her. It's the only way to end this. The person who's cursed *has to die*."

I didn't want to be the one to tell her that when Jennie had shown me Violet's death, it wasn't supposed to happen for decades. And her death was peaceful. Serene. She could expect to live until a healthy old age . . . unless, of course, it was possible that our fates changed with each passing second, and the circumstances of Violet's inevitable death depended on when and how they were being predicted. But even so—Jennie said that wasn't the way.

"I don't have time to explain how I know this, but that won't work. Even if we play the game right now, and make Violet kill herself—"

Violet shouted in protest, "Hey! I'm right here!"

"I know. Sorry. It still wouldn't work. Technically, we'd be the ones forcing her to die, and the curse would just jump back to one of us," I said, pretty confident in my assumption based on the answers Jennie had already given me. Seeing that the wildness in Mischa's eyes wasn't dissipating, I added, "That would put us right back where we started."

"You're wrong," Mischa snapped, her eyes filling with tears. A strange smile pulled itself across her face. "We don't have to make her kill herself. She already knows how guilty she is." She bent her neck to address Violet directly. "I don't even know how you get out of bed and make it through the day, honestly. You're a murderer, and you've killed more innocent people than we can even count. You owe me this. You owe it to all of us to save my sister's life for what you did to Olivia and Candace!"

"I already know for sure that your plan won't work," Violet said in a trembling voice, "because when I inherited the curse and realized what I was going to have to do, I tried that."

We all fell silent. I looked to Henry in surprise, and even Mischa took a moment to digest that. "Liar," she finally said.

"It's true," Violet insisted. Mischa loosened her grip on Violet just enough to allow her to stand up straight enough to look at us, and I was surprised at how different she looked from the last time I'd seen her. Her complexion was paler, which could easily have been explained by the brutal winter, but she had greenish rings beneath her eyes, and looked a little jaundiced, too. I remembered Cheryl mentioning Violet's extensive absences from school and wondered fleetingly if she'd actually been sick that winter.

"I overdosed and my parents sent me off to Arizona for six weeks of rehab. Last December—after I had to kill this girl I knew from school named Brianna. I was stuck there for Christmas and New Year's. You can look her up, if you don't believe me. I have a shirt from the rehab place upstairs in my drawer."

This genuinely took me by surprise. Violet had poured her heart out to me back in January, after we'd successfully lifted the curse off of her, but she hadn't told me that she'd ever been that desperate to free herself from it. I hadn't thought it would be possible to ever feel sympathy for her, but I did at that moment.

"The thing is, the spirits won't let you die. If the curse is on you, they just won't let it happen! You can step in front of an eighteen-wheeler truck, and it'll swerve out of the way instead of hitting you. You can be ready to jump off a bridge, and someone will come along at the last second and tackle you," Violet explained.

"You expect me to believe you tried all those things?" Mischa asked. She was silently crying so hard that her nose was running, but she didn't seem to notice.

"I tried one thing—one thing that should have worked—and it didn't. If you want to save your sister's life, then I'm telling you . . . any of us dying *is not the solution*."

This was the first thing Violet had said that seemed to matter to Mischa. She erupted into sobs, and for a moment I thought she was going to release her hold on Violet. But then she yanked Violet toward her and gripped her even more tightly. "No. Amanda's doctors are saying that she's probably suffering permanent brain damage, and the longer she's on the respirator and feeding tube, the worse her chances are for *ever* recovering. We're playing the game again, *now*. I want this thing *off me!*"

Henry and I exchanged loaded glances. That changed everything. On the drive over here, I'd thought we had more time to find a way to break the curse: twelve days until the next new moon, and three before I had to fly back to Florida. But Amanda's time was running out fast.

"Okay, okay," Henry told her. "We'll play the game again. Just let Violet go so that we can talk about the best way to do this."

Mischa shook her head. I was starting to wonder if Henry was going to tackle her to get her to release Violet. Violet was swinging her arms, having more difficulty breathing now that Mischa had strengthened her hold. If her face was turning red or even blue, we couldn't tell because it was tilted toward the floor, and her dark hair obscured it.

"We can call Kirsten at the bookstore and ask her to help us," Henry offered.

Still, Mischa adamantly refused. "No other people. We can't wait around for anyone to drive all the way up here from Chicago."

"Mischa, let her go. She can't breathe!" I cried out.

"It's going to be okay, Mischa," Henry assured her. "We're going to figure this out."

As much as I adored Henry and appreciated his being there, I knew that his words of comfort for Mischa were just meaningless platitudes. He may have lost Olivia to Violet's game, but I still didn't think he fully understood what we were up against. I thought of Amanda in her hospital bed, presumably hooked up to ventilators and IVs, and couldn't stand the possibility of Mischa losing her entire family.

Violet grunted and tugged at Mischa's arm. She attempted to pinch Mischa's skin with her fingernails, and Mischa swatted her fingers away. Mischa wrapped her other arm around Violet's neck and squeezed even more tightly. Violet reached forward as if hoping to grab on to something to steady herself, but there was nothing in front of her. She kicked one of her legs out in desperation.

Henry's chest rose dramatically as he inhaled deeply. As if Mischa could sense that he was preparing to tackle her, she took a giant step back and shook her head. "Don't do it," she warned. "I can break her neck faster than you can get over here."

I could tell from the tremble in Mischa's voice that she wasn't kidding around. She'd worked out somehow in her head that killing Violet that day would make things better in one way or another, even though it was clear to me that we had two separate and distinct problems to solve. Which was why I said in a tiny voice, "Transferring the curse to someone else won't save Amanda."

Before Mischa had a chance to react, I added, "I need to borrow someone's phone."

CHAPTER 7

HENRY GATHERED ALL OF THE CUTLERY FROM the butcher's block and silverware drawer the moment we stepped into the Simmonses' enormous kitchen, and he stashed them somewhere on the house's second floor to keep them out of Mischa's reach. It seemed like the announcement I'd made about having a plan in mind had calmed her down, but neither Henry nor I wanted to take a chance on having to witness a bloodbath that day.

At my request, Mischa downloaded a radio app to her phone and tuned it in to AM 1354. I popped her AirPods into my ears, hoping I'd be able to hear Jennie's voice coming through, even though I feared that if I was successful in being able to communicate with her, my rapt audience would expect me to deliver answers. And I knew Jennie had none.

My only idea—sacrificing myself—*wasn't* a good one. It was a rash, desperate attempt to buy more time until I could figure out how to lure the spirits out of Mischa.

And I wasn't sure if Jennie would agree to it.

Or that Amanda would ever regain consciousness at this point—even if we successfully took her out of the queue to die.

Mischa leaned forward across the table. "Can you hear her?"

"I don't understand what we're doing, here," Violet admitted impatiently. "Your *dead twin sister* is going to talk to you through the phone?"

Henry glared at her and angrily shushed her with a finger held up to his lips.

"Not yet, she's not," I said as I listened intently. Just as I was about to give up, I heard the crackle of static and Jennie's voice greeting me.

"Hello?"

"It's me," I said, and then felt like a fool. Who else would it be? Who else would be able to hear her? "I have a big favor to request."

Turning my head to avoid making eye contact with Mischa, I asked, "So . . . would it be crazy for me to allow Mischa to predict my death so that maybe her sister's life is spared?"

For a long, uncomfortable moment, Jennie didn't reply. Then she said, "Yes, it would be crazy. And dangerous."

"But would it work?" I asked, glad that none of my friends could overhear Jennie's voice over the AirPods so that I could digest her reply before they could.

I took Jennie's silence as a yes.

I held my finger up for my friends, suggesting they should wait, and I stepped into the sunroom.

Once outside on the patio in the surprisingly cold afternoon, I asked, "If I let Mischa predict my death, would it be my real, natural death in the future? Or would the spirits come up with some kind of violent story that would happen before the next new moon?"

"Don't know," Jennie admitted. "If they want you, then you'll die before the new moon."

I stole a glance over my shoulder into the house through the glass panels of the sunroom. Panic and adrenaline were coursing through my veins as if I was about bungee jump off a bridge. No one was forcing me to do this, I knew. The next new moon was on April twenty-second—in just shy of two weeks. I wasn't exactly giving myself an abundance of additional time to figure out how to get the curse off Mischa, but was possibly making all the difference in saving Amanda.

"Is there any other way to save Amanda's life?"

"No," Jennie told me. "She's first in line."

Right. *A life for a life, an even trade.*

It was all a big gamble.

"Could you show Mischa a fake death for me? Something that would seem real to the spirits so that they'd back off Amanda—but that obviously won't actually happen?"

Jennie was silent for a long beat. "Not sure. The curse was originally put on Violet's grandmother, and Violet inherited it. So she had a stronger connection to the spirits than Mischa does. They were able to make it clear whose soul they wanted, and provide visions of the death predictions to Violet for her to describe.

"But Mischa's connection isn't as strong, so they're going to give her more like . . . flashes." Jennie told me. It seemed like she was struggling to describe exactly how the spirits would communicate the death predictions to Mischa, but I got the picture. "It might not be as easy to trick them this way."

"But you can try?" I asked. I would have only volunteered myself for this if Jennie was willing to try, and I believed with all my heart that she would find a way to deliver whatever she promised. She'd managed to spare me from Violet's death prediction back in September, and she'd delivered a prediction for Violet back in January that had saved the lives of a lot of people.

Jennie replied, "Trying isn't good enough. I'll convince them."

I was about to thank her when I heard her continue, "I hope you're not doing this for me."

"For you?" I asked, confused.

"Yes. Out of some sense of guilt that I'm here, and you're there," she explained. "This was always the way it was supposed to be. It's my responsibility to protect you, and I'm happy to be here, doing this."

It took a few seconds for me to swallow the urge to cry. It wouldn't do me much good to walk back into Violet's kitchen with tears in my eyes, but Jennie had just answered one of the biggest questions I'd been wanting to ask her. She wasn't jealous that I was alive and she . . . wasn't. "Thank you," I managed to say, wanting to elaborate but knowing there wasn't time.

"You aren't alone," she reminded me. "We're together, always." I headed back inside with an icy feeling lining my stomach despite Jennie's reassurance that she would show the evil spirits a fake prediction for my death. It intensified when I noticed that Mischa and Violet were anxiously awaiting my return. With numb fingertips, I pulled Mrs. Robinson's gris-gris out of my shirt to remind myself that it was still there, hanging around my neck.

"Okay. This is the plan," I said, folding my hands on the table and trying my hardest to prevent them from trembling. "Mischa's going to predict my death so that I can take Amanda's place in line, and then we're going to figure out how to break the curse."

Both Henry and Violet looked at me in abject horror.

"No. Absolutely not," Henry stated emphatically.

"Just . . ." I cut myself off. It seemed like a bad idea to explain the logic, and better for Mischa—and the spirits who'd be conducting their evil through her—to fully believe that what we were doing was real. "This is the only way to save Amanda. You guys have to trust me."

"McKenna, no! That's insane!" Henry insisted. "What about your mom? You can't do this to her. It's . . . selfish."

I glared at him and gave a small shake of my head, trying my best to convey that he should just trust me. Reminding me about how much my mom had already lost wasn't making me feel any more confident about my proposal. Under the table, I reached for his hand and squeezed it. "It's the only way."

Henry's mouth twisted into an angry frown. He slid his hand out from my grasp, got up from the table, and shook his head furiously. "I won't watch this." He balled his hands into fists at his sides, and then pointed a finger at Mischa. "If you do this to her, you're a monster," he said, before marching out of the kitchen into the living room.

Mischa looked like she was about to start crying again, but then whispered, "Are you sure?"

"Yes," I said, trying my best to sound convincing. It wouldn't have been fair to make Mischa feel like she was being selfish when all she really wanted was to save her sister.

Anticipating that we'd be playing the game that afternoon in one way or another, she'd brought a deck of tarot cards with her. As she began shuffling, I chewed my lower lip and felt my fingers turn increasingly cold with fear. When I'd first thought of this idea, it hadn't occurred to me that if something went wrong, I could expect to die at any second—even as soon as on the drive home from Violet's house. Before I ever saw Mom again. Before I had a chance to find out if Rhonda was having a boy or a girl.

But it was too late to rescind my offer. I had to have faith that Jennie would protect me, and that Amanda's condition would improve. After all, what I was offering wasn't all that heroic. Mischa had lived with the knowledge of her own impending death from September until January. What I was subjecting myself to wasn't any worse than what she'd already endured, but I was still scared.

Mischa handed the deck to me and said in a timid voice, "You have to shuffle these while thinking about how you want the cards to predict your death."

Grim, I thought. To make light of the situation and try to get her to smile, I performed a fancy pivot cut shuffle. Mom and I often played War at home, and I'd practiced shuffling moves as a kid. Neither Mischa nor Violet seemed impressed. I realized suddenly that the shoestring on which the gris-gris hung around my neck began to make the skin it was touching itch with a burning sensation while I handled the cards, and I quickly handed them back over to Mischa. Dread pooled in my stomach. "Tough crowd," I tried to joke.

"Are you sure?" she asked me. "Are you sure you're done shuffling? You have to be sure."

I took a shallow breath and said, "Yes." How can anyone ever be sure when they're shuffling a deck of cards that will predict the end of their life? I didn't want to touch the deck again, though. I wanted this over with.

"Okay," Mischa said. She set the deck facedown in front of her on the table. "I'm going to take the first five cards and set them down, and then . . . I'm not sure what will happen."

Violet lost her patience. "How can you not know what will happen? McKenna's trusting you with her life!"

"Because that's all they've shown me!" Mischa snapped. "I'm supposed to put five cards down, and then they'll take over."

Five. A chill ran down my spine.

I still had Mischa's AirPods in my ears, and her phone was set in front of me on the table. Jennie had remained quiet since I'd returned inside, but the time had come for me to ensure that she was still engaged. "Jennie, if you're listening, Mischa's going to draw the top five cards from the deck."

"I'm always here," Jennie told me. I was starting to get the sense that it required less effort from her to repeat certain phrases.

I nodded at Mischa, giving her permission to begin.

As she reached for the deck and touched her fingers to the top card to peel it off the stack, my scalp broke into a raging fit of tingles. Violet and I locked eyes, both of us sensing in unison that the spirits were now present. When Mischa set the first card facedown on the table, I thought perhaps I was imagining things when the table shifted almost imperceptibly. But Mischa noticed the subtle movement too, and her hand hesitated over the stack before she reached for a second card.

This time, right as she placed the card on the table, the table jolted as if hopping up off the floor.

"Um . . . ," Violet said, with enormous eyes. "Maybe we shouldn't be doing this."

It took every ounce of courage I could summon to look at Violet and say, "It's fine. We have to keep going."

The third card was set on the table, and the table rattled and shook on its own as if an earthquake was occurring in the Simmonses' kitchen. Its legs knocked loudly against the kitchen floor, and I slid my chair back a little bit, in fear. Oddly, despite the table's erratic movements, the stack of cards remained intact without spilling, and the three cards Mischa had already placed in an array stayed fixed to the tabletop as if they'd been glued there.

"I don't like this," Mischa said as her fingers hovered over the deck.

"It's too late. I already shuffled, I already set my intention," I reminded her. "We have to finish it."

She set down the fourth card, and a breeze swept through the kitchen, catching all three of us by surprise. Our hair was swept up over our heads and across our faces. A stack of mail on the counter behind Violet scattered across the room.

And somehow, the shoestring of the gris-gris became unknotted at the base of my neck. The leather pouch slid down my chest and hit the table in front of me.

The first rush of wind died down to a moment of alarming stillness before another—stronger—blast of air stirred around us. Cabinet doors opened and slammed shut. A wire rack suspended from the ceiling over the stove from which copper pots and pans hung began swaying, and the pots and pans clacked and clanged. I was grateful to Henry for having taken the knives upstairs because it seemed entirely likely that if he hadn't, there would have been blades flying through the air. Petals were torn from the spring bouquet set atop the kitchen counter in a crystal vase, and bits of pink and peach miniature carnations flew past our faces. The vase skidded across the countertop toward the edge, but none of us dared to get up from the table to keep it from falling off. The table continued to shake, now rocking back and forth on its four legs.

I wondered how it was possible that Henry hadn't heard the commotion from the next room, but for all I knew, he'd driven himself home.

The blood had drained from Violet's face, and unexpectedly seeing her appear so genuinely afraid made me more anxious about what was happening than the hurricane unfolding around us. She raised her voice to be heard over the raging wind. "Something isn't right! We should stop!"

But nothing had been right for months. Fear wasn't an adequate reason to give up. In fact, if I'd learned anything so far in my dealings with Violet's spirits, when they were trying to scare me, it was usually a good indication that I was on the right track.

"Jennie, should we continue?" I asked breathlessly. The crystal vase slid over the edge of the countertop and shattered on the tile floor a few feet behind Violet, startling all of us.

Before Jennie could reply to my question, Mischa squealed. A fifth card was rising above the deck entirely on its own, levitating in the air for a moment before drifting into the row on the table to join the other four cards. "I didn't do that!" she exclaimed. "I didn't even touch it!"

Violet bolted upright from her chair so quickly that it toppled over behind her. "Enough." She reached forward to swipe the cards off the table, but in a flash, four of them burst into flames, igniting the sleeve of her sweater.

I jerked backward. I could handle ghosts and *loa*, shattered windshields and even avalanches on ski slopes. But fire zapped my courage completely. It had made me nervous even to light candles every morning to cast the protection spell on Mischa's family; even the smell of smoke made my pulse accelerate in terror.

"Oh my God!" Violet screamed, shaking her arm. The fire devoured the cashmere, and in less than a second it looked like her entire right arm was covered in flames. She dashed to the sink and threw on the water, but Mischa's voice returned my attention to the table.

"McKenna?" Mischa asked.

The two of us watched as the one remaining card of the five— the other four had been turned to black ash—levitated up from the table, which had finally fallen still. The fire from the other four cards had spread to the edge of the circular table, and small tongues of flame danced around the circumference of the table as if it were the main ring of a hellish circus.

The lyrics that had haunted me all morning creeped into my mind. "I fell into a burning ring of fire . . ."

"Are you watching this?" Mischa asked me, her voice barely audible over the water blasting in the sink and the wind blowing through the kitchen.

"Yes," I whispered in reply. I was too terrified to reach out and grab the card, although it was hovering in the air to suggest that I should do exactly that.

"I don't want to do this anymore," Mischa said, shaking her head. A single, fat tear rolled down her cheek. "This was a bad idea. I don't want you to die either! I can't lose you!"

"Shh. It's going to be okay." My voice was quivering. The flames crackling around the edges of the kitchen table were nearly a foot tall, and I'd have to reach over them if I wanted to pluck the card out of the air.

"Don't touch it!" Either Jennie had been silent all this time, or I hadn't been able to hear her over the roar of the wind. But now she was adamant. "That's what they want!"

At the sink, Violet had turned off the water and was clutching a towel to her right arm, but her eyes were filled with tears, and she was yelling something inaudible at me and shaking her head.

Suddenly, Mischa leaned over the flames and grabbed the hovering card. Simultaneously, the smoke alarm went off. Henry appeared in the doorway a split second later. An expression of absolute confusion bloomed on his face when he clocked the envelopes blowing around the room, the pots swaying overhead, the table on fire, and Violet cowering at the sink. Without uttering a word, he tore through the room and vanished into the sunroom, returning with a fire extinguisher.

But the moment he yanked out its safety pin, the flames vanished. The wind stopped abruptly.

"What the hell?!" Henry yelled at no one in particular.

Mischa, Violet, and I looked around the room—which had just been in total chaos—completely baffled. The letters and petals dropped to the floor. The kitchen table didn't show a single sign of just having been on fire . . . although the four tarot cards Mischa had set on it remained piles of ash.

Violet sobbed softly as she inspected her right arm. The sleeve of her sweater looked as if nothing at all had happened, but it was rolled up over her elbow. "My arm was just completely burned. I could feel it blistering! I thought I was going to have to go to the hospital."

Mischa's lower lip trembled as she glanced at the tarot card in her hand. "Ten of Swords, reversed," she said. She held it out toward me so that I could see it for myself.

The card that had been chosen by the spirits for me had an illustration on it of a guy wearing a tunic lying on his stomach with what appeared to be a bunch of swords jabbing into his back and neck. It took me a second to piece together what was being depicted, since Mischa was holding the card upside down, so at first it looked like someone lying on top of a picket fence. Never having had my tarot cards read before, and having no familiarity with the practice at all, I was clueless as to what this meant.

"Ten of Swords is about resistance. It's usually shown to a person combating inevitable change or loss," Mischa explained, her eyes enormous. She tossed the card down on the table and yanked her hand back as if the card were a dirty tissue. "Someone who has a choice to move on with their life after a bad situation, but they may not realize that they're free to welcome change."

"I don't like any of that," Violet said as she joined us at the table and took a look at the card.

"But because they showed it to you upside down, that's a reversal," Mischa continued, her tone growing more serious as she shook her head. "I'm not very good at this yet, and we can Google the meaning if you want, but I think they're trying to tell you that you've already lost a battle, and you just refuse to accept the loss. You still believe a victory's possible, but it's not. It's time to call it quits."

I huffed loudly in annoyance. "How is that supposed to be a death prediction?"

Mischa bit her lower lip and hesitated, making timid eye contact with me before continuing. "It's part of the suit of Swords in the minor Arcana. Wands is associated with air."

"Air," I repeated numbly. My heart stopped for a second before it occurred to me that perhaps this had been Jennie's way of protecting me. She'd shown the spirits her own death instead of mine when we'd played the game with Olivia, tricking the spirits into thinking my soul wasn't theirs to claim—maybe she'd done the same thing again. Air could mean . . . smoke. "Jennie?" I asked, clinging to hope that she'd been in control this whole time. "Did you show them the fire?"

All I heard over Mischa's AirPods was static.

"Jennie? Are you there?"

No answer.

Once, in fourth grade, when I had been roughhousing on the playground during recess with Roy Needham, who'd been doing fake karate moves, he accidentally kicked me in the solar plexus. I'd doubled over, unable to breathe, incapable of piecing together how he had totally incapacitated me with one swift blow. The realization that Jennie might not have been able to protect me this time around, and that I might actually die in a way related to air within the next twelve days, made me feel just like I had on the playground that day.

I would be boarding another airplane on Tuesday morning. In four days.

Henry set the fire extinguisher down on the kitchen floor, crossed the room, and wrapped his hand around my wrist. "We're leaving."

CHAPTER 8

WE BARRELED DOWN THE LONG PRIVATE DRIVE and through the gates of the Simmonses' property in stiff silence. Once we rounded the corner, however, Henry pulled over to the shoulder, yanked the parking brake, and pounded on the steering wheel with his fists.

"Why did you do that? Why did you have to offer yourself up like that?"

I'd never seen Henry so emotional before, not even at his own sister's wake. His face was pink, and he angrily wiped his eye with the back of his wrist. When I opened my mouth to explain that I'd thought I had it under control, I found that I was at a complete loss for words.

I'd taken a huge misstep, and now it was too late to take it back. I'd been overly confident about Jennie's ability to protect me—*and* herself—and now I was next in line to die. Henry had been in such a hurry to leave that I'd left Mischa's AirPods and phone behind before trying to see if I could find Jennie's voice on a different channel. She'd *just* told me that she was always with me, and now she was gone. Maybe forever. Mrs. Robinson had said Jennie was in a "dark place," and I'd been so focused on trying to be a hero that I hadn't paused to wonder if Jennie was endangering herself by helping me. Now, if Mischa's prediction for me came true and I died within the next few days, I couldn't assume I'd be reunited with my twin . . . which was just as detestable as the idea of death, itself.

That thought was devastating enough to make me gasp before I could reply to Henry. Eternity, all alone.

When Violet had been the storyteller conducting the game, there had never been a violent spectacle like what I'd just seen at her house . . . although I guess in retrospect I'd been suspicious the night of Olivia's party that the flames in the fireplace were burning just a little too high.

But still . . . there'd been no windstorm. Nothing had burst into flames. Not like the hellish display I'd just witnessed.

"That was just so—so—stupid!" Henry exclaimed. "What am I going to do if you die?"

I swallowed hard, not wanting to promise him that I wouldn't die, because I'd never felt more distracted and out of touch with reality in my whole life than I did while staring out his windshield at that moment. It seemed not only possible but likely that I'd die before I'd ever arrive back in Tampa. Before I'd ever see Trey again. And the way Henry had been acting since we'd arrived at Violet's house that day was making the reason why he'd been FaceTiming me every day for the last few weeks very clear: He cared more about me than I'd allowed myself to realize.

I was distractedly worried about Trey, what had happened to him at Northern to make him escape, and where he was at that very moment. But I could no longer deny that I felt a powerful attachment to Henry, too. His brimming tears made *me* feel like crying.

"You'll . . . keep trying to figure this thing out . . . get the curse off Mischa."

Henry squeezed his eyes shut and shook his head. "What's the point of figuring this out if you're not here? What's the point of"—he looked up and winced at what he saw through the windshield: gray sky and bare trees—"any of this if you're not here?"

I couldn't speak; the same thoughts had been occurring to me for the last few weeks about going through the motions of life in Florida without Trey. What was the point of anything if we couldn't be together? Realizing that Henry felt that way about me made me acutely aware of how insensitive I'd been toward him. I had been flattered by his attention. I'd grown accustomed to receiving it. But while I'd been eager to end the game that Violet had started so that I could secure my future with Trey, Henry had remained involved in the effort more out of a desire to prove himself to me than to avenge Olivia.

Even though he knew I was in love with Trey.

Even though it was clear to me now that he'd left Wisconsin for France to try to get over not only Olivia's death, but his feelings for me.

And instead, once he'd gotten there, we'd fallen into a daily habit I had to admit that—despite the conflict in my heart and my loyalty to Trey—I loved.

I wanted to assure Henry that I'd find a solution. There had to be a way to get the curse off Mischa, and with the guidance of Kirsten and Mrs. Robinson, we'd figure it out. But for the first time since my mom had gotten me up in the middle of the night to tell me that Olivia had been in an accident, I'd lost all hope that anything in our lives would ever be okay again. Maybe the only option was for all of us to save ourselves, to walk away, and to let the cursed person figure out terms for collecting souls that they could justify, in the same way that Violet's grandmother had.

"You'll need to get justice for Olivia," I reminded Henry in a trembling voice, not wanting him to suspect how much darkness had crept into my thoughts. "You'll keep searching for answers."

He switched off the truck's engine and turned to face me. "I don't care about answers anymore. Maybe I used to want to understand why Olivia had to die, but answers aren't important anymore. Just ending this—however we can—*that's* important."

"I don't know. I just . . ." I wanted to give Henry a reason to believe that there was still a way out of this, even though I couldn't connect my thoughts together well enough to decide what to do next. "Jennie said the spirits are, like, inside of Mischa. We have to draw them out of her using some kind of bait if we want to get the curse off her."

"I don't care. I don't want to hear about it anymore. I don't want to—"

He stared blankly out the windshield and continued, "I thought if I went to France and was in a new place, meeting new people, keeping myself busy with tennis, that all of this would fade into the background. This town. What Violet did to my sister. My parents and—and—my mom's just, like, plummet into depression."

I held my breath as I waited for him to admit he was angry about our routine of talking every morning. Hearing him express regret about that would have made the tears gathering in my eyes start to fall. Talking to Henry had been the best part of my day every day in Florida, in many ways even better than my restricted phone calls with Trey because I'd had to be so careful about the words I chose on Tuesday nights.

"But I don't *want* to move on. I know everybody talks about how much Willow sucks and how there's nothing to do here, but this is the only place I ever really want to be. And you're the only person I ever want to be around."

Henry fell silent and slowly raised his eyes to meet mine. Before I knew it, he was leaning toward me, and since he hadn't buckled his seat belt in his haste to leave Violet's house, he slid across the seat and took my face in his hands. His lips were on mine before I realized what was happening. From the instant our mouths connected, I knew intellectually that it was wrong, that I was only supposed to kiss Trey and him only. But Henry's kiss felt so safe and filled me with so much warmth—it was like crawling under a heavy comforter during a thunderstorm—that I didn't pull away.

I didn't want to pull away at all.

And as his lips moved against mine, I realized that I wanted to keep kissing Henry forever, as if the homecoming dance hadn't been rescheduled, as if we'd fallen in love that night, and Olivia hadn't pitied Violet enough to invite her to her birthday party.

Maybe my life would have been better if I'd never fallen in love with Trey. The way I felt about him was incomparable to anything else in my life, but if I'd never experienced it in the first place, I wouldn't have known what I was missing. In a normal world, without evil curses inflicted on all of us by the sinister history of the Simmons family, this simple sensation of feeling adored and protected by Henry would very likely have been mine to enjoy.

But it wasn't.

At that very second, Trey was probably somewhere in Willow. Trey, the guy who would do anything at all to protect me, even at the expense of his own safety and comfort. As he entered my thoughts, I opened my eyes, and the magic moment between me and Henry was abruptly severed. I pulled away, our lips parted, and I was plunged back into the harsh reality of what I'd just done to myself back at Violet's house. "Sorry," I apologized and hung my head. "This is just—we shouldn't."

Henry sighed and tilted his head back, his eyes fixed on the truck's ceiling. "I'm sorry. I know you and Trey are . . . I just wish things were . . ." He paused, and then said, "You know what? I'm not sorry. I wish things were different, but I'm not sorry."

The windows of the truck had started to steam up. All at once the cabin of the truck filled with awkwardness, and Henry buckled his belt and started the engine. Through my window, I looked back at the Simmons mansion over the wall that encircled their property and the tops of the evergreens that maintained their privacy. From where I sat, I could see only the steep gables of the house, and its many chimneys rising up from the shingled rooftop.

Forcing the kiss out of my mind, I focused on what Jennie had told me. *Half.* An aspect of the curse involved half the house. A cold feeling of doom had crept into my chest, and I didn't want to think about the Simmons family or curses any more that day. I needed to get my hands on a phone or radio so that I could ask Jennie exactly what had happened and whether or not I could expect to die at any moment.

"What do we do now?" Henry asked, sounding exhausted.

"I don't know," I admitted. "Do your parents have a radio? Or could I use your phone? I should probably try to get back in touch with Jennie. I mean"—I didn't want to give myself a single reason to have hope for saving myself, but—"I didn't touch the card at the end of whatever that was. Mischa did, but I didn't. So maybe my prediction wasn't complete."

Henry said, "My dad has an old radio in the garage for emergencies."

We stopped back at my house so that I could tell my mom I was going to the Richmonds', assuming that she'd be more likely to agree if Henry accompanied me. When Mom heard us enter through the front door, she called from the laundry room, "McKenna? Where have you been all this time?"

"I walked to town," I replied, eager to deal with her quickly to avoid becoming emotional. "And I ran into Henry Richmond at the pharmacy. He's here."

She entered the living room carrying a basket of laundry. It struck me for possibly the first time ever that my mom actually looked *young*. Even compared to the other moms in town—moms who had the gray dyed out of their hair, moms who wore yoga tights to the grocery store after their morning kundalini class at the community center—she didn't look nearly as old and tired of life as I had grown accustomed to thinking of her as being. Perhaps she had a new energy about her because of Glenn. But it was possible she looked different to me now that I was looking at her through the lens of the likelihood that she'd probably outlive me, instead of the other way around. I pushed the thought away.

"Well, hello, Henry. I thought you were back in France at that resort job of yours."

"I came home for Mr. and Mrs. Portnoy's funeral," Henry said, which was only partially true. "Plus, the resort tends to empty out over Easter weekend, so it's not like I'm missing much."

Not wanting to waste a single moment of my remaining time, I asked, "Is it okay if I go to the Richmonds' house for a little while?"

The flash of objection I saw on her face made me feel a pang of guilt. I'd given her every reason to be suspicious of me. Before January, she'd been much more trusting of Henry, too, but I suspect it had unsettled her that he'd been in Michigan with me and Trey at the time of the avalanche, since Henry had graduated the previous June and had no business being on a ski trip with a bunch of eleventh graders.

Sensing her objection, Henry chimed in, "My mom's home. She's sorting through all of Olivia's things to donate to charity."

As he probably knew it would, this softened Mom's expression. She asked how Mrs. Richmond was doing, and I told Henry to wait a second while I dashed down the hall to grab a heavier sweater.

My bedroom was startlingly cold, and my eyes instinctively traveled straight to my window, which was cracked open. Before I even saw my phone on my bed, I realized that Trey must have made it back to Willow. Heat crept into my cheeks at the thought of how Henry's soft lips had felt against my mouth just fifteen minutes earlier. Now that I knew Trey was very close by—he may have even been in my bedroom while I'd been kissing Henry—my betrayal of him felt as bitter as I knew deep down that it was. I had no idea how he'd managed to change his flight or hitch a ride from Green Bay to town, but he'd set my phone on my bed underneath a book, right next to the weekender bag I'd brought home with me. For a moment, I wondered if there was any reason why he'd taken a book off my shelf to cover the phone, or significance to the book he'd chosen (*Rebecca* by Daphne du Maurier). But then I reasoned he'd probably just placed the book over the phone in case my mother peered into my room and saw the phone there, which would have made her wonder how I could have lost it in plain sight.

Dread overwhelmed me as I plugged my phone in to charge its dead battery. Trey was obviously in some kind of serious trouble, but he had still found a way to return my phone, which made me deeply regret what had happened in Henry's truck. Trey hadn't left a note or any other sign to indicate that he'd stopped by my house, but I figured that was for my own safety as well as his, since both of our mothers were under the assumption that he would eventually find a way to contact me. After a minute or two of my phone recharging, I was able to turn it on, and was heartbroken to discover that Trey hadn't even left me a text note or other message on it—or anything else that might have suggested to me where he was going next or how to find him.

I needed to find him. Dealing with what had just happened at Violet's house had to be my first priority. But finding Trey was a pretty close second.

Afraid that my mom was giving Henry the third degree in the living room, I didn't want to leave him out there with her for too long. But, unable to resist my curiosity about whether or not I'd be able to connect with Jennie on my own phone, I popped my earbuds into my ears and tapped open my radio app. "Jennie?" I asked quietly, straining my ears over the static on our channel for her voice.

All I heard was static. I double-checked to make sure the radio app was still set to AM 1354, and my chest ached when I saw that it was.

I wondered if maybe Violet's spirits had been able to find Jennie in the dark place while she was communicating with me during Mischa's card trick. Maybe they'd pieced together what she'd done the first time Violet tried to predict my death, and were punishing her.

Or maybe, I desperately hoped, she had just switched communication over to a different frequency to trick the spirits, and I'd be able to find her on Mr. Richmond's radio. I stuffed my phone and my charger into my tote, not feeling focused enough to concoct a credible lie for my mom's benefit about where I'd found my phone.

"Be home by six, McKenna," Mom told me as I stepped past her to leave with Henry.

"Okay, Mom."

"You're welcome to join us for dinner, Henry," Mom offered as we passed through the front doorway. "I'd love to hear what you've been up to in Europe."

When we climbed back into Henry's truck, I told him, "Don't come for dinner. I'd love the company, but it's going to be super awkward." I went on to explain to him that Mom had a new boyfriend who was staying with us temporarily.

"Yeah . . . well, speaking of super awkward, I'm warning you in advance that our house is a bit of mess. I mean, more than a bit. Thing have gotten out of control with my mom while I've been away, and my dad's been encouraging her to get help, but I haven't had a chance to clean up yet."

"What do you mean, clean up?" I asked, but then was distracted by an incoming text message on my phone.

813-555-0172 3:11 P.M.

Hey this is Ernesto from school. Call me back if you can.

My mind went blank for a second before I remembered: *Yes, Ernesto. The kid who saved my life yesterday morning.* "This is weird," I muttered. "Some kid from Tampa I barely know just texted me. I don't even know how he got my number."

"What does he want?"

I was about to say that I didn't know when my phone vibrated again with a second text.

813-555-0172 3:12 P.M.

My grandmother says she knows you

Without wasting a second on filling Henry in, I tapped my phone to call Ernesto. "Hey," I said when he answered. "This is McKenna Brady. You texted?"

"Yeah. Cool, thanks. My grandmother lives in a assisted living facility called Oscawana Pavilion? She randomly called me today and asked if I know you," Ernesto said. I could hear the television on in the background on his end of the call. "She says you work there?"

"Let me guess," I said, wondering why tingles hadn't broken out on my scalp yet—because this situation was a perfect example of when they usually would. My heart was ballooning with hope. "Mrs. Robinson is your grandmother?"

"Yeah. How weird is that, right? What a coincidence," Ernesto said, sounding genuinely amused.

I had stopped believing in coincidences months earlier. "Are you there with her right now?"

"Yeah."

I asked to speak with her, and Ernesto put me on speakerphone.

Henry and I parked in front of the Richmonds' house and sat there with the engine off while I explained to her what had happened at Violet's house, and how I'd fallen out of touch with Jennie. "So, what do you think? Am I next in line to die?"

Mrs. Robinson replied, "Well, you shuffled the deck and set an intention. You opened yourself up to it, didn't you?"

"Yes, but . . ." She was right. I had initiated this mess. "I thought my sister could trick them."

Mrs. Robinson's warm laugh trickled through the phone, angering me. This was serious—a timer had been set on my life—and she was *laughing*. "Haven't you ever heard the expression *fool me once, shame on you, fool me twice, shame on me*? They're on to you, girl. They know exactly what you're up to now. None of those tricks you used before will ever work again."

I stole a glimpse at Henry and shook my head at his concerned expression to indicate that this conversation was not going as well as I'd hoped. Figuring Mrs. Robinson wouldn't mind, I tapped my phone to put her on speaker on my end too.

"That's why I had my daughter call Ernesto at school and tell him to get his butt over here on the bus. I had a dream about you last night, and I just knew you were getting yourself into trouble," she said.

"I put you on speaker so my friend Henry can hear you, Mrs. Robinson. He's helping me," I told her. "How can I know for sure if I'm next?" I asked. If Kirsten were around, she'd be able to see my aura. But we couldn't drive down to Chicago just for that.

"Well, it's a good thing you brought me all those oils, because technically you bought them, and they're your possessions. So I can do some work tonight once the sun goes down and let you know in the morning."

The morning. I wasn't sure I'd be able to sleep at all without an answer.

"What about breaking the curse?" Henry asked with eager eyes fixed on my phone. He was tightly gripping the steering wheel even though he hadn't released the parking brake yet.

"That's Henry," I clarified for Mrs. Robinson's sake. "Mrs. Robinson? This is my friend Henry. Henry, this is Mrs. Robinson, my"—I hesitated, unsure of exactly what Mrs. Robinson was besides a treasured mentor—"friend from Florida. My sister said we'd have to lure the spirits out of the girl who has the curse on her as a first step in breaking it," I said.

"Sounds about right," Mrs. Robinson agreed.

I asked, "How would I do that? I mean, how could I possibly get them out of her soul and then keep them from going back in?"

Mrs. Robinson paused for a moment, and I could hear what sounded like *Wheel of Fortune* in the background on her television. "You can draw them out by tempting them with a better host. Think about what they like to do, and who would be good at it."

"Either someone powerful and good at bullying people into doing things, or someone super trustworthy," Henry mused. Oddly enough, when he put it that way, I guessed Violet had probably once been more of the latter and had become better at bullying people over time. In fact, when we'd first played the game with her, she hadn't really pressured us at all. She'd made it sound like it would be fun.

"Then what? Is there something we have to chant? Some kind of ritual we have to perform?" I asked. I didn't know much about the practice of voodoo, but I knew enough to hope that Mrs. Robinson's recommendations didn't include any kind of animal sacrifice or blood. I also didn't much like the idea of the spirits fleeing Mischa's body and then roaming freely around town. My assumption was that we were going to have to somehow either destroy them or capture them.

"Well, you've got to decide who your bait's going to be and figure out how to get them close to the afflicted person. Real close. Same room, just a few feet away. In fact, touching would be best. The spirits aren't going to want to travel far. No, they're not," Mrs. Robinson told me. "When you figure that part out, call me back, and I'll tell you what to do."

Henry and I sat in the cab of the truck in silence for a moment after Mrs. Robinson ended our call. Who in the world could we possibly ask to serve as bait—and get them to agree to *touch* Mischa so that the spirits would attempt to leap from her soul—and into theirs? We'd have to do it at the memorial—Mischa would obviously definitely be in attendance, and there's no way she'd agree to meet us anywhere else. I said so out loud to Henry.

After nodding, Henry raised an eyebrow at me. "I thought you said you lost your phone."

"I did," I replied, trying to sound casual and not defensive even though I felt so. "But I just found it when we stopped by my house."

Henry removed the keys from the ignition, but neither of us moved to get out of the car. He stared forward through the windshield. "You know, Trey's missing from his school."

I bit my lower lip in fear that Henry was about to call me out for plotting with Trey and leaving him out of the loop.

"There was a story in the *Gazette* this morning. Police in town are asking people to keep an eye out for him in case he shows up around here," Henry continued.

"I know about the article," I admitted. "I didn't read it. But I heard that Trey's missing. I think he's in trouble." Guilt twisted my mouth as I thought about how foolish it was for me to have insisted that Trey follow me back to this town, where so many people were on the lookout for him. I hoped wherever he was at that moment, he was well hidden, and that he'd contact me before nightfall.

I could tell there was more that Henry wanted to say or ask me, but instead he simply said, "I think you're in more trouble than he is."

With that, Henry reached for the door handle, and I did the same.

Henry hadn't been exaggerating about his house being a mess. Newspapers were stacked in columns throughout the living room, forming a wall around the couch. Boxes that looked like they'd been shipped from online stores were stacked like inconsistently sized bricks along one wall, nearly reaching the ceiling. A faint smell of mildew wafted through the living room, making me wish we could step back outside for fresh air.

Trying not to let my discomfort show on my face, I followed Henry into the kitchen to enter the garage through the interior door, and I pressed my lips together in shock when I saw more of the same: orderly columns of paper bags, mountains of emptied, washed aluminum cans, flattened cereal and frozen dinner boxes, stacked and tied with twine.

"What's going on, here?" I asked Henry. The Richmonds' house had always been spotless and beautifully decorated. Even back in

January, when Henry and I had crashed here the night I'd broken out of the Sheridan School for Girls, the house had been thoroughly vacuumed and smelled like fresh potpourri. Seeing it in such a state of clutter made me feel like we'd crossed over into the twilight zone.

Henry tossed me a bottle of water from the fridge. "My mom's obsessed with saving everything. She keeps saying maybe it can all be used later for something else."

"You mean . . . hoarding?"

"Yeah. My dad's been trying to get her to speak to a therapist. She's always been into scrapbooking and saving souvenirs and stuff, you know? Seems like losing Liv has kicked her tendency to want to save and cherish things into high gear." He looked around the kitchen with a look of defeat on his face. "Part of me pities her, and another part of me is really angry that she's let it get this bad."

Henry didn't seem to want to elaborate, and I didn't press him for details. Mrs. Richmond had seemed okay to me when I'd interacted with her back in January. She'd offered us the use of her credit card during our trip to Michigan, and had kept the secret of our destination, even though she must have known we were venturing directly into danger. But now, on second thought, it was clear to me that her actions were not those of an adult in the best state of mental health. I suppressed the urge to suggest having my dad call Mrs. Richmond to provide help. I might not live long enough to see that offer through.

Henry flipped on the lights in the garage, and my breath caught in my throat. A red Prius—Olivia's sixteenth birthday present—was parked in the second spot. I hadn't seen it since the day she died; I'd passed it in the high school parking lot that morning and felt a pang of envy. I'd never—in all the months that had passed since September—wondered who'd traveled out to the mall in Green Bay to pick it up after the accident. But now, seeing the forlorn expression on Henry's face when his eyes landed on it, I had my answer.

"I think the radio's over here, with his tool stuff," Henry murmured, passing me to cross the garage and reach steel shelving that was heavily loaded with shrink-wrapped flats of bottled water from Costco and cardboard boxes. Mr. Richmond's radio wasn't hard to find, but it required a fresh pair of nine-volt batteries. "I guess they didn't use this thing the day of the tornado," Henry remarked.

Fortunately, since Mrs. Richmond's tendency to stock up on seemingly trivial items and store them was not a new one, Henry was able to find the exact batteries he needed in the kitchen.

He popped the new batteries into the radio, and then turned the on/off knob. After a second, the chords of an old Bon Jovi song trickled out of the old device, sounding like the radio waves carrying them to our ears had originated somewhere very far away—like the other side of the galaxy. "We're in business. How do we find your sister?"

I switched the frequency to AM and twisted the dial all the way to the left before slowly, slowly turning it to the right. Leaning forward, I turned my head to position my ear closer to the radio's speaker. "Don't laugh at me. I know I look ridiculous," I told Henry.

He smiled at his feet and jammed his hands in the pockets of his jeans. "It's a little late for either of us to worry about looking ridiculous."

I had scanned all the way across the dial, twisting as slowly as my fingertips would allow when I arrived at AM 1354. "Jennie?

Can you hear me?" I asked self-consciously. Even though Henry had seen me dashing through snowbanks without a coat, posing questions to a pendulum, and getting tossed out of Violet's house by meatheaded seniors, it still felt a little odd to have him witness my attempt at paranormal communication. But he'd handled everything that had happened at the occult bookstore and on the mountainside in Michigan in stride, so I didn't think he'd be freaked out by my growing abilities to communicate with Jennie. If I was actually able to reach her, I was pretty Henry would have been impressed.

But all I heard was the crackle of static, followed by mariachi music originating too far away for the signal to come through clearly. "Maybe FM," I said, trying to stay hopeful.

"What are you listening for?" Henry asked.

Once he'd asked, I had to admit that I couldn't quite explain it. "It's not really a sound. It's more like a vibe. So I guess I'm not even really listening for it, exactly. I mean, I can hear noise, or a voice. But it's more like my ear feels a certain way—it kind of tickles my skin, and I sense that something's sending me a message. It's only worked a few times, so it's not like I'm an expert, or anything."

Henry nodded as if this made perfect sense to him, although *I* didn't even completely comprehend how it worked. All I knew was that every time Jennie had reached me through radio waves, it had been easier to understand her.

After just two twists of the dial across the FM frequencies, I heard a distinctive female voice asking, "McKenna Brady, are you listening?"

I flinched in surprise and smiled at Henry. "Did you hear that?"

Henry's eyes traveled to the radio as if he might be able to see evidence of what I was claiming to have heard. "Hear what?" He looked at me with a flash of dismay, like either he thought I was pranking him, or he was jealous that he hadn't heard what I had.

"Can you hear me? Say something if you can hear me."

"I can hear you!" I said to the radio as if the speaker was a microphone.

"Geez. I was starting to think I was just babbling to myself."

Although the voice coming across the radio sounded female, I was sure it didn't belong to Jennie. I raised one eyebrow at Henry, wondering if he had figured out who'd contacted us through the radio at the same time I had. But he was completely oblivious to what was happening in front of him. "You really don't hear anything?" I asked him, and he shook his head.

"Just static," he admitted. Despite the fact that he was wearing a heavy sweater, he crossed his arms over his chest and rubbed his upper arms. "But it's freezing in here all of a sudden. Can you hear your sister?"

I shook my head.

"He can't hear me. He's not a freak like you."

"Thanks, Candace," I laughed, feeling overjoyed and emotional, while looking Henry in the eye. I was thrilled to hear my deceased friend's scratchy voice, even though connecting with her instead of Jennie made me even more worried about what had happened to Jennie when Mischa had read my card. I had to wonder why I was suddenly able to hear Candace; had she been trying to reach me since the fall? Or was my ability to hear souls' messages growing stronger? "Could you give Henry some other kind of sign that you're the one talking so he doesn't feel left out?"

"Ugh."

The overhead light flickered. Henry startled and squatted as if he'd felt the ground move beneath his feet and he was bracing himself for an earthquake. His eyes looked upward, and he pointed at the light fixture. "Candace did that?" he asked.

"Tell him that's nothing compared to what I do at Isaac's house," Candace said. "He's hooking up with Hailey West now. Did you know that? I haven't even been gone six months."

"Sorry," I told her. Isaac Johnston was just about the last person on my mind those days. "Candace. The place where you are. Is it . . . dark?"

There was a long pause before she replied—long enough to make me fear our connection had been broken.

"What's she saying?" Henry asked.

"Shh," I said.

She finally said, "It's hard to explain because things aren't really light or dark in the way you'd think about where *you* are. Here, it's just . . . nothing. There's nothing around me in any direction. I can see you guys, but it's, like, through a thick screen, sort of."

I was wondering, of course, if Candace had ended up after death in the same place as Jennie. "I can't talk for long," Candace continued, making me realize that pursuing this line of questioning to try to establish communication with Jennie again was selfish of me and wouldn't necessarily solve my most urgent problems. "They don't want me talking to you."

I didn't have to ask who she meant by "they." "They know she's talking to me," I informed Henry, and he also immediately knew which "they" I was referring to.

"Ask her about getting the spirits out of Mischa," he urged me.

"Candace, Violet's curse is on Mischa now. We have to use someone else as bait to—"

She interrupted me. "You don't have to fill me in. I already know all of that. And you already know who the best person is."

I shrugged at Henry and replied, "I promise you, I don't already know."

Candace sighed, exasperated, and I could vividly imagine her rolling her eyes at me. "Come on! Someone who easily influences other people, either through charm or by bullying?"

I mentally ran through all of the names and faces of kids I knew at Willow High School. Many of them were people who had never even registered on Candace's radar. Roy Needham was a bully, but more of the kind of guy who started fights in the parking lot than someone who had mastered the art of peer pressure. Sophia Diaz, a senior, was rumored to have flirted her way into the starring roles of several theatrical productions of the drama club, but wasn't exactly beloved by her peers. Besides which, I barely knew either of those people well enough to loop them into a plot involving Mischa. "Just tell me," I demanded.

"You're standing right next to him!"

Although I consciously tried to keep my eyes focused on the radio, they drifted up to Henry's face anyway. "Bad idea," I told her, hoping Henry hadn't inferred what we were discussing. His blank face and eager eyes suggested that he was completely oblivious. "That's not an option."

"Um, hello. It's the *best* option," Candace insisted. "Mischa knows him and trusts him, and he's already clued in to what's happening. So you wouldn't have to lie to him about the plan."

"Too many complications if anything goes wrong," I said, not wanting to elaborate in front of Henry. If the spirits were to somehow latch on to Henry and burden him with the curse, it wouldn't be fair to him to expect him to reap souls after losing Olivia. He'd already suffered enough, and so had his parents. And furthermore, I just couldn't imagine Henry having the heart to kill someone else, no matter the consequences for refusing to follow orders.

The radio emitted a long stretch of crackling static before Candace replied, "That's my recommendation. But if you think you know better—"

"Not an option," I repeated.

The static was increasing, making it more difficult for me to discern Candace's voice from the hissing and popping. All I was able to make out from her reply was, ". . . going to have to choose, eventually."

"Choose what?" I asked impulsively. *Choose eventually.* My impulse was to believe she was referring to Trey and Henry. *But choose which one of them for . . . what? Love, or as some kind of sacrifice?*

"They're here," Candace said, sounding alarmed. The overhead light in the garage flickered again, catching Henry's attention. The volume of audio coming from the radio momentarily cut out, and when the static returned, it was noticeably quieter. "Are the batteries dying?" I asked Henry.

"Those are brand-new batteries," he reminded me.

I slapped my palm against the top of the radio, not ready to end my conversation with Candace just yet. "Candace, I'm losing you," I shouted. Inside the Richmonds' house, muffled by the garage door, the smoke alarm in the kitchen began going off.

"What the hell?" Henry muttered. He took a few steps toward the door before hesitating. "I don't smell smoke. Do you?"

"I don't think there's a fire," I told him, distracted by my eagerness to maintain my connection to Candace. But the static was so thick that if she answered me, I couldn't hear her, and her "vibe" was gone. Desperate, I flipped the radio over to check the battery compartment again, and swore when I saw sticky brown liquid oozing out from the plastic panel door.

"Don't touch that," Henry warned as I instinctively reached to pop the door open. I set the radio upright on the workbench again and slapped the top of it, causing it to spit out one last burst of static. With it, I heard just the last snippet of Candace's voice uttering the last name—other than Henry's—that I wanted to consider for the role of bait.

And then . . . the radio went silent.

"What's happening?" Henry asked. "Can you still hear her?"

I twisted the radio's tuner in both directions, but Candace was gone.

CHAPTER 9

I T SHOULD BE ME."

Henry had ignored my request that he turn down my mom's invitation to our house for dinner, and had rung our doorbell at six o'clock carrying a bouquet of flowers from the grocery store. When I answered the door, I looked up and down the block in a state of heightened paranoia, terrified that Trey might be lurking behind a bush, watching and making an incorrect assumption about why Henry had come over. But I had to assume that Trey's instinct was to stay as far away from our street as he could get, which didn't make me feel much better since most businesses in town were still closed because of tornado damage.

I was grateful for Henry's company. His presence at the dinner table distracted Mom from the fact that I felt too queasy to eat. I still hadn't put together any kind of strategy for finding Trey, and had yet to find any comfort in Candace's recommendation. I was mentally freaking out a little bit.

We sat in the kitchen, speaking in hushed tones over cups of coffee while Mom and Glenn watched a British baking show in the living room.

"No," I disagreed. "It can't be you! We have no idea what we're doing. What if we mess something up and you get stuck with the curse? I may be dead within the next two weeks. Then you'd be on your own."

Henry refused to look me in the eye. "Don't say that."

"Well, it's true," I insisted. "Watch this." I reached for the salt shaker at the center of the table and poured a little mountain into my cupped hand. Then I overturned my hand to dump it on the table, which was covered in a white tablecloth.

"What are you doing?" Henry asked.

I answered, "Look. It's gone."

As soon as I'd gotten home from his house earlier that afternoon, I'd tossed salt to the east, suspicious that what had happened at Violet's house that day might have changed the outcome of Mrs. Robinson's salt test. No longer was salt that I'd touched turning red when it hit the ground. Now it was simply vanishing the instant it left my hand.

Henry patted the tablecloth where the salt should have landed, and then licked his fingertip, touched the tablecloth, and held his fingertip up to his eye for close examination. "What the hell?!" he exclaimed. "How did you do that?"

"I didn't do anything. But I'm pretty sure that means I'm scheduled to die next," I said, hoping that my nonchalant attitude didn't reveal my panic.

"Look," Henry said with his head hung. "I wasn't the nicest guy in high school. In fact, I was a total dick to a lot of people, including your boyfriend, and probably a lot of other people I don't even remember. A lot of people avoided me, or were nice to me because

139

they were afraid I'd make fun of them and get other people to join in. Honestly"—he looked up at the ceiling—"I probably even got better grades than I deserved from some teachers because they didn't want me to confront them, and didn't want to have to deal with my dad if I failed a class."

I didn't say anything because as much as I'd grown to genuinely like Henry after getting to know him that year, much of what he was saying was true.

"If we're serious about using someone as bait to get the spirits out of Mischa, I'm our best bet. We might not get a second chance to do this. I mean, there's no way Mischa's going to cooperate more than once." Henry had made up his mind, and he was absolutely correct on all counts.

But still . . . I was never going to agree to risk his safety. Not even with my own life in the balance.

"Candace suggested someone else," I informed him. "And I don't like that option much more than using you, but . . ." It took effort for me to lie with a straight face. "I think she may be a better choice."

Henry demanded that I tell him who the alternate suggestion was, and I refused; I had to first decide whether or not I could go through with risking the fate of someone so undeserving and unsuspecting. I promised that I'd call him first thing in the morning with my decision, and it felt as if my intestines were tied in knots as I waved good-bye to him from the front door when he pulled out of our driveway.

Not surprisingly, I didn't sleep at all that night. Around two in the morning, I admitted defeat, got up, opened my laptop, and wrote a detailed history of how I'd come to understand the curse on

Violet and how it not only had claimed the lives of my friends, but had also resulted in the death of Stephani deMilo and nearly killed several other eleventh graders over the winter. Knowing better than to leave something so alarming on my laptop, I drafted the file in Google Docs, carefully wrote an e-mail containing a link to the file and a password to open it, and scheduled it to automatically send to Henry on April twenty-third, twenty-four hours after the next new moon. It was the most efficient way I could think of to make sure that he'd have all the information he'd need to continue trying to break the curse in the event that I died in the next few days.

As I reached across my nightstand to turn off my lamp, my eyes fell upon the copy of the book that Trey had placed over my phone earlier that day. With an electric jolt blasting through my body, I suddenly knew exactly what he'd been trying to communicate to me in a way that my mom wouldn't have understood if she'd happened to enter my bedroom before me.

Books.

The *library*.

Trey was hiding out at the library in town. Not the library at the high school, which would have been foolish, even for him. The big library, the one that had built its second floor with a charitable donation from Violet Simmons's millionaire grandfather. I smiled widely in the dark, delighted not only that I'd figured out where he was, but that I knew him well enough to understand his clue. After the apocalyptically bad day I'd had, my renewed sense of connection to him made my heart swell.

His choice was a wise one: There were comfortable couches at the Willow Public Library, plus vending machines, bathrooms, and heat. The security system there was probably also somewhat lo-fi, since there probably weren't many people in town interested in breaking in to steal anything other than the ancient laptops at the Internet stations.

My heart was beating so rapidly that I could hear the blood coursing through my ears. Outside my window, the rising sun was turning the sky pink. I was furious with myself that it had taken me so long to figure this out.

I needed to get to him as quickly as possible. Henry hadn't been kidding; there'd been a story about Trey in the *Gazette*, and if everyone in town was keeping an eye out for him, Trey would be crazy to stick around for long. It was Saturday. If I waited until the library opened for business at ten o'clock, there was a chance Trey would have already taken off. The grim realization that this might be my last chance to see him—*ever*—rocketed me out of bed.

I quickly pulled on jeans and a sweater, taking care not to make any noises that would wake Mom or Glenn, and slipped into the garage to see if Mom's bicycle was still in working condition. Aside from having flat tires, which were easily inflated with the old pump, it seemed to be in decent shape until I realized after hopping onto it outside the garage that the hand brakes didn't work at all.

Fortunately, at that early hour on a Saturday, there wasn't much traffic on the roads leading to the library, so the busted brakes weren't a problem. But my joints were jittery, and every movement of my body felt like I was bracing myself for a fatal blow. Potential death was everywhere I looked. Now I knew what Mischa's plight had been like in the fall, when she'd been terrified of eating and drinking for fear of choking to death. Death by air could mean anything. It could include any of the tree branches under which I rode, many damaged and weakened by the storm, falling on me. It could manifest in debris blowing in front of a passing car, and that car blindly swerving and hitting me.

By the time I neared the library, I had convinced myself so thoroughly that I was going to die before ever arriving that I hopped off the bike and walked it toward the building as soon as it came into view. The Willow Public Library, a small brick building with an oddly modern added-on wing in the back, was located on the same street as our park district and shared a parking lot. As I grew closer, I could see the town swimming pool, still empty and desolate, as it would remain until Memorial Day. It was likely that the soccer fields would be buzzing with activity within a few hours, as soon as parents started dropping off kids for their matches. But at that hour, it was a safe bet that no one saw me roll Mom's bike around the back of the library and rest it on its kickstand outside the children's section.

Then I had to figure out how to contact Trey inside the building without setting off any kind of alarms. I paced the perimeter of the building around to the front again, and settled on trying to get his attention with the book return. The oversize metal drawer led to a chute that ended in a bin behind the front desk, and assuming that Trey was on the building's first floor, I figured he'd probably be able to hear me if I called to him through it.

"Hey! Is anybody home?" I called into the empty drawer after pulling it open with the handle. "Hello . . . ?"

Just as I was starting to feel self-conscious, I heard a tapping noise to my left. There was Trey, shaking his head and grinning at me in amusement on the other side of the library's clear front doors, as if whatever terrible circumstances had landed him here were of no concern.

"I know. Very funny," I joked. As always, upon seeing his face, I momentarily forgot about everything bad that had happened in the last twenty-four hours. He was safe; we were together. Seeing him smiling at me from ten feet away was all I could have wanted . . . until I remembered that now *I* was the one in trouble, most definitely more urgent trouble than his. Everything had changed since our brief encounter at the airport less than a day ago.

I swallowed hard, hoping that my sudden wave of sadness wasn't showing in my eyes.

"I was starting to think you weren't going to stop by," he said, scratching his head, which looked like it had been recently shaved. He had less than half an inch of dark hair all the way around his skull, making his face look thinner and his features look more delicate than usual.

I gestured at the library. "It took me a while to figure out your clue," I said apologetically. "How can I get inside?"

"There's a security system," he said, thumbing at an electronic device with an LCD screen on the wall. "They should be trying to get more people in here instead of trying to keep them out, if you ask me. But hold on a second."

He walked the length of the entryway and disappeared behind the library's front desk. I took a step closer to the door to see him better through the glare, and noticed that he wasn't wearing socks or shoes. When he returned a moment later, he was holding an index card, which he held up to the door so that I could see it.

"They left the security locking and unlocking instructions on the staff bulletin board," Trey informed me. Written on the card in draftsman hand-lettering were numbered steps for setting the system at night, and disarming it in the morning. "What do you think the odds are that these are still current?"

It was risky to turn off the security system; if Trey entered the wrong code, presumably an earsplitting alarm would sound and the library's security firm would send someone over to investigate. But we decided to go for it, figuring it was a safe bet that our town's librarians were organized. Trey tapped in the six-digit PIN and pressed the pound key. Then we both held our breath for a moment until the word DISARMED blinked twice on the LCD, and the tiny light at the bottom of the security panel switched from red to green.

Trey pushed the door open for me, and I threw myself at him, wrapping my arms around his neck. Before I was even aware of my emotions, the sound of sobbing filled the foyer, and it took a second for me to realize that it was coming from *me*. Being terrified that I might die and of the grief it would cause my parents—who'd already suffered so dearly—was one thing. But being heartbreakingly regretful that I may very well have compromised the life I wanted to one day enjoy with Trey was too much to bear.

Although I'd missed Trey terribly, I'd forgotten what it was like to be in his presence. To look at his face. To feel his breath against my ear. It was impossible to remember so many sensory experiences in perfect detail when we were apart, but what I was reminded of as we stood there was how I never felt more like my true self than when I was with him. I'd been going through the motions in Tampa for so long . . . being the daughter my dad wanted me to be, playing the role of McKenna Brady, new girl at school. Even around Henry,

I was hyperconscious of my behavior, the tone of my voice, and trying to come across as capable and courageous. But with Trey, I didn't have to calculate any element of my impulses, reactions, or expressions.

"What's all this?" Trey whispered into my hair as he held me so tightly against his body I could barely breathe. "I'm here now. We're together. Whatever's happening with Mischa, it can't be worse than what we've already seen."

He loosened his embrace so that I could wipe tears off my cheeks with the backs of my hands. "So much has happened in the last day. Amanda Portnoy—Mischa's sister—is still in a coma, and—"

"Wait. Before you say anything, just . . . listen," he said, staring into my eyes so fervently without blinking that I wondered exactly what had been going on at Northern to cause him to leave. "I can't stay here, in Willow. I have to leave now. This morning. I only came back here hoping I'd have a chance to talk to you, like this. I really was on my way to Florida yesterday when I ran into you at the airport, and thank God I did, or else I don't know how I would have gotten in touch with you again. Being here—in this town—is really dangerous for me."

My heart ached. "Why now? You'll be eighteen in July, and then you'll be free to do whatever you want. They'll probably erase your record," I reminded him, although even as I spoke the words, I knew they'd stopped being true the moment he'd broken out of his school for the second time.

Trey squeezed his eyes shut and shook his head. "I wouldn't have survived until July if I'd stayed."

"What do you mean?" I asked. Trey knew everything there was

to know about surviving reform school. He'd told me before I arrived at the Sheridan School for Girls to keep my head down, avoid calling attention to myself, and keep myself out of situations in which I might rack up social debts to other people. Even though I knew Trey loved earning the ire of teachers at Willow High School, he'd made a point of keeping a low profile at Northern Reserve.

Trey led me farther into the library, to the bright red couches in the children's area where story hour for kids was held. It was odd to find myself there—enveloped in its unique and peculiar smell of old paper—a place where I'd spent so much time in junior high scouring the stacks for books to check out. Dust, illuminated by morning rays of light, danced in the air around us as we sat down. The library, to me, had always been a haven, providing security and promising magic. It was ironic that this particular section of the library had been built by Trey and Violet's grandfather, and now here we found ourselves, discussing our future, which had been wrecked by Violet and her deceased sisters, his descendants.

"Two weeks ago, at the end of March, I had a visitor, okay? And that's weird because I never have visitors. My mom's only driven up to visit me twice since November. So when I went into the cafeteria that day, I had no idea who or what to expect, but the person who'd come to see me was a lawyer. Lawrence Strohmann."

My heart skipped a beat. That name was familiar, but in the same way as the verse of a song you can't quite remember.

"Ekdahl, West & Strohmann?" Trey said, and realization flooded me. Of course. Mr. Simmons's attorneys from Green Bay, the ones who had attempted to bribe Trey's mother into terminating her pregnancy after her affair with Violet's father. When I'd been home in January, I'd come across a letter from them sent to Trey's mom to inform her that she was being sued for accepting payment from them but failing to comply with the terms on which they'd agreed.

I asked, "Was it about the lawsuit? How could you possibly be expected to come up with the kind of money they were . . ."

Trey shook his head. "I think it's connected, but I'm not sure how. He was there to draw up some sort of agreement with me. I don't know how much of this I should believe. But he told me that Violet Simmons has some genetic disorder and will probably die before she turns twenty-one without a kidney transplant."

"What?" I asked in a flat, dubious voice.

Trey exhaled loudly to express his doubt, and continued. "He was there with this huge envelope of paperwork for me to read. It wasn't just one contract, but a bunch of them. Basically, he wanted me to agree to get tested to see if I could be an organ donor, and if I said yes, they'd drop the lawsuit against my mom. And if it turned out that I was a match and was willing to give Violet one of my kidneys, then they'd create this, like, financial trust for me that would mean I'd get money when I turn twenty-four and then more money when I turn thirty-five."

None of this was making any sense at all. But I remembered Violet mentioning how her life hadn't been easy since the curse was lifted from her, and wondered if this was what she'd meant. "Why you?" I asked. "I mean, obviously, you're related. But you can't be the only possible donor!"

"Well," Trey said with a smirk as he leaned back on the couch and folded his hands on his abdomen, "turns out I am. Violet's blood type is B, same as mine. Her mother's blood type is A, so she's incompatible. Her dad is also type B, but Violet's doctors think his kidney might be too large for her system, besides which, according to the lawyer, he has high blood pressure, which disqualifies him. Violet's uncle refuses to have his kids tested because of the whole debacle with the will," he explained.

"The will," I repeated. Violet had told me about how her grandmother had left everything to her out of guilt because she'd also passed along the curse. I vaguely remembered her telling me something about her uncle, who'd wanted to sell the Simmons mansion and split the profits with her father.

"So I'm it. Violet's only hope," Trey said.

Although everything Trey was telling me tracked with things Violet had shared with me in the past—as well as her sickly appearance the day before—something about the proposal seemed suspicious. "You didn't say yes, did you?" I asked.

"No! Of course not. I didn't even take the contracts from him to read over. I wished him luck and went back to my room. But . . ." He hesitated and his expression changed. "The very next night, as soon as the guard on our floor stepped into the stairwell to smoke like he always does at ten o'clock, two guys came into my room wearing pillowcases on their heads and beat the crap out of me. One held me down while the other came at me. My roommate just sat on his bed, watching, like he'd known it was going to happen and was just staying out of the way."

"Your eye," I whispered and reached out to gently touch the greenish-yellow bruise around his right eye. My lip quivered as I tried to imagine the scene he'd described, being attacked while utterly defenseless in an environment where the authorities didn't care what happened behind closed doors. He probably never would have told me so, but he had to have feared for his life. Hearing the awful truth about what had driven Trey to flee Northern made me feel even sicker about having to tell him my news. "Is that how you ended up in the infirmary?"

"The eye was the least of my problems," Trey joked, but I could tell that he didn't think any of this was funny. I appreciated that he was trying to make light of it for my benefit, but I wasn't in the mood to dismiss either of our plights as humorous. "None of it was serious enough for me to have been sent to an outside hospital, which I'm sure was intentional. And then, on Monday, that big envelope of contracts was delivered with my mail, and I had a note from the office saying I could expect a visitor on Thursday. Then I kind of pieced it together; the beatdown was a warning. But this time I'd be expected to either agree to everything or be ready to negotiate. Saying *no thanks* was not an option."

This was a different kind of terrifying from the visits from ghosts and predictions for deaths we'd been dealing with since the fall. Everything I knew about Mr. Simmons suggested that he was ruthlessly greedy and selfish. He was a man who had cheated on his wife while she was enduring devastating fertility challenges, a man who'd made empty promises to a young woman who believed his lies. He'd relied on a team of attorneys to handle his personal business when he was too much a coward to own up to his responsibilities. Mr. Simmons and the power that his vast wealth afforded him, as well as his apparent lack of a conscience, scared me. It was one thing to be afraid that spirits on the opposite side of reality might threaten our safety, and quite another to know that a very alive, very capable man just a few miles away could inflict whatever kind of pain he wanted on us with little likelihood of repercussions.

It hadn't escaped my attention, or Trey's, back in November, when we were first sentenced by Judge Roberts to separate boarding schools, that Trey's operated much more like a minimum-security prison than mine. Now it seemed obvious that Mr. Simmons had had a say in that.

"But he can't just make you donate an *organ*. That's extortion!" I exclaimed. "Besides, you're not even old enough to sign contracts."

Trey picked at his chewed-down fingernails. "My mom knows all about it. They sent her copies of the contracts too. She wants me to agree to whatever they want—the testing part, at least." He fell silent for a moment, obviously hurt by the position his mother had taken. It was hard for me not to butt in with my opinion that Mrs. Emory's encouraging Trey to cooperate with the Simmons family was a deep betrayal. "I get it, you know? It's not fair to my brother that they're selling the house. There won't be any money for college, for me or for Eddie. I could change all that. But it's not even the kidney, you know? I wouldn't think twice about the surgery if it were for someone else, like you, or my brother. I just don't want to take orders from *him*."

My lower lip started trembling uncontrollably, and I swallowed hard to keep myself from crying. Trey was facing the biggest crisis of his life, just as big as what I'd been up against back in September, and there was nothing I could do to help him. He'd helped me research ghosts and curses, and he'd done everything I'd asked for and more when we first realized what Violet had done to my friends. But now I couldn't think of a single way in which I might be able to help him.

"What should we do?" I asked in a tiny voice.

Trey leaned toward me and cupped my face in his hands as a new energy filled his eyes. "I've been thinking a lot about Violet, and Olivia, and Candace—but mostly you and me." He smoothed the hair back from my forehead and tucked it behind my ear. "We're in over our heads, and this isn't our battle to fight, McKenna. I know you have this—this—*thing* inside of you that won't let you abandon someone in trouble. Maybe because you lost Jennie so young and were too little to save her. But it's not selfish to want to have a normal life, okay? We tried. We did our best, but now all I want is to go somewhere with you—somewhere else. Somewhere safe. I don't care if we're penniless, and Mischa ends up killing every single person in this goddamn town. All I want is to be with you and leave all this behind."

His face was bright with hope, and I could tell that he expected me to agree. God, how I wished I could. Nothing sounded better than just getting on a bus or a train with Trey and never thinking about the Simmons family, tarot cards, or Willow games ever again. But I couldn't nod. Couldn't speak.

"I know I'm asking a lot of you, and I'll understand if you say no, or need more time to think about it. But if we leave together now, we can go anywhere. I could get a job on a fishing boat in Alaska, and you could get your degree. Or if we go to California, you could go to community college for free! I just think if we stay here, and keep falling deeper into this thing with—with—the Simmons family, and ghosts, and town history? One of us is going to end up dead."

A fat tear escaped from my eye and rolled down my cheek.

"What is it?" he asked tenderly. "Is it your parents?"

I shook my head and managed to choke out, "It's not that. I'm— I'm *next*."

It took a second for the impact of my admission to register on his face, and he blinked, speechless.

"We had to do something to save Mischa's sister, and I thought Jennie could protect me, but something bad happened yesterday. And I'm next."

Trey's face went pale and he dug his fingers into my upper arms. "No. Oh, God."

"The next new moon is on the twenty-second."

"Why? Why would you do that?" he asked hoarsely, sounding like he might also start crying. He leapt up from the couch and started pacing the rug in between the two bright red couches.

I clapped my hands over my face and released a few sobs before catching my breath enough to tell him, "I can't leave. You should go. I mean, the longer you stay in Willow, the likelier it is that someone's going to spot you."

"How can I leave now if there's a chance that you're going to . . ."

A torrent of tears poured down my cheeks. And since without either one of us saying as much but both of us knowing that morning in the library may be the last time we'd ever see each other, Trey kissed me.

I'd assumed since the first time we'd ever kissed that eventually Trey and I would have sex when the time was right. I thought when the moment finally arrived, it would be romantic—like the physical version of a promise. But instead, it felt more like a desperate, reluctant farewell. I never would have thought that the first time we'd have sex would be quite possibly the only time we'd ever have the chance.

CHAPTER 10

WE AGREED THAT TREY WOULD STAY IN WILLOW at least until Sunday night—until after Mr. and Mrs. Portnoy's memorial service, at which I would attempt to lure the spirits driving the curse out of Mischa's soul. It suddenly seemed like a fortunate twist of fate that tornados had torn through town a few days earlier, because a perfect solution had occurred to me. "I think you could probably stay at my mom's boyfriend's house without any-one noticing. A tree fell on it and damaged the roof, but it looks pretty stable. It'll be cold, but unless it rains, you'll probably be fine there. And I'm sure there's food in the kitchen."

I gave Glenn's address to Trey and told him to take my mom's bike to get there before too many drivers were out on the streets of Willow. Since my mom hadn't ridden her bike in ages, I figured she wasn't likely to notice it missing that weekend. But saying good-bye to him before we went our separate ways was grueling. I studied his face, trying to memorize the details of it—the exact curve of his nose, the exact shade of blue of his eyes—wanting that moment to be fresh in my mind. If there was a chance my life was going to flash before my eyes within the next two weeks, I would have been happy for the memory of that morning with Trey to have been preserved.

Trey hugged me so hard it felt like I was about to board the *Titanic*, and we both knew that I was going to end up in the cold waves. He remained behind in the library so that he could rearm the security system and slip out after it officially opened for business so as to not arouse suspicion. After the door closed behind me, I didn't allow myself to look over my shoulder at him through the library's front doors. If I didn't keep my feet moving in the direction of home, I might very well have agreed to run off to the train station in Ortonville with him, despite already having a pretty good idea of how that adventure would end.

As I began my long walk home across town, the residents of Willow began waking up and emerging from their homes. Despite the chilly temperature the day before, the earthy scent of spring hung heavily in the air, and I suspected the temperature was going to be pleasantly warm later on. The normal routine of a Saturday morning had commenced, and this was the first time in my whole life that I was experiencing it as an observer, taking notice of every chirping bird and lazily rolling cloud, because I might not ever witness all of this again. It was upsetting to think that I was already several hours into what might have been the last Saturday of my life.

The honk of a car horn behind me tore me out of my reverie, and I turned to see a green Mini Cooper slowing down along the shoulder of the road. I cursed under my breath as my stomach soured; the last thing I wanted to do that morning was be around Violet, even just in passing. But there was nowhere to hide; she already had an advantage over me in that there wasn't any plausible reason for me to be walking along the side of the road so far from home at that hour.

It would have been pretty easy for her to have guessed the reason why I was up so early, and on the other side of town.

Violet lowered her passenger-side window and called out to me, "Hey. Do you need a ride?" A Top 40 song trickled out the window after her voice. Inwardly, I recoiled at the sound of it; I didn't feel like hearing an upbeat melody.

My first instinct was to decline, but it was almost nine in the morning, and Mom and Glenn were definitely awake by then, probably wondering where I was. If I could endure Violet for just five minutes, I'd be home, and wouldn't have to conjure up lies in an hour about where I'd been all morning. So I opened the passenger-side door and climbed in.

"You're up early," Violet said. To her credit, she sounded like she was making lighthearted conversation instead of accusing me of something.

I fastened my seat belt and replied stoically, "I couldn't sleep."

"Understandable," she said, with what sounded like genuine sympathy. "Were you able to find out if you're . . ."

"Next in line? Yeah, I'm pretty sure I am."

My answer dangled in the space between us for a few uncomfortable seconds before Violet attempted to rekindle our conversation. "I was just on my way home from yoga in Ortonville. I keep hoping a studio will open here in town, but . . ."

I clocked her bright blue yoga top and pants, and the rolled-up mat in the back seat. To deflect her obvious attempt to get me to share my reason for being out, I replied, "The park district has yoga classes every single morning—for senior citizens, new moms, and advanced students." Certainly, smug Violet thought of herself as too sophisticated to get her flow on at the park district.

But she reacted in mild surprise. "Oh, really? I didn't know that. I'll have to check it out."

I stared out my window, doing my best to banish my thoughts of Trey, and the rush of heat that accompanied even just a brief flash of him across my mind. But what he'd told me about her loomed heavily on my mind; she didn't look like she was ailing so much that she needed a kidney transplant. Not that I had any idea what someone in need of an organ would look like.

Sensing that I was holding out on her, at a stoplight, she said, "I don't know if you've been in touch with Trey, or what, but if you know how to reach him, he should know that half of my inheritance is technically his."

With my eyes fixed straight ahead on the road, I tried to keep any kind of reaction from showing on my face.

She continued, "I mean it. No strings."

Thinking about Trey's black eye, I couldn't resist snapping back at her, "How in the world would you share half of your inheritance with Trey without your mom finding out?" Back in January, Violet told me that her father had clued her in about her secret half brother, but Violet's mom had no idea that Trey Emory, Willow's most infamous juvenile delinquent, was her husband's illegitimate son.

Violet slowly eased on the gas when the light changed. "My dad could find a way," she stated.

"But no strings, right?" I challenged. "Because I'd say a kidney definitely qualifies as *a string*."

We'd reached the corner of Martha Road, and Violet pulled over to the curb to let the engine idle. She turned toward me, and I dared to glance at her face. She looked truly flabbergasted. Offended, almost. "What are you *talking about*? Did Trey *tell you* that? That he'll get half of my inheritance if he agrees to give me a kidney?"

I shrugged, trying to keep a level head. Now that I'd made the mistake of revealing that I knew about that proposition, I had to make sure it didn't seem like I'd just heard about it two hours ago, from Trey's own lips, here in Willow. "We talk on the phone, you know. Every Tuesday."

Violet blinked twice as if she couldn't believe what she was hearing. "What the hell . . . my dad, I swear." After a pause, she continued, "Half of the inheritance is his, if he wants it. All he has to do is agree to a blood test to confirm paternity. There was a clause in my grandmother's will about Trey, and it turns out for the last two years, that's been why my dad and my uncle have been fighting. I guess my uncle didn't take too kindly to the idea that my grandmother cut his kids out of her will, but provided for my father's secret son."

I thought back to what Violet had said in January about how she'd come into her inheritance. The money her grandmother had left in her name, as well as the Simmons family mansion, were a bribe of sorts—because along with those material things, Violet's grandmother had bequeathed to her the awful burden of having to condemn someone to death with each cycle of the moon. It didn't make sense to me that Grandmother Simmons would have included Trey in the will and shafted her other son's children unless, like Violet, Trey had inherited some kind of obligation related to the curse.

"That's not what your father told Trey," I informed her.

"Well, I've seen the will. I've overheard my father speaking with his attorney, and what I'm telling you is true." Probably aware that I didn't trust her at all, she added in a softer tone, "I do need a kidney. Or rather, I will need one, eventually. I have this hereditary thing called Alport syndrome, which I guess I got from my mom, but she's never had any problems other than high blood pressure. My doctors are shocked that my symptoms came on so suddenly two months ago, because usually patients have hearing or vision problems—or some kind of kidney issues—that show up much earlier before the disease advances. But . . ."

She looked dreamily through the windshield, her voice sounding flat and defeated. "I think while I had the curse on me, the spirits were preventing the disease from progressing. It's only started to manifest since January, and it's moving fast. They tell me it's rare for a female to experience kidney problems so quickly. Lucky me, I guess."

It was my instinct to doubt everything Violet told me, but this all rang true.

"I heard you missed a ton of school recently," I said.

"Yeah, well, dialysis," she said. "Please don't tell anyone. I don't exactly want to be known around school as the sick girl. I'm doing everything they're telling me to avoid having to do it again soon."

We both fell silent, and I looked down the street toward my house. So, all this time, the curse that Violet's grandmother had cast had not only guaranteed Violet's healthy birth, but it had warded off the advancement of this disease, as well. I thought of those five other Simmons daughters who'd been stillborn or died as infants, and suddenly it made a lot more sense why Violet was the only one to have survived. Although I didn't want to trust her, the tiniest bit of sympathy for her crept into my heart. She didn't ask for her grandmother to start her down this horrific road of murder and guilt. "I don't know what to say," I admitted. "That sucks."

She smiled weakly at me with shiny eyes. "So I guess we both know what it's like to be doomed. Although in my case . . . I guess I deserve it." She paused and released her parking brake. "If you're in touch with Trey, wherever he is, that's the deal. I mean, if he wanted to give me a kidney and was able to, that would be amazing. But I hardly expect him to want to do anything for me. Or for any of you to care, for that matter."

My natural impulse was to reassure Violet that of course I'd be open to showing her kindness, so I stubbornly pressed my lips together. She'd apologized for what she'd done to Olivia and Candace, and I knew enough now to know that she really hadn't had much control over what had happened. But I still couldn't forgive her—especially now that I could expect to die at any second.

When we pulled up in front of my house, she asked, "So, is there a plan yet? For breaking the curse? Because I've gotta admit, I'm afraid of Mischa. She knows how to get into my house, and my parents aren't the best when it comes to remembering to set our security system. And if we lose you? This will *never* end."

The front door of my house opened, and Glenn stepped outside with Maude and his two dogs on leashes and waved at me. He wore a heavy winter coat over his robe and pajamas, which was so disarmingly dorky that I kind of understood what Mom saw in him. I unfastened my belt, climbed out of the car, and replied, "Working on it."

Just as I was about to slam the passenger-side door, Violet blurted, "Can I help?"

It would have been my strong preference to tell her that she couldn't help, not in any way. But since Trey wouldn't be able to get anywhere near Gundarsson's Funeral Home without everyone in town losing their minds, I figured it might be good to keep Violet around in case I needed an extra pair of hands. "Just be at the memorial for Mischa's parents tomorrow," I told her, knowing that showing up to support Mischa was probably the last way in which she wanted to make herself useful.

I said hi to Glenn and mumbled something about having gone to yoga with a friend when I passed him on the front steps on my way into the house. Running into Violet had turned out to be a blessing in disguise. What she'd said about the curse never ending if I died was probably true; it was only my ability to communicate with Jennie that had led to us saving Mischa back in January. Without someone who could get reliable direction from a spirit on the other side, Violet, Mischa, and Henry really didn't have much of a chance of ever breaking the curse completely.

And for that reason, I knew I needed to find the strength to be selfish. I had to draw inspiration from Violet and take advantage of someone innocent in order to save myself, as well as everyone else. Exposure to her attitude was the reminder I needed about doing whatever was required of me, even if I hated the idea of it.

In my room, I called Mrs. Robinson at Oscawana Pavilion, hoping that she hadn't chosen that day to suddenly start socializing with her fellow residents and hang out on the patio or in the TV lounge. But fortunately, she picked up on the third ring after the front desk transferred my call to her room.

"Mrs. Robinson. It's McKenna Brady," I said. "The aide at the assisted living facility?"

"I know who you are!" she replied. "I may be old, but I'm not feeble. Not yet, anyway!"

"Sorry, sorry," I apologized. I went on to explain that we'd decided on a person to lure the spirits out of Mischa's soul. "But I need you to tell me what that process looks like because whatever happened yesterday, I think my connection to my sister has been broken. I don't know what happened to her; she's just *gone*." My entire body deflated when I heard myself say the word "gone." I wasn't prepared for the possibility that Mrs. Robinson would confirm my worst fear: that I'd finally reconnected with Jennie again only to lose her.

And that I might realistically die before I could find her, and still be unable to communicate with her in whatever followed my time in this life.

It sounded like Mrs. Robinson was making clucking noises and smacking her lips together on the other end of the call as she tried to figure out how to reply to me. "Hmm . . . She's not gone. Can't be *gone*."

I exhaled in relief so powerfully that I fell over on my back across my bed. Jennie wasn't gone. I didn't want to know how Mrs. Robinson could be so sure; I figured she knew about all the places where souls might end up just like I knew what radio static sounded like when someone's spirit was trying to contact me through it. As long as Jennie was *somewhere*, I could hang on to hope.

"Do you think the spirits did something bad to her?" I asked.

"No, they can't harm her. But they can block the channel between the two of you. I imagine that's probably what's happening—they're just causing interference."

I imagined Jennie in "the dark place," and couldn't help but think of her as being vulnerable there, wherever "there" was. The thought of her connection to me being blocked—especially in light of how happy I'd been to finally be able to communicate with her again after eight long years—was enough to bring a lump to my throat. But I couldn't cry; not then, not until I had some kind of plan in place to fix things. "Can you tell me how to get this evil out of Mischa, and what to do with it once it's out?"

"You need to get yourself a bottle or a jar," she informed me. "Now, that's for the last part, but there's no point in doing all the other stuff if you don't have something good to capture them in. Something that can be sealed off with a cork or a tight lid."

Mrs. Robinson went on to explain exactly what I'd have to do once I had both Mischa and the bait in the same place. As she rattled off directions, I took notes on a piece of paper and wondered just how the hell I was ever going to pull this off—in public, no less, with my entire community in attendance.

"Don't forget the drums," Mrs. Robinson reminded me after I thanked her for her guidance. "It may not seem important, but *loa* can't resist a strong beat!"

Drums. Right. Mrs. Robinson gave me the phone number for her room so that I wouldn't have to reach her through the assisted living facility front desk anymore, and I added it to the contacts list in my phone. She assured me that she'd work on trying to reestablish my connection to Jennie but encouraged me to collect all of the items I'd need and not leave any until the last second. "Things have a way of disappearing out of the blue when you need them most for magic work," she mused.

I thanked her again wholeheartedly. Despite the fact that Mrs.

Robinson had given me instructions in a matter-of-fact way that made me think that my task the next day would be quite straightforward, I was still keenly aware that this might be the last time we'd ever speak. "I'm so lucky to have met you, Mrs. Robinson. I don't know what I'd do if I didn't have your advice."

After a moment, Mrs. Robinson replied, "You'd do your best, child. That's what we're all doing, all of the time. The best we can."

For the rest of the afternoon, I dodged my mom's requests that I help out around the house by instead collecting the bizarre items that Mrs. Robinson had specified. Animal blood, red brick dust, rum and cornmeal. And, of course, drums.

Getting my hands on animal blood was the easiest of all, given that Glenn was a veterinarian who did house calls. When he'd moved into our house temporarily, he'd brought with him his minifridge for storing samples and vaccinations. As I stashed a small sample vial in the top drawer of my dresser, I prayed that Glenn wouldn't notice it missing in the next twenty hours. I really had no idea how I would ever explain myself if Mom found that in my room.

Then I vacuumed the living room and hallway so that my mom would stop nagging me for a little while, and texted Henry to see if there was any chance his parents had a bottle of rum in the house.

HENRY 2:19 P.M.

Yeah, of course. My mom loves dark & stormies.

Without providing a reason, I asked him to bring a thermos or water bottle full of rum to the Portnoys' memorial the next day. He agreed, and texted me back again to see if I wanted to hang out and talk through the plan, but I couldn't find the words to reply. My feelings toward Henry were as impossible to sort through as different colors of glitter combined. I very much wanted to hang out with him and lock down our plan for the next day, but at the same time, I didn't want to see him at all—because I wasn't sure how I'd feel around him after having seen Trey earlier that morning.

The truth was, I didn't want to feel anything at all except platonic affection for Henry, and I wasn't sure that would be the case.

So I didn't text back. Eventually, I would have to speak with Henry or see him in person to explain the role he'd have to play at Gundarsson's. But I wasn't ready, not just yet.

Cornmeal. In a lot of other people's houses, there might have been a Tupperware canister of it in the pantry, or a dusty, unopened bag at the back of a cabinet. But my mom was not the type to randomly be inspired to whip up a pan of corn bread from scratch. Fortunately, cornmeal was an easy enough thing to purchase at the grocery store; it was by far the simplest remaining prop on Mrs. Robinson's list to obtain. So I mentally set that requirement aside.

But red brick dust posed a different kind of problem. There weren't voodoo shops in Willow where I could buy a mason jar full of the stuff. A quick Google search and a tutorial on YouTube told me I could make my own, but first I had to get my hands on a brick. I scoured the website of the *Willow Gazette* in search of any mentions of construction around town where I might be able to find a stray red brick because I didn't know if it was possible to buy one—just one single, solitary brick—at the hardware store. When my search results came up dry, I had an epiphany. There had to be bricks scattered all over Mischa's subdivision from the tornado's path of destruction.

The Portnoys' gated community was a long walk from my house, but not impossible to get to on foot. But everything I'd heard about the state of the Portnoys' neighborhood suggested that the tornado hadn't done much damage anywhere but to their house, so I had every reason to believe there would be a guard stationed at the gate, and I might be turned away if none of the residents at Timber Creek were expecting me as a visitor. That being the case, I might have to climb over a fence or push my way through thick hedges to trespass.

I tied the shoestring on which I'd hung the gris-gris three times at the back of my neck, hoping that might make it harder for any spirits with evil intentions to unknot it. Then I shook a little salt into each of my shoes and set out. I told Mom I was going to walk to the grocery store to buy something for dinner, figuring I could perhaps pick up both the cornmeal and the brick in one trip.

The journey would have been more pleasant if I'd brought Maude along with me, but I thought better of taking that risk. Even though I'd already decided what I would have to do the next day, the long walk across town felt like a just punishment—or at least part of one. Unable to shake my fear of a car veering off the road and striking me, I walked all the way to Timber Creek on the grass after the sidewalk ended. I was less than twenty-four hours away from attempting to break this curse, and surely the spirits were aware. Every experience I'd had with them since September suggested that they would find a way to try and stop me from making it to the Portnoys' memorial. There was no precaution too silly or extreme for me to take that day.

"Air" could mean anything.

Sure enough, when I reached Timber Creek, I spied a bored

guard sitting inside his little station, watching a video on his phone and laughing. So I continued on past the main gate and rounded the corner, walking the perimeter of the subdivision until I reached the unmanned side gate, which was flanked by pine trees. Perhaps six months earlier I would have felt like a creep lurking beneath pine trees until a driver came along and tapped the security code into the security panel to raise the gate, but sneaking into Timber Creek was a breeze compared to sneaking *out* of the Sheridan School for Girls. Within five minutes, a maroon SUV rolled up. Its driver-side window lowered, and a middle-aged woman tapped in the code. The gate rose, and as soon as she'd driven through, I trotted behind her onto the property as the gate began its descent.

The reports that the tornado had *only* damaged the Portnoys' house hadn't been exaggerated. Aside from a few broken shutters on houses along their street and some overturned patio furniture, nothing looked askew—until I arrived in front of Mischa's house. Its roof had been torn clean off, and half of the westernmost wall was gone too, making the house look as if an enormous monster had taken a bite out of it. My mother liked to jokingly refer to houses in Timber Creek as McMansions, implying that they were cheaply made status symbols. I had to admit that there appeared to be truth to her assessment from the way the drywall seemed to have just been blown away by the wind, with bright pink insulation hanging out of the top of the damaged wall. Yellow police tape had been wrapped around the base of the house, and a fluorescent orange sign had been fixed on the front door: CONDEMNED.

There were bricks, of course. They were scattered all over the front lawn and the space between the Portnoys' house and the next amid family photos, kitchen plates, underwear, pages of books, fridge magnets, pillow stuffing . . . just about every kind of household tchotchke and kitchen accessory imaginable. There were bricks everywhere. They were more orange in color than red, but I picked one up from the Portnoys' front lawn and slipped it into the tote bag I'd brought with me.

Standing there, in their front yard, I could see directly into what remained of Mischa's purple bedroom on the second floor, right next door to Amanda's room. Her bed had been carried by the wind close to where the floorboards had been torn up, and it looked like another strong gust might blow it down to the living room. Her closet doors had been torn off the hinges and were long gone. As I carefully picked through some of the detritus in the grass, I thought it was shameful that no one had come by to clean all of this up and store it for Mischa. But then, who would? Prowling through a family's belongings out on their lawn wasn't any less intrusive than breaking into their home.

Just as I was about to walk back to the side gate, I noticed a photo on the ground as I almost stepped on it. As I bent to reach for it, I realized it was one of those goofy old-timey fake Western photos that you can have taken at the theme parks in Wisconsin Dells. In it, Mischa, Olivia, and Candace, all around thirteen years old, were dressed as Depression-era gangsters with newsboy caps and blazers. Mischa was chomping on a cigar and holding a fake machine gun. Candace's wide smile revealed braces on her teeth. They must have had it taken on our eighth-grade trip; I had a similar photo of myself posing with Cheryl and Erin somewhere at home.

My connection to Jennie had only been broken for a day, but

I already missed the tingling sensation she'd send me whenever I needed to be mindful of my surroundings or take notice of something. Although I'd gotten a creepy sense that my stumbling across that photo was no accident, I still shouted when a floorboard in Amanda's bedroom gave way behind me. Her nightstand crashed to the first floor, and the WHAM it made upon impact stopped my heart.

A wind kicked up around me, strong enough to stir some of the papers on the ground surrounding the house. Wind. Air. My feet began carrying me back to the gate before I was even aware that I'd ordered them to do that. By the time I reached the side entrance and squatted behind one of the two columns flanking the gate to hide myself from approaching drivers, the wind had died down, and the afternoon had gone completely silent.

Eerily silent.

Deadly silent.

I hadn't been paying particular attention to the soundscape of the neighborhood until it was suddenly gone. A dog had been barking in the distance, but it had stopped. I was sure that occasional cars had been driving down the next street over, and that I'd subconsciously been listening to traffic speed past on the main road beyond the gate. There had been birds, too—not many, but chirping. Now? Nothing. It suddenly felt like I was the last living creature on Earth. I couldn't remember having been this uncomfortable during the day before. The sky overhead was blue, and a handful of cheerful clouds floated past, but there was an electric charge in the air—just like there had been after school the day Olivia died—as if a storm was coming.

Slowly, I became aware that I wasn't alone. Something was watching me, waiting for me to make a move.

I felt a strong urge to turn my head and look back at the Portnoys' damaged house. But something deep inside of me refused to let me turn my head. I slid the photo I was holding into the back pocket of my jeans, figuring there was a reason it had literally crossed my path that day. The creaking of the gate as it rose distracted me, and a vehicle from a private security firm passed through at a slow speed, so I inched around the column to remain out of view before making a run for it.

I ducked beneath the gate and took off as fast as I could, not caring much if the security officer who'd just driven past me could see me in his rearview. I ran in the direction of the grocery store, the brick in my tote bag slamming into my hip with every step, and I paused on the corner of Glenn's street because my lungs felt like they were on fire. As I doubled over to catch my breath, I debated whether or not I should stop by Glenn's house to check in on Trey. There was no good reason why I should do that, I knew. There was a chance that one of Glenn's neighbors would see me, or Trey, and that would be the worst scenario possible. But still . . . the urge to walk in that direction was powerful.

I thought of how confused and distracted I'd become the day that Trey and I had chased Violet through Willow High School to grab her locket. This was a similar sort of feeling, and despite acknowledging that my thoughts were probably being manipulated, I remained frozen on the sidewalk even after catching my breath, staring down Glenn's street toward his house. However, when I pressed the grisgris I wore around my neck between my thumb and the knuckle of my index finger, I suddenly—almost magically—had the strength to turn away and continue to the grocery store.

The fact that Mrs. Robinson's magic actually seemed to work gave me hope for the next day. The sun had set, and the temperature had dropped by the time I crossed my front yard carrying my brick and my purchases from the grocery store: two mason jars, a bag of cornmeal, two cans of coffee, and ingredients for a modest salad to justify my walk across town in case Mom asked. In the kitchen, I dumped ancient flour out of an old Tupperware container into the trash, rinsed out the inside of the container, and poured the ground coffee from both cans into it. Then I placed the plastic lids back on the now-empty cans, and voilà: two makeshift bongos—at least the closest thing to drums I was going to get my hands on before the next day.

Realizing I could no longer put Henry off without jeopardizing our plan, I called him from my bedroom and ran him through the steps we'd have to take at Gundarsson's. He did not dismiss the plan or doubt its potential because it sounded ridiculous. But he did say, after mulling everything over, "If we pull this off, it's going to be a miracle."

"Don't say that," I warned him, thinking about the approaching new moon. "This *has* to work."

The tutorial I had watched on YouTube about making red brick dust had suggested all I needed to do was set down some newspaper on concrete to catch the dust, place the brick on it, and hit it with a hammer while wearing safety goggles. I knew without checking that we didn't have safety goggles in the house, so I fished Mom's swimming goggles out of the linen closet in the bathroom.

Outside in the driveway, I was numbly focused on setting about this task. The day had been emotionally draining; all I really wanted to do was curl into a ball in my bed and pretend that none of this was happening. But there was no one coming to save me. Although I knew I had my friends, I was going to have to fight for myself if I wanted to live.

So I set down a large sheet of newspaper, placed the brick on it, secured my goggles, and took a swing at the center of the brick with a hammer from the garage, expecting the brick to split in half, or at least crumble.

Instead, a shockingly powerful jolt of pain shot up my arm, surged past my eyes, and throbbed at the very top of my skull, in which it felt like my brain was rattling. I felt the impact of the hammer striking the brick in the very roots of my teeth. White orbs blinked and swirled in front of my eyes, making me truly wonder for a moment if I was dead.

After recovering enough to think straight—and realizing I should have lightly but steadily tapped a corner of the brick instead of striking it with all my might at its strong center—I looked up at the waning gibbous moon in the clear dark sky. Surely, Violet's evil spirits were having a good laugh at my expense.

Within eleven days, I'd be dead, and there I was, squatting in my driveway, hammering away at a brick in the moonlight, wasting what very well might have been the last Saturday night of my life—while the boy I loved slept across town, his own life endangered by his sinister lineage.

CHAPTER 11

FROM THE MOMENT I STEPPED INTO THE KITCHEN wearing my black funeral dress, I began to suspect that everything was going to go wrong that day.

First of all, Mom was wearing a black pantsuit at the kitchen table, where she was poking at a plate of scrambled eggs. It wasn't a common occurrence for Mom to get dressed *at all* on Sundays, so I immediately knew something was up.

"Are you coming with me to the memorial?" I asked, praying that she would say no.

"Of course," she said. My stomach soured; there was probably no way I could do everything Mrs. Robinson had said without causing a scene at the memorial—at least a small one—and having my mom present was going to be an issue. "I mean, I feel so terrible, especially after reconnecting with Elena back in January when we had that little fender bender. She was so thoughtful back in those days after the fire."

Damn it, I thought to myself as I poured myself a glass of orange juice.

"Is Glenn coming?" I asked innocently. I prayed that he would be, and that he'd serve as a distraction.

"He's working. The clinic's Easter egg hunt is today, remember?" Mom got up from the table to clear her place. I felt like I'd been punched in the solar plexus. Of course—it was Easter Sunday.

As if on cue, Glenn wandered into the kitchen with an expression of confusion on his face. "This is the darnedest thing. I must have misplaced one of the samples I took from some heifers the other day. I'll have to go take new ones. I've never lost a sample in twenty years of farm visits."

He joined Mom at the sink and pecked her on the cheek, and she rubbed his upper arm to console him. "Well, you're under a lot of stress with everything that's happened in the last week. It's easy to be distracted when you're in a new routine."

With my back to them, I rolled my eyes.

On the drive over to the funeral home, I ran through Mrs. Robinson's directions repeatedly in my head. My phone buzzed almost constantly inside my bag with texts from Henry and Violet, and they were adding to my anxiety. The rum had to be mixed with the cornmeal. Our bait would have to be positioned near that mixture; Mrs. Robinson claimed that it, like the drums, was appealing to evil spirits and would help to draw them out. We'd have to create a barrier of red brick dust on the ground between our bait and Mischa. That would serve to protect our bait and prevent the spirits from invading her soul. And the drums? Henry would have to start improvising a drumbeat as soon as our bait came within three feet of Mischa.

Everything was going to depend entirely on timing and placement.

And surprise.

I hadn't mentioned anything to Mischa about Jennie's theory. Perhaps the spirits inhabiting her soul knew what was coming. But they would have to exert enough power to control her thoughts and body if they wanted her to thwart our plan. That was a gamble I had no choice but to take.

The parking lot at Gundarsson's was packed that afternoon even though we were arriving relatively early. As Mom parked, I grimly thought to myself that the owners of our town's small funeral home had to be raking it in that year, with so many unexpected deaths.

In the crowded lobby, black fabric had been hung over the two hanging decorative wall mirrors. Candles arranged on a credenza burned brightly. According to Jewish tradition, they were supposed to burn for the entire shiva, or mourning period. They reminded me of the seven-day candle that Kirsten had given Mischa over the winter for protection; Mischa had kept the flame burning continuously that entire week out of fear for her life. There weren't many Jewish families in Willow, but Gundarsson's had done their best to honor Jewish tradition. Some guests in attendance helped themselves to black ribbons set out in a basket, which they fastened to their dresses and coat jackets with safety pins as a means of performing the custom of keriah, or tearing one's clothes during shiva, without actually destroying their outfits.

I scanned the guest book log to see who'd already arrived. Michael Walton, Mr. Dean . . . so many people from school I hadn't thought much about since moving to Florida. A stack of cards stood in a crystal dish, and they were printed with Mr. and Mrs. Portnoys' wedding photo on one side, and a prayer I didn't recognize, El Maleh Rachamim, on the back.

Mom slipped into the crowd to say hello to a few people, and upon feeling a hand on my shoulder, I turned to find Henry standing behind me, holding a stainless steel water bottle. Standing so closely to him again after having had sex with Trey the day before brought heat to my cheeks, and I prayed I wasn't blushing. It was stupid to be so self-conscious—it wasn't like virginity was *visible*, like a suntan. But I still hoped he didn't notice anything different about me.

"Hey," I said as I took a small step away, intent on maintaining the gap of two feet between us. My commitment to Trey had strengthened since the last time I saw Henry in person. If we could successfully pull the evil spirits out of Mischa and trap them that day, then my next priority would be to figure out how keep Trey safe— even if that meant leaving my entire life behind to be with him. I was sure that if I vanished, Henry would be deeply hurt—especially after the kiss we'd shared in his truck. But I would have to worry about that later, once I knew for sure that I had a future to plan.

"Are you ready for this?" Henry asked. He nodded toward the main viewing room, and I followed his eyes to where Violet sat next to Pete in the last row. Henry had taken on the task of filling Violet in on her role in today's game plan. She half smiled at both of us to acknowledge our presence, and then tilted her head in the direction of the front of the room to where Mischa stood at the center of a small crowd.

I patted my oversize, overstuffed tote bag. If my mom was the kind of person who ever thought about fashion, she might have questioned why I was bringing what was essentially an enormous gym bag to a memorial service. But thankfully, she didn't notice that kind of stuff, and it was a weird memorial service anyway, since a lot of people were wearing their pastel Easter church outfits. I'd brought one mason jar of red brick dust, another jar, which was empty, a Ziploc bag of cornmeal, two empty coffee cans, and a vial of cow's blood. "As ready as I'll ever be."

Two closed caskets were arranged at the far back of the viewing room amid enormous floral arrangements, and Mischa was positioned just a few feet in front of them. She'd brushed her hair since Friday, and looked like she'd showered, too, although her eyes were sunken and her nose was red. I wished with all my heart that circumstances were different, that I could embrace the enormity of Mischa's loss and dedicate myself to comforting her that day. I'd known both of her parents my whole life, and I felt guilty that I wasn't at their shiva simply to mourn them. With both Olivia and Candace gone, I should have been someone on whom Mischa could rely for emotional support. Instead, I couldn't even bring myself to look in her eyes.

She was holding hands with Matt, who wore an ill-fitting suit and had his hair gelled down. On Mischa's other side stood a short but handsome middle-aged man that I instantly realized must have been her infamous uncle Roger, occupant of the Portnoys' summer home up near Lake Superior. Rows of upholstered chairs were arranged on both sides of a center aisle, down which a girl I didn't recognize—presumably one of Mischa's classmates at St. Patrick's—walked to tearfully greet her.

In bits and pieces of the conversation surrounding us, I heard snippets of gossip that suggested Amanda was recovering, with the voice of Tracy Hartford's mother cutting through the din as clearly as a church bell. "Her doctors called it a miracle. She woke up out of the clear blue. They're hopeful she may regain the use of her arms."

News that Amanda was not only still alive, but thriving, made my heart beat faster. An improvement in her condition meant that the sacrifice I'd made (even if it was unintentional) had served its purpose. It also probably meant that the spirits were already counting on my death occurring in exchange for Amanda's.

I'd been to enough memorial services in the last year to know that this would probably be the routine for the next two or three hours, whether it was Jewish tradition or not. Guests would arrive, sign the book, and walk down the main aisle to greet Mischa before lingering in front of the closed caskets for a few moments and then taking seats. This was what I'd expected, but observing it with my own eyes made the complexity of what I was going to have to pull off at any second more difficult. If Mischa stepped away to get a cup of coffee or to use the restroom for a few minutes, that might throw off the whole plan. I visually measured a length of about three feet from Mischa's body on the floor, and noted where I'd have to pour the rum-and-cornmeal mixture on the rug.

I reached into my bag and handed the cornmeal, which I'd wrapped in a plastic grocery bag in an attempt to be somewhat covert, to Henry. "Like a watery paste," I reminded him. He nodded, took one more look at Mischa, and vanished to the men's bathroom.

In Henry's absence, I felt self-conscious and was reminded of my status as a person of intrigue around town. People from Willow High School—some of whom had cheered when Mischa and I had been tossed out of Violet's New Year's party, but who'd still shown up to pay their respects—stared at me and whispered behind hands cupped over their mouths. From across the room, Mrs. Gomez, my former Spanish teacher, smiled weakly at me but made no attempt to walk over and say hello. Tracy Hartford glared at me from over the top of her Styrofoam coffee cup, and then giggled when Michael Walton whispered in her ear.

Tracy Hartford. I'd risked my life to save hers, not that I had expected her to appreciate it.

Once upon a time I'd loved this town. I'd considered our community tight-knit because of the way everyone had come together to support my family after the fire, because of the way that everyone's parents would buy chocolate or cookies during school fund-raisers, and because everyone knew their neighbors. Now I could see how easy it had been for them to kick me out of the circle, and it made me sad to realize how badly I wanted to be welcomed back in.

I took a quick peek at my phone. It was two fifteen. Cheryl had been done with her shift at the juice bar for an hour and fifteen minutes, which I had assumed when plotting my timeline to be just about as long as it would take for her to drive home, change into a black outfit, drive over to her boyfriend, Dan Marshall's, house to pick him up, and then arrive at Gundarsson's. It was—terrifyingly—showtime. At any second now, we could expect her to appear in the wide double doorway with Dan, and we'd have to be ready for action.

Sweet, unassuming Cheryl. I bit into my lower lip and felt a flash of hesitance about doing this to her. Candace's parting advice for me was to use Cheryl as bait if I flat out refused to consider Henry. On one hand, Cheryl wasn't someone I would think could easily talk victims into requesting their own deaths. Not the way that Violet had been able to do at Olivia's party, or even in the festive way she'd predicted deaths at her New Year's party. What had made Violet so skillful in managing her curse was that people always wanted to cozy up to her, earn her admiration.

Plus, Cheryl was too kindhearted to ever intentionally hurt another person. But what Cheryl had going for her was her eagerness to please others. Her genuine willingness to be a good friend. No one would ever suspect Cheryl of having evil intentions . . . and that was exactly why she'd be an irresistible conduit for the spirits' soul-reaping.

The only reason I'd settled on Cheryl after ruling out Henry was that Mrs. Robinson had seemed so confident that I would pull this off, lure the spirits out and trap them without ever endangering Cheryl. I wasn't so naïve as to think I could conduct this ceremony without Cheryl having any idea what I was doing. She'd definitely know I was doing something weird. But if I could dare to hope that I'd capture the five evil spirits in a mason jar and seal them off from the world, what was the harm in hoping Cheryl might not be too mad at me?

I hadn't told Henry that Cheryl would be our bait that day, which meant that Violet also had no idea. While it was better that way—even if only so that neither of them could make me feel guiltier than I already did—it meant that I was solely responsible for getting the timing correct.

Just as Henry returned to the viewing room, Mischa began sobbing loudly enough to catch our attention. He handed me the water bottle, and we both watched as an enormous man with a buzz cut—easily twice the size of Mischa, with shoulders as wide as a refrigerator—walked down the aisle toward her. He practically lifted Mischa into the air when he reached her. The mere sight of him seemed to break Mischa out of whatever shell had been repressing her emotion since we'd arrived, and now the floodgates were open as he rocked her in his arms.

"That must be her gymnastics coach," I told Henry. Amanda and Mischa had been training with the same coach in Ortonville since they were both toddlers. Mischa had told me that Coach Armoudian was kind of like a second father to them. The moment that thought occurred to me, it was followed by my hope that nothing bad would happen to him. Mischa had lost more than any of us now. It just wouldn't be fair for her to have to say good-bye to another loved one.

As Henry and I watched Mischa and her coach, Mom appeared at my side holding a cup of coffee for me. "How are you holding up?" she asked me, assuming that I was torn up about the deaths of Mischa's parents. I mean, I *was* upset. But I was also a little preoccupied with wanting to prevent my *own* tragic death. I reluctantly took the cup from her, planning to ditch it at the first opportunity. I needed to keep my hands free, and glanced nervously at the entrance to the viewing room in search of Cheryl.

"I'm okay," I replied.

Henry nudged me in the side with his elbow. Mischa's coach was leading her out of the room with a strong arm wound around her shoulders. Panic surged through my veins. I turned to Mom and mumbled something about going to check on Mischa to see if she was okay, and then race-walked out of the room with Henry following me.

The lobby of the funeral home was crowded, and it took a moment for me to find Mischa in the sea of bobbing heads. Or rather, I saw her coach's buzz cut towering over everyone else, and realized that he was escorting her outside to get some air.

Even though it was a sunny afternoon, conducting this process outside was unpredictable. Outside was *not* the plan.

I set down the coffee Mom had given me on a side table, and Henry and I wormed our way through the crowd to reach the front doors. Outside, a cluster of people were smoking cigarettes. I spotted Mischa's coach walking her along the sidewalk that ran in front of the funeral home toward the garden on the side of the building.

"Where are they going?"

Turning in unison, Henry and I saw that Violet had followed us outside. She looked distressed, and I wondered if maybe she was more invested in helping break the curse than I'd originally assumed. Neither of us answered, but all three of us watched with bated breath as Mischa and her coach rounded the corner of the building and disappeared around the brick wall. I knew what they'd find there: two cement benches, a trellis that was covered with bougainvillea in the summer, and a fountain that was dry because the temperature was still freezing at night. The fountain had been dry the afternoon of Jennie's memorial too.

"Will this work outside?" Violet asked in a panicky voice.

"There's no reason why it wouldn't work," I said. "But it's going to be a lot trickier—"

Without any warning, my scalp broke out into a fit of hot tingles. It was like Jennie was suddenly back in full force, desperate for me to notice something happening at that very moment. I wondered if Mrs. Robinson had been able to restore our connection. But before I could even consider calling her or asking my pendulum—

"Hey, guys. How's Mischa?"

Cheryl had arrived. She wore a black sheath dress that looked like it would have been appropriate for a job interview. How typically and adorably Cheryl, always looking older and wiser than a teenager. Dan Marshall stood behind her in a blazer and a pair of khakis.

My heart was racing. This was not how Cheryl was supposed to arrive. It was not where she was supposed to greet and embrace Mischa. They were supposed to be inside, facing each other in a narrow aisle, where it would be easier for us to crowd around them as Cheryl hugged Mischa to prevent her from backing away too far. But this was it—our only chance. If Cheryl and Dan entered the funeral home before Mischa went back inside, it was possible that Cheryl would skip greeting her altogether. Then I'd be boarding a flight bound for Tampa on Tuesday, certain to die before April twenty-second.

I took a shallow breath, looked Henry in the eye, and then unzipped my bag to make it clear to him that we had no choice other than to act right there, right then. "She's not doing so great," I told Cheryl, feeling queasy about manipulating her into partaking in our plan with half-truths. "She's taking a moment to pull herself together over there with her gymnastics coach. It would probably be nice of you to say hi to her now before she goes back inside. You know? Just in case she gets emotional again."

Cheryl looked at me with a confused expression and said, "Why? I'll just give her some space and say hello later."

"Both of her parents just died," Violet jumped in, sensing what I was driving at, which was that we needed to shepherd Cheryl to the side of the building to get her in front of Mischa. "And just about everyone in town is here. It's a little overwhelming, you know? You guys have all known each other since, like, preschool. It would probably mean a lot to her if you speak with her one-on-one. Now. Before she goes inside again."

Cheryl looked at me for confirmation, and I nodded. We were wasting time, and I could practically feel seconds ticking by in my bones. I forced a smile and extended my arm in the direction of the garden to suggest that Cheryl and Dan should take the lead. Still looking uncertain, Cheryl finally stepped ahead of the rest of us and walked down the path toward the garden. Following, I reached into my bag and handed the empty coffee cans to both Henry and Violet. To Henry, I also passed the mason jar of red brick dust, and he removed its lid to be prepared to toss its contents. I twisted off the cap of the water bottle and dropped it into the tote bag, then pulled the rubber stopper out of the top of the vial. In my haste to have everything prepared by the time I turned the corner and came into Mischa's view, I dropped the stopper into my tote bag, realizing after the fact that it was probably smearing cow's blood all over the interior.

When I stepped around the edge of the building, seconds after Cheryl and Dan, I saw Mischa rising from the bench where her coach remained sitting. ". . . so nice of you to come," Mischa was saying.

This was the moment.

Cheryl stood about five feet away from Mischa, and it looked like either Mischa would take a few steps closer, or Cheryl would move to give her a quick hug. My scalp burned with tingles; this was exactly what I'd been waiting for, so I wasn't sure if Jennie—if the tingles were even being caused by her—was trying to warn me, or why. There was no time to think. Henry and I dashed forward to arrive on both sides of Cheryl. As he reached in front of her to pour a shaky line of red brick dust near her toes on the sidewalk, I tossed the vial of blood at Mischa.

"What the . . ." Mischa looked down at the front of her black dress. There hadn't been more than about two tablespoons of blood in the vial, but the substance was still recognizable against the dark fabric. "Is that *blood*? Are you *serious right now*?"

The blood begins the ceremony, Mrs. Robinson had told me. *It's how you tell the spirit world you're getting started: with a sacrifice.*

Cheryl reached for my arm, trying to stop me from doing whatever I was up to. "McKenna, what are you . . ." But I shook her hand off of me. Henry and Violet stood on either side of Cheryl, facing Mischa, both tapping the plastic lids of the coffee cans they held to the beat established by Henry.

The drums summon the spirits.

Ignoring Cheryl and Dan, I tried not to notice that Mischa's hands were balling into fists at her sides, and her scrunched-up face was turning red with fury. And despite the fact that her Hulk-size coach had gotten up from the bench, I continued.

I dropped the empty glass vial to the sidewalk and transferred Henry's water bottle from my left hand to my right to give me more control over it as I poured it onto the sidewalk on Mischa's side of the line of red dust Henry had scattered between her and Cheryl. As I tilted the water bottle over and fragrant yellow sludge slid out and down to the pavement, I chanted the French words Mrs. Robinson had instructed me to practice: *"Sortez, sortez, méchants."*

The spirits can't resist the smell of rum and cornmeal.

"What is going on here?" Mischa's coach yelled at me in a thick European accent.

"McKenna, this is just . . ." Cheryl shook her head in confusion. She reached for Dan's hand and turned away from me as if she was going to walk back to the parking lot. But anticipating this, Violet stepped in front of her to block her path. *This* was why conducting this ceremony inside would have been ideal; if Cheryl made a run for it out here, we'd be in serious trouble.

But Cheryl wasn't the type of person to ever make a run for it.

And Mischa—or the spirits inside of her—had figured out exactly what we were attempting.

Mischa narrowed her eyes at me with a devilish smirk on her face. "You have no idea what you're doing," she taunted me in a sing-song voice. Although Mischa was often sarcastic, I had no doubt that these words and the voice that had spoken them were not her own. It had to be a sign of progress, or at least I hoped it was, that the spirits were revealing themselves to us.

"Stop this!" the coach yelled at us.

To my right, I heard Dan say to Violet, "Come on, Violet. Let us go. This is freaky."

We were almost done—*so close*. If only Cheryl would stay still for a few more seconds.

Tease them out. Tempt them, Mrs. Robinson had advised. This wasn't like an exorcism in the movies. She had seemed confident that these spirits would not respond well at all to one of us commanding them to leave Mischa's soul. They had to leave of their own accord, and temptation was the most likely way to make that happen.

I threw the empty water bottle into the grass and reached into my tote bag for the second mason jar—the empty one. With one quick flick of the wrist, I took off its lid inside the bag, where Mischa couldn't see my hands.

"*Sortez, sortez, méchants. Venez dans votre nouvelle maison.*"

Clearly furious but still seemingly amused, Mischa took another step closer to the cornmeal mix on the sidewalk, maintaining eye contact with me. Challenging me. She raised her right leg as if she was going to step over the scant red brick dust barrier on the sidewalk separating her from Cheryl. But instead of setting her foot down on the other side, she kept it suspended in the air below her bent knee, as if the dust was a kind of force field preventing her from passing. Either that, or she wanted me to believe that it was.

Henry and Violet continued their tapping on the coffee can lids. Cheryl raised her voice to Violet, saying, "You guys are crazy. Seriously!"

And then, suddenly, Mischa's hands flew to her throat and clasped around it. She appeared to be choking on something. Her eyes popped open so wide they looked like they might fall out of their sockets. She struggled to cough, her chest heaving, but no sound escaped her mouth, as if her airway was completely blocked. "Mischa!" her coach shouted in alarm. He reached around her waist to perform the Heimlich maneuver.

But I knew that Mischa wasn't choking on anything.

She was strangling herself.

Or rather, the spirits inside of her were making her do so. Mrs. Robinson had warned me that they did love a spectacle. They'd do anything to resist the effect of the drums, the rum, and the cornmeal. And they'd resort to theatrics to try to make us stop. Choking . . . a sarcastic nod to the death Violet had predicted for Mischa back in September? Even though I had been expecting something along these lines, it was still horrifying to watch. If it weren't for my own life in the balance, my love for Trey and desperate desire to have a future with him, the dramatic display might have made me lose my courage.

I had warned Henry about this. His and Violet's drumbeat slowed, and I snapped at both of them, "Keep going!"

"She can't breathe!" Dan shouted at me.

Cheryl shook her head angrily at me. "Just stop this, McKenna!" she shouted.

Ignoring Cheryl, in as soothing a voice as I could manage, I said again, *"Sortez, sortez, méchants. Venez dans votre nouvelle maison."*

Suddenly, the day went completely still, just as it had when I'd gone to the Portnoys' house to fetch the brick. Car noises from the nearby parking lot were silenced. Chatter from attendees of the memorial service who were smoking around the front of the building faded away. The rhythm of Henry and Violet's tapping took on a strange, monophonic audio effect, as if the sound waves were being slightly flattened.

Mischa's coach pumped his clasped hands upward beneath Mischa's rib cage as if trying to dislodge whatever she was choking on from her windpipe. She broke free from his tight hold on her, surprising him, and she leered at me. The blood had drained from her face, but her speech was unencumbered, making it obvious that she'd never actually been choking.

"Even after all this time, you think you can outsmart us," she hissed, no longer sounding anything like herself. "And all you do is just keep making this easier."

A chill ran through me. I'd never heard the spirits address me directly like that before. Without taking my eyes off of Mischa, and with my scalp burning so badly that all I could think about was scratching it, I shouted to Henry and Violet, "Keep going!"

Their beat continued.

I repeated, *"Sortez, sortez, méchants."*

Then Mischa's body contorted. She doubled over, writhing, and clapped her hands over her nose and mouth. Her hands flattened against the skin as if she was trying to keep something from escaping either out through her nostrils or her lips, and her eyes darted wildly.

"Mischa!" her coach exclaimed.

"This is it, you guys," I warned Henry and Violet, who in turn increased the speed at which they were banging on the tops of their cans.

And then—the moment I'd been hoping for—Mischa's petite body lurched forward, and she vomited watery foam onto the sidewalk. It hit the ground with a *splat* that sounded deafeningly loud in the otherwise eerie silence, which was otherwise only punctuated by Henry and Violet's drumming on their coffee cans. Hoping with all my might that Mrs. Robinson had been correct about this part of the ceremony, I held the empty mason jar up in front of Cheryl's stupefied face as if I was expecting to catch something inside of it, then clapped the lid over it and twisted it shut.

It was impossible for a few seconds to know whether or not I'd caught the evil spirits in the jar. Mrs. Robinson had warned me that they were invisible. But she had told me that spirits create condensation when they're captured during those first few moments of distress, when they realize that they're trapped. Henry and Violet both stopped tapping on their cans in amazement and focused their attention on me.

I held up the jar so that Henry could also peer inside of it.

First one drop of condensation formed on the inside wall of the glass.

Then a second.

I became keenly aware of a car behind us driving slowly through the lot, and the song playing on its radio. The weird sound bubble around us seemed to be fading away, and the world was returning to its normal volume.

Mischa gasped sharply as if she'd been stabbed, and stood straight up with raised eyebrows. For just a fraction of a second, she looked completely shocked—as if she didn't recognize her surroundings. But then she blinked and relaxed her posture as her coach fussed over her. She wiped her mouth on the back of her hand.

"Did it work?" Violet asked with enormous eyes.

Relief flooded over me with such power that I stumbled backward and caught myself before falling over. I really and truly believed we'd been successful. Overhead, fat clouds rolled across a bright blue sky. Everything seemed normal. For the first time since Trey and I had thrown Violet's locket into White Ridge Lake, I was confident that we'd finally freed ourselves from the Simmonses' evil.

"I don't know what you guys were doing, but that was really not cool," Dan told me before turning and yanking Cheryl's wrist to make her follow him. She lingered for a moment, frowning at me as if I'd just deeply betrayed her.

Feeling guilty, I called after her, "I'll explain later!" She didn't reply, though; she and Dan were already stepping off the curb and marching back across the parking lot.

Mischa's coach glared at the three of us and pointed his meaty index finger at us. "You should be ashamed, playing games on a sad day like this."

For once, Henry didn't try to assuage the situation. I took a step back to be closer to him and Violet, all of us watching for any sort of change in Mischa. But instead of announcing that she felt weak or unburdened, or that the curse was broken, her lips curled into a slow, mischievous smile. She raised one eyebrow as she asked me, "What's in the jar?"

As Mischa smiled at me over her shoulder while her coach ushered her back toward the entrance of the funeral home, muttering Russian curses under his breath, the raging fire on the top of my head gave way to a cold sweat. A strong shiver rippled through my body from my head to my toes, strong enough to make my teeth chatter. Because although there had always been a sparkle in Mischa's eye, a little hint of ferocity, what I just saw was something new. Unfamiliar.

"What . . . the hell . . . ," Henry said.

"Didn't she sound weird? Just now?" Violet asked, looking at me and then over at Henry. "That didn't sound like Mischa."

With a trembling lower lip and a sharp lump in my throat, I raised the mason jar in my hand and looked at the two small drops of liquid clinging to the inside of the glass. My breath was so shallow that I was becoming light-headed as I found my voice despite my fear. This couldn't have happened. It was too horrible to believe. My mouth could barely form the words, "I don't think that was Mischa."

Henry shook his head. "No. We were both right here, watching!

I mean, did you notice what happened with the sound around us? We did something just now. I think we broke the curse."

But Violet pointed down at our feet, and when my eyes followed her finger to the sidewalk where I'd poured the rum and cornmeal, I knew that we were in real trouble—worse than ever before. What had just, moments ago, been a bright yellow, grainy liquid was now unrecognizable from its original form. It was completely black and charred, as if it had been baking in the hot sun for days. Mrs. Robinson hadn't mentioned anything at all about spirits actually consuming the rum and cornmeal, or transforming it into something. Even with my limited knowledge of the occult, I guessed that any kind of matter suddenly being burned to a crisp was a very, very bad sign.

"We have to find her," I whispered. "Whatever we just did, we have to undo it. Now."

Without waiting for Henry or Violet to agree with me, I spun on my heel and broke into a run in my uncomfortable shoes. Frantic thoughts raced through my head as I wondered what the hell we could have possibly gotten wrong. I'd followed all of Mrs. Robinson's directions. Even with the unanticipated change in location, we'd done everything right. "Do you think the spirits went inside Cheryl?" I heard Violet ask Henry behind me.

"Cheryl seemed fine," Henry replied.

There were even more guests inside the funeral home when I burst in through the front door than there had been when we'd stepped outside. More people from Willow High School and others I didn't recognize. "Excuse me," I mumbled as I squeezed my way among clusters of people, trying to reach the viewing room.

Mom spotted me across the crowd and waved. We'd been there almost forty-five minutes. That was about as long as she could tolerate any social situation. But I couldn't leave yet—not without figuring out what we'd done. I flashed a half-hearted smile at Mom but didn't wave back, instead ducking my head down and turning sideways to squeeze in between two large men.

When I finally stepped through the open French doors into the viewing room, it became very obvious that whatever we'd just done to Mischa was bad. Very bad. Henry caught up to me and stood on my right side, Violet on my left, and the three of us watched in sickening wonderment as Mischa returned to her place at the back of the room.

With each step she took, the atmosphere seemed to sour. The velvety petals of the orchids in the flower arrangement closest to the two caskets began to wilt, shriveling up and turning into blackened buds among the greenery. Then the same thing happened to each of the other flower arrangements. Roses wrinkled, and the buds dropped to the carpet. Bright white petals dropped off daisies and were scraggly and yellowed by the time they hit the floor. The black shroud placed over the mirror at the back of the room slipped off on its own and landed in a pile.

None of the guests standing around sharing memories of Adam and Elena Portnoy seemed to notice anything at first. But the powdery, floral scent of the funeral home was slowly overpowered by a musty, rotten stench, and attendees tried to respond politely as they became aware of it by covering their noses with their hands and handkerchiefs. Mr. Gundarsson—not the owner of the funeral home, but his adult son—sniffed the air delicately and stepped out of the room, presumably to alert his housekeeping staff that something strange was happening.

Mischa turned away from the guests, and her eyes landed on me, Henry, and Violet. She stared at us with a firm frown, expressing that this was her territory, and we were intruding on it. Matt approached her, slipped an arm around her waist, and whispered something in her ear. She twisted her neck to face him while replying, and whatever she said to him was surprising enough that he backed away from her with his jaw hanging open and retreated to the other side of the room, where his mom was seated with his brothers.

"There you are. I've been looking all over for you."

Mr. and Mrs. Richmond arrived, and Mrs. Richmond kissed Henry on the cheek. She looked as well put together in her black dress and cashmere coat as she always did, although now that I'd seen the piles of clutter in the Richmonds' house, I thought of her differently. As she greeted me with a warm smile, my eyes fixed on her gold earrings, which were shaped like crosses. I knew I wasn't imagining it when the crosses slowly turned upside down in her earlobes.

"Your mother? Is she here?" Mrs. Richmond was looking at me with a concerned expression on her face. I snapped out of the daze the earrings had put me in, realizing that she'd already asked me once about Mom.

As if on cue, Mom appeared next to me. "Ready to hit the road?" she asked me. She looked down dubiously at the mason jar in my hand. "What's with the jar?"

I nodded. There was no way we were going to be able to undo what we'd done to Mischa that day without guidance from Mrs. Robinson or Jennie. "It's just a . . . project."

Henry and Violet both looked panicky as I waved good-bye to them and promised in a shaky voice to text them later. It took all of my focus to act "normal," not wanting my mom or anyone else at the funeral home to have any sense that I'd probably just sealed my grisly fate, as well as doomed the entire population of Willow. It felt like an absolute admission of defeat to leave without correcting my mistake. Mischa, or whatever was masquerading as her, could skip town that very afternoon. I might never see her again and have another chance to beg or bargain for my life, if there was a chance either might work. All I could do was follow my mom on wobbly legs toward the French doors.

I didn't bother taking another look at Mischa over my shoulder as Mom and I left. It was already painfully evident that the girl in the black dress splattered in cow's blood was not Mischa.

In the hallway as I waited for Mom to fish my coat out of the closet, I looked at the two drops of condensation in the mason jar I carried with a stabbing pain beneath my rib cage. What if I'd lured a soul out of Mischa's body and caught it in the jar after all, only it wasn't evil?

CHAPTER 12

"I SWEAR, IF I DON'T GO TO ANOTHER MEMORIAL service again for the rest of my life, it'll be too soon," Mom said as we walked across the parking lot.

I couldn't bring myself to chat, but Mom didn't seem to notice. I climbed into the passenger seat, fastened my belt, and held the mason jar in my lap. Until I figured out exactly what had gone wrong, I had to consider whatever that jar contained to be precious cargo.

Mom hesitated for a second before starting the car's engine. "I'm sorry, McKenna. About everything that happened in the fall. I know you don't want to tell me why you and Trey did what you did to that girl from Chicago. And I get it. I guess when I was your age, I kept secrets from my mother too."

"Mom, I—" I really did not have the mental capacity to get into an argument with her about everything that happened since Violet had moved to Willow in the fall. Knocking her down in the high school parking lot and stealing her locket was *nothing* compared to what Violet had done to Olivia and Candace, although my mom would never believe the truth.

"No, no. You told me that there was something strange going on in this town with . . . so many tragedies, and I tried to convince you that they could all be explained by coincidence. But now, I've got to admit . . . this just doesn't seem normal."

I appreciated Mom's admission, but this was absolutely not the right time for me to unload the truth on her. There would probably *never* have been a good time to fill Mom in, at least not about all of it. Not about the night we played the game, or how we made Violet play it again in Michigan, and *definitely* not about having been in touch with Jennie. "I don't know what to say, Mom. Sometimes bad things just happen. I think you and Dad were right. It doesn't mean there's a reason why."

Mom's lips parted as if she was about to say something else, but then she started the car. As she backed out of the spot, her mood changed. "What if we stop by Bobby's and get some pie? We haven't done that in a long time."

Under ordinary circumstances, I would have enthusiastically agreed. But when she'd started the car's engine, the radio had filled the car with music. And not just any music.

"Love . . . is a burning thing. And it makes a fiery ring . . ."

In pure terror, I looked at the radio in the dashboard. "What radio station is this?" I asked in a hoarse whisper.

Mom idled at the exit of the funeral home with her right turn signal clicking. "I don't know. It's satellite. Glenn's always changing it."

Whatever it was, I was certain that my mom didn't regularly listen to music stations that would play Johnny Cash songs. My scalp broke into another fit of tingles, and this time they were strangely painful. "Mom," I said in a trembling voice, not wanting to alarm her—not wanting to be right about what I suspected was happening at our house at that very moment. "We need to go straight home. Fast."

Mom pulled out onto State Street at a moderate speed. There weren't any other cars headed in our direction. "Why? Are you okay?"

I couldn't find the words to even lie to her about having to go to the bathroom. With my fingers wrapped tightly around the mason jar, I just stared ahead through the windshield and thought about the text Mischa had sent me the day after the tornados touched down.

This is your fault, and I'm going to make you pay.

Maybe those spirits had completely taken over Mischa's mind and body now, but they probably still had access to her memories. They'd been in her soul when she'd sent that text, anyway, and they'd obviously been paying close attention to me since that first night at Olivia's house. So I knew as we drove the streets of our small town back to Martha Road that the deep sense of doom I felt wasn't just an effect of paranoia.

The bitter smell of smoke tickled my nostrils before we even reached our corner.

"Oh God!" Mom shouted behind the wheel, noticing black smoking drifting upward from the middle of our block and instantly realizing that it was coming from our rooftop. She hit the gas so hard that my head was thrown back against my seat, and then she slammed on the brakes seconds later when she parked haphazardly in the middle of our street. Elderly Dr. Waldbaum, a retired dentist who lived down the block, was pacing in front of our house with his cell phone pressed to his ear.

"No," I said where I sat in the front seat of the car, watching

Mom sprint across our lawn. All these months, I'd managed to elude the spirits. I'd tried to undo everything. Everyone kept telling me that I was so brave. But now I regretted my courage. It was a fair assumption that the spirits that carried out the curse had always been restrained up until that point by the will of the unfortunate person who was issuing death predictions. But they'd never been able to inhabit a human body as if it were their puppet before, like they could now. I couldn't even imagine what they might be capable of with Mischa's body as a host, leveraging her physical strength and the fact that everyone in town pitied her at the moment.

They were coming for me. *She* was coming for me. Maybe I was going to die within the next ten days, but Mischa—or whatever she'd become—was going to make me suffer before then too.

Ravenous flames engulfed our entire roof. The living room windows were blown out, but smoke and not flames escaped through them. Before Mom reached our front steps, Glenn burst through the front door with a soot-covered face, his right arm wrapped in a towel. He was carrying several framed photos. I heard the roar of sirens behind me as two red fire trucks whipped around the corner.

In a slow-moving daze, I opened the passenger-side door and attempted to climb out, not realizing until I felt the strain of the seat belt against my chest that I'd forgotten to unfasten it. The fire trucks parked in front of our house, and Mom led Glenn to the driveway while the firemen rigged up their hoses to the closest hydrant. The sirens brought more of our neighbors out onto the lawn. I walked toward Mom and Glenn with a heart weighed down by the knowledge that this was my fault.

". . . smelled smoke, so I put the dogs out, but I couldn't figure out where it was coming from," Glenn was telling Mom as the firemen began tackling the flames. Another high-pitched siren blared at the end of our street, and an ambulance turned the corner, honking and slowing down to wait for curious neighbors lingering in the middle of the road to step out of its way. "By the time I went back into the kitchen, convinced I was imagining things, the flames had already broken through the wall."

Mom gently placed a hand on the side of his face. "Why didn't you get out sooner? What were you doing in there?"

"I thought I could put it out," he said, shaking his head. "It just moved so fast."

A team of paramedics opened up the back doors of the ambulance and had Glenn take a seat on a gurney so they could check his vitals. Mom spoke with one of the firemen, and he took notes. She pressed her fingers to her temples, unable to tear her eyes away from our house as flames consumed it. Maude and Glenn's dogs were running laps around the backyard and barking, and we all knew that his cat had been hanging out at the Waldbaums' since the day before because Mrs. Waldbaum left food out for him.

Glenn had managed to save the family portraits and framed photos of me and Jennie from the living room, but had burned his arm badly enough that the paramedics insisted on sedating him and taking him to the emergency room. Mom tearfully told him she'd follow behind the ambulance in the car after settling the dogs at the Emorys' house. The ambulance pulled away, and one of the firemen told me and Mom that they believed the origin of the fire to have been electrical in nature, to which I wanted to shout, *Yeah, no kidding!* They assumed that it had started in the kitchen but had spread through the wall separating the kitchen from the living room, and when it finally broke through the drywall, it released overwhelming amounts of black smoke.

"We'll do our best to save what we can," the firefighter assured us, "but there may not be much left standing by the time the fire's put out."

I don't think Mom could stand to watch the firefighters continue to blast water at our home, or to watch its blackened remains smolder once they were done. She'd already watched fire devour all of her possessions once before, and experiencing that once in a lifetime was enough. And I knew what Mom was thinking: The few remaining material objects that had once belonged to Jennie during her short life were gone now. It was obvious from the position of the flames that the garage and everything inside of it was destroyed past the point of salvation. For Mom, not a single thing in the house mattered more than that handful of items boxed in the garage.

Not knowing what else to do with myself and not having anywhere else to go, I accompanied Mom to the hospital in Ortonville, carrying the mason jar along with me. Once Mom was settled in the waiting room, I told her I'd fetch her some coffee and a sandwich from the cafeteria, considering that she hadn't eaten since breakfast that morning. As I passed the intake desk, I asked the nurse for a piece of tape and a marker, wrote MISCHA and my phone number on the piece of tape, and applied it to the side of the jar—just in case I happened to misplace the jar at some point and someone mistook it for trash. Once I walked the length of the first-floor hallway to reach the cafeteria, I sat down at a table and placed the jar before me.

The smell of detergent overpowered the scent of french fry

grease and stale coffee. I knew from past visits to the hospital that the noxious vapors would follow me out of the building when we left that night, clinging to my clothes and hair. I already smelled like a campfire, since tiny particles of my incinerated home covered my skin and clothing. I was so exhausted that my muscles ached, but the fluorescent lighting overhead was harsh enough to prevent me from getting drowsy.

I probably should have called my dad to tell him about the house. There was a chance he might have thought I should extend my trip to help Mom get settled, since he would have known better than anyone how devastating this must have been for her. But there was still a chance he would have insisted that I change my ticket and fly back to Florida the next day instead of on Tuesday—which would have been perfectly reasonable if it weren't for the fact that I'd accidentally made the situation with the curse exponentially worse that afternoon.

So instead of calling him, I tapped Mrs. Robinson's name on my contacts list, and fervently prayed that she'd answer.

"Well, Happy Easter," Mrs. Robinson greeted me cheerfully. "He is risen!"

"Uh, yeah," I said. The religious significance of the traumatic day was totally lost on me.

She sounded very pleased with herself when she asked, "Did your sister reach out to you yet? They put her behind kind of a curtain, can you believe that? It took me some time to find her—yes, it did."

"Yes. Thank you. I can't believe you were able to find her, but I sensed her this afternoon. I haven't had a chance to connect with her," I admitted. It didn't seem fair to burden Mrs. Robinson with the details about the house fire, so I didn't mention that I was calling her from a hospital cafeteria. "Mrs. Robinson, I'm sorry to bother you. But something went terribly wrong today when we followed your directions."

Mrs. Robinson sounded surprised by this. "This was a very simple procedure. Draw the spirits out, catch them in the jar."

"I did catch something in the jar, but I don't think it's the five spirits of Violet's dead sisters," I said, side-eyeing the jar on the table.

"Well, let's back up. You had your rum and cornmeal?"

I confirmed that we did.

"And where'd you get that from?"

I told her that we'd used rum from Henry's parents, and plain old cornmeal from the grocery store.

"And the drums? You had some kind of a beat?"

I waffled before replying; we'd had something *similar* to drums, but maybe that was where we'd gone wrong? "My friends were tapping on coffee cans, like bongos. Not real drums, but close enough, don't you think?"

Mrs. Robinson sounded stumped. "Hmm. Yes, definitely close enough. I would have been worried if you'd said you'd just used a recording, because that wouldn't have worked. What about your red brick dust? Did you put that down to protect your volunteer?"

Cheryl hadn't exactly volunteered, but I didn't want to admit that. "Yes."

"And where'd you get your dust from?"

I told her that I'd made it; I'd sat in my driveway for two hours tapping a brick with a hammer to fill half a jar with red dust.

"Where'd you get the brick?" she asked.

Now my mouth twisted and my breath dragged as I exhaled. My thoughts returned to the spectacle of Mischa's damaged house, with its roof gaping open like an angry mouth. "There was a tornado in town earlier this week, and some buildings were damaged. So I went over to the house of a friend, where I figured some of the bricks would be scattered, and took one of those."

"Mm-hmm," Mrs. Robinson said knowingly, confirming my fear. "This wouldn't have been the house of the girl who's possessed, would it?"

I couldn't even say the words *it was*. Now, in hindsight, my ignorance seemed so obvious. Maybe I wasn't a voodoo priestess, but using something that belonged to Mischa was clearly a mistake.

"You used a brick from the girl's own *home*?" Mrs. Robinson asked. "Do you know why we use red brick dust in voodoo? Bricks build our homes. They are the physical manifestation of security. They're used to build walls. Borders. If you used dust from your friend's house, then you weren't creating security around the person you were trying to protect. You were setting up—like, like—a *force field* around your possessed person. You lured those spirits out, but they didn't have anywhere to go but back in!"

My face burned with humiliation as well as anger at myself. Even after all this time, the spirits were outsmarting me. They'd even changed the atmosphere around Mischa's house the moment I'd picked up the brick and I'd been too scared to realize what it meant. They'd been warning me, teasing me, cocky about my ignorance.

"Do you think," I asked in a tiny voice, "there's a possibility that Mischa's soul was lured out along with the evil spirits, and that maybe I caught *her* in the jar?"

Mrs. Robinson fell silent for a moment and then hummed a little melody before answering. "I've never heard of *that*. But I guess it could happen. If you're dealing with some *real* bad spirits, then I guess they could have pulled the good out along with them and then locked her out."

Locked her out. That sounded about right.

As well as horrifying.

If we weren't sure how we'd allowed her to be locked out of her own body, how were we ever going to help her get back *in*?

"If Mischa's not in her body, then can the *loa* do whatever they want with her?" I dared to ask.

"Well, I would imagine they could."

I had to remind myself that it wasn't fair to expect Mrs. Robinson to have an answer for every one of my questions. No matter what she'd seen growing up in Louisiana, I was sure that what was happening right there in Willow was more outrageous than anything she'd ever personally witnessed. "Is there any way to know for sure?" I asked. "I'm sorry to be so desperate, but I don't have a lot of time to figure this out."

"Well, you'd have to get close to your friend again to observe her behavior. If someone's possessed by more than one *loa*, then they're probably fighting over which one's in charge. You might be able to hear them talking over one another in her voice. Or see her shaking as they all struggle for power over her movements. Sometimes possessed people have seizures, and this is why; the *loa's* inhabiting an unfamiliar body, and it doesn't always know how to operate it properly."

Great, I thought to myself. It was already dark outside, and there was absolutely no way I was going to show up on the Galanises' door-step and demand to see Mischa. Not when I wasn't even sure where Mom and I were going to sleep that night. I didn't have a change of clothes with me. And it was truly by pure luck that Glenn and the pets hadn't been killed that afternoon. I couldn't risk infuriating the spirits again without having a solid plan in place to banish them; there was no doubt in my mind that they had sparked the fire in our walls the second they'd settled into Mischa's body. Getting anywhere near Mischa before arming myself with knowledge was a bad idea, and it occurred to me for the first time since leaving Gundarsson's that I had better hope like hell *she* didn't come looking for *me*.

Trying my hardest not to become emotional—because at that moment it truly felt like there was nothing I could do to save myself or Mischa—I asked, "If I *did* actually get Mischa's soul locked out of her body, is there any way to put it back in?"

"Of course there is. But you'd best make it a more hospitable environment before you try."

If Mrs. Robinson said it was possible to rectify this situation, I had to believe her and try—as she liked to say—my best. Although I didn't know her well, I could tell she wasn't the type of person to placate me just because I was young. She assured me that when it came to voodoo, there was always a way to undo what could be done . . . except, of course, bringing the dead back to life. And even after saying that, she hesitated, but then perhaps thought it wise not to continue.

I said good-bye after thanking her again and tapped to end our call. At least it kind of sounded like Mrs. Robinson was enjoying herself. Since it didn't seem like her daughter much appreciated her religious beliefs or knowledge of occult practices, it might have been a long while since she'd had an opportunity to advise anyone on these kinds of things.

The clock on the wall overhead in the seating area gave the time as ten after six. I pressed my fingertips to my forehead, wishing with all my heart that I could just go home, climb into bed, and wait for Trey to tap on my window. But my bedroom was gone. Every single thing I'd ever owned and loved—music boxes, teddy bears, books— was gone. Trey would never climb through my window again.

Trey.

I had to find a way to warn him. Glenn had a sister in Green Bay, and there was a good chance that either she or Mom would head over to his house to grab some of his things. This meant that on top of the Mischa mess, I was also going to have to figure out another place for him to hide while I developed a new strategy.

But if I dawdled in the cafeteria for too long, Mom might have freaked out in light of everything else going on, so I ordered a turkey sandwich for her and leaned against a column while it was being prepared. After popping my earbuds back into my ears, I tapped the radio app on my phone to see if Jennie was really back. As expected, all I heard at first was static. Trying not to get upset just yet, I tapped the volume buttons on my phone to spare my ears from the crack- ling, and then said, "Hello?"

"Mayo?" the guy behind the counter asked as he built Mom's sandwich.

"Please," I said, and then I heard garbled words on the radio that ended with, ". . . house is gone!"

"Jennie?" I cried out, ecstatic to hear her voice again. I'd blurted out her name so loudly that the sandwich guy shot me a look over the counter. But I didn't care if he thought I was being rude; I believed I only stood a chance at fixing the mess I'd made and preventing my own death if I had Jennie's help. "Were you able to see what happened?"

"Yes. Not while it was happening, but I can see what's left. Everything burned except for the big things inside like the fridge and the oven," she told me.

Once again, I pictured my bedspread, all of my yearbooks, my color guard uniform—not to even mention all of Mom's clothes, her computer, our couch—all burned to ash. But there wasn't time to mourn any of it. They were just objects, and if I didn't stay focused, I'd die. "Were you watching us at the funeral home? When we were with Mischa?"

The sandwich guy gave me an odd smile as he handed me the sandwich on a paper plate and I mouthed, *Thank you*, at him.

"No," Jennie replied as I carried the plate over to the only open cashier. "I couldn't find you. I couldn't see what was happening. Everything was dark."

"Well, we tried to, uh, get something bad out of Mischa." I selected my words carefully so as to not sound insane to the bearded man standing in front of me, awaiting his turn to pay. "But I think we messed it up, and now they're stronger than ever."

I took a step forward as the line advanced.

"They are," Jennie confirmed. "Before, they could only take one soul for each cycle of the moon. But now they have much more flexibility to hurt anyone who tries to stop them."

The cashier rang up the sandwich, and I smiled politely as I handed her cash. After walking out of earshot from the checkout area, I griped, "I still just don't understand *why*. *Why* would the souls of Violet's dead sisters want to collect a new soul every month? Just to keep Violet alive because she has this degenerative disease?"

"It doesn't have anything to do with Violet anymore now that its connection to her has been broken. The physical world likes cycles. Not just the moon. Photosynthesis. The carbon cycle. Matter and energy fall into patterns, and so does evil. This evil is going to keep repeating as long as it can."

Something Violet had mentioned to me back in January crept back into my thoughts. She'd referred to the spirits as belonging to her five dead sisters, but had said that maybe they were something else, pretending to be her sisters. I hadn't asked her what she'd meant by that. But before I had a chance to ask Jennie about it, the familiar prickling sensation broke out across my scalp and down the back of my neck.

"Don't step into the hallway yet!" Jennie warned me just as I was about to pass through the cafeteria doorway and back into the hall. Holding my phone and Mom's sandwich in one hand and the mason jar in my other hand, I stepped aside and pressed my body against the wall so that anyone about to walk past wouldn't easily spot me.

A second later, I heard a man's voice saying, ". . . see if they'll make an exception because it's a holiday." I dared to lean forward by a few inches to catch a glimpse of who was walking toward the elevator bank, and I flinched in surprise when I saw Mischa and her uncle Roger. They both still wore all black, as if they'd come straight from the funeral home to the hospital to visit Amanda.

"If they won't let us in to see her, then you can just drop me off at Matt's house. I'm tired," Mischa replied to him, sounding like she wasn't the least bit interested in visiting her sister. Then, just as I thought my presence had gone unnoticed because they were about to clear the entrance to the cafeteria and press the button to summon an elevator, Mischa slowly turned to look over her shoulder directly at me, and she smiled.

"Look away," Jennie commanded me over my earbuds. I maintained eye contact with Mischa for another long moment before tearing my eyes away, and in that second, the overhead lights flickered. Other people sitting in the cafeteria murmured in surprise, even after the lights stabilized. With my eyes focused down on the beige-flecked tile floor, I forbade myself to raise my head and glance in Mischa's direction. "They're just trying to intimidate you."

"Yeah, well, they burned down our house today without even being anywhere near it. So it's working," I whispered.

Farther down the hall, a musical ding sounded as the elevator doors parted, and a moment later, Jennie told me, "It's okay now. They're gone."

But it wasn't okay. Nothing was okay. Glenn was still in the hospital, and if Mischa was so easily able to manipulate electricity then he wouldn't be safe there—no one would. His injuries were my fault; he'd burned his right arm, which was the arm he used to perform surgeries on animals. The mistake I'd made with the ritual may have cost him his career. If I made another, the man who'd restored my mother's belief in love might end up dead. My *mother* might end up dead.

"What should I do now? How do I fix this?" I asked, feeling completely helpless and defeated.

There was a long pause before Jennie replied, "You need to command them out of Mischa's body and then banish them so that she can return."

Eager to get out of the hospital now, I began walking toward the waiting area. "Like a *real* exorcism?" Trey and I had sought help from Father Fahey, the pastor at St. Monica's, in the fall. He'd turned us away, claiming that aiding us would expose the other priests who lived in the rectory to more danger than he could allow. I didn't think there was any way he'd entertain the idea of helping us now, not when breaking the curse was even *more* dangerous.

"Yes. But you're going to need help. And you shouldn't be near Mom right now," Jennie told me.

"She needs me, though. She's super upset." I didn't want Mom spending the night alone at the only motel around for miles. This fire was probably going to cause nightmarish memories to resurface for her. And to be perfectly honest, if I was going to die within the next ten days, I wanted to be around her as much as I could while I still had time.

"You're making it too easy for them if you're around her. It's hard for them to apply energy in more than one place at a time. If you and Mom are in different locations, they'll fight over who to torment. They won't be able to come after you simultaneously," Jennie explained.

This, strangely, made sense to me. Perhaps the evil spirits had the ability to know what I was doing at any given second, which gave them the upper hand in always being one step ahead of me. But I'd been thinking of them as if they had futuristic powers, and in reality, they were probably a lot less sophisticated in terms of formulating complicated plans than I was giving them credit for being.

In the waiting room, Mom was so distraught that she hadn't seemed to notice that I'd been gone almost forty-five minutes. Glenn's doctor had met with her and told her that she'd be allowed a brief visit that night in an hour or so when he came out of sedation. They expected he might need a skin graft on his right arm, and two of the fingers on his right hand were in bad shape, but it was too soon to tell.

Mom told me she was going to hang out around the hospital until she was permitted to visit with Glenn, even if it was just for a few minutes. She thanked me for the sandwich and ate a few bites of it while I wondered how in the world I was going to separate myself from her, and where in town I could possibly go. The sad truth was that I had already burned all of my bridges in town. Cheryl was probably still disgusted with me for what I'd dragged her into earlier that day. And even though my mother loved the idea of my spending more time with Henry Richmond, sleeping at his house for even one night was a last resort.

But I didn't have to think too hard about finding a solution, because one found me. Just as Mom started talking about how she thought we should go to Glenn's house that night since the bedrooms hadn't been damaged and the contractors were supposed to start working on the roof the next morning, I got a text from Violet.

VIOLET 6:53 P.M.

R U OK? Just heard about your house.

Violet.

Not too long ago, she would have been the last person on Earth I wanted to ask for help. But now she was in some ways my best option. I wouldn't have to lie to her about my reason for needing to stay away from my mom at a time when it seemed completely insensitive to leave her on her own. And although I didn't want to disclose anything about Trey's presence in town to her, she'd also understand the importance of keeping him hidden just a little while longer. She had seemed genuinely willing to help me over the last few days, and she had nothing at all to gain by doing so. I had to admit that if I were in her position, having been finally freed from the curse, I might not have been as eager to pitch in.

As a plan came together in my mind, I told Mom, "I don't think it's a good idea for us to stay at Glenn's at all. I mean, the damage to the roof may be more complicated than just what we see. There could be electrical issues. And besides, it's *cold*."

To my surprise, Mom actually seemed to agree. "Well, we could stay at the Waukechon Inn in Ortonville. I guess one night wouldn't break the bank. But I hate the idea of being so far from the house. You know, the police said they'd post someone there overnight to keep people off our property, but I just don't know."

She was playing directly into my hand, which made me feel both good and guilty. "Mom, why don't you spend the night at the Emorys' so that you can keep an eye on things, and I'll just sleep over at Cheryl's?" I proposed. Then, to really drive home my point, I added, "You know you won't sleep at all tonight if you're worried about the house, and Glenn's going to want to see you first thing in the morning."

Mom yawned unexpectedly and said, "You're right. That's an excellent plan." She wrapped an arm around my shoulders, pulling me into a hug. "What would I do without you?"

I tried my best to banish negative thoughts from my mind and to instead appreciate her sentiment. But the nightmare of this day was my fault. There were a million things I could have done differently to avoid ending up in the hospital waiting room that night, ranging from declining the invitation to Olivia's birthday party to refusing to fly back to Willow to attend Mischa's parents' wake. Since I'd first suspected that Violet was to blame for Olivia's death, I had foolishly believed that I could get to the bottom of the curse and protect Candace and Mischa. But now I was realizing that belief had been narcissistic. It might not be possible to save everyone, including myself, and I regretted not choosing more carefully *whose* lives I wanted to protect most.

Mom left me in the waiting room to visit Glenn, and I fought the urge to ask her to take the stairs instead of the elevator for her own safety, since Mischa was probably still somewhere in the building. I hoped with all my might that spending the night apart from Mom would serve to protect rather than endanger her.

CHAPTER 13

IT WAS PURE LUCK THAT MOM PULLED INTO Cheryl's driveway, idled until I reached the Guthries' front steps, and then drove away. It would have been awkward if she'd lingered until I rang the front doorbell or worse, until someone answered the door, since I hadn't called Cheryl in advance. But I had other plans.

From the Guthries' driveway, I could hear the television in their living room. I already knew what a cozy night at Cheryl's typically entailed: a movie on TV, buttery popcorn, and a highly competitive round of Trivial Pursuit with her family. My heart yearned for the days when I was a frequent participant in nights like that, but a quick glance up at the moon overhead in the night sky—it was just about half-full—was a sharp reminder that I had no choice but to keep moving.

In my black pumps, which had been rubbing blisters onto my feet for hours, I walked to the corner of Cheryl's street and waited for Violet to arrive. The temperature had plunged when the sun had gone down, and now I shivered as I lowered the zipper on the front of my coat to tuck the mason jar inside, pressed against my chest, so that I could shove my right hand into my pocket for warmth. I wondered as I stared down the dark street if I could really trust Violet to help out with whatever was required of us next. There was a tiny chance that she thought she'd earn herself a kidney, but I don't think that was her motivation for driving across town to pick me up. She may have agreed to fetch me from the Guthries' corner and give me a place to crash for the night out of a sense of guilt. But I was starting to get the sense that Violet had an appetite for closure similar to Henry's. She seemed to really want to help end this thing, as long as I was willing to take the lead.

My sigh of relief released a white puff of condensation into the night air when Violet's green Mini Cooper pulled over to the side of the road and I saw Trey slouching in the back seat. He flashed me a *what the hell?* expression as I opened the front passenger door and climbed in after deciding it would be rude to get in the back next to him.

"Thank you so much," I told Violet through chattering teeth.

"I almost didn't make it because your friend, here, nearly killed me," Violet said as she pulled away from the curb and gave Trey a dirty look in the rearview mirror.

"What did you think was going to happen when you broke into a stranger's house?" Trey snapped. "Sorry I didn't greet you with milk and cookies."

I had called Violet on the sly from the hospital waiting room while Mom had gone up to the ICU to visit Glenn, and requested that she pick up Trey first at Glenn's address before meeting me on Cheryl's corner. Not too long ago, putting my fate as well as Trey's into the hands of Violet Simmons would have seemed like a terrible idea. But I had to acknowledge that she'd exceeded my expectations at the funeral home. Besides, if I was going to drag another person into peril, I felt considerably better about that person being Violet instead of Henry.

"Gee, I don't know. Maybe I expected you'd thank me for canceling my plans with my boyfriend at a moment's notice and driving over to save your ass?" Violet shot back at him.

I had never before considered the possibility that Violet and Trey shared personality traits as half siblings, but it took effort not to laugh at their similar stubbornnesss. "You broke into Glenn's house?" I asked Violet in amusement.

"I just popped the lock on the front door with a credit card. Not a big deal. And only because I knocked for like five minutes, and Trey wouldn't open the door," Violet said defensively. "You should really tell your mom's friend to get a dead bolt installed. This quaint little town isn't nearly as safe or as welcoming as you all like to think it is."

"Sorry," I told Trey though the space in between the front seats. I was trying to compartmentalize my emotions to stay focused on the biggest issues I faced, but thinking about all of the events of the day threatened to make me burst into tears. "I don't know if Violet told you, but my house burned down today right after we confronted Mischa." I stopped speaking as I felt myself choke on the phrase *burned down*, knowing that sobs weren't far behind.

"Violet told me everything," he said to relieve me from the burden of having to explain in greater detail. He reached forward to rub my neck under my hair. "I'm so sorry. I don't even know what to say. It's just not fair."

I knew what he was implying: It wasn't fair that my mom and

I were being punished for what his and Violet's grandmother had done. But there wasn't time to bemoan injustice. And even though I was feeling less chilly toward Violet, I still didn't want her to see how devastated I was. So I concentrated on the present moment and the fact that we were headed to the Simmons mansion with no plan in place. "Well, apologies for the mystery and drama. But it wouldn't have been safe for you to have stayed at Glenn's, not even overnight. My mom's probably going to drive over there first thing in the morning to pick up some of his clothes because everything he had at our house is gone now."

We reached the main intersection in town, right near the entrance to the shopping center where the grocery store was located. Violet slowed to a stop for the red light. We were in the exact location where Mom's brakes had failed back in January and had caused her to get into an accident with Mischa's mom.

"Were you able to figure anything out about what went wrong this afternoon?" Violet asked me.

I reached inside my jacket and withdrew the mason jar. Those two little drops of condensation were still clinging to the inside of the glass. "Current theory is that I accidentally pulled Mischa's soul out of her body along with the evil spirits, and they went right back in and locked her out."

Trey asked, "What does that mean? Is Mischa . . . dead?"

"Not dead, exactly," I said with an exhausted sigh, praying that Mrs. Robinson was right about all this. "Just displaced. I'm pretty sure she's right here, in this jar. And . . . probably really pissed off."

From the back seat, Trey asked, "Where exactly are we going?"

Violet hung a right turn onto the rural highway that led to her house. "My parents had to reschedule their trip to St. Barts over Christmas because my mom got sick. So they left on Friday night, and they'll be gone until Tuesday." She hesitated and then added, "I probably shouldn't be telling that to either of you in case you decide to murder me as soon as we get to my house, but that's the truth. You can both stay until Tuesday if you need to. No one will know."

Trey lurched forward in the back seat. "No. No way. I'm not going into that house!"

"Trey, we don't have much of a choice," I reminded him over my shoulder. "We've really only got tomorrow to end this thing, or—"

"No. Anywhere but there. I'll sleep in Tallmadge Park if I have to."

"Sleep?" Violet scoffed. "If we accidentally pushed Mischa out of her own body, and McKenna's supposed to die before the next new moon, then I don't know why you guys think we have time to *sleep*."

We. She'd said "we." For whatever reason, Violet seemed to really be in this. Although I was grateful, I didn't say anything for fear she wasn't aware of what her choice of words had implied.

She slowed to a stop just a few feet before the gated entrance leading to her family's mansion. Her car's high beams cast cones of light outward into the forest. The display on her dashboard gave the time as 9:17 p.m. and the temperature as thirty-eight degrees Fahrenheit. It was way too cold for anyone to consider sleeping outside.

"So, what's it going to be?" Violet asked. "Do you want to sleep on a park bench, or do you want to put our heads together and figure out how the hell we're going to prevent McKenna from dying?"

After a tense couple of seconds when I could practically *smell* Trey fighting the urge to tell Violet to go to hell, he finally grumbled,

"Fine," and she flipped on her turn signal. I shifted in my seat to turn around and smile at him as Violet pulled the car forward, lowered her window, and tapped in the security code to open the gate.

Once again, the eerie sense of being transported into another world came over me as we were swallowed by the trees lining the private road to the Simmons mansion. I never could have known the very first time I'd crossed onto this property back in the fall, when I was simply trying to get closer to Violet to gather information, that I'd be returning to this place so frequently. And every time I came back, it seemed to be under much more abysmal circumstances.

In the side-view mirror, I caught a glimpse of Trey where he sat behind me. His eyes stared straight ahead as he took in the grandeur of the house and fountain out front. I wondered if he was estimating the value of the house, and how much of it was rightfully his as Michael Simmons's biological son.

Violet parked in the circular driveway at the bottom of the front steps, and led us up to the front door. She tapped a long code into a security panel on the brick wall next to the doors, and the doors opened in unison with a click as a green light flashed on the panel. She stepped inside first and held the door open to welcome us.

Trey couldn't help but marvel as he entered the foyer, just as I had the first time I'd entered this house. An enormous arrangement of peach roses and white tulips was set in a swirled glass vase atop a marble table in the center of the entryway, behind which sprawled the grand staircase leading to the house's second floor. The imposing portrait of Grandmother Simmons was hung on the wall along that staircase, which kind of made her seem like she was frowning down at the parlor area to our right.

"Shoes off, please," Violet said.

As Trey kicked off his sneakers, he joked, "Does the butler have the night off?"

Violet didn't even turn around to look at him when she replied, "Of course. It's Easter Sunday."

Trey shot me a frown, and I shrugged. I'd never seen hired help at Violet's house before during previous visits, but it seemed reasonable that her family had at least a small part-time cleaning staff. The house was enormous—far too big for all of the rooms to be used often by its three occupants. I couldn't imagine Violet's parents, both of whom worked full-time, spending their weekends maintaining the vast property.

We followed Violet into the parlor area and then onward to the kitchen. "So, I think we need to conduct an exorcism on Mischa," I said as I sat down at the table.

Violet took three glasses out of a cabinet and set them on the counter. "Exorcism," she repeated dubiously as she opened the fridge and removed a bottle of water. "Are you guys hungry?"

I hadn't thought about it until that moment, but I hadn't eaten anything all day. If I had to guess, Trey probably hadn't eaten much over the last two or three days either. "Kind of," I admitted, although depending on more of Violet's kindness made me uneasy. She handed both me and Trey glasses of water, and then, without saying a word in response, she took a frozen pizza out of the freezer. She then turned on the oven to preheat it before sitting down at the table with us.

"So, how do we go about performing an exorcism?" Violet asked as casually as she'd once asked me to come up with fund-raising ideas for the junior class trip.

"How should I know?" I said. I was next in line to die, didn't she understand? I was exhausted from everyone always expecting me to have answers. Violet had been dealing with the curse for far longer than I had; I was starting to get annoyed that the strategizing always fell on my shoulders. "Please don't think I'm some kind of witch doctor or ghost hunter, because I'm not. I don't know any more about this than you do. I just have a slight advantage in being able to ask my sister questions."

"I'm sorry," Violet apologized. "I didn't expect that you'd know. Honestly. I was just wondering aloud. I mean, I guess we'll need a priest, right? That's usually how those things go?"

Trey rolled his eyes. He replied with a distinct air of sarcasm in his voice. "Yeah. Any idea where we can find one of those?"

Violet looked at me with an expression communicating, *What is his problem?* But before I could reply, Trey stood up.

"Is there a bathroom around here?" he asked.

Violet thumbed over her shoulder. "Back through the living room, on the other side of the staircase."

Trey nodded and stepped through the doorway.

Once I was sure he was out of earshot, I explained what had happened in the fall. "We went to Father Fahey at St. Monica's for help, but he basically turned us away."

"Father Fahey," Violet murmured as if she recognized the name. "My grandmother knew him. He might have even married my mom and dad. They got married here in town, you know. At St. Monica's."

I was surprised by that. Although I'd known that Violet's father had grown up here in Willow, I figured her mother would have wanted to get married somewhere in Chicago. Somewhere more impressive than our little one gas station town.

Just then, we both sat up straight up in our chairs as we heard footsteps overhead.

"Did Trey . . . ?" Violet began to ask, but I rocketed out of my chair because I already knew what he was doing. He'd slipped up to the house's second floor to either look around, or to look *for* something. Whatever he was up to, and no matter how much I sympathized with his curiosity about the Simmons family, I feared he was overestimating Violet's coolness. Sure, she'd invited us into her home. But if she thought he was snooping or stealing anything, I didn't think she'd hesitate for a second to call the police.

Unable to tear my eyes away from Violet's alarmed gaze, I called loudly, "Trey?"

Sensing my panic, she, too, stood up from her chair. Then, in an unexpected burst of energy, she bolted out of the room. I followed her, and we both raced up the grand staircase in the living room. We scaled the steps with such speed that my feet slipped on each hardwood step, and when I reached the landing I couldn't believe that I'd made it to the top without having fallen. Ahead of me, Violet trotted down a long hallway past two open doorways until she arrived at a door that was closed and jiggled its brass doorknob. It was locked, so she pounded on the door with her fist.

"Hey! Unlock this door!"

I caught up to her, and we both stood there, slack-jawed, listening for signs of activity from inside the room. I could vaguely hear a noise that sounded like drawers opening and slamming shut. "What's in here?" I asked Violet.

She side-eyed the door and whispered, "It's my dad's office."

Of course. Trey was probably looking for anything he could find detailing Violet's illness or the contract that Mr. Simmons had drawn up to pressure him into donating a kidney. I had to trust that he knew what he was doing; his plight was just as dire as mine. But I feared Trey might have forgotten what a delicate situation we were in.

"He shouldn't be in there," Violet said, looking terrified. "My dad will know if anybody's been going through his stuff."

"Um, Trey? What are you doing?" I asked, entirely for Violet's benefit.

His voice was muffled as it reached us through the door. "I'm just looking for something."

Violet bit her lower lip and told me in a quiet voice, "That's the one room of the house I'm not supposed to go in. He keeps confidential client files in there."

Sensing that Violet might break at any second, I knocked on the door again. "Trey? Whatever you're doing, you're freaking Violet out, and that's not the wisest thing to be doing right now."

Finally, the door opened, and Trey stood before us, holding a laptop cracked open as he smiled from ear to ear. "Found it," he announced.

"Found *what*?" I asked.

"Proof!" he exclaimed.

Violet pushed past him and stepped into the office, surveying the messy piles of paper on top of the desk and the file cabinet drawer abandoned on the floor. The office looked kind of like the private chambers of a comic book villain, with heavy drapery flanking windows that overlooked the gardens below, and a thick rug under the desk. An antique lamp with a green shade stood next to an oversize monitor on the desktop.

And there, next to the base of the lamp, was a handgun. My eye was drawn to it, even before Violet marched across the room toward it. As if she'd known all along that this was the *real* thing that Trey had been searching for in the office, she picked it up with a familiarity that suggested she'd handled it before, squinted at Trey, and asked, "Where did you find this?" Answering her own question, she placed the gun back in the ajar top drawer and locked it with a key that had also been left out on the top of the desk.

"Um, is that a *real gun*?" I asked. A lot of people in Wisconsin were into hunting, so certainly rifles were prevalent around town. It wasn't uncommon at all for people my age to get their hunting licenses for their twelfth birthday. In fact, I would have bet that Henry had one. But I'd never seen a handgun in person before in my entire life.

"Of course. My dad just has it for protection, and it's supposed to be *locked up* at all times," Violet snapped, her eyes fixed on Trey. "Do you think you're investigating *crimes* or something in here?"

Trey thrust the laptop toward us for emphasis. "Your father paid someone to assault me."

Violet shook her head at him. "Is this more of that kidney BS? I already told McKenna, my dad would never *extort* an organ from someone, okay? Besides, you could easily just *sue* him to establish paternity and get him to pay child support, which I'm sure he knows."

Violet stepped out from behind the desk and took a few steps in Trey's direction, and he swiveled to prevent her from grabbing the laptop away from him, assuming that was her intention. "It's right here. An invoice from your father's law firm detailing costs for preparing a contract for me, Trey Emory. Fees for in-person delivery with the address of my school, and then another pass-through fee described simply as 'payment for services rendered,'" Trey informed us. "Fifteen thousand dollars in 'services.'"

Despite the fact that Trey sounded convinced he'd discovered something important, I had started tuning out both him and Violet. My scalp had broken into a rage of tingles, and I was getting the distinct sense that Jennie wanted me to inspect Mr. Simmons's bookshelves on the other side of the room.

Violet rolled her eyes. "That's not proof of anything! He had to pay his attorney to draft up whatever contract he gave you to accept your half of the inheritance."

Trey looked over at me in confusion, and from where I stood in front of the bookshelf, I shrugged. Distractedly, I told him, "She knows about the contract." In front of me, the shelves were lined with finance journals and nonfiction hardcover titles about foreign investment strategy. What could Jennie have possibly wanted me to notice? I'd left my phone on the kitchen table with the mason jar, and considered running back downstairs to grab both.

Behind me, Violet and Trey continued bickering. "Great," Trey snapped in my direction. "Did you tell her about how he paid one of the administrators at my school to arrange for me to be beaten up?"

"That's a little far-fetched," Violet was shouting at Trey. "Maybe someone just beat you up at your school because you were asking for it with your charming personality."

I did my best to block the two of them out. "What is it? What do you want me to see?" I asked Jennie aloud in a tiny voice. And then, as if she'd physically redirected my eyes upward, I noticed a leather-bound Bible on the top shelf. Why on earth would a businessman who didn't regularly go to church have a *Bible* in his office?

"You guys," I said loudly enough to interrupt them. "Look."

I reached for the Bible and pulled it off the shelf, already suspecting what I'd find inside. Sure enough, a folded piece of paper was jammed into the middle, and when I opened it, my pulse sped up as if I were being chased. It was a handwritten note on a sheet of personal stationery, which had yellowed with age. At the top was printed FR. JAMES G. FAHEY.

When Trey sidled up beside me and saw what I was holding, he muttered, "What the . . ." Trey understood why I was stunned to find any kind of communication from Father Fahey inside the Simmons house. The priest had allowed us to relay the entire history of what had happened—from the moment Violet had predicted my friends' deaths all the way up to the hauntings I'd been experiencing in my bedroom—and he hadn't breathed a word about being acquainted with the Simmons family. He'd even warned us that it sounded to him like Violet had a very powerful bond to the spirit (or spirits) that were enabling her to predict deaths with such accuracy.

Trey exhaled in disgust as, like me, he must have been reflecting on everything that Father Fahey had told us. He was the one who'd told us that an object tied Violet to the spirits. It was at his suggestion that we'd attacked her during a basketball game back in November to tear away the locket that she wore around her neck, and we'd led cops on a high-speed chase up to the Lake District so that we could dispose of it. All of that had been for nothing, obviously.

In fact, it now it seemed as if perhaps the pastor at St. Monica's had deliberately misled us.

"He knew," Trey murmured, arriving at the same realization as mine. "He told us to break the connection to throw us off. Don't you remember? As soon as we mentioned that the new girl in town was involved, he got a lot more interested."

Violet joined us and took the piece of paper from me. "Are you guys saying that a priest at St. Monica's told you to steal my locket?"

"Something like that," I admitted.

She scanned the note with furrowed eyebrows. "What the hell does this even mean? It looks like something on a poster at a yoga studio."

I took the note back from her to examine it. What was written on it looked like a poem in masculine-looking handwriting, all capitals.

> 3X
> AS YOU DIG, BE MINDFUL OF CREATING SPACE.
> AS YOU SPREAD THE ROOTS, BE MINDFUL OF
> ENCOURAGING LIFE TO FLOURISH.
> AS YOU PAT THE SOIL IN PLACE, BE MINDFUL OF THE
> FRAGILITY OF LIFE.
> THE NEW MOON, FEB 1, 2003 4:48 A.M.

"It's a spell," I said, recognizing immediately that these were directions for planting something, intended to be repeated three times. Kirsten had told me that a lot of spells were most effectively cast during full or new moons. New moons, in witchcraft, signified the beginning of a new phase or chapter.

"Spreading the roots?" Trey asked. "That sounds like rosebushes. The roots are always in a ball."

Kirsten had told me that she'd been able to determine that whoever had cast the original spell that had resulted in the curse had planted three rosebushes on the Simmonses' property, one for each of the daughters Vanessa and Michael Simmons had lost. Two had been planted later, after Violet was born. We'd always assumed that Violet's grandmother had cast the original spell. In fact, Violet was the one who'd told me that her grandmother had planted the rosebushes.

But we never considered that Father Fahey had instructed her on how to do it.

"What was happening in February, seventeen years ago?" Trey wondered aloud.

"It was two months before I was born," Violet informed us. "My mom had been diagnosed with preeclampsia and put on bed rest right around that time, at least that's what she told me. If my grandmother was afraid that my mom was going to lose me, then it makes sense that she would have cast the spell then."

She shook her head slowly at the piece of paper and asked the question on all of our minds. "Why would a *priest* at St. Monica's have written these directions down for her?"

CHAPTER 14

THE FRONT DOORS OF ST. MONICA'S WERE LOCKED, which wasn't surprising considering that it was after ten o'clock on a Sunday night.

"Great," I muttered, pulling on the handle of the front door despite already being aware of the futility. I was so tired I could barely see straight, I reeked of smoke, and now we were standing outside a locked church late at night in the freezing cold. A lump formed in my throat. Becoming emotional wasn't going to improve my circumstances at all, but the idea of just going back to Florida and simply hoping I wouldn't die in the next ten days was starting to hold an undeniable appeal.

"I've got an idea," Trey announced, and without waiting for either Violet or me to reply, he hopped down the cement stairs and followed the path that wrapped around the side of the church.

Violet frowned at me. "I'm *not* breaking into a church on Easter Sunday."

I shared her sentiment. I'd done enough breaking in, snooping, and sneaking around for a lifetime. But we needed to get our hands on something in particular before we did anything else, and I was too exhausted to think of any other place in town where we might find an object that would meet the criteria. So I trudged down the stairs after Trey, and Violet begrudgingly followed me, huffing and puffing with each step.

We found him holding open a side door, through which a wedge of pale light spilled onto the path. "I had a feeling this wouldn't be locked," he told us. As Violet and I entered, we realized that we had stepped into the small chapel off to the left side of the altar. Although Mom and I hadn't made a regular habit of going to church for many years, I vaguely remembered this side chapel was where baptisms were usually held. Dim overhead lights had been left on inside the church, which was fortunate, since I had no energy for poking around in cold, dark places filled with objects of religious significance at that hour. A surprisingly sweet and floral scent tickled my senses, and I noticed Easter lilies lining the center aisle of the nave.

"How did you know there was a side door?" Violet asked Trey.

"Believe it or not, once upon a time, I was an altar boy."

With one earbud in my ear so that I could hear Jennie's voice over the radio, I walked down the center aisle between the chapel's pews toward the altar. "We need something that Father Fahey either owns or handles a lot," I reminded Trey and Violet.

"The sacristy," Trey said, and gestured for us to follow him.

Violet flashed a smirk at me, impressed and amused by Trey's totally unexpected familiarity with St. Monica's. Sure enough, when we passed through a doorway at the back of the sanctuary, we entered into a narrow carpeted hallway. Trey reached into the first open doorway along it and flipped on the light switch. He led us into a small, cramped room containing a mahogany wardrobe and two desks. There was a small crucifix hanging on the wall and a cork bulletin board over the desks, to which Easter greeting cards and palm crosses were held in place with pushpins.

"This is where they keep the vestments," Trey told us.

He reached into the wardrobe and pulled out a vibrant purple tunic on a hanger. "He would have worn this one to say mass today. Purple, for Easter."

I ran my hand over the smooth fabric and asked Jennie, "Will this work?"

Violet mumbled, "Do you think we'll all go to hell for blackmailing a priest?"

"We haven't blackmailed anyone yet," Trey reminded her.

I shushed them so that I could hear Jennie better. "It's good enough," she told me. "Just keep your hand on it in one place long enough for me to get a sense of him."

I pressed my hand against the purple fabric. We were there because we had agreed that confronting Father Fahey at the rectory about his involvement in spell-casting probably wouldn't get us anywhere. There was no reason for him to tell us the truth, and nothing to stop him from calling the police and telling them that Trey was back in town. We needed to better understand *why* he'd helped Violet's grandmother, and we needed evidence of just how far his interest in the occult reached. Basically, we needed leverage to *make* him agree to help us conduct an exorcism on Mischa.

So yes. As much as I preferred to think of it under different terms, we were essentially there, at the church, using Jennie's help to gather information for the purpose of blackmailing a priest.

"What's she saying?" Violet asked.

"It's outside," Jennie told me. "Something outside, on a brick? There's writing."

I listened for more.

"It has to do with Ann Simmons and the rosebushes."

"Okay," I said, avoiding Trey and Violet's eager eyes. "What about other people? Has Father Fahey ever cast spells for other people in town?"

Behind us, something struck the carpeted floor with a muffled sound. All three of us flinched at the sudden, unexpected motion, and Violet clapped her hand over her heart. "Jesus!" she exclaimed.

It was a small silver key, and I squatted to pick it up. It seemed to have fallen off the top of the wardrobe, and I knew without asking that Jennie must have exerted as much energy as she could gather to move it.

"It opens the drawer," Jennie told me as I held the key up to inspect it more closely. A drawer made sense; the key was too small for a door's lock. "Top drawer on the larger desk."

Of the two desks in the room, the one on the left was slightly larger than the one on the right. FATHER JAMES G. FAHEY was etched into a triangular glass nameplate on that desk, and I nodded in its direction. "Jennie says this key opens the top drawer."

Trey stepped aside to allow me to pass, and the key fit into the lock on the top drawer perfectly. I pulled the drawer open to discover an orderly arrangement of office supplies: paper clips, a box of staples, a stack of business cards . . . and a small red spiral notebook.

"This," I said, lifting the notebook for Trey and Violet to see. I didn't need Jennie to tell me that the notebook was what we'd hoped to find. When I lifted the card-stock cover, I found each lined page to contain a name, a dollar amount, and a note about a request or issue. Some of the notes were more cryptic than others, but all were written in Father Fahey's distinctive all-caps handwriting.

LINDSTROM, $50, MOTHER.

CORTESI, $100, MARRIAGE.

DEMILO, $75, CROP.

As I ran my finger over Father Fahey's handwriting on each page, Jennie showed me a flash of an image detailing why each person had sought the priest's help, kind of like little movies running behind my eyes. I saw an elderly woman lying in a hospital bed with a scarf wrapped around her head and knew that Marie Lindstrom had asked Father Fahey to cast a spell to allow her ailing mother to pass away peacefully after a long battle with cancer. When I turned to the next page, Jennie showed me a middle-aged woman holding up her husband's cell phone and reading his text messages with a horrified expression on her face; Jody Cortesi had reason to believe her husband was cheating on her and asked Father Fahey to end the affair in an effort to save her marriage. And then I saw Stephani deMilo's dad riding a tractor across a field of soybeans in the hot summer sun, and understood instantly that Stephani's family had been in danger of losing their enormous farm because of dwindling crops each fall.

On page after page, Jennie showed me familiar faces from around town dealing with heartbreak, financial problems, grief, loneliness, and unrequited love.

"What does it say?" Trey asked me.

I turned to face him and Violet. "This seems to be like a record of requests for help and the amounts of money that Father Fahey charged," I said. I handed the notebook to him so he could take a look for himself.

"That's it! It's perfect!" Violet whispered with a smile. "We can take pictures and back all of this up, and he'll have no choice but to help us. People in town would freak out if they knew the pastor of their church was doing all this freelance witchcraft!"

Trey frowned. "Yeah, except that half of the population of our town is in here, so they must already know." He handed the notebook back to me. "Besides, this basically looks like a list of people who asked him to say a special mass for them. People do that, you know? My grandmother tells me all the time that she has her priest say mass in the hope of saving my soul."

"Secrets," I heard Jennie's voice say over the earbuds.

Frustrated to have been wrong, Violet frowned at both of us. "Well, Father Fahey's *boss* wouldn't find it amusing that he's casting all these spells. I can't imagine the *Vatican* would think too highly of that. Even if it looks on paper like he's taking requests for special mass offerings, he's charging a lot of money for it. What's he doing with the money?"

"You're right," I told Violet. "We should take pictures of all of these entries as backup, because if he refuses to help us with the exorcism, we can do something with them. But Jennie seems to think he'll help us because he won't want everyone in town to know how often he's doing this. He knows the secrets of everyone in Willow."

Violet set about taking a picture of each page in the notebook with her phone, and Trey slipped his fingers through mine and squeezed my hand. "Does Jennie really think we can convince him to help us?"

"What do you think, Jennie?" I asked aloud.

She reminded me that it was difficult for her to predict the future when someone's free will was involved.

"He's got that room in the basement of the rectory," I reminded Trey. "I mean, he's definitely performed an exorcism before." But even as I listened to myself speaking, I knew that we were getting ourselves deeper into a mess that was larger than all of us. If Father Fahey had given Violet's grandmother directions on how to cast the original spell, then maybe he'd also advised Trey's mother on how to cast *her* spell, the one that had caused all the trouble. It could be very dangerous for us to cross him, but I had nothing to lose anymore.

When Violet was done, I tucked the notepad into the interior pocket of my coat, and we headed back outside into the cold night. Violet and Trey turned right to follow the path to the rectory, which was behind the church. But sensing that there was still part of the puzzle we needed to see, I blurted, "You guys, wait. Jennie said something about writing on a brick."

Trey waved in the direction of the enormous church. "There are a lot of bricks here, McKenna."

"Just hold on a second," I urged him. "Which brick, Jennie? Which one ties Father Fahey back to Violet's grandmother?"

"Across," Jennie told me.

"Across where?" I asked. Straight across from the chapel door were tall hedges. "I'm going to need you to be more specific, because it's cold out here, and it's getting late."

"The other building."

Other building? The only other building besides the church and rectory in the St. Monica's complex was the elementary school, which was past the hedges and across an enormous parking lot. I walked down the path to where the hedges ended so that I could take a better look at the school building, and my head rose as if invisible hands were repositioning it. The two-story school building in the distance had been built with limestone, and its windows were dark behind the paper Easter decorations that had been hung in them.

Trey and Violet joined me and both gazed out across the parking lot at the school in wonderment. Without saying a word, the three of us walked past Violet's parked car and over the dark expanse of the lot until we reached the grassy lawn surrounding the school. In the lead, feeling as if my feet were being guided by Jennie, I walked toward the front corner of the building. My eyes came to rest on a bronze plaque hung on the brick wall, level with my eyes.

Violet read the words embossed on the plaque aloud. "'St. Monica's Elementary School, August 2003. Many thanks to the generosity of Harold and Ann Simmons . . . ?"

"That doesn't make sense. My mom went to St. Monica's when she was a kid," Trey said. "That was way before 2003."

I looked down the length of the building, past the double doors of the entrance and toward the back, where I knew the gymnasium was located. "They built onto it. Here, in the front, and the gym. See how the limestone's a different color here than near the front doors? And look at the roof over the gym."

Unlike the roof over the rest of the building, the roof of the gym was peaked, with brown tiles covering it. I couldn't recall ever having been inside, but it made sense—especially if it had been constructed decades after the original building—that the architects had sloped the roof because of the excessive snow our area of Wisconsin received every winter.

"You didn't know that your grandparents donated a ton of money to build onto the elementary school?" I asked Violet, doubting that she could possibly have been so ignorant. "I mean, they added onto the library, too."

"And the community center," Trey chimed in. "Haven't you ever noticed the sign by the pool? They closed it one spring when we were kids to renovate and build the toddler pool. I only remember because the pool didn't open that year on Memorial Day weekend because the construction wasn't done yet, and everyone was angry."

Violet shrank a step back from us as if we were attacking her. "I had no idea! God! Obviously my grandparents invested a lot around this town. But I didn't grow up here, so how would I have known?"

"Donating money to build an addition on a Catholic elementary school is kind of suspicious, especially if your own kids don't attend that school," I gently pointed out to her. "Did your dad and your uncle go here?"

Violet looked uncomfortably at Trey and then at me. "They went to boarding school in Connecticut."

"Of course," Trey mumbled.

I checked the time on my phone and saw that it was a few minutes after eleven o'clock. Perhaps Father Fahey had written down a two-digit number in his red notebook to account for Ann Simmons, services rendered. But the plaque on the school was proof enough to convince me that the favor he'd done for her was a *big* one, one worth millions. I glanced up at the sky. The moon had waned down to a little more than a half—a waning gibbous, to be precise. A visual reminder of the clock running out.

Even though I felt like I might fall asleep standing upright, I couldn't risk getting killed in an accident on the way back to Violet's house. It had never been more urgent to just keep pressing forward. "Let's go," I told Trey and Violet. "This can't wait until tomorrow."

We walked past the creepy white statues of various blank-eyed saints out in front of the rectory. From the patchy lawn below, it looked like everyone inside the building had turned in for the night. But when I tilted my head up toward the rectory's second floor, I saw the cyan glow of a TV screen through the horizontal blinds hung in the windows. Someone was still awake inside, although the only residents of the rectory I knew of were Father Fahey, elderly Father Nowicki, and a visiting priest from Africa.

Ignoring the business hours for the church office posted near the front door, I pressed the doorbell three times in fast succession. The night was so quiet that all of us cringed as we heard the shrill ring ripple through the three-story rectory. Moments later, I held my breath as I heard footsteps coming down the stairs. Trey stepped up alongside me and gripped my hand so tightly it felt like he was trying to cut off circulation to my fingertips.

The locks on the door twisted open, and we found ourselves face-to-face with Father Fahey, who wore a threadbare brown terry-cloth robe and held a mug of tea. While he hardly looked happy to see us, he took a long look at Trey, most likely recognizing him and assuming we were there for an unpleasant reason. Nonetheless, he greeted us through the screen door with a polite smile. "To what do I owe this late-night visit?"

I tugged the earbuds out of my ear, jammed them into my coat pocket along with my phone, and flashed the red notebook at him with a frown. "We need to speak with you."

His smile faded when he saw the notebook in my hands. "I'll let you in because it's my duty," he told me. "But I hope that the three of you come in the name of the Lord and don't have any ill intentions."

The familiar smell of the rectory—alphabet soup mixed with Murphy Oil Soap—overwhelmed me as we stepped inside, along with the memory of having passed through here with Trey just six months earlier. In a low voice, the priest told us, "Father Nowicki is already asleep, so please keep your voices lowered."

We followed him to the kitchen, where he gestured toward the table indicating that we should sit down.

"Don't you want to go downstairs?" I asked. "Maybe you don't recognize us from the fall."

"Oh, I recognize you," Father Fahey told me, leaning against the back of the empty fourth chair at the table instead of sitting on it. "And you must be the Simmons girl. Ann's granddaughter," he said to Violet.

She nodded. "How'd you know?"

"You look so much like her—well, when she was young," Father Fahey said.

Having had enough of the pleasantries, Trey said, "We're not here to chat. We need you to help us perform an exorcism, and don't even waste our time by telling us you don't know how to do it. You told us you did last time we were here."

Father Fahey looked at Violet with an amused expression on his face. "An exorcism? This girl isn't possessed!"

241

It took me a moment to realize why he thought Violet was the one in need of an exorcism; when Trey and I had visited in the fall, the curse had still been on her.

"It's not her," I clarified. My temper shortened by tiredness, I rudely snapped, "Do you really think someone in need of an exorcism would just walk onto church property?"

Most likely to put me in my place, Father Fahey replied, "Well, it would depend on what said person was possessed by. Demons get a thrill out of parading around in churches and on hallowed ground."

Trey shot me a look, and I noticed that his eyes were watery. Although it didn't seem wise to tell him as much, Father Fahey was our last hope. If he refused to either help us perform an exorcism or instruct us on how to do it ourselves, I was as good as dead. And there was no telling what Mischa would do to Trey and Violet, or anyone else who'd ever try to put a stop to the spirits' killing.

Knowing how critical this meeting was, Trey raised his voice at the priest. "This is *serious*, man. Do you get that?"

Violet laced her fingers together and set her hand atop the table. "Listen. We know that you helped my grandmother cast a spell seventeen years ago."

"And that spell was corrupted," Trey added. "Now people are *dying*. That's *your fault*. Aren't you afraid of going to hell?"

Father Fahey shook his head regretfully. "All I did was offer advice." He looked at Violet before continuing, "Your grandmother was desperate. Who knows what she might have tried if I hadn't given her a little hope?" He paused before continuing. "I'm sure all of you believe that prayer is ineffective. Young people tend to think of it as a silly hobby of old people."

I didn't dare break eye contact with him, but he was right. After Jennie had died, my mom had said lots of prayers. Hundreds. Thousands. None of them had made a difference; she'd still cried herself to sleep at night for years.

"What none of you understand is that sending focused energy out into the universe, which is in many ways exactly what a prayer is, can be quite powerful. Can it cure cancer? Bring someone back from the dead? Most certainly not. But the Bible details many instances of desperate people making sacrifices to gain favor with God. And there are similar ways of making sacrifices to endear oneself to Lucifer and his legion of fallen angels."

A chill ran up my spine.

"So, what? You counsel your parishioners on how to make bargains with God for *profit*?" I asked.

"Not in the slightest." Father Fahey finally sat down at the table with us and shook his head. "If someone comes to me in a state of despair, asking for help, I provide them with instructions for how they might request special consideration from the Lord, or at least reshape their thoughts about their predicament so they can more clearly see God's intentions for them. There are no guarantees. I'm not a warlock."

"What about the money?" Violet asked with an arched eyebrow. "Does the Catholic church know that you're running a little side business here at St. Monica's?"

"The money I accept for offering this type of advice goes directly toward the hospital bills of a little boy in Ortonville named Aaron Somer. He suffers from myelomonocytic leukemia. I donate it anonymously, and I don't particularly care if the three of you believe me or not," Father Fahey told us.

My heart was steadily breaking. I had been so convinced that his guilt would be a slam dunk. I *needed* him submit to our demand that he help us, but with each word that left his mouth, it was becoming clearer that he considered himself to be some kind of Good Samaritan. He'd justified all of his actions long ago, and my hope was draining as our case against him fell apart.

"And what about gaining Lucifer's favor, for those times when God isn't taking care of business?" Trey asked with an edge in his voice. "Because it seems to me that whatever kind of advice you gave to Violet's grandmother, it wasn't very *heavenly*."

Father Fahey folded his hands and set them atop the table before fixing his eyes on Trey. "My boy. I have a master's degree in theology from Trinity College. Don't you think that someone who yearns to know as much as possible about God would also want to learn as much as possible about God's greatest enemy?"

None of us had a response for that, and I, for one, was not eager to keep talking about the devil. Violet was the first to break the silence in the kitchen by asking, "What about me? Why do you think the spell you gave my grandmother actually worked?"

The priest sighed deeply. "Your grandmother wanted your parents to successfully bring a child into the world at a time when it was not God's plan to allow such a thing. I warned her. I don't know if the spell I provided to her actually worked because I prayed on her behalf, or because her belief in it somehow physiologically influenced your mother, or if your mother would have delivered you even if your grandmother hadn't sought my help."

My skin began tingling, and without even reaching into my pocket for my earbuds to ask Jennie for direction, I knew what she wanted me to ask. "What did you warn Violet's grandmother about?" If he'd warned her, he'd predicted something like the curse was possible.

Father Fahey looked at me with an expression so stern, it made me shrink in my seat. "That when you refuse to accept God's design, even if your will manifests, the outcome will *always* be vulnerable." He smiled with sad eyes at Violet. "Your grandmother came to see me not long after you were born, and told me about the . . . orders she'd been receiving. She was terrified, of course. Not only of what might happen to you if she didn't comply, but of what might become of her soul if she did what was being asked of her. We both knew then that some . . . *outside force* had compromised the spell she'd cast."

I didn't dare steal a peek at Trey even though the two of us knew exactly what that outside force had been. His mother had cast her own spell on Violet's mother, and Kirsten had told us that was what had made the passage of the five evil entities into our plane possible. It was as if evil had piggybacked onto the spell originally cast by Grandmother Simmons.

Which kind of made Trey's mom the villain responsible for my upcoming death before the new moon.

Father Fahey turned from Violet to face Trey and me. "I truly had no idea how to stop it. I hoped with all my heart that the evil that had attached itself to Ann had rid this world of itself when she passed away last year."

"Yeah . . . well, it didn't." A tear rolled down Violet's cheek and she made no effort to wipe it away. "She passed it to me."

The priest continued, "When you came to me in the fall, I guessed that it had been transferred to someone else. But I couldn't wager a guess as to who had interfered with your grandmother's spell. For all I know, it was someone I've never met."

Although he seemed to pity our situation, it was obvious that he took no responsibility for the role he'd had in creating it. His righteousness was infuriating.

I set the mason jar down on the table without explaining what it contained to Father Fahey. "Well, now it's been transferred again. And it's worse than ever before, because whatever it is—whatever these five things are—they pushed our friend Mischa's soul out of her body."

He weakly smiled around the table at the three of us and shook his head as if wanting to console us, but shrugged to make it clear without saying as much that he wasn't volunteering to involve himself. "Part of the spell that I provided to Ann Simmons involved planting a rosebush during a new moon in honor of each of the souls that had been lost. My best advice to the three of you would be to destroy those bushes—burn the roots, burn every petal. Put the ashes in a place where they can never contribute to the growth of another living organism. And," he said, leaning back in his chair and resting his folded hands atop his belly, "be sure to do this during a *full moon*. The end of a cycle."

With panic in her eyes, Violet looked across the table at me. "It's too late for that. I already had our gardeners cut them down. The roots might still be there, but that all happened a few days after a new moon back in January. I don't know what they did with the bushes or the flowers, but I'm pretty sure they didn't burn them."

Trey shook his head and looked down at his lap. "Jesus Christ," he muttered. "Everything we've done has been wrong."

Father Fahey appeared to be lost in thought for a moment and stroked his beard. "I truly hope you didn't come here tonight intending to extort exorcism services from me by using that notebook for leverage. An exorcism isn't what you need. If these incorporeal fiends have taken complete control of the host's body, then they're already too powerful to be withdrawn by prayer. Even if you found a way to draw them out, they'd need a place to *go*. In a typical exorcism, my job would be to make the host's physical form too inhospitable for the demon to remain. Eventually, it would choose to return to hell. But these spirits . . ." He shook his head. "I fear they are something else, and they work together."

At last, he'd come around to issuing advice on the topic we were there to discuss, but he was telling us exactly what I didn't want to hear: that there was no way for me to save myself. An exorcism wouldn't work. Game over.

"There has to be something we can do," I pleaded, my voice barely more than a whisper. We'd botched Mrs. Robinson's best advice. Father Fahey was our last resort.

"Then your best bet would be to destroy the physical form of the possessed person. Quickly and suddenly, before the spirits have a chance to suspect what's coming. And while doing everything you possibly can to protect yourselves with the Lord's grace until they find a new life-form to attach themselves to."

My mind raced as I tried to process the priest's instruction. *Destroy* a physical form? I suddenly felt overheated and realized I was sweating beneath my winter coat.

"What are you saying?" Trey demanded angrily, voicing my thoughts.

"Are you recommending that we *kill Mischa*?" I shouted. I was on the razor's edge between life and death, and now I found myself in the same awful predicament that Mischa had been in since January: kill or end up dead. The whole point of everything I'd done since the fall was to try to prevent more people from dying, and now my only chance at saving myself was to murder Mischa.

"I'm recommending that you render her body incapable of supporting life." Father Fahey nodded at the mason jar on the table. "I'm afraid Mischa may not ever be able to return to her body, anyway."

CHAPTER 15

I CANNOT BELIEVE A PRIEST IS TELLING US TO *murder* someone!"

Trey couldn't contain his outrage on our drive back to Violet's house. I was just as upset as he was by Father Fahey's advice, but I was too distraught to express it. In fact, I was so distracted by fear of my imminent death that I could barely form complete thoughts. Whether Mischa's body was inhabited by five forms of pure evil or not, there was no possible way I could bring myself to hurt her. I was willing to do a lot to save Mischa's life, but not to end it forever.

I'd known Mischa since we were in Mrs. Martindale's preschool class together. She'd been headstrong and outspoken even at the age of five, insisting on turning cartwheels when the rest of us put down mats for naptime. I couldn't imagine life without her. How could I move forward in life with any hope of ever being happy if the memory of dooming her in order to save myself was in my heart? "You have to talk to your sister and ask her if there's another way," Violet told me in a shaky voice. She was so keyed up that I was glad there weren't more cars on the road at that hour; she was driving erratically.

I was texting a reply to Henry, whose messages I'd been ignoring all evening. Kirsten, the clerk at the occult bookstore in Chicago we'd met back in January, had texted him out of the blue and said that her sister had taken her to London for her birthday as a surprise. That explained why she'd been so out of touch for the last few days. When she arrived home that evening from the airport, the soybean plant she had potted as part of a protection spell she'd cast for my benefit was dying, and she assumed that something was very wrong. I hadn't previously known and didn't especially like that Kirsten had cast a protection spell on me, but it was a relief to know that she hadn't been in touch because she was traveling and not because she was sick of us.

Apparently, Henry had driven over to my house after dinner to check on me, and completely freaked out that my house had burned down. Now that I was finally texting him back, I felt awful for not having replied sooner. He'd assumed the worst, and the fire department wouldn't release any information. I couldn't bring myself to dump any more bad news on him, so I didn't mention that we'd struck out with Father Fahey.

"Right now, I have to take a shower and get some sleep," I said after tapping to send my message assuring Henry that I was fine. "I'm not even thinking clearly anymore."

"But we've only got tomorrow!" Violet argued. "If we don't figure this out before the funeral, we probably won't have a chance to even see Mischa again before you're scheduled to leave. I mean, who knows where she'll go after tomorrow? Either she could leave town with her uncle or just . . . vanish."

From the back seat, Trey said, "McKenna's right. We're not going to come up with any good ideas right now."

"Okay," Violet said as we pulled up to the security gate on the outskirts of her property. "Your call. But we're getting up early."

My scalp was tingling and I sensed that Jennie very badly wanted to tell me something, but I didn't take my phone out of my pocket, and I did my best to block her out. If she thought we should find a way to kill Mischa, I didn't want to know.

Violet led me up to her bedroom and set out a clean towel for me. I'd been there before, the first time she'd invited me over to bake cupcakes, but I'd forgotten how oddly sophisticated it was in decoration for a teen resident. Her bed had a natural, rustic oak headboard and footboard, and it was covered by a white pin-tucked comforter. Neatly framed concert posters of 1980s bands like the Cure and New Order hung on the walls, and plush gray carpeting covered the floor. A wide desk with an enormous iMac screen atop it was arranged so that Violet could gaze out at the gardens through her windows whenever she sat there doing homework. Bookshelves lined the opposite wall, and at the foot of Violet's bed was a beautiful wooden chest that perfectly matched her bed frame.

As she opened the door to the adjoining bathroom, she said, "I'll leave a change of clothes out for you. You smell kind of smoky. I can wash your clothes tonight if you want."

"Thanks," I mumbled, closing the door behind me. I wearily undressed and thought to myself how odd it was that Violet was turning out to be so surprisingly . . . likable. For the last six months of my life, I'd put so much energy into hating her that I didn't even want to admit to myself that I'd never really had a chance to get to know her before terrible things began happening. As I stepped beneath the piping-hot water, it crossed my mind that she really wanted to make amends.

But I was too exhausted to contemplate whether or not Violet had ulterior motives. It seemed obvious that she might, especially if her own long-term health was in danger. Instead, my thoughts drifted toward the idea that I was washing the smoke and ash of all of my most beloved possessions out of my hair and off my skin. It was odd to think of the detritus of my childhood circling a drain at Violet's house, but in many ways, it was practically metaphoric for the impending end of my life.

After I toweled off in the bathroom, I stepped into Violet's bedroom and found that she'd set out a pair of pajamas and underwear for me, as neatly folded as if I were staying at a luxury hotel. Almost delirious with tiredness, I pulled them on and realized with amusement that Violet's wealth had done nothing to shelter her from terror. There had been times when I'd been jealous of people at school for their nice clothes or cars, but now I realized that those things were meaningless. They didn't protect you from anything—or make death any less terrifying.

With a towel wrapped around my head because the Simmons house was drafty, I decided to carry the mason jar down to the first floor even though I knew it was ridiculous to take it with me everywhere. As I descended the stairs, I heard Henry's voice coming from the kitchen, and I instantly blushed. I wasn't prepared to be in the same room as both him and Trey, and I'd said good night when I'd ended our call to discourage him from even thinking about driving over to Violet's house.

He shot up from where he sat at the kitchen table with Violet and Trey the moment I entered the room. When his eyes met mine, and I saw the relief in them, I felt as if I were on a roller coaster speeding down a 250-foot drop. I'd suspected it before, but really didn't *know* until then: Henry was completely in love with me.

Perhaps I shouldn't have even noticed or cared, especially with Trey sitting less than three feet away from him. But my chest felt constricted, and I could barely breathe. I wasn't in love with him in return, at least not the way I was in love with Trey. However, the realization of the depths of his emotions had me completely flustered. And that had to mean *something*.

"You didn't have to drive over here," I told Henry as I sat down. My cheeks were still pink, and I kept my eyes on the mug of tea that Violet slid toward me to avoid looking over at Trey. Since I was hyperaware of Henry's feelings, I was paranoid that Trey was too. Out of the corner of my eye, I noticed that Trey had changed into a pair of sweatpants and a sweater, presumably belonging to Violet's father.

Henry shook his head as he sat down again. "Of course I did. I didn't even know if you were alive all afternoon. Your house *burned down.*"

Violet had heated up the pizza she'd taken out of the freezer hours earlier and a second one, and she sat at the table across from the guys as the two of them devoured both. "We saved you some," Trey told me as he motioned for me to sit down at the table next to Violet.

"It did burn down, but there's not much any of us can do about that," I grumbled, hating myself for suddenly being in such a sour mood.

Henry continued, "I know. But you're not safe. None of us are safe."

Violet gestured across the table at Henry. "That's what *I* keep saying! We don't really have time to rest. We should at least sleep in shifts so that somebody's awake, keeping an eye on things."

Especially annoyed that Violet was inferring that she and Henry were on the same side, I mumbled, "That's probably a reason for us to stay away from each other as long as possible." I lifted a slice of pizza to my lips and took an unenthusiastic bite.

With a confused frown, Henry pressed on. "McKenna. You know we're running out of time."

I felt the weight of everyone's stares on me, and I tossed my piece of pizza onto the plate in front of me. They were all waiting for me to say something, do something. As always.

"What!" I exclaimed. "Of course I know that, Henry! Do you guys think I'm holding out on you? That I'm just going to whip up a way to fix this after running around all day? After watching a fire destroy my house—and having to follow my mom's boyfriend to the hospital because he got hurt—and knowing it's all my fault? I'm out of ideas, guys, okay? I'm tired!"

As I pushed myself away from the table, feeling like I was about to start crying, Henry pleaded, "Come on, McKenna. You know I don't expect you to have all the answers."

I hurried out of the kitchen and into the dimly lit living room before it occurred to me that I wasn't in my own home and didn't really know my way around. So I collapsed on one of the uncomfortable antique sofa settees moments before Trey followed me into the room and sat down beside me. We were both silent before he finally said, "I wish I could tell you that you didn't have to do this. That we'd take care of it, and you didn't have to worry." He laced his fingers together where his hands hung between his knees and looked down at his feet. "But we don't stand a chance without you. And as much as it sucks about Mischa? To be honest, at this point, all I care about is finding a way to save *you*."

If I attempted to speak, I knew I would cry. So instead, I leaned against Trey and rested my head on his shoulder.

"If that's what it comes down to, McKenna, you have to promise me you'll save yourself." He stroked my hair, and I held my breath to avoid breaking into sobs. Because if I started crying, I might never stop. "If you think putting yourself first is selfish, then think of it as doing what's best for me, or for your mom."

I shook my head, doing my best to tamp down the sob I felt crawling up my throat. "I don't know if I can save *anyone*," I admitted. All of the boldness I'd had in the fall about toppling Violet and breaking the curse was gone. The idea of spending the last few days of my life chasing Mischa and watching both of my parents suffer was starting to seem like a heartbreaking waste of time. I could just lovingly bid my mom farewell and go back to Florida, where I could help Rhonda and Dad set up the nursery for the baby and at least leave something meaningful behind.

"What can I do to help?" Trey asked me.

I sat upright and looked into his clear blue eyes. The yellowing bruise around his right eye hadn't faded much since the day before. "I'm just scared, all right? I'm scared. If we fail tomorrow, then I'm going to die. And the rest of you might die too."

"Okay," Trey said resolutely. "We should get some sleep before you even ask Jennie for advice. What if we all just sleep in here? Does that seem like it would be okay?"

I nodded. I didn't like the idea of falling asleep in a strange place, especially now that it seemed Violet and Henry were right: We weren't safe anywhere. As much as I suspected we were putting ourselves in danger by gathering in one spot, the idea of us splitting up around the enormous house seemed like it would make us even more vulnerable. Trey returned to the kitchen to tell Violet and Henry that we were going to crash in the living room for a few hours, and Violet asked me to follow her upstairs to fetch pillows and blankets for everyone.

At the end of a long hallway, past the door to her father's office and her bedroom, Violet opened a door to reveal a large linen closet. As she handed me a stack of folded blankets, she said, "If anything bad happens to you in the next few days, I'm not sure who would take it worse, Trey or Henry." There wasn't a hint of snark or bitterness in her tone.

"I know," I admitted, not really wanting to discuss it with her.

Violet offered me a weak smile and said, "It's not the worst problem to have, right?"

I tried and failed to grin. With each passing hour, it was seeming more likely that Mischa's prediction for me would come true. As much as I wanted to believe that my heart was wholly Trey's, I didn't like the idea of leaving Henry behind either.

Henry set his phone alarm for six in the morning. That would give us seven hours to plan before Mr. and Mrs. Portnoys' funeral was scheduled to begin at Gundarsson's before the procession to the Jewish cemetery on the far side of town. For safe measure, I double-checked to make sure that the lid on the mason jar was twisted tightly shut.

Falling asleep on the settee seemed impossible. I couldn't get comfortable, no matter how I shifted positions, and every time my thoughts began to fade toward sleep, the strong sense that Jennie wanted to speak with me stirred me awake again. Although I definitely had more urgent concerns, the thought that I was never going to sleep in my old bedroom ever again was weighing heavily on my heart. Making matters worse, the tall grandfather clock standing at the foot of the staircase chimed once every half hour and then again, repeatedly, every hour. Its somber melody seemed to fill every corner of the enormous house, even blanketing the sounds of Henry's deep breathing and Violet's sniffling.

Giving up on sleep, I took my phone and crept from the living room into the kitchen intending to get a glass of water. But once I stood in front of the sink and reached for the tap, I found myself staring into a beam of moonlight pouring in through the window. As I took a sip of water, I gazed out at the Simmonses' wintry garden, unable to remember exactly where the rosebushes had originally been.

On my right, one of the cabinet doors creaked open, and I knew Jennie wouldn't wait any longer for me to connect with her. While leaning against the counter, I popped my earbuds in my ears and listened.

"Mom is upset," she finally said.

"Yeah, well. The house is gone. She has every right to be upset," I said numbly. "What can you tell me about Mischa? Is she . . . with you?" I wasn't sure what to think of the state of Mischa's soul. She wasn't alive; she wasn't dead. Was she even aware that she was trapped in a mason jar?

"No. She's probably in the same place as me, which is more like a situation than a place," Jennie explained.

"The dark place."

"Yes. But it's not really dark. More just . . . empty. If she's here, I can't sense her. And she can't sense me either. So we could both be here, but not be together."

Something that hadn't occurred to me previously crossed my mind, and I asked, "Jennie, are you in the dark place by choice? I mean, do you stay there so that you can talk with me?"

There was a long paused filled with radio static before she replied, "I can leave whenever I want."

For eight long years, Jennie had had the option of leaving, presumably to enjoy eternal peace, whatever that may have meant for her. But according to Mrs. Robinson, Jennie had stayed in the dark place because she was worried about me. The idea of her being there by herself by choice, especially because she'd told me that she couldn't predict the future and hadn't ever known whether she'd be able to make contact with me, filled me with sorrow. She'd missed me as much as I'd missed her, and while I'd had no choice but to move on with life after her death—start a new school year every September, make new friends—she'd just been waiting. Now, I had to wonder, would she remain in the dark place until I joined her?

"So," I said. "The priest who set this all in motion said a traditional exorcism won't work. I don't know if we can even trust that he's not lying, but I'm all out of ideas. This honestly feels like"—I hesitated—"the end. Maybe we'll be together again soon."

After a pause, Jennie said, "We're together now. I know you can't understand, but even if you were on this side with me, we would be just like we are now. So it's better for you to stay where you are, because you're connected to so many people there."

I thought of Gundarsson's and what it might be like for my own wake to be held there. And what would become of Mischa if I died before rectifying her situation? Her soul might remain suspended in the gap between the worlds of the living and the dead for all eternity. "That might not be possible. I've messed up pretty badly."

"There is only one way," Jennie told me. "And I don't know if it'll work."

"Just tell me," I urged her. "I have nothing to lose. If it doesn't work, I'll be dead in the next ten days, anyway." After the words left my mouth, I realized how insensitive I sounded. Jennie *was* dead, after all.

She hesitated. "If it doesn't work, it might be worse for you than dying. Worse for me, too."

I couldn't find words to respond. It was awful enough that Mom was sleeping at the Emorys' house without even so much as a change of clothes to her name. Poor Glenn was probably going to need surgeries for his burns. Trey was trapped in a web of problems that I couldn't help him navigate. But putting Jennie in some kind of danger? That, I could not consider.

"Behind you," Jennie said. The cabinet she had opened to get my attention was still cracked open behind me, and I opened it further to see that it contained teacups, saucers, and a shelf of mismatched coffee mugs. "Take out two teacups," Jennie ordered, and I obeyed.

"Where should I put them?" I asked.

"On the counter." I took a few steps forward and set the cups gently down on the floating island.

"Turn them over," Jennie advised. "Upside down."

I carefully turned them over and set them down again, and I awaited further instruction.

"See the porcelain canister near the toaster? Lift the lid and take out one coffee bean."

I'd never realized before just how very aware Jennie was of the details of my surroundings. She was right on the money; the porcelain canister she had instructed me to open was full of aromatic coffee beans.

"Now set one coffee bean underneath the teacup on the left," Jennie told me.

Amused, I asked, "Are we going to play the shell game?"

"Just watch," she told me. And the two teacups began moving on their own in circles, swapping places and swerving around each other—slowly, at first, and then so rapidly that my eyes couldn't keep up with them. I was impressed that Jennie was able to harness enough energy to produce so much motion. The teacups stopped suddenly, appearing to be back in their original positions. Jennie asked, "Which cup do you think the bean is under?"

They'd been moving far too quickly for me to have had any chance of following the bean. But to play along, I raised the cup on the left. Not surprisingly, there was nothing underneath it. So I lifted the cup on the right to find that the bean wasn't there, either. "I'd be impressed if you weren't a ghost who can do magic tricks," I teased Jennie.

"But you understand what I'm suggesting, don't you?" Jennie asked. "Check under the first cup again."

I lifted the teacup on the left once more, this time to find that the bean was back. And suddenly I understood.

Jennie was proposing that we trick the spirits again, but this time in a different way. It would be similar to how she showed them her death the first time I played the game with Violet, but actually swapping souls with me this time right when they were about to claim mine. "If we do this, can you send them away?" I asked in a whisper. "To a place they can't return from?"

"I'm not sure," Jennie admitted. And without her explaining in detail, I understood why she had prefaced her demonstration of what she planned to do with such a stern caveat. If we hid my soul from the spirits and tricked them by making them interact with hers instead, and she failed to banish them to a place from which they couldn't escape, it might be Jennie who'd end up trapped there. And . . . me too.

There was one element of Jennie's plan I didn't comprehend. "But they won't want my soul. They already think they've got it lined up. I'm supposed to die next."

I could hear the alarm on someone's phone quietly buzzing in the next room. It was only a matter of time before Henry, Trey, or Violet would wander into the kitchen and interrupt our conversation. When we'd gone to Michigan in January, Trey and Henry had collaborated on our strategy to confront Violet out on the ski slopes to force her into playing Light as a Feather, Stiff as a Board again. But this time, I got the sense that only Jennie and I would truly understand the game plan. Her voice came across the radio through the static. "They can only claim your soul if you die according to their prediction."

Of course. That made sense. But their predictions always came true. They hadn't specified exactly how I'd die, but I didn't doubt for a second that it would have something to do with air.

"So, what are you suggesting?" I asked.

"They might be willing to leave Mischa's body to try to prevent you from dying if they think you're at risk of dying in a way other than how they predicted," Jennie explained. "You're going to have to decide which of your friends you trust the most, and ask them to kill you . . . because they may have to."

CHAPTER 16

WE HAVE TO GET MISCHA BACK TO THIS HOUSE somehow."

Trey, Violet, and Henry sat around me in the living room, listening with such intensity that it made me even more nervous that I didn't have much of a plan to share with them. The sun was rising outside, turning the sky lavender, from the sliver of it that I could see through the heavy curtains on the windows. Violet had made a pot of coffee, but I didn't want caffeine to worsen the anxiety that was already making my hands tremble.

"Why *here*?" Violet asked in outrage. "I don't want those *things* back in my house!" She was curled into the far corner of the sofa on which she'd slept, and she leaned against the pillow from her bedroom that she'd placed against its arm.

Jennie hadn't specified that we bring Mischa back to the Simmons mansion, exactly. But she'd said we'd need to get Mischa to an area we could control, where there were fewer chances of the spirits surprising us with locked doors, falling tree branches, and unexpected curveballs of that nature. It didn't seem right to put Henry in a position of placing his parents in danger, and the high school was locked up for spring break. Since my house was no longer an option—and for obvious reasons, neither was Trey's—that left us with Violet's house.

I explained Jennie's reasoning to everyone and created a related task for Violet, since I knew that would appeal to her desire to be more integrated into our group. If I had anything at all in common with Violet, it was an irrepressible—almost pathetic, honestly—desire to be included.

"You know these spirits better than any of us," I reminded her. "So we'll be depending on you to predict their behavior."

"Predict their behavior and then . . . do *what* about it?" Violet asked sarcastically. "If they want to burn down my house—just like they did yours—even while we're all standing inside of it, there's nothing I'll be able to do to stop them."

"Just hold on a second." Henry squeezed his eyes shut and shook his head. "How the hell are we going to get Mischa over here? Because she's not Mischa anymore. She's—she's . . ." His eyes drifted over to the mason jar on the coffee table at the center of our circle. "She's *them*. And they're not going to take orders from us."

Trey, who was stretched out and practically reclining on the same sofa as Violet—but sitting as far away from her as possible—chimed in, "How do we even know she's going to show up to this funeral? Those things are what killed Mischa's parents. They don't care whether or not her parents are laid to rest."

Violet sat up straighter and said, "She'll be there. They're going to do their best to act like Mischa, because they're only going to be able to do what they want if people either like being around her or are intimidated by her—but not so much that they avoid her entirely."

"Okay, so we see her at the cemetery, and then what? We invite her over here for frozen pizza?" Trey said.

"This is serious, man." Henry shot him a death glare.

Trey fired back, "I *know* it is! We only have one chance at this, so our plan needs to be airtight!"

Henry's eyes darted over to land on me. "Do you have any idea how we're supposed to get Mischa here?"

The truth of the matter was, Jennie and I hadn't worked out any of the details. The only part that we knew would have to happen—that the spirits inhabiting Mischa would need to genuinely believe that I was about to die in one way or another that didn't involve air—I couldn't even share. When the moment arrived, either Trey or Henry—whoever I *didn't* ask to pretend to kill me—was going to need to believe the threat on my life was real too. I hadn't yet decided which of the guys I'd ask to take on the most important role of the day because I had reservations about both of them being able to carry out the task.

I wrung my hands and admitted, "I don't know. I'm open to ideas."

"We could drug her," Trey suggested earnestly. "If Violet's right, and the spirits are limited by the state of Mischa's body, then maybe we could knock her out long enough to bring her back here."

"Drug her with *what*?" Violet asked.

"Don't your parents have fancy designer drugs around here? We could crush Ambien into a cup of tea or something," Trey said.

Violet shook her head in frustration. "You obviously don't understand how sleeping aids work. And besides, you guys should know by now what happens when the spirits suspect we're up to something. Even if we could disable Mischa's body, they'd still *know* what we were doing and try to stop us."

Henry piped up, "Why don't you ask that woman?"

"Mrs. Robinson?" I took a moment to explain for Trey and Violet's benefit who Mrs. Robinson was.

"Call her," Violet urged me. "It can't hurt."

With the time difference between Wisconsin and Florida, it was seven fifteen in the morning in Tampa. Far too early to be making phone calls on a Monday. But most of the residents at the assisted living facility were up with the sun. I just didn't know whether or not Mrs. Robinson was one of them.

Mrs. Robinson's phone rang three times before she answered and greeted me with, "Who is this?"

"It's McKenna Brady," I replied.

"McKenna Brady," Mrs. Robinson repeated. "When are you coming back to work? I need you to bring me some needles and black thread. One of these girls on the housekeeping crew complained to the building manager about my salt, and I need to teach her a lesson."

I smiled in spite of my anxiety about the day ahead and the grim likelihood that I'd never return to Oscawana Pavilion. "Mrs. Robinson, is there a way we can convince a possessed person to come with us to a safe location?" After I explained to her that Jennie thought she might be able to banish the spirits to the dark place, Mrs. Robinson thought for a moment. "The only way I can think of to get the *loa* to do anything at all is to offer them something they'd want."

Intimidated by the three sets of eyes fixed expectantly on me, I turned my back on the others and walked into the kitchen before saying, "Well, they want souls, and they've already got mine. I don't know what more I could offer them that I could actually *give* them."

Mrs. Robinson hummed a few notes that didn't sound like they belonged together in a melody. "Well, they do love making deals. You know, that game you played with them really was a deal—just a *shady* one. You had to figure out the terms on your own, after the fact."

I shuddered. Of course. A *deal*.

In a tiny voice, I asked, "Why would they want to make a deal with us when they can just take whatever they want?"

"That's the thing! They can't just take things outside of the rules of the spell. To do that, they always need to make an agreement. They need your cooperation. At the end of the forty days that Jesus spent in the desert, the devil took him up to the top of a mountain and tried to tempt him into proving that he was the son of God. . . ."

I couldn't recall Mrs. Robinson ever mentioning the Bible before, but I guessed it wasn't impossible for her to know her Bible stories and also believe wholeheartedly in voodoo.

"So he could *trick* him into handing over the Lord's kingdom. The *loa* are like the devil," she continued. "There's always something more they want, and it always has to do with power over our world. They can't get enough of it," Mrs. Robinson explained.

There were five of them—I'd seen them with my own eyes—and only four of us. And among us, there were only three souls they had yet to claim. Based on what Kirsten had told me about spell interaction, and how the spell cast by Trey's mom had subverted Grandmother Simmons's original spell, I wasn't even sure they'd want Violet's soul, or Trey's. In the fall, Violet had told us that they "didn't have a story" for Trey, which meant they would refuse to predict his death. If we stood any chance of successfully luring Mischa over to Violet's house that day under the guise of making a deal, all we really had to offer them was Henry.

And I really, *really* didn't want to do that.

After a prolonged moment of silence, Mrs. Robinson must have sensed my terror, because she added, "You'll have to take some precautions. I would recommend you make some voodoo dolls, if you've got the time."

"We don't have much time. Do you really think the dolls would help?" I asked.

Mrs. Robinson went on to explain why the dolls were important; that their purpose had been distorted in mainstream media. They were most effectively used for protection rather than to inflict pain and suffering on others. We were going to have to make voodoo dolls of *ourselves* as a way of deflecting the full force of the spirits' power. "They don't have to be anything fancy. Just make sure they've got heads, arms, and legs."

She also said that black pushpins were essential; the color black was associated with power, and we'd want to stick a pin in the head and chest of each of the four dolls we created to bolster our individual strength. "And you'll need to take the pins out of your doll at the right moment for your sister to do whatever you're thinking," Mrs. Robinson reminded me. "She won't be able to reach any of your souls either, as long as the pins are in."

Making dolls and even finding black pushpins were the least of my worries that morning. Staying focused the entire time we were dealing with Mischa, and convincing her at exactly the right moment that I was going to die—so that Jennie could swap our souls and do her part—*that* was going to be a lot more difficult.

"You don't actually have to follow through on the deal once you get them where you want them," Mrs. Robinson assured me. "You just have to be careful if you're planning on double-crossing 'em. Because they'll know, and they'll be ready to trick you."

I appreciated Mrs. Robinson's reminder to be cautious, but I was already well aware that the spirits were capable of outsmarting us at every turn. She didn't ask me to let her know how everything went. We both knew that if I wasn't successful, I wouldn't be calling back.

No one seemed relieved when I shared Mrs. Robinson's advice with them, although I did my best to sound confident about our chances for outsmarting Mischa.

"Let's text Mischa right now and invite her over here," Henry suggested.

I shook my head, wishing it would be that simple. "I don't want to give them time to think about what we're up to. We need to put them on the spot and force them into an immediate decision to come here."

"Okay, so we go to the funeral," Henry agreed.

"We confront Mischa there, tell her we want to offer her a deal—but we'll only discuss it here, at my house. And then what?" Violet asked me.

I tried to remember exactly what Jennie had told me. "I need you guys to remember not to specify what kind of deal we want to discuss, okay? And it's super important that after I tell Mischa what we want to negotiate, none of us respond to anything she says or does, got it? We don't want to accidentally consent to anything she proposes, and she will *definitely* try to trick all of us into doing exactly that. So . . . no head nods, no blinking—be mindful of every single thing you do."

Violet and Henry had questions about what would happen once we got back to the Simmons house. "It's better that you don't know," I explained. "Because if *you* know, then *they'll* know."

Then I told them about the voodoo dolls. I expected all three of them to balk at the idea of us stitching together toys in the precious few remaining hours we had, but Violet announced that her grand-mother had been an avid sewer and dashed up to the second floor. She returned five minutes later with fabric, scissors, needles, and a pincushion that looked like a tomato, loaded with colorful pins.

"I'll be honest, I did not expect that I'd be making a doll ver-sion of myself when I drove over here yesterday," Henry mumbled as he sat cross-legged on the floor whipstitching two pieces of fabric together. "Or . . . ever."

The one thing Violet didn't have on hand was stuffing, so we dissected the embroidered throw pillows in the living room and used their innards to fill our dolls. Per Mrs. Robinson's instructions for personalizing the dolls, each of us cut off a small lock of our own hair to stuff inside with the fluffy white Poly-fil before we sewed up the heads—except Trey, whose hair was too short. Instead, we clipped his fingernails and brushed the clippings into the doll he'd made of himself.

Violet distributed black pins from the pincushion to all of us, but we were three short and had to resort to coloring the heads of purple pins black with a Sharpie. When we were done, I arranged the four dolls on the music rack of the baby grand piano in the corner of the room. The dolls wouldn't be visible to anyone standing in the living room unless they stepped around the piano as if intending to play it.

It was almost ten in the morning. My eyes fell upon my own voodoo doll, on which I'd drawn eyes and a smile. Someone was going to have to remove the black pins from my doll's head and chest at the exact moment when someone *else* was going to attempt to kill me. This entire afternoon was going to have to operate like a well-choreographed Broadway show, and I hadn't assigned any of the featured roles yet. I was running out of time, and I couldn't blame anyone but myself for my indecision.

My phone buzzed over on the end table where it was charging.

MOM 9:54 A.M.

Visiting with Glenn this morning. I'll pick you up at Cheryl's around noon?

Contacting both my mom and dad that morning and having what might very well have been my last conversations with both should have been a top priority. But I knew that hearing either of their voices would wreck me, saying anything that felt like good-bye would feel like a concession to the spirits' power, and I might chicken out if I thought too much about the danger I'd be leaving my parents in if I failed that day. So instead, I texted Mom back and informed her that I'd be going to the Portnoys' funeral with Cheryl, and Cheryl would drop me off at the Emorys' house later on.

"The funeral starts at Gundarsson's, and then everyone's driving over to the Mount Zion Cemetery," Violet told us as she read Mr. and Mrs. Portnoys' obituaries on the *Willow Gazette*'s mobile website.

"No way are we going inside," I announced.

Henry said, "One of us will have to. You usually have to get a sticker to put on your windshield that says you're part of the funeral procession."

"We don't need the sticker. We can just drive with the other cars," Trey insisted.

"Seems like a perfect way for us to get separated from everyone else if something's trying to stop us," Henry said in a cautionary tone. "Like, if we come across a red light, and everyone else drives ahead? That's the kind of stuff they like to do."

"We need the sticker," I agreed. "Can't take any stupid risks today."

"I can't be the one to go inside," Violet said, holding up her phone toward us as if it was the reason. "Pete's been texting me all morning about whether or not I'm going. If he sees me there, it'll just complicate everything."

"That can't happen," I agreed and turned to Henry. "Henry will go inside. But you have to avoid Mischa at all costs, okay? Try not to even let her see you."

"I need to be there," Trey insisted when Henry suggested that his presence would become a distraction if he was recognized—and it certainly would be, considering that so many of our classmates would be in attendance. "I don't want McKenna facing off with Mischa unless I'm around."

While I was flattered by Trey's wanting to protect me, we agreed as a group that having Trey cause a stir and possibly draw cops to the cemetery would be a disaster. However, we might still need his help in dealing with Mischa before we got her back to the Simmons house, so he'd come with us. "We'll take my car," Violet announced.

"We can all fit inside of it. I don't like the idea of us splitting up."

There was some debate about the danger of us all riding together, relying on one vehicle. But eventually Henry shrugged, consenting to this strategy, even though I knew he probably didn't like the idea of Violet being behind the wheel. In high school, Henry had been a big shot. It had to bother him that there wasn't much of a leadership opportunity for him in our loosely planned endeavor, but I appreciated how cooperative he was being.

And finally, we all came to the consensus that there was no point in discussing our plan anymore. We were talking in circles, and it was after eleven. We needed to start getting ready to head into town, even though my eyes were burning with tiredness and a headache loomed on both sides of my head behind my ears.

"Maybe you guys should, like, call your parents or something," I suggested, consciously omitting the second half of that sentiment, which would have been *just in case.*

Violet and Henry looked at each other with hopeless frowns and shrugged, both coming to the same conclusion that I had earlier. It was probably in everyone's best interest to not reach out to parents and engage in conversations that might turn into farewells, for whatever advantage that might give Mischa over us.

I didn't dare look over my shoulder at Henry as I ascended the grand staircase to the second floor with Trey trailing behind me. If Henry's feelings were hurt that I was spending time alone with Trey, I couldn't allow myself to be distracted by guilt.

Already, the day had taken on an air of mourning, even though we hadn't left the house for the cemetery yet. Violet had generously washed and dried the black dress I'd worn the previous day to the shiva, and it hung on a hanger over the top of the door of her private bathroom. She had washed Trey's clothes too, the ones he'd worn since he had escaped from Northern Reserve. Despite both Trey and I being fully aware that this might be the last few moments we'd ever get to spend together alone, we both dressed in silence. Trey pulled on the navy pants and white T-shirt that were part of his Northern uniform, and then wiggled back into the black sweater that Violet had presumably pinched from one of her father's drawers for him.

"Zip me?" I asked as I stood in front of the full-length mirror that was balanced against one of Violet's walls. In the mirror's reflection, I watched Trey step up behind me and pull the zipper of my dress up my back. When he reached the top, he gently touched my shoulder to urge me to spin around to face him. When I did, he pulled me toward him, winding his arms around my waist and holding me against his body while burying his face in my neck.

We stood like that for what felt like several minutes until he whispered, "Can't we just stay here forever, like this?"

"I wish we could. You know that I wish we could." I pressed the side of my face against his chest, hearing his heartbeat beneath Mr. Simmons's sweater.

Trey's shoulders lifted as he inhaled deeply, his exhale a downward glissando. "Whatever happens today, we'll be together. Whether it's here, or somewhere else, later." Placing his hands on my shoulders, he leaned back so that he could look into my eyes as I felt tears welling up.

"Okay" was all I could manage to say. When we'd parted ways in January, he'd asked me to wait for him. Our lives were intrinsically woven together. We belonged with each other; we were two parts of a larger whole in much the same way that Jennie and I were linked across the divide between life and death. Trey and I had both been a part of this network of evil and consequences for far longer than either of us had been aware.

"Later today, when we get Mischa here, I might need you to . . . ," I began, and then the request vanished from my tongue. There was no way that Trey could be the person who would pretend as if he was about to kill me that day—certainly not if he had to follow through on the threat if the spirits who inhabited Mischa called his bluff. He wouldn't be able to bring himself to harm me; they would know it because *I* knew it. The undeniable truth, which made my heart ache, was that Trey would hurt himself before he'd ever hurt me. He would sacrifice himself before he'd let me die.

"What?" Trey asked as he looked deeply into my eyes. His face was so perfect, his features so beautiful, I didn't want to consider the possibility of death depriving me from ever seeing him again. "Anything. You know I'll do anything for you."

But he couldn't do the one thing I needed him to do, and I couldn't ask him. And so my decision was made, as uncomfortable as it was going to be to ask Henry to own that task.

"Explain all of this—everything that's happened—to my mom one day," I said. That was a request I could make of him on which I knew he'd follow through.

Trey solemnly nodded and then pulled me against his chest again. He said into my hair, "Let's hope we pull this off today so that you can tell her yourself."

An hour later, as I followed Trey out of the Simmons mansion and stepped over the threshold, I looked over my shoulder once more at the house's first floor. I took in the oil portrait of Grandmother Simmons hanging over the grand staircase, the stodgy furniture in the living room, the flocked wallpaper and hardwood floors. We'd done a minimal job of cleaning up our indoor campsite, leaving folded blankets on the coffee table and pillows stacked on antique sofas. If everything we were about to attempt actually worked out, the next time I'd see this place, it might be within the last few minutes of my life.

A few feet ahead of me, Henry paused to wait for me as Trey and Violet climbed into the car. This was the moment when I needed to ask Henry to kill me when we returned to the house, but I lost my nerve when he smiled at me and said, "You could sit this part out, you know. We could go to the funeral and tell her she needs to meet with you here to make a deal."

His thoughtfulness astounded me; he was always proposing ways to soften the burden on me, even if his suggestions weren't realistic. But that struck me as equally problematic as it was endearing, considering what I needed him to do when we returned. "Henry," I began, knowing that everything I was about to say put the entire plan's chance at success in jeopardy. It might very well have been the equivalent of closing the lid on my own coffin now that I knew what was in Henry's heart. But I couldn't ask him to risk his life if there was a chance he was doing so with any expectations.

"Before we do this, I need you to understand that Trey and I . . . we're . . ." I couldn't find the right words to communicate that I'd made my decision, or more accurately, that there really had never been a decision to make—even though I cared so much

276

about Henry that it was painful for me to make sure he understood the truth.

Henry shook his head and said, "It's okay, McKenna. You don't have to say it."

"No, I do," I insisted. "I hope you're not doing this to prove anything—or to try to win my heart," I said as gently as possible. "Because you already have it, in so many ways . . . just . . ."

"I get it," Henry said gruffly. "And I want to be a part of this anyway, because I love you whether you love me back or not."

Before I could reply, Henry descended the stairs and joined Violet and Trey in the car. I felt like I'd just been struck by lightning—unable to move and speechless, my mind completely blank except for the words Henry had just spoken.

Overhead, a crow cawed, pulling me back into reality. It was time to go. I reached for the door handle behind me and took one last look at the parlor. It was then that I thought of the gun Violet had put back in the top drawer of her father's desk.

And my scalp began tingling.

The previous day, in Mr. Simmons's office, after she'd returned the handgun to the drawer where Trey had found it, Violet had slipped the key to the top desk drawer into the pocket of the black pants she'd been wearing. But Violet was a planner, and although she'd been far more helpful in the last two days than I ever would have expected her to be, she *did* know these spirits better than we did. And I was absolutely certain as my eyes scanned the parlor and came to rest on the sofa on which she'd slept that she had stowed the handgun beneath her pillow at some point before we'd all fallen asleep. She'd wanted to keep it close to her during the night, and now Jennie had directed my eyes to the exact place where it was stashed so that I'd know Violet had already taken precautions to protect herself.

And in doing so, she'd made it abundantly clear to me what role I would need her to play.

CHAPTER 17

THE PARKING LOT AT GUNDARSSON'S WAS EVEN more packed when we arrived that day than it had been for the memorial. Storm clouds had rolled in, but the weather report didn't predict rain until later in the afternoon. I sat in the back seat of Violet's car next to Trey, who slouched down as low as he could, and with Violet behind the wheel, we waited in tense silence for Henry to emerge.

"This is taking way too long," Violet mumbled. We'd all thought he'd be able to step inside, nab a sticker, and leave, but he'd been in there almost ten minutes. "Maybe he ran into that Eastern European gymnastics guy from yesterday."

"Something's wrong," Trey said, shaking his head. "One of us should go in there and see if he's okay."

"No," I said sternly as Violet unbuckled her belt. "If Mischa sees more than one of us in there, it'll tip her off." My scalp wasn't tingling, and I popped one earbud into my ear and opened my radio app just to confirm with Jennie that there wasn't reason for us to be concerned. "Jennie, is Henry in trouble?"

There was a long stretch of crackling static before I heard her reply: "I can't tell. He's too close to them, so I'm sensing danger, but that could just be *general* danger."

Trey, whose eyes were fixed on the entrance to Gundarsson's, said, "Look," and shifted on the seat next to me. Mourners dressed in black had started exiting the funeral home. I saw Michael Walton walking hand in hand with Tracy Hartford, followed by two of Matt Galanis's brothers, both looking uncharacteristically dressed up.

I said, "The prayer service must be over. This is normal. They're just walking to their cars."

We all breathed a sigh of relief when we saw Henry step through the doorway carrying a bright yellow sticker. He walked toward Violet's car at a brisk pace, checking twice over his shoulder as if he feared Mischa was following right behind him. The second he opened the front passenger-side door, Violet barked, "Did she see you?"

"No, I don't think so," Henry told us as he set the yellow label in the windshield.

Two black hearses pulled out from around the funeral parlor's side lot, then drove slowly past its entrance and toward the parking lot's exit lane. Cars all around us were backing out of their spots and assembling in a line that formed behind the hearses, which had turned right from the lot onto State Street. Through my window, I saw Pete walking with his mom, who had been friendly with Mischa's mother. "We should go," I told Violet.

She started the engine, and suddenly we all cringed in pain. The radio came on at top volume, blasting music. Wincing, Violet clapped her hands over her ears before reaching to turn the radio off on the dashboard. "Jesus!" she shouted. "That wasn't on before I turned off the car."

When I managed to calm down, I said, "Turn it back on. I need to know what song was playing."

I would have been thoroughly freaked out if the radio had been playing "Ring of Fire." But when Violet twisted the knob to turn the radio back on at a lower volume, the last few seconds of Alicia Keys's "Fallin'" played through the speakers.

". . . the way that I love you. Oh baby, I-I-I-I'm fallin', I-I-I-I'm fallin'."

Falling. I shot a look at Trey, who frowned at me in response. Falling had everything to do with air. This was a warning. I had no doubt.

"Ugh," Violet snorted. "This song is, like, a million years old. I don't even know what station this is." She threw the car into reverse and politely waited her turn to merge with the vehicles in the procession.

The Mount Zion Cemetery was all the way on the far side of town, in the direction of Green Bay. The long procession of cars, at least forty in total, stretched the length of several blocks, and at a slow speed we continued right through intersections without stopping. Traffic slowed to a crawl when the front of the procession reached the ornate gates of the cemetery.

When it was our turn to drive through the tall wrought-iron gates, we saw why the procession had decelerated so much. The street that wound through the cemetery was barely wide enough for two lanes of traffic, and it snaked through hills covered with tombstones. In some places, the paved road was almost impassable where cars had already parked in the other lane. Some cars ahead of us in line were pulling over to parallel park while others continued onward to stop closer to where Adam and Elena Portnoy would be laid to rest.

Henry said, "We should probably park back here so that if we need to leave quickly, we aren't boxed in."

"Good point," Violet said, and flipped on her turn signal. There was a spot a few feet ahead into which her tiny car would fit.

Trey leaned forward in between the two front seats. "Actually, just drive a little farther. I don't want to be all the way back here if you guys are on the other side of that hill. I won't be able to see anything from here."

Without saying a word, Violet obliged and turned her signal off. We continued onward over the hill.

My stomach began to sink. I hadn't eaten anything that morning before leaving the Simmons house, and for that I was grateful. It was starting to feel like we were on our way to the gallows to be executed in front of an audience.

Violet shut off the engine, and we all looked through the windows on the right side of the car to where the pallbearers were carrying the caskets. The hillside was crawling with people dressed in black, and from where I sat watching, the scene looked almost horrific—as if the mourners were insects scurrying toward their destination. I squeezed my eyes shut, knowing that I was seeing what Mischa wanted me to see. She—or rather, the spirits masquerading as her—wanted me to be intimidated. I had to remember that this was just a funeral, nothing more. Just two caskets being lowered into the ground with plenty of witnesses around, keeping their eyes on Mischa.

There was no reason to be scared . . . yet.

"I guess this is it." Violet slid a pair of oversize Gucci sunglasses with black frames up her nose and climbed out of the car, with Henry following her.

Seizing my last seconds with Trey and knowing that the moment had arrived when I had to assign his specific duty to him, I inhaled deeply. "When we get back to the house, there's going to come a moment when I'll need you to pull the black pins out of my voodoo doll."

Hurt flashed across Trey's face. He'd probably assumed all along that Jennie had given me more description about what would have to happen that day than I'd shared with the group. It was fair for him to feel a little betrayed. "That's all I can tell you," I told him.

"I thought the pins were supposed to protect us," Trey said.

"They are. But there's going to be a moment, and I can't describe exactly how you'll know it's time—but I think you'll know when you'll have to take them out." He nodded, staring deeply into my eyes. "I wish I could tell you more, but that's all I can say."

"I'll be ready," Trey assured me in a small voice.

I unfastened my seat belt so that I could lean over and kiss him gently on the cheek, and then climbed out of the back seat.

Henry was already walking ahead of Violet toward where the large group of mourners had gathered. I trotted to catch up with Violet, suddenly wishing I'd handled this matter before leaving the Simmons house. It didn't seem like a great idea to bring it up now, in such close proximity to Mischa, but I couldn't put it off any longer. Impulsively, I grabbed her by the wrist and spoke in a low voice.

"I have to ask you to do something when we get back to the house, and only you can know about it," I said, speaking rapidly.

Violet's lips parted as if she was about to object, but then she asked, "What?"

"The gun," I told her. She wrinkled her eyebrows as if she was trying to act like she had no idea what I was talking about. But we didn't have time for feigning ignorance. "I know you had it under your pillow last night, and you left it in the living room. I don't care; that's not why I'm bringing it up."

"I was just—"

I cut Violet off. "Listen. At some point, once we get Mischa back to your house, once we start negotiating the deal and we come to an agreement on whatever the terms will be, I'm going to need you to threaten to shoot me."

Violet blinked twice and shook her head. "What?"

"The spirits have to believe that you're going to kill me and prevent their prediction for me from coming true. So that means I need you to pick a fight with me, or I'll attack you—I don't know exactly how this will play out. It's going to have to be convincing. But you might"—I looked over Violet's shoulder to her parked car, where Trey had hidden himself in the back seat—"actually have to shoot me."

"You're crazy. I'm not *murdering* you."

"Violet," I said. It didn't seem like an appropriate time to remind her that she'd already essentially murdered a lot of people. "If you do, then it dies with me. You know it's the only way, and you said yourself that the spirits most likely won't let that happen."

"No. I said that they won't let whoever is cursed kill themselves," Violet argued.

Ahead of us by about twenty feet, Henry had noticed we weren't following behind him, and he'd paused to watch us. I grabbed Violet by the shoulders to make her pay attention. "I need the spirits to try to get inside of me, okay? That's all I can tell you, and scaring them into thinking that I might die in a way that doesn't deliver my soul to them is the *only* way. Promise me you'll do this."

Violet scrunched up her face and shook her head again. I wasn't getting through to her at all, and I was starting to panic. "Violet," I repeated, but then my attention was captured by a voice behind me.

"McKenna."

I turned to find myself looking into the face of Mrs. Emory, and couldn't prevent myself from gasping in surprise. She looked much more polished than usual, with her hair blown out and rosy blush brushed onto her cheeks, despite the fact that her eldest son was missing and she was presumably providing temporary shelter to Mom as well as all of Mom and Glenn's pets. I hoped with all my might that she hadn't seen us driving in the procession, when she might have spotted Trey sitting next to me in the back seat of Violet's car.

"Hi, Mrs. Emory," I said uneasily. Though it would have been laughable to suggest that anyone—especially me—could have been considered a bad influence on Trey, I was sure that her opinion of me wasn't far off from that.

She glanced disapprovingly at Violet, and I was painfully aware of how difficult it must have been for her to even acknowledge Trey's half sister; Violet took for granted all of the benefits of being a legitimate Simmons that Trey had been denied. She was a living, breathing reminder of the life that Mrs. Emory had wanted for herself.

But Mrs. Emory didn't seem interested in Violet at all. She fixed her pleading eyes on me. "If you've heard from Trey—"

"I haven't," I blurted. There couldn't have been a more inconvenient time for her to have begun interrogating me about Trey's whereabouts. "I don't know where he is, and I'm worried about him, too."

Mrs. Emory took another step closer to me, and now there was urgency in her eyes. "Well, if you do, tell him that he should accept what's rightfully his," she said as her expression turned sour, and she side-eyed Violet. "Your father's attorneys have been in touch with me, and I understand they've reached out to Trey, too. I don't know what your father's motivation is to finally be acknowledging Trey as his son, but it's about time he did." Returning her attention to me, she said, "Tell Trey that he can have his inheritance placed in a trust and access it from wherever in the world he chooses to go. He doesn't have to come back to Willow. But it would mean everything to me to know that he's safe."

I didn't know how to reply; it was best that she had no idea I knew anything about Trey, the attorney who'd been threatening him, and Mr. Simmons's sudden interest in forcing an inheritance on him. So I nodded foolishly and said, "If I hear from him, I'll let him know."

With her face hardening, Mrs. Emory gripped my shoulder. I instinctively flinched, startled that she'd touched me. In a low, gravelly voice, she told me, "Remind him about cutting his hand when he was eight. Ask him to remember how that happened. That," she said, looking me straight in the eye, "is part of this."

Mrs. Emory let go of me and took a few steps backward, still maintaining eye contact with me as if daring me to look away. Instead of returning to the group of mourners, she walked down the slope toward the road, presumably to her car. Violet and I watched her in silence, and she turned to look at me once more over her shoulder. As I returned my attention to Violet, intending to continue our conversation about the gun, I realized that Henry had backtracked to fetch us and was standing right behind us. "Sorry to interrupt," he said, looking genuinely apologetic. "But they're getting started. We should get up there."

I shot Violet one more loaded look, hoping that I'd effectively communicated how very, very important it was for her to fulfill my request. But she refused to look my way from behind her sunglasses, instead holding her head high as she forged ahead of Henry and led us toward the funeral ceremony. I offered Henry a weak smile, feeling guilty that now he suspected I was keeping secrets from him—as well as simultaneously protective of him, because although I'd spent hours deciding whether to ask Trey or Henry to make a threat on my life, it was obvious to me now that Violet was the one who'd been my only real option, all along.

The voice of a female rabbi speaking in Hebrew soared over the crowd that had gathered at the graves as the three of us stepped into the large group. There were enough people assembled that I wasn't sure where Mischa stood, although I was sure she was in the front row. I inched up toward the middle-aged couple standing in front of me and peered into the gap between their heads. But I couldn't see past the extremely tall older gentleman standing in front of them.

On my right, Henry nudged me in the arm with his elbow, and nodded his head on an angle to suggest that I should take a few steps to the right along with him. The three of us inched over by a few feet, and suddenly I could see Mischa.

Or rather, she could see me.

She was standing on the left side of the two polished, slate-gray caskets, which had been arranged side by side, both set atop the straps of lowering devices arranged over the rectangular graves that had been dug in the ground. She looked more serious and mature than I'd ever before seen her in a fitted black wool coat. Her uncle Roger stood beside her and rested his hand on her shoulder.

But I could tell even from her posture that Mischa was not *Mischa*. And she didn't seem the least bit surprised to see me as our eyes locked. A barely there grin curled at the corners of her lips. The expression on her face informed me that I was right where she wanted me.

"*Y'hei sh'mei raba m'varach l'alam ul'almei almaya,*" the rabbi said as everyone listened politely. A tiny redheaded woman standing next to Mischa's gymnastics coach sniffled and dabbed at her nose with a handkerchief. The rabbi switched to English to continue praying the Mourner's Kaddish. "Blessed, praised, honored, exalted, extolled, glorified, adored, and lauded be the name of the Holy Blessed One . . ."

A bitterly cool breeze rustled the bare branches of a nearby tree, and everyone in the crowd shuddered. But I was barely paying attention to what was happening around me. All I could focus on was Mischa's face, and the menace that I saw in her dark eyes. I'd stowed my earbuds and phone in the pocket of my coat, which still stank like smoke, hoping to make it less easy for the spirits to realize that the phone was my method of communication with Jennie—just in case they weren't already aware.

Even as the caskets were slowly, ever so slowly, lowered into the ground, Mischa's eyes remained fixed on me. She only looked away when the rabbi handed her a small shovel, and she stepped around the two open graves to raise a scoop of dirt to dump into her father's grave, and then her mother's. As soon as Mischa handed the shovel to her uncle Roger so that he could take his turn, and her gymnastics coach and his wife embraced her in a group hug, her eyes returned to me.

With that same, cunning hint of a smirk on her face.

The group around us began to disperse as people walked toward their cars. In the distance, thunder rumbled. Cars pulled away from the curb, and I resisted the urge to look over my shoulder and back at Violet's Mini Cooper.

But Henry, Violet, and I remained where we stood, all of us watching Mischa as neighbors, friends, and relatives shook her hand, and she politely filled them in on Amanda's prognosis.

Pete emerged from the thinning crowd and made a beeline for Violet.

"No, no, no," I said to Violet under my breath. "He can't be here right now. Get rid of him!"

Without acknowledging me or Henry first, Pete reached for her and tried to kiss her on the mouth, but his lips landed on her cheek when she didn't turn her head. "I thought you weren't coming," he said, and then shot Henry a sheepish look with his head slightly hung. "Hey, man."

Henry nodded stoically in response. "Hey."

I didn't think Henry and Pete had ever spoken since the fall, when Pete had started going out with Violet shortly after Olivia's death. At one point, before Henry graduated, they'd run in the same social circle: the jocks, the privileged guys who drove nice cars. It *had* to bother Henry that his sister had been so quickly replaced, but today was not the day for him to confront Pete about his romantic choices.

"My mom and I are going to Bobby's," Pete told Violet. "Come with us. I barely saw you all weekend."

Violet ran her hands over the front of his wool coat and told him, "I can't. I have plans. But we should go to a movie or something tomorrow."

Pete gave me and Henry a look, as if he didn't want us to hear him. He leaned closer to Violet and said in a low voice, "But your parents will be back by then."

Highly aware that there were only a few people remaining at the grave site expressing their condolences to Mischa, Violet stood a little taller and said, "I'm sorry. I just have to do something today."

Now Pete took a step back, perhaps humiliated that she'd dismissed him in front of us. He narrowed his eyes at us and said, "I don't understand what's going on, here—why you're hanging out with these people."

Surprising me, Violet took a step closer to me. "Just . . . I'll call you later, okay?"

Her shoulders slumped when he turned and walked back to his mother, clearly miffed at Violet. It was easy to see that their exchange had upset Violet, too. "Stay focused," I reminded her. "Don't think about him anymore."

It was then that Mischa finished her conversation with the rabbi and turned to face us. She stepped around the graves as she walked toward us at a pace so leisurely that it made my heart beat faster. She seemed to ignore Violet and Henry, and focused all of her attention on me. The hairs on the back of my head stood on end, and I felt my skin prickle beneath the heavy sleeves of my winter coat.

"It was so *kind* of you to come today," Mischa said when she reached us. "Although I suspect your reason for being here isn't to pay respects to my dead parents. After all . . ." She batted her eyes at me and flashed me a petty grin. "They're dead because of McKenna's foolhardy belief in herself, aren't they?"

It was difficult to remember that this wasn't really Mischa talking, blaming me for her parents' deaths. I'd told Violet and Henry to let me do all the talking, and per Jennie's advice, I tried to keep my response simple and direct. "We're here to make a deal with you," I said, trying my hardest to keep my voice from shaking.

Mischa's face remained unchanged—frozen in a hollow grin— for just long enough to make me uncomfortable. Then I realized that the spirits were waiting to reply in the hope that either Violet or Henry would speak up so that they could start pitting us against one another. Instinctively, I reached out and wrapped a hand around each of their arms to remind them to remain silent.

Mischa finally threw her head back and cackled. "That's hilarious. A deal? You don't have anything to trade."

"I think you'll be interested in what we have to offer you. But we're not discussing terms here. If you're interested, you have to come with us," I said.

Again, Mischa laughed, and I could feel my heartbeat echoing throughout my entire body. The spirits must have sensed that we were there with serious purpose. "Why would the three of you think I'd have any *interest* in anything you have to offer?" With a sneer, she nodded in the direction of Violet. "*She* is useless to me. And *he*"—she pointed her chin at Henry—"is just a soul, as useless as all the rest." She narrowed her eyes at me and leaned forward to make it clear she was really only speaking to me. "You know as well as *we* do that he's too *weak* to carry the curse. He's *too weak* to be of much use to anyone."

I felt Henry's muscles tense under my hand, and I squeezed his arm to remind him to not interact with the spirits.

"Guessing what we're proposing to offer is a waste of time," I replied. "If you're interested, get in the car and come with us." The spirits crossed Mischa's arms over her chest. Sensing that I was failing, and quickly, I threw out my wild card. If this didn't do the trick, I didn't have another idea for how we might lure Mischa back to the Simmons mansion without using force. And I highly doubted that we were strong enough to get her there on our own, even with Trey's assistance. "But you know, I might be worth more alive to you than dead. I'm sure you're aware that I have an ability that's somewhat rare. It could be of use to you."

An eyebrow on Mischa's face rose at me as if the spirits were doubting everything I'd just said, although the fact that they were still standing there, listening, was evidence that they were at least mildly intrigued. "Your ability, as you call it, isn't worth anything to us! But you have something else we might want—under the right circumstances."

"Then let's go," I said, eager at that point to get them in the car.

"Not so fast. We don't agree to anything without *something* in return." They set Mischa's hands on her hips.

Violet turned to me in objection, but I replied, "I already told you. We won't negotiate here. If you want to strike a deal, you have to come with us."

Gambling on my own future, I turned and began walking toward Violet's car, still holding on to Violet and Henry's arms to make sure they followed me. We'd walked a good ten feet—and I'd started to truly panic that I'd blown my only shot at saving my own life—when I heard Mischa say behind us, "Fine. Have it your way." Although it was a victory that the spirits had finally agreed to come with us, my chest tightened and my lips trembled.

This was really happening.

When we reached Violet's car, she unlocked the doors with a quick flip of her key fob. I hoped I was the only one who noticed that her fingers were shaking. I opened the back door, and Trey sat upright in the back seat. Once he saw that Mischa was standing behind me, he slid over to the far side, and I gestured at Mischa to climb in.

"We'd prefer to sit in the front," the spirits said, and Mischa's face smiled sweetly at Henry just as he opened the front passenger-side door.

He hesitated, unsure of how to handle the request, until I snapped at Mischa, "You sit in the back, or you walk."

Mischa grinned and wiggled her fingers at me as if pretending to be afraid, but she crouched and climbed into the car as told. The back seat of Violet's car wasn't wide enough to have an actual middle; it was an uncomfortable, unsafe squeeze for three people to sit back there. But Mischa didn't say a word as she pressed her knees together, and Trey and I buckled our seat belts.

Violet started the engine and carefully pulled away from the curb. She knew, just as the rest of us did, that she had to focus more intently on driving safely than she ever had before in her life. Because there was simply no telling what the spirits might do to us now that—for the first time, ever—we had them where *we* wanted them.

CHAPTER 18

"WHAT AN UNEXPECTED DELIGHT TO BE BACK
here," the spirits said in Mischa's voice as we stepped through
the front door of the Simmons mansion. Her eyes wandered around
the large foyer as if she were the owner of the mansion, returning
home after a long trip. "We didn't expect we'd ever have occasion to
return to this place."

Violet shot a furtive look at me as she hung up her winter coat
on the rack near the front door. My phone—my connection to
Jennie—was in my pocket, and I pulled it out after a split second
of hesitation before handing over my coat when Violet reached
for it.

Though Mischa hadn't even watched me do that, with her back
turned to me, the spirits said, "Of course. Wouldn't want to play any
games without your precious sister."

I felt Trey's hand on the small of my back, and I knew that he
was thinking the same thing I was: We may very well have been in
way over our heads. From the wide doorway leading into the parlor,
Henry looked over at me. I could see the rise and fall of his chest as
he inhaled and exhaled. I was more terrified than I'd ever been—even

more than in the moments following the avalanche we'd survived in Michigan, when I'd been buried in snow.

"You're right, we wouldn't," I replied, using the spirits' acknowledgment of Jennie as an excuse to place one of my earbuds in my right ear and tap my radio app on.

"Well, we're all here," Trey said, leaving my side, walking past Henry, and strolling into the parlor. "Might as well get down to business."

Mischa confidently followed him into the parlor and stood at its center with her arms extended outward, like the ringmaster of a circus welcoming a crowd. "Yes. Let's."

I swallowed hard, listening for guidance from Jennie over the earbuds. Although I could sense her presence, she was silent, and I assumed that she was remaining quiet for our safety.

Henry, Violet, and I stepped into the parlor and fell into a circle formation around Mischa, who sat down on one of the sofas, facing us. The mason jar containing the real Mischa's soul was set on the coffee table in front of her, and she smiled at it. I tried with all my might not to think about the handgun stashed under the pillow on the sofa behind me. Violet had stationed herself directly in front of it, presumably so that she could reach behind herself and grab it when she needed to.

"We'd like to propose playing a game with you," I said, ad-libbing. I'd rehearsed this part in my head at least ten times since Jennie and I had devised this plan at dawn, but I still wasn't certain what was going to come out of my mouth next. I knew that no matter what I offered Mischa, it wouldn't be good enough, and she'd counter with something else far more dangerous. "Double or nothing. If you win, you get me and my twin sister. And if you lose, you lose your claim on me, now and forever."

I was already expecting the spirits to refuse this proposal because it was flimsy, nothing more than empty words. But I still bit my lower lip when she raised an eyebrow as if considering, and then viciously cackled. "That's not much of an offer! It's more like *nothing* or nothing. We came all the way here to make a deal, and we're sure it won't surprise you that we already have a proposition in mind."

Perhaps because the spirits weren't trying very hard to convince anyone present that they were Mischa Portnoy, teenage gymnast, Mischa had gone pale since we'd arrived. Veins throbbed beneath the skin of her face, delicate blue webs of blood coursing beneath her eyes, up her temples, and into her hair.

This would have been the perfect moment for Violet to have instigated an argument with me to put the pressure on Mischa to agree to a game. It would have been ideal for the spirits to have tried to prevent me from dying *before* they specified their offer, before whatever I stood to lose had been defined. With a tight frown, I glimpsed at Violet, but her eyes were fixed on Mischa. My fingers curled into my palms, forming loose fists. Maybe Violet truly had no intention of acknowledging my request. I tried my best not to let my anxiety show on my face; our success that day entirely depended on Violet. I had to believe she could do this. If she didn't, she was likely going to doom us all.

"You have access to something *very* special," Mischa said, folding her hands in her lap and fanning her fingers in a way that was so hypnotic that I averted my eyes. "Or, rather, you will . . . soon." I wasn't sure what the spirits were referring to, but my chin wrinkled in disgust at Mischa's enthusiasm. "There's nothing we love more than innocence. And there's no one who can fulfill our desires with as much ease as a child."

A *child*? I didn't know any children.

But just as I wondered what in the world the spirits were getting at, the answer occurred to me.

Dad and Rhonda's baby.

"If you want to play another game with your soul as the prize, then your half brother is the only thing you have that we're willing to bargain for," the spirits told me, never tearing Mischa's eyes away from mine.

A *brother*. Although I felt as if I'd had the wind knocked out of me, I marveled at the unexpected news that Dad would be having a son. He and Rhonda probably didn't even know their baby's gender yet.

"If you lose? Then we'll evacuate this body and relocate to yours. We'll return to Florida tomorrow instead of you, and we'll find a way to infect that baby's soul as soon as he's old enough to speak. After all, no one ever says no to a baby. He'll be able to summon the souls of whoever we choose for many, many years."

Suddenly aware of Jennie's voice breaking through the static in my right ear, I heard her say, "No! Don't agree to that!"

"What half brother? Am I missing something here?" Henry asked me.

Ignoring him, I struggled to find my voice, and my objection came out as a whisper. "Not that. Not the baby."

"What are you doing?" Violet hissed at me, her face scarlet with rage. "Just say yes so we can play the game and get this over with!"

I shook my head at Mischa. "What do you even get by capturing all these souls?" I asked. "What's the point of all of this? What has the point ever been?"

"Your sister is in a state you've heard described as 'the dark place,'" the spirits reminded me. Her eyes were now as dark as charcoal, so dark that the pupils had blended in with the irises. The veins beneath her skin looked darker, almost blackened, like actual cobwebs beneath a thin veil of translucent skin. "As long as we collect souls, we keep ourselves out of a place much, much darker. We like it here, among all of you, where there is work to be done and there are games to be played."

On my left side, Violet pointed at me, looking furiously from Henry to Trey. "She's tricking us! She and her sister are doing something to screw us over!"

She sounded so hysterical that I wasn't sure if she was following through on my request or actually accusing me of selling everyone else out. Henry and Trey both looked at me in uncertain wonderment.

"She's going to make them take our souls instead of hers! She doesn't have a brother! This is all a trap!" Violet shouted and took a step backward—toward the sofa behind her and away from both me and Mischa. "I'm not going to die," she announced. "Not after everything I've gone through. You're not going to take me like this!"

Still unsure of what was actually happening, I argued, "I'm not tricking anyone, Violet. Honestly." And just to be safe, I whirled around and snapped at Mischa, "I *don't* agree. We're not playing any games for the baby."

Mischa stood up from the sofa on which she'd been sitting. "Then there's nothing to—"

The spirits went silent as Mischa's eyes fell upon something behind me, and a wide, wicked smile stretched across her gruesome face. I turned around to see that Violet had pulled the gun out from under the pillow and had it aimed at me.

"Jesus, Violet!" Henry exclaimed as he extended an arm and outstretched his fingers toward her. "Is that *real?*"

Instinctively, I threw my hands in the air—as anyone would if a loaded gun was pointed at their chest. "Violet, don't," I begged. None of this seemed like a viable plan now that the spirits had mentioned Dad and Rhonda's baby. How could Jennie and I have been so careless as to have not taken the baby into consideration? I had barely given Dad's announcement much thought since leaving Tampa, but now it seemed like an enormous oversight.

"It's real," Trey said calmly. He made eye contact with me, and I could tell that he was afraid, but he understood that this was what I had warned him about. He glanced over at the piano, which was a good fifteen feet behind where Mischa stood. He was remembering what I'd told him about the pins, and trying to determine how he might make his way over there without rousing the spirits' suspicion.

"Put it down!" Henry urged Violet. "There's no reason for anyone to get shot."

"No," Violet refused in a voice amplified by fear. She waved the gun at me. "We're playing any game they choose, *right now*. Give them whatever they want."

"Shall we play?" the spirits asked me in Mischa's voice.

Static filled my right ear, and I was about to object, when Violet commanded, "Say yes, or I'll shoot. I swear, I will. I'll tell the police that you guys broke into my house and that I was acting in self-defense."

Jennie had told me to be prepared for whoever I asked to actually make good on their threat to kill me, but now that I was actually in that situation, I was wondering if I'd live long enough to ever step outside of the Simmons house again.

It was all starting to fit together in my head: the foreboding sense that had overcome me the first time I'd ever visited this place with Violet; the way that the trees along the private drive seemed to envelop this house, hide it from the outside world. I would die here, and I had felt that in my bones every time I'd ever come here.

"No," I told Violet.

On my right, I heard Trey say, "McKenna, just play the game. Please."

But I shook my head again. This was the plan. Jennie's plan, *our* plan. It was time to prove to myself that I was brave enough to see it through.

Violet's arm shook violently, and her lower lip trembled. "McKenna," she warned in a hoarse voice. A tear spilled from her eye and down her cheek.

"Don't do this, Violet," Henry said from behind me.

"This is the only way. We have to make her die in a way that's different from how they predicted. This ends it. I know. I've been dealing with this longer than all of you."

Violet was going to squeeze the trigger. It was at that moment that I knew the gun was going to be fired, and it was all I could do to look over at Trey one last time. His blue eyes were already fixed on me. It took every ounce of strength I had to resist the urge to even allow a muscle in my face to twitch so that he would know that this was the moment—*right now*—when he had to remove those pins from my voodoo doll. The spirits were sure to notice anything I communicated to him, so gesturing or shouting was unthinkable—

And then . . .

Bang!

A powerful force, sudden and unexpected, knocked me off my feet. I smelled something like burned sugar before my eyes opened, and it took a second for me to make sense of what I was seeing. Violet stood several feet in front of me with her eyes squeezed shut. She still gripped the gun, which continued to quiver in her raised hand. My heart was thumping so loudly in my chest that I *felt* like I'd been shot; adrenaline flooded my body in a way that made me feel as if I could jump through the ceiling.

But I hadn't been shot. I was alive. I'd been hurled against the sofa, and I'd fallen halfway onto it at an odd angle. My arms were spread across the cushions, but my hips hadn't quite cleared them, so my legs were sprawled on the floor—

And Henry lay across them, his body, unmoving, turned away from me.

My hands cupped over my mouth, and when Violet opened her eyes and saw what she'd done, a high-pitched noise emerged from her body, a noise I didn't know a human was capable of making.

Kindhearted, courageous Henry. Just earlier that day I'd decided I couldn't ask Trey to kill me because I believed he'd die before he'd let anything happen to me, and now Henry had taken a bullet for me. It hadn't ever occurred to me that Henry would give up his life to save mine—primarily because I never would have asked him to make a sacrifice like that. The way he was slumped over on his side, I didn't see the blood at first. But then it began to pool around him, dark as ink, pouring from the left side of his chest, which was pressed to the floor.

I attempted to turn my head to the right to see if Trey had made his way over to the piano to take the pins out of my voodoo doll. But my neck didn't twist immediately, and when it did, I became distinctly aware that my body seemed to be operating on a delay. My eyes didn't automatically follow the movement of my head. I felt disconnected to my physical motions, as if someone else was controlling my body like a puppet and I was simply observing.

Then my realization of what had happened when Violet had fired the gun clicked into place. Trey had pulled the pins out at the exact right second. I wasn't the one operating my body anymore. I wasn't really even sure that I was *in* my body anymore.

Jennie was.

Trey was there, behind the piano, looking over at me in such terror that I don't think he was even breathing. And Mischa's body had slumped back against the sofa where she'd been sitting. Color was returning to her face, and the spidery veins visible beneath her skin were fading. But her glassy eyes stared straight ahead, showing no sign of life behind them.

Confirming my worst suspicions about having been pushed out of my body, I heard my own voice yell across the room at Trey, "Open the jar!"

He hesitated during a moment of suspended animation, looking confused as to whether or not to trust me. But then—still carrying the gun—Violet, who was closer, leapt toward the coffee table. She set the gun down and twisted off the mason jar's lid, then gaped at the open jar in horror as it occurred to her that she'd just released Mischa's soul into the expanse of her parlor.

Just then, I looked down and saw my own hands clutching at my throat as if I was trying to strangle myself. Strangulation. That was a death associated with air. That might have been the spirits' prediction for me all along.

I heard my garbled voice shout, "Under her nose!"

Violet yanked Mischa's head upright by a handful of the hair on the back of her head. She shoved the open jar underneath Mischa's nose, but Mischa's expression didn't change. "Come on, breathe!" Violet shouted at her. Trey dashed across the room to assist, and clapped a hand over Mischa's mouth, giving her no choice but to breathe through her nose if, in fact, her lungs were actually working. Then, switching tactics, he frantically pumped on her chest as if giving her CPR, and hopped backward when she suddenly sputtered.

As Mischa blinked and coughed, Trey reached across the coffee table to grab the handgun. Violet was a split second ahead of him, snatching the gun and aiming at him. "Don't even," she warned.

Both of them turned to face me—or my body, rather—as I heard myself coughing and sputtering. I was detached from my body but still watching the outside world through my eyes, and I couldn't hear anything but static coming across the earbud nestled into my right ear. But surely the five spirits were inside me, wrestling with Jennie for control of my body. We hadn't considered what this experience would be like for me while she tried to send them to the dark place, and I panicked, believing that even a few seconds of this was a sure sign that something was wrong. Jennie was outmatched. They were too powerful for her. . . .

And of course they were.

How had I ever thought she could take them on by herself? After all I'd endured since the fall, after all that Trey and I had done . . . Now Henry was either dead or dying on the floor, and Mischa was blinking around the room as if she didn't recognize any of us or her surroundings.

There's no way to accurately describe in mere words the sensation that I felt next, because it was incorporeal, but I sensed myself— my soul—being pulled further into the core of my body. Not into the core as in my stomach, but inward, as if being sucked into a whirlpool leading to another place. Another dimension, perhaps. I sensed Jennie vanishing there, as if she was being pulled into a black hole, but tightening her hold on me as she slipped. She was pulling me with her.

I could only trust that it was best for us to stay together. As much as I loved Mom, Dad, and Trey, nothing was quite the same as the bond I shared with Jennie. If she wanted me to accompany her wherever it was that the spirits were taking her, then I would go. I sensed my presence in the living room fading away. Violet's voice was shouting, "What's happening?" Trey was yelling my name. My view of the room bounced up and down, and I realized it was because he had grabbed my body by the shoulders and was shaking it.

Then, suddenly, everything changed.

A cold blast of air blew right through me, or at least it felt as if it swept right through my body—from my feet, up, and out of the top of my head. I had no idea what had happened except that all of my bodily sensations returned in an overwhelming rush. My fingers were wrapped tightly around my neck, and I released them, allowing air to pass into my windpipe and lungs in a dizzying gust. I felt warm wetness on my feet and realized that Henry had been bleeding onto me, soaking my shoes. My left hip ached from where it had hit the wooden frame of the sofa, and a scratchy burn crept up my throat. I hacked to try and clear it, as well as catch my breath.

I knew, without even checking the radio waves, that Jennie was gone. Our connection was broken. My attempt to command my fingers to remove the earbud from my right ear failed; I couldn't seem to make my hands obey all of my mind's orders yet.

But Trey and Violet weren't paying attention to what was happening to me. They weren't looking at Mischa, either, where she sat as if hypnotized. Both of them had fixed their eyes on the front door, and when I found the strength to raise my head, I understood why.

Mr. Simmons was barreling toward us. I hadn't even heard the front door open and close, and yet he was there, racing through the room. His ice-blue eyes darted from Henry's body on the floor to where Violet stood in front of me with the gun dangling from her fingertips at her side.

"What the hell are you doing?" His voice echoed strangely after he roared, but I had gained back enough awareness to recognize that the echo was all in my head as my soul settled back into its rightful place within my body. He wasn't supposed to be back yet. This was all wrong.

Violet stammered something about being sorry, but she was breaking into sobs. Mr. Simmons grabbed the gun away from her, and in a nightmarish flash, he aimed it at Trey.

I was regaining clarity and control over my body by the second. Fast enough that when Mr. Simmons addressed Trey, there was no echo or delay in the words leaving his mouth. "You. You have no right to be here!"

Never one to resist an opportunity to stand his ground, Trey didn't hold up his hands as if to plead for mercy or beg for his life. Instead, he stared his biological father right in the eye. "According to the attorneys you sent to threaten me, I have just as much right as your precious daughter to be here. That's what you wanted me to believe, right? Why am I not surprised that it's turned out not to be true?"

Mr. Simmons was so furious that his lips quivered. Violet gestured toward her father but didn't dare take a step toward him, or toward Trey. "Daddy, please! You don't understand what's going on! He's here to help us! Something terrible has been happening. We're just trying to make it stop!"

Mr. Simmons seemed to calm down long enough to glance down at the floor and truly register that Henry had been shot—with the gun that he now held in his hand. Although Violet had been holding the gun when he'd first walked in on us, he focused his ire once again on Trey. "You did this? You shot someone in my *home*?"

Finally able to find my voice, I managed to bark out, "Call nine-one-one."

Crying tears of terror now, Violet sputtered, "Where are they? Where are the spirits?"

Mr. Simmons turned to Violet and shouted, "You said this was over! You said it had moved on to someone else!"

I could hardly believe what I'd just heard. Unable to contain myself, I gasped, "You knew." Either Violet had told him, or he'd known all along. And it made perfect sense that he'd known. It was his mother who'd cast the original spell, possibly at his insistence so that Violet's mother wouldn't leave him.

Mr. Simmons narrowed his eyes and scowled at me. "This one." With one swift flick of his wrist, he aimed his gun at me. "This never had anything to do with you. You should have minded your own business."

Now Violet placed her hands gently on her father's forearm as if urging him to lower the gun. She tried to smile convincingly through her tears. "Just listen, Daddy! We figured it out! We know how to end it! McKenna's next, so we're going to trick them into thinking she's dying some way other than how they predicted, and then it's over!"

She was describing our plan as if we hadn't already executed it, making me realize that she and Trey had no way of knowing that it was over. They hadn't sensed Jennie carrying the spirits away with her like I had, and Violet had just given her father a simple way to protect his family—by killing *me*. I could see in his eyes that he was thinking exactly that. He raised the gun and pointed it at me again, and I backed away, feeling nauseous as I saw Henry's body lying there, immobile.

"No, no, no," I murmured. "Don't do this!"

In my panic, I dropped my phone to the floor, and it yanked the earbud out of my ear on its descent. There was nowhere to run. Mr. Simmons was less than ten feet away from me and advancing as quickly as I was maneuvering around the sofa. He stepped over Henry as if Henry were nothing more than a pile of clothes, and instantly I understood how he was planning to carry this out. He was going to kill me and tell the police that Trey was responsible for my murder and for Henry's.

"This ends now!" he roared. But as he squeezed the trigger, Trey barreled toward him and knocked him over. Mr. Simmons's arm shifted just as he fired the gun, and the bullet grazed my shoulder blade as I dashed toward the front door.

"Run!" Trey yelled.

I extended my fingers for the door handle as my feet carried me into the foyer, and Mr. Simmons fired again. The bullet ricocheted off the brass of the handle, missing my hand by centimeters. I snapped my hand to my chest and ran in the only direction my brain seemed to acknowledge: up the grand staircase.

As soon as I began scrambling up the stairs, I knew I'd chosen poorly. The black pumps on my feet were just loose enough to be treacherous when I tried to move quickly. I didn't know my way around the upper floors of Violet's house beyond the hallway leading to her bedroom and Mr. Simmons's office. Doors and windows could be locked. There was a back staircase that led into the sunroom—however, I didn't know from where on the upper floors I could access it. But there was no time to change my mind. I could hear Mr. Simmons's heavy footsteps on the stairs behind me, and he was skipping steps to catch up to me. At least he'd temporarily forgotten about Trey and was completely intent on catching me. But as I reached the top of the staircase and stole a glimpse over my shoulder, I saw Trey chasing after us at the bottom of the steps.

A chunk of drywall inches from my eyes exploded, and I realized that Mr. Simmons had fired again, this time at my head. Without another fraction of a second to spare, I bolted down the hallway and ran past the open doorway of Violet's bedroom, and past the closed door of Mr. Simmons's office.

But in this narrow hallway, although I was a moving target, it would have been hard for Mr. Simmons to miss me if he took another shot. My left shoe fell off, and I didn't give it a second thought as I continued on, hobbling for a few steps until I kicked off my right shoe. Looking ahead, I could see that the hallway turned a corner at its end, and presumably wrapped around the perimeter of the house. With all my might, I tried to run faster, but still screamed in surprise when I heard the gun fire again behind me. This time, the bullet whizzed past my left shoulder and struck the window toward which I was running. I heard the glass pop but not shatter as the bullet broke through it.

Just as I thought for sure that I didn't stand a chance of rounding the corner without Mr. Simmons hitting me with his next shot, I heard a scuffle behind me. When I reached the corner, I threw myself around it, took a deep breath, and realized I didn't hear footsteps from the hallway, but *thud*s and grunting instead. I dared to peek around the edge. Trey had thrown himself at Mr. Simmons and pulled him to the floor. One of his knees pinned Mr. Simmons's shoulder down, but even as Trey attempted to grab at Mr. Simmons's neck, it was clear that he wouldn't be able to subdue him for long.

Mr. Simmons's gun had been thrown in my direction. It was probably about eight feet from where I stood watching, angled on the long vintage runner rug.

"Get the gun!" Trey shouted, snapping me out of my reverie.

I dashed forward and bent my knees to raise the gun, which was heavier and colder in my hand than I had expected. I aimed it at Mr. Simmons, but he was entangled in such a way with Trey that there was no way I could get a clear shot at him—even if I'd known what I was doing with the gun, even if I'd had practice aiming and firing it.

So instead I spun on my heel and ran.

CHAPTER 19

I TORE AROUND THE CORNER AGAIN, THIS TIME running down the next stretch of hallway lined with windows, and paused in front of a closed door at the very end of it. My scalp tingled, although so lightly that I wondered if I was imagining it out of desperation. As I reached for the ornate brass doorknob, from behind me I heard a ragged voice shout threateningly, "Don't go up there!"

It was Mr. Simmons, standing at the far end of the hallway with a bleeding lip and his hair on end. *Up there*. Whatever was behind this door would take me to the higher floors of the house. I twisted the knob, and behind the door, I found another staircase, this one far more narrow and plain than the one in the front foyer. I ran up the first flight and didn't bother opening the door on the landing. There was no time to think clearly, but I guessed that this floor only had bedrooms and bathrooms on it. At the time that this estate was built, there were probably servants hired to run the household, so this floor was probably where they were boarded. Small bedrooms, possibly *locked* small bedrooms, would only have been helpful to me if I could have ducked into one of them to call 911. But I'd left my phone in the living room.

So I dashed across the landing to the next flight of stairs, climbed them, and at the top, I found myself faced with a choice: either opening a door directly in front of me, or running around another landing to my right, at the end of which a second door awaited. Hearing footsteps below me, I panicked and opened the door in front of me.

I'd entered into a small room cluttered with cleaning supplies and ladders. It smelled musty, and dust sparkled in the dim light creeping into it from a tiny window overhead. It appeared to be a utility closet, and it was most certainly not in frequent use. Another set of stairs, a much shorter set, ascended toward a small landing with a hatch door on its ceiling, and I noticed once my eyes adjusted to the dark that the small window was part of the hatch. Barely thinking about the danger in climbing higher, I dashed up the stairs and fumbled with the dead bolt on the hatch door. The door creaked on old hinges when I pushed it upward to throw it open, and I hesitated momentarily before climbing the last two steps and hoisting myself out into the harsh daylight.

I'd reached the roof, only that fact didn't fully register in my mind until I saw clouds overhead.

The roof. I was standing atop what was probably the tallest building in town, aside from the high school.

The door below me at the bottom of the stairs opened, and Mr. Simmons burst through it. Although he'd been chasing me like a crazed animal, when our eyes connected, I could see that he was in complete control of his actions. He knew exactly what he was doing; he was going to kill me.

I should have raised the gun and shot him right there and then.

The space was so small that I couldn't possibly have missed if I'd found the strength to just pull the trigger. But instead, I pulled my legs through the opening, slammed the hatch door, turned, and took a step forward.

A cry of frustration escaped from my throat when I realized the mistake I'd made. I had stepped out onto a small widow's walk, only about five feet square and surrounded by an ornate wrought-iron railing. I spun around in absolute fright, realizing that the rooftop of the mansion on all sides of the enclosed walk was a series of steep peaks. I'd known that, of course, before climbing out there. The house was a fake Tudor; its peaked rooftop poked out above the tree-tops encircling the property, visible from the street.

Figuring it was more for my safety than for Mr. Simmons's, I flung the gun into the trees with all of my strength. Before I could even watch it sink into the sea of pines below, the hinges of the hatch door squeaked behind me, and Mr. Simmons scrambled out to join me on the rooftop. Once standing, he raised his arms out toward me almost as if he was advancing forward to embrace me. "You know that this is the end," he told me calmly. "You want to save your friends? This is how you do it."

Since Mr. Simmons was about to kill me in a way that would fulfill the spirits' prediction for me even though they'd been banished, I became even more terrified about what had happened to Jennie when we'd been torn apart. Maybe we'd managed to get the spirits out of Mischa's body, but it seemed as if my prediction was about to come true, anyway. Falling off a rooftop and plunging over fifty feet to the pavement below would definitely qualify as an air-related death.

If I died the way in which they'd predicted, even if they were somewhere inside of either my body or conscious, struggling with Jennie, I had every reason to believe that the curse would continue. Maybe my death would even release the spirits back into this world. Nature likes cycles, Jennie had said. My death would complete one, and per the curse, a new one would begin. My death— and everything I'd done for the last few months—would have been for nothing.

I dared to look over the low railing and down the shingled peak to the circular cement driveway and fountain below. A black Range Rover had been parked haphazardly near the fountain, a few feet away from Violet's Mini Cooper. I raised one leg to step over the railing, highly aware that if I slid, there would be nothing to grab on to. About twenty feet down, there were two smaller peaks in the roof, built over decorative windows on the third floor. But if I lost my footing, there wouldn't be any way to angle my trajectory toward either of them. Nothing would prevent me from falling over the edge.

"That's it." Mr. Simmons encouraged me, taking another slow step forward. "Keep going."

Terrified that he'd spring at me and cause me to tumble backward, I lifted my other leg over the railing too. Through the sheer tights I was wearing, I could feel that the shingles on the roof were as rough as sandpaper, but treacherously slippery because of the silkiness of my stockings. Already sensing that my balance was waning, I took a tiny, prudent step down the peak.

Encouraged that I was now in direct danger, Mr. Simmons crossed the widow's walk to stand on the other side of the railing from me. If he wanted, he could reach over and shove me. Sensing that he might do exactly that at any moment, I extended my arms outward at the shoulders to try to keep my balance, and I inched down a little farther.

"I was doing you a favor by insisting that the judge send you away," he told me in a voice so calm that I understood he wasn't the least bit anxious about killing me. The tiniest drop of cold rain fell onto my forehead, and then another hit my cheek. The thick clouds in the sky beyond Mr. Simmons's head had darkened with the arrival of rain. "It was for your own good, since you were smart enough to piece together this whole puzzle even before I could."

"You don't have to do this. We ended it," I croaked, not wanting to face him but fearing I'd fall if I turned and looked down the slope. My throat was tight with tears. I couldn't imagine how this might possibly end any other way than with me plunging to the ground and breaking my head open on the bright white cement. I would never see my mom or dad again. None of my hopes of getting older with Trey after all of this was over would ever come true. And poor Henry—Henry, who only ever wanted to make things right in his sister's honor—was inside, possibly already dead. My life would end today. Here. "This is what they predicted would happen. You're making it come true. You might make it start all over again if you do this!"

Mr. Simmons frowned at me, and I could see traces of Trey in his features. "I'm willing to take that chance and find out. You should have known how far I'd go to protect my family. But it's your own fault that now you have to—"

He lurched forward, chest first, as if he'd been struck by a powerful wind from behind. The railing only came up as high as his midshins, so he fell over it, arms flailing . . . headed directly for me.

I only caught a glimpse of Trey standing on the widow's walk—his eyes locked on mine, blazing with fear and regret. I could see the fury drifting off of him like steam rising off a lake on a cold morning. But before I could fully appreciate that Trey had followed us up to the roof and pushed Mr. Simmons from behind, Mr. Simmons's shoulder knocked into mine and we both tumbled chaotically.

I fell backward, knowing the instant my foot budged that I was doomed. I fell onto my back and slid, feeling the pull of gravity drawing me toward death at what seemed like hyperspeed. Mr. Simmons grabbed at the sleeve of my dress as we fell in unison, but the fabric slipped from his loose hold. He somersaulted down the peak in a way that made it look like his body had folded over at the neck, and we reached the edge of the roof at the same instant. He disappeared over it as if rolling like a log on his side, his head mere inches from mine.

But my hands found the edge of the roof and—not even fully aware of what I was doing—I clamped on to it. A split second later, I felt my arms snap at the sockets, the full weight of my body coming to an abrupt, shocking halt. A nightmarish *boom* sounded from far below me a few seconds later, and I didn't dare look, fearing that even a turn of my head would require more energy than I could spare. I already knew that was the sound of Mr. Simmons hitting the hood of the Range Rover.

"Hold on!" Trey shouted hysterically from the widow's walk. He was pacing and shaking his hands, and finally set his palms on the railing as if he intended to climb over it to descend the peak and save me.

"Don't!" I called up to him, but fell quiet in realization that any effort I exerted shouting was better spent hanging on. I squeezed my eyes shut, believing that each passing second was my last. The pain in my arms was so extreme that my fingers felt like they were slipping— even though they might not have been.

I became keenly aware that I smelled smoke. Not house fire smoke, but sweeter smoke, the gentle smoke of birthday candles. Behind my closed eyes, I saw Mom, much younger—without a strand of gray in her hair and with no bags beneath her eyes— carrying a cake with two glowing candles in the shape of a "3" on top of it—toward me and setting it down in front of me in an otherwise dark room. I recognized the cake; Peppa Pig had been drawn on top in icing. I turned to my right and saw Jennie next to me, and heard distant voices singing "Happy Birthday."

A blur of smiling faces followed—schoolteachers, classmates, neighbors. And memories I'd long forgotten: trick-or-treating with Jennie around our neighborhood with Dad trailing behind us wearing a werewolf mask, shopping for school supplies, sitting in reading circles at Willow Elementary School, and slurping milk through straws from cartons in the lunchroom.

I wasn't going to be able to hold on to the edge of the roof much longer. Memories were running through my mind's eye so fast that I could barely process them, but in a level of detail that reminded me comfortingly of things I hadn't thought about in so very long. The smell of sticky white classroom paste. The floral patterns of the matching patchwork quilts that were once spread across Jennie's and my beds. Powdered donuts—Dad's favorite treat on Sunday mornings.

Then I saw myself peering down at tree branches and grass from high above and heard childish laughter. I was at the top of the tree that used to be in the Emorys' front yard. The summer that Jennie and I were six, we followed Trey in climbing all the way to the top, and we were too afraid to climb back down. Trey remained up there with us to comfort us, even though he'd climbed up and down that tree hundreds of times. Mom called the fire department to pull us down, and we went back up the very next day.

In the distance—in my mind, I realized—I heard faint sirens. They grew louder as the whirlwind of memories continued. Bickering with Jennie over her butchering of a doll's hair. The warmth of Moxie, our dog, sleeping in a ball on top of my feet in my bed at night. Playing Cat's Cradle with Candace on a field trip bus ride—Candace had lost her teeth before everyone else and always knew the best games.

And then sirens were blaring, and the smell of smoke was growing more pungent. I knew the time had come for the worst memory of all: waking up in darkness, choking. Running my hand against the wall of the long hallway and feeling my way out of our old house on Martha Road. Stumbling out onto the lawn in my pajamas with Moxie running in circles and barking around me. And looking back over my shoulder to see Jennie's silhouette in the living room window. She could see that I'd made it outside, but she'd inhaled too much smoke to do so herself.

Just when I was expecting to see a continuation of memories that followed the night of the fire—and sensed my fingers releasing from pure exhaustion—I felt strong hands wrap around my wrists, and a voice told me, "I've got you."

I opened my eyes to find myself looking up into Trey's face. He'd made his way down the peaked roof toward me on his belly. Hanging on to my full weight was making his arms tremble from muscle strain, and through gritted teeth, he calmly told me, "See if your feet can reach the wall."

"What?!" I asked in desperation, terrified that I was going to pull him over the edge.

"The wall in front of you. Try to touch it with your feet."

Trying to swing or kick my legs in any direction after holding as still as possible took quite a bit of effort. It was also very cold outside, and moving around made me more aware of the temperature. But to my great shock, Trey was right: The roof's overhang was only about six inches deep. My chest swelled with joy as I pressed the soles of my feet against the smooth wall.

"Can you reach it?" Trey asked.

I was concentrating too hard to reply while trying to get firm enough footing so that I could use the muscles in my legs to boost myself back onto the roof. Trey was in no way weak, but he wasn't going to pull me up to safety on his own. The effort required to hoist myself up high enough so that Trey could pull me up a few inches farther made me grunt.

But when he'd managed to raise me so that my rib cage was level with the edge of the roof, the sound of a bloodcurdling scream from four stories below made us both startle. The scream was unmistakably female, and I knew immediately that it had come from Violet. She must have stepped outside and seen her father's dead body crumpled on the hood of his vehicle.

"Don't listen to her," Trey commanded me. "You're almost all the way up. One more big boost."

I repositioned my right foot higher on the wall and hoisted myself once more with all my might. This time, Trey had to inch backward to give me enough room to clamber over the edge and back onto the roof. Once I was finally able to set my knees down, I threw my body forward and pressed myself against the shingles, almost unable to believe that I'd made it.

"Are you okay to climb up?" Trey asked me, nodding his head in the direction of the widow's walk at the top of the peak.

I could barely catch my breath, and dug my fingernails into the rough roof tile. Nothing felt or seemed real, and I wondered if my disorientation was a side effect of having cheated death. I had no sense of Jennie's presence, and wondered exactly what had happened earlier in the parlor, and if she was safe. If I'd managed to survive the spirits' death prediction for me, it would have been a bitter victory if something terrible had happened to Jennie to make that possible.

But I didn't think that the curse had been broken. I didn't feel any different.

"McKenna," Trey said, his voice cutting through the fog of my terror about Jennie's status. "You have to try to climb to the top." Then, with a slight hesitation, as if he almost didn't want to resort to mentioning this, he added, "We have to help Henry."

Henry. How much time had passed since he'd been shot? How much blood had he lost? Was it even still possible that he'd survived?

Climbing higher seemed impossible, too risky. It wasn't too late for me to fall over the edge, after all. It felt much safer to cling to my exact position, to that moment, to not take any more chances. But concern for Henry dragged me out of my fear and forced me to consider a few undeniable realities. With Mr. Simmons now dead and Henry either dead or dying, we probably had less than an hour to figure out what to do next. It occurred to me as strange that not only had Mr. Simmons come home early, unannounced, but Violet's mother hadn't been with him.

I had to find the courage to climb to safety and get a sense of exactly where things stood.

Trey urged me again. "Come on. You can do this."

Following his lead, I inched my way up the roof, clinging to it almost as if I were a snake slithering uphill. When I finally reached the flat landing at the top of the peak, and the railing surrounding the widow's walk was within reach, I fought the urge to burst into tears. Trey stood on the landing and stepped over the railing first, and then turned to offer me a hand as I joined him. Even once safe, I didn't dare look over my shoulder at the parking area below. Instead, from our vantage point, in the opposite direction, I could see the Simmonses' vast gardens, which stretched all the way to the line of trees at the edge of the property. I could now see bald patches of grass where Violet's gardeners had dug up the five rosebushes that had once grown back there, and I remembered that their roots were probably still beneath the surface of the ground, their evil still poisoning this land.

We slipped back through the trapdoor and made our way down to the house's first floor, and with each step I took, I grew more paranoid about what Violet was doing at that very moment. If she'd called an ambulance for either Henry or her father, then we'd be hearing real sirens within seconds. Sirens would lead to questions. Questions we couldn't answer.

And if Violet had summoned her father home early to thwart

our plans for some reason, then we were in serious danger, because we had no idea what awaited us downstairs. Violet had seemed so vulnerable and sensitive when she'd come to me in January and shared her version of how the curse had manifested—and she'd been so seemingly helpful in paying for my travel back to Willow that weekend—but now I had to wonder if I'd been tragically naïve about her motivation.

When we reached the last flight of stairs in the stairwell, which opened into the sunroom (as I had suspected it would), I whispered, "Trey," at the top. He paused and seemed to understand that I was suggesting we wait for a moment. "We should be careful," I whispered. "There could be more weapons in the house."

Trey nodded. We tiptoed the rest of the way down the stairs and slowly crossed the sunroom. Both of us lingered cautiously in the doorway of the kitchen, listening for signs of movement elsewhere in the house before daring to take a step into the parlor. But then we heard not one voice, but two. Violet was tending to Henry, and upon hearing him beg her for help, I dashed out from where Trey and I were lurking to see how badly he was hurt.

"Just call an ambulance," he told Violet.

"I can't yet," Violet told him. She was kneeling on the floor beside where he sat upright, propped up against the sofa. The white towel she was pressing against his left shoulder was crimson with blood, and his pallor was grayish. I was genuinely shocked that she was caring for him and trying to calm him down even after having seen her father's body outside. She must have assumed that either Trey or I had pushed him off the roof. Her face was tearstained, and her voice kept cracking, but she remained focused on keeping Henry calm. "As soon as we call for help, there won't be anything more we can do to save McKenna. Do you understand that?"

"Save me?" I asked in surprise. "It's over. Jennie took the spirits away."

Violet barely paid any attention to me as I approached and crouched alongside her. I'd never seen someone injured as badly as Henry appeared to be. Even though I didn't know anything about gunshots other than that he'd already be dead if the bullet had gotten anywhere near his heart, he still looked very bad—bad enough to lead me to believe he was dying.

"It's cold in here," Henry mumbled. "Why's it so cold?"

It *was* cold in there; the enormous house must be difficult to heat, with its high ceilings and tall windows. But I had a feeling Henry was cold for a reason other than the chilly draft in the living room, and Trey confirmed my fear.

"He's in shock." Trey stood at a safe distance behind me. "He's going to need medical assistance soon, or his organs will start to fail."

Mischa was sitting on the couch where we'd left her after opening the jar, staring at Henry with an expressionless face and blank eyes. I wondered if her soul had made its way back into her body, because she didn't seem to be fully . . . there. But Henry's situation seemed more urgent, so I switched my attention back to him.

"Just call an ambulance," I insisted. My pulse was still racing from the ordeal on the roof, scattering my thoughts, and without confirmation from Jennie, I could really only assume that the curse had been broken. But we were going to lose Henry if we didn't get help for him. I still had nine days remaining before the new moon to save myself if the curse hadn't been completely broken; Henry might have been down to minutes. "We have to do something," I said.

Violet shook her head. "We have to get the curse off you first."

"There isn't time!" I exclaimed, fully aware of the outcome on which I was insisting. How we spent the next few minutes might determine whether Henry or I would die, and there wasn't a chance that I was going to choose my life over his.

"McKenna," Trey said softly. "We have to at least try."

"Try what?" I snapped. "I don't even know if the curse is still on me. Maybe I beat it by not dying on the roof."

But the more I thought about the fact that the prediction had been issued and not fulfilled, the more it seemed possible that I wasn't in the clear yet. Violet confirmed my fear when she narrowed her eyes at me as if she was angry. In an emotionless voice, she said, "You didn't beat it. It's still on you."

"How do you know?" Trey challenged her.

"There are still nine more days before the new moon," she said in my direction. "Something changes about people who've gotten their prediction. I can't explain it. It's like normal people have this electrical charge around them, barely noticeable unless you're trying to detect it. And people who are going to die soon *don't*."

I remembered back to holiday break, when we'd met Kirsten at the bookstore in Chicago, and she'd been able to tell that Mischa was doomed because she didn't have an aura. Maybe Violet had a touch of the same awareness Kirsten did, or even a version of the same abilities I had. Whatever the source of her sense may have been, I didn't doubt that she was right.

"If we don't find a way to end this thing *right now*, before anyone finds out what happened to my dad, then we won't. Not ever. You'll die, and those things will find their way back to Mischa," Violet said, sounding absolutely convinced. She had raised an arm to point at Mischa, who looked at her in confusion as if she had no idea what Violet was talking about.

My phone was still on the living room floor on the other side of Henry, on top of a dark, black pool of blood, which had saturated the rug. When I picked it up, I noticed that the battery had less than 20 percent of power remaining; Before I even placed my earbud in my ear I knew I wouldn't hear anything other than static, but I was hoping with all my heart that Jennie would reply and tell me what to do.

Then we heard a car approaching outside. All of us raised our heads and our eyes shot toward the front windows, but the heavy brocade curtains were mostly drawn, and the sheer panels hanging underneath them made it difficult to see what kind of vehicle was pulling into the driveway.

"Who is that?" Trey asked Violet. "Did you call someone?"

With her brow wrinkled as if she was going to cry, Violet began, "It could only be—"

The slamming of a car door and a bloodcurdling scream cut her short. Mrs. Simmons had arrived home, and would be calling for an ambulance as soon as her horror subsided enough for her to remember how to use her hands.

"It's my mom. She and my dad drove separately to the airport on Friday after work when they left on their trip," Violet said as she stood. "We have to go upstairs."

I didn't want to budge. My eyes passed from the window to Henry. There was no way he was going to be able to walk upstairs on his own, and we couldn't move him.

Desperate, I said into my phone, "Jennie, is it safe for us to move Henry?" But of course, all I heard in reply was static.

"It's better to leave him," Trey said decisively. "Your mom will call an ambulance, and we need to get upstairs before she comes inside." He squatted next to me to be eye level with Henry, who was having difficulty keeping his eyes open. "Help is on the way, man. You're going to be okay."

We heard the voice of Mrs. Simmons, as clear as a bell, from outside as she shouted at a 911 operator on her phone. The sound of the automated front door lock being activated caused Violet to fold Henry's right arm so that his right hand held the towel against his left shoulder. Then she rocketed upright. "Come on. Now."

I reached for Mischa's arm and pulled her to her feet as Violet tore out of the living room in the direction of the grand staircase. To my great relief, Mischa was able to stand on her own and seemed to sense the urgency in our dash out of the room.

The front door opened behind us as we ran across the foyer and up the stairs. I looked over my shoulder to see a bewildered Mrs. Simmons standing in the doorway. "Violet!" she shouted, as if she feared Violet was in danger based on the state in which she'd found her husband.

But then she saw the four of us running up the stairs. Violet weakly called out, "It's okay, Mom!" Although, obviously, nothing was okay.

Mrs. Simmons threw the bag she carried over one shoulder onto the floor, balled her hands into fists, and screamed from the very bottom of her core, "What is happening?"

"Everything's fine!" Violet shouted.

We reached the top of the stairs, and followed Violet to her bedroom. She slammed the door behind us and twisted the delicate lock above the knob. That lock might have kept Mrs. Simmons out, at least as long as she was in a wild state of confusion and trauma, but it wouldn't take long for someone—likely the police—to make their way into the room.

We had only minutes remaining to solve a mystery that had baffled us for months.

CHAPTER 20

Trey WHEEZED, HIS CHEST RISING AND FALLING as he caught his breath. He snapped at Violet, "What the hell?! You said your parents would be gone until tomorrow!"

Violet scowled. "What, do you think I *arranged* for my dad to—"

From behind us, a small voice said, "I don't feel normal."

All of our heads turned toward Mischa, who was touching her throat as if she was as surprised that she'd spoken as we were. Suddenly concerned, Trey asked, "How do we know this is really Mischa and the spirits haven't found their way back into her head?"

With a confused expression on her face, Mischa insisted, "It's me. I feel like I've been asleep for a long time."

We heard another high-pitched scream from the house's first floor, which suggested that Violet's mom had just noticed Henry. Her outburst put all of us back on task.

Violet waved her hand at the phone I held in my hand. "Can you hear your sister at all?" she asked with tears in her eyes.

I shook my head. I heard nothing but the baritone voice of a radio announcer on another AM frequency creeping through the static in bursts. But I did feel the slightest sense of tingling across my head. I hoped Jennie was the cause of it, and not the pure terror that we were all about to be held accountable for breaking into the Simmons house, holding Violet hostage, shooting Henry, and killing Mr. Simmons. And that I'd then go on to die in a horrible plane crash or in some other way, alone, on my return to Florida.

"Just try to reach her," Trey encouraged me in a hoarse voice. "Ask her to help you."

My pulse was bounding, and my heart felt like it was thundering in my chest. "I can't concentrate," I admitted. I had to be in a certain mind-set to be able to hear Jennie, and at that moment, I was way too frazzled to tune in to her energy. Somewhere, far away, I heard a chorus of voices chanting something that sounded like *history, history*, which reminded me of how sometimes words would get stuck in my head over the winter, before I'd been able to connect with Jennie over radio waves.

But "history" didn't make sense. The entire curse was rooted in history. I couldn't pore over every detail of the last eighteen years to figure out how to unravel everything in the seconds remaining. Where to begin? With the moment Trey's mom stepped into Violet's father's lecture hall eighteen years ago? Or the moment when Grandmother Simmons visited Father Fahey for help?

Never before had I tried to communicate with Jennie under quite this much duress. My ears pricked at the distant sound of sirens, and it took me a second to realize that I wasn't simply remembering the night of our house fire again. These sirens were real, and they were growing stronger.

"Just relax," Trey commanded me as he reached for my upper arms and gently squeezed them. "Here, let's sit."

The four of us sat down in a circle on Violet's carpeted floor.

"What are we doing?" Mischa asked innocently. She clearly had limited awareness of what had happened since she'd been evicted from her body the day before, but there was no time to fill her in.

"Trying to break the curse," I mumbled. As much as I wanted to feel calmer, instead I felt even more wary of the seconds passing by. But with the pleading eyes of Violet, Trey, and Mischa weighing on me, it was all I could do to mutter hopelessly into my phone, "Jennie, can you hear me?"

Not surprisingly, even when I strained my hearing and tried to steady my heart rate despite the sound of vehicles screeching to a halt, I still didn't hear any sign of her. The distraction of the voices coming from the front of the house outside only added to my anxiety. Mrs. Simmons had seen Trey with us. If she'd recognized him from the courtroom and had already called the cops, then we could expect them to show up with guns raised, ready to apprehend him. Police in our town would also recognize Mischa as the girl who'd gone missing over the holidays and then reappeared with no memory of where she'd been. With Mr. Simmons dead in a grisly mess outside, and Willow's three most problematic teenagers holed up in a bedroom with its wealthiest, there was no telling what would happen when authorities made their way upstairs.

My mind kept whirling with thoughts of that nature, making it even harder to listen for Jennie. *History, history. Tell history*, the voices urged.

"Keep trying," Trey urged.

I squeezed my eyes shut and tried to reach Jennie with my mind instead of my voice. *Please, please. If you're there, if you can hear me . . .*

My heart sank. I couldn't sense her presence at all.

It was pointless to keep trying. I was going to have to accept that we'd failed, and that the spirits had done something terrible and irreversible to my sister.

Just as they would do to me within the next nine days.

I opened my eyes as I admitted, "I just can't . . ."

But when I saw the expressions on the others' faces, I fell quiet. They were looking at something behind me. I turned to see what they were marveling at, and I couldn't believe my eyes. The wooden chest at the foot of Violet's bed had opened, its lid tilted backward on its brass hinges. And from within it, two stuffed animals had floated up into the air. They hovered over the chest, at least two feet above our heads where we sat on the floor.

"What . . . the hell . . . is happening?" Trey asked.

One of the stuffed animals was a beige dog with floppy ears and a brown nose. It was levitating on its back, just as Olivia, Candace, and Mischa had when we'd played Light as a Feather, Stiff as a Board at Olivia's party. The second plush animal was a white teddy bear, and it floated below the dog, positioned in the air as if it were standing.

Now, I felt the tingling under my hair more strongly. This was undoubtedly Jennie, reaching out in what must have been the only way she could.

"It's Jennie," I whispered.

The voices weren't encouraging me to think about history. They were saying, *Your story. Your story.* They wanted me to tell the story of my death, the death that should have just occurred.

Violet flinched at the sound of heavy footsteps coming up the staircase, accompanied by loud male voices. The police had probably arrived, and they were now inside the house, on their way to find us. "Is she saying we need to play the game again?"

"Yes, sort of," I said, trying to understand what Jennie was demonstrating. The white bear floated higher as the beige dog was lowered, and then the white bear was angled on its side as if lying down, taking the position that the dog had held. Then both stuffed animals fell back into the chest. "I think she's suggesting that I—"

Fists pounded on the other side of Violet's bedroom door. "Open this door!"

Trey's alarmed eyes shifted from the door to me. "Whatever she wants you to do, just do it!"

"Open up!"

"Okay," I said, trying to ignore the barrage on the door. "We should hold hands or something. Just like when we played the game the first time. I think the game always requires everyone's participation."

Without any resistance, Violet, Mischa, and Trey linked hands. Mischa and Trey, on either side of me, each reached for one of mine. I closed my eyes and tried to remember exactly how it had felt to be on the Simmonses' roof, when I'd been certain that I was about to die. I tried to imagine what it was like having all of those scenes from my life play inside my eyelids.

Then I took a deep breath, knowing this would be my last chance to save my life. "It was a cold day in April, and McKenna Brady had just attended the funeral of her friend Mischa's parents with Violet Simmons, Henry Richmond, and Trey Emory. McKenna had arrived at the funeral with the intention of bringing Mischa back to Violet's house later that afternoon to make her play a game. The purpose of the game was to trick evil spirits that had overtaken Mischa's body into abandoning it by making them believe that McKenna was about to die. To do this, Violet was going to aim a gun at McKenna and shoot her, if necessary."

I was cutting corners, but I could hear a metallic clanging noise on the other side of the door, making me think that whoever was out there was trying to break the lock.

"But when Violet raised the gun, Henry jumped in front of McKenna and blocked the bullet. Moments later, Violet's father arrived home unexpectedly after a vacation, and was shocked by what he saw occurring in his living room. He chased McKenna up to the house's rooftop, and she climbed over a railing and descended a dangerously steep peak to try and escape him."

I hesitated, knowing that if I told the story accurately from this point onward, Violet would know that Trey was responsible for her father's death. But I had only seconds remaining, and couldn't risk this game not working out of fear of offending her. So I continued, "Trey had followed Mr. Simmons and McKenna up there, and he surprised Mr. Simmons by shoving him from behind. Violet's father fell forward, over a railing, and when he reached the place where McKenna was clinging to the shingles, he knocked into her. Together, they fell off the edge of the roof."

This was the critical moment, the point at which Jennie's instructions would either work . . . or fail. Whoever was on the other side of the door had successfully removed the doorknob, and was peering at us through the hole left in the door. I blocked that out, and focused on trying to tell the rest of the story—the story of how I would have died if Trey hadn't saved me—as calmly as possible. When Violet had been the storyteller on the night of Olivia's party, she'd gone all out on the gory details, so I did my best to imagine my death as it would have realistically occurred.

"McKenna tumbled through the air, falling over three stories to the pavement below. Her skull cracked when she hit the ground, and her neck snapped. She died instantly, spraying the cement and nearby fountain with blood and brain matter."

From outside the door, I heard a male voice say, "They're having some kind of séance or something!"

I looked around the circle at Mischa, Violet, and Trey and said, "Two days later, her family and friends gathered at Gundarsson's funeral home, where her twin sister was waked eight years earlier. Her body lay in a closed coffin. Light as a feather, stiff as a board."

Already knowing what was expected of them, Mischa and Violet chanted, "Light as a feather, stiff as a board." Trey joined in, and the four of us continued to repeat the phrase. Our voices faded as if someone were turning down the volume on the audio around me. Within seconds, it was as if everything happening in Violet's bedroom was on mute, or like my brain had been enclosed in something soundproof. I saw the lips of the others continue to move as they chanted, and in my peripheral vision, I saw men in navy-blue uniforms burst into the room after throwing the door open.

Then everything went dark.

When I opened my eyes, I was in a hospital bed.

I held very still as I gained awareness of my surroundings, at first wondering if somehow I'd reversed time and was eight years old again, back at St. Matthew's Hospital, where I'd been taken after the house fire that had killed Jennie. Or maybe this was part of the dying process, revisiting one of my strongest memories. I recognized the location by its antiseptic smell before even noticing the TV on the wall across from my bed or the IV in my arm.

As soon as I made sense of the fact that it was daylight—and sunny outside my window—I realized that the women on the television show on my room's TV were discussing the current president. I hadn't traveled back in time. Then I felt a jab of pain in my heart.

Henry.

The last thing I could remember about being in Violet's bedroom was the door opening. I had no idea if Henry had been taken away in an ambulance, or if he'd even lived long enough to be treated by the paramedics when they'd arrived at the Simmons mansion.

And I definitely didn't remember being injured, so I wondered how I'd ended up there.

Just as I was leaning forward in bed, wondering if I could drag the stand on which the bag of saline solution attached to my IV was hung, I noticed Violet, of all unexpected people, sitting in the corner with a cup of coffee.

"You're awake," Violet said, sounding pleased. "Your mom just stepped out for a few minutes to check on your stepdad."

"He's not my stepdad," I croaked, surprised by how crusty my voice sounded and how sore my throat was.

"You were intubated," Violet said, gesturing at her own throat. "They just removed your breathing tube about two hours ago, if you're wondering why your throat hurts."

"Henry," I managed to say, feeling tears forming in my eyes as I assumed the worst.

Violet leaned forward, closer to me, and lowered her voice. "That's why I'm here. I was hoping I'd get to talk to you before the cops. I've been telling everyone that my dad came home early from his trip and thought there were intruders in the house, and that *he* shot Henry."

That didn't answer my question. I tried to prop myself up on my elbows and found that my left shoulder was strangely stiff. Bandages, I realized. I vaguely remembered a bullet grazing my shoulder blade; someone must have tightly bandaged it. "Is he alive?" I asked fearfully.

Violet smiled widely. "Of course he's alive! He's upstairs, recovering from the surgery he had yesterday. He just lost a lot of blood."

My entire body went warm with relief. Then I remembered the chaotic moment when the police had burst through the door of Violet's bedroom. "What about Trey? And Mischa?"

"Trey's fine," Violet said. "And Mischa's . . . weird, but I think fine. Listen, this is important." Her eyes flashed toward the door to make sure no one was entering the room. "I told the police that we were all hanging out on the roof for fun when my dad came home, and he thought we were burglars. Then, after shooting Henry, when he went up there? You stumbled, he realized who you were, and he fell off the roof while trying to save you."

"None of that makes sense," I said, wondering why in the world the police would ever believe that story.

Violet shrugged. "It makes more sense than trying to get the police to believe that my dad chased you to the roof to kill you and break an evil curse."

I wondered why Violet was acting so nonchalantly about her father's recent death, and why—after everything we'd both survived in the last six months—she was willing to lie to the police to spare Trey from having to take responsibility for what was *definitely* a murder. As if reading my mind, she said, "Look, I'm as relieved this is over as you are. I loved my father very much. But I know that he played a big role in architecting all of this. I think he knew what his mother was doing all those years, and that he at least suspected it had been passed on to me. But he let it continue. He never offered to help me make it stop. He didn't even apologize when I told him about it in January, when I thought this was over."

A tear escaped her eye and rolled down her cheek. Lost in thought, she let it linger there before wiping it away. "I guess we probably are all gonna need some serious therapy."

I thought of poor Ms. Hernández back in Tampa, and her attempts to get me to spill my guts. "Or something," I agreed, pretty sure that therapy wasn't going to be the answer to any of our future problems. "You just said you're relieved that this is over. Is it?" I asked. "Over?"

Violet nodded. "I think so." She reached for me and rested her hand on my arm. "You're normal again, at least. It's off you."

Five days later, on Saturday, Trey and I walked the long distance across town to the abandoned house that had belonged to his grandparents before he was born. It was the house in which his mom and her sister had been raised, where Mary Jane Svensson had dreamed about her life beyond the limits of Willow, Wisconsin, before venturing off to college and crossing paths with Michael Simmons. It was located, ironically, on the road that ran alongside the rural highway that headed south, toward Chicago—almost as if Trey's mom had literally been born on the path leading to her destiny.

"When did your mom's family move away from here?" I asked as we came to a stop in front of the one-story house on Frontage Road. It was almost impossible to see it from the street due to the overgrown grass and shrubs out front.

"My grandparents died in car crash when I was a baby, and the house has just sat here, empty, since my mom's younger sister moved to Ohio," Trey said. The bruises on his face from Northern had faded into a barely visible shade of yellow, and he looked like he'd gained weight during the last few days while he'd been living back at home with his parents. "I think my mom tried to sell it, but it was already in pretty bad shape, and she didn't want to put in the time or energy to repair things that would have increased its value. We used to come here on weekends when I was a kid to try to keep up with the yard work and scrub off the graffiti, but eventually it just got to be too much work. This isn't a place that held a lot of happy memories for my mom, anyway."

Between us, we'd lugged a shovel, gardening shears, and thick gardening gloves all the way over from his garage on Martha Road. Mom and I were still staying in a motel in Ortonville, and I was due to fly back to Tampa the next morning. I had spent two days at St. Matthew's Hospital after the day of violence at the Simmons house, unknowingly having suffered a condition referred to as "suspension trauma" after hanging off the roof for so long. My doctor had been amazed that I'd remained conscious for as long as I had after Trey had pulled me back up to safety; they'd explained I had passed out in Violet's bedroom because the oxygen level in my blood had been dangerously low.

When Trey had come to visit me in the hospital, he'd already been reunited with his mother. In a strange turn of events, the police in Willow had been so preoccupied with the tragic death of Mr. Simmons that they'd completely chilled on their pursuit of Trey. It didn't seem like Northern Reserve was eager to welcome him back, and without Mr. Simmons making demands on Judge Roberts to banish him from town, there was no longer any urgency around making sure Trey served out the rest of his punishment. It was frustrating to think that our lives had been so controlled by Mr. Simmons's influence in Shawano and Suamico Counties, but I was trying my best to focus on being grateful that we were both still alive and that Violet's willingness to invent a cover story had spared us trouble with the cops.

I hadn't had a chance to ask Trey at Violet's house about how he'd cut his hand when he was eight as his mom had advised me to ask at the Portnoys' funeral. But Mrs. Emory had reminded him that he'd cut his left hand so badly on a thorn from this rosebush at his grandparents' old house that he'd needed stitches across his palm. She had also told him that if he and I believed that the Simmons family was involved somehow with all the recent deaths around town, the rosebush she'd planted was the beginning of it all. It might not have mattered that Violet had cut down the bushes on her family's property, or that she hadn't taken care to destroy their roots. *This* rosebush still bloomed every spring.

Our oversight in not having taken care of this over the winter back when I'd first found the spell that Trey's mom had tucked away in her journal was glaring; we should have known better.

I had texted Kirsten that morning about our plan to destroy this bush, and she had messaged me back immediately.

KIRSTEN 10:08 A.M.

Be careful. Remember the rule of 3. Trey's mom cast that spell in anger.

The rule of three, of course. It was a basic principle of witchcraft specifying that any spell cast to bring harm to another would back-fire threefold. But Trey and I weren't the ones who'd cast the original spell. Even if our destruction of the rosebush might have brought bad luck to Trey's mom, he and I were both in agreement that we had to do this, anyway. After all, Violet had visited me in the hospital and assured me that my electric "charge" was back, but there were still four more days until the next new moon.

I wasn't about to take any chances.

"There it is," Trey said, nodding in the direction of the front of the house. Underneath one of the front windows, an enormous rose-bush grew. For the last few days, the temperatures in Wisconsin had warmed considerably, and the bush had sprouted fresh green leaves. It felt like it had been winter for ages, but now bees buzzed around us, and birds sang overhead, announcing the long overdue arrival of spring. Since the ground had thawed enough that week for Mr. and Mrs. Portnoy to be buried, I wondered if Stephani deMilo had finally been buried in St. Monica's cemetery. When she'd died over the winter, it had been too cold.

There weren't any buds on the bush yet. But that was just as well.

We had walked all the way over to ensure that this particular bush never, ever bloomed again.

This was the bush that Trey's mother had planted upon learning that her lover's wife was expecting a baby. As Trey stared at it, he told me what his mother had shared with him in the days that had passed since the dramatic events on Monday at Violet's house. "My mom told me that when I was about four months old, she decided to drive down to Chicago to confront him." He couldn't bring himself to even say Mr. Simmons's name, and I didn't blame him. "Kind of shady. She was already married to Walter at that point, which makes me think I haven't really appreciated how much he must have cared about her, you know? To marry her when she was six months pregnant with some other guy's kid? And she was still head over heels for Violet's dad, really hoping he'd take her back. I guess she got it into her head that if she just showed him his son, he'd change his mind. She thought he'd at least want to be involved in my life."

I tried to imagine Trey's mom when she wasn't much older than we were, making the long drive down to Chicago alone with an infant buckled into a car seat. Desperate. Scared. Probably feeling a little like all of us had been since October.

Trey continued, "She's embarrassed about the whole thing now, obviously. She said she was young and hopelessly in love, and she didn't understand then that people from families like his don't just marry young, uneducated girls from families like hers."

I couldn't help but feel sympathetic toward Trey's mom.

"When she confronted him on campus, he was furious. She'd accepted a ton of money when she'd agreed to terminate the pregnancy, and the moment he saw me he started threatening her with legal action. He told her that his wife was expecting a baby, and that she was stupid to think he'd leave the woman he loved after the fertility troubles they'd been experiencing to instead run off with some hick from his hometown."

"What did your mom do with the money?" I dared to ask. When I'd pinched a letter from Mr. Simmons's attorneys out of the Emorys' mailbox over the holidays and read it, it had said that Mr. Simmons was attempting to collect almost two million dollars from Trey's mom.

"Turns it out wasn't that much," Trey admitted. "It was like a hundred and seventy-five thousand dollars. And to my mom, back then? That seemed like a fortune. It was enough to buy the house on Martha Road with cash. The two million dollars they were trying to squeeze out of her was based on some kind of penalty for violating the contract and an insane interest rate that they'd applied. But they only started really pushing her for that money last fall, when Simmons and his family moved back to Willow."

I shook my head. "A likely story."

Trey gestured at the seemingly innocuous rosebush again. "So she was angry. And embarrassed. And eager to do anything to hurt him and his wife."

"Do you think she had any idea this would work?" I asked. The spell that Trey's mom had cast in a moment of fury had resulted in the deaths of Olivia, Candace, Stephani deMilo, and countless others for whom Grandmother Simmons and Violet had issued deaths. It had nearly killed Tracy Hartford and Mischa, and—in a roundabout way—had resulted in the deaths of Mischa's parents and Michael Simmons. Amanda Portnoy and Henry had both come very close to dying, too, and both of their lives would be forever changed due to injuries they'd incurred . . . all because of the fateful words that Mary Jane had chanted while planting this very rosebush by the light of the moon.

Trey shook his head. "I doubt it. My mom told me that after a while, she really did fall in love with Walter. I mean, at least she loves him now. She loves him enough to have kept all of this a secret because she didn't want to hurt him—at least until recently, when the threats about the money became more demanding. She thinks the money was just about Simmons wanting to scare her into moving our family far enough away that his wife would never find out about me."

I rested my hand gently on his shoulder and asked, "She knows now, doesn't she?"

Trey hesitated, thinking about Violet's mother. She'd looked out of her mind with horror when we'd seen her last at Violet's house, shortly after she'd discovered her husband's body. "They're reading the will on Monday, and the Simmonses' lawyers requested that my mom and I be present. So I guess, yeah . . . Violet's mom must know *something*."

I didn't want to press him for more details about the will. Whether Michael Simmons had bequeathed anything to Trey, and Trey's acceptance required him to do anything in exchange for his inheritance, I already knew that Trey would refuse. Listening to the reading of the will was simply a formality.

Trey went on to tell me that his mother had been so angry after her trip to Chicago that she'd driven straight back to Willow and immediately set about researching ways to punish Michael Simmons and his wife using witchcraft. "Actually, she said she'd thought about just murdering them outright. But she had me to worry about, so at least she wasn't completely out of her mind."

"How much did you tell her about what's been happening?" I asked. I'd still not told my mom much, although I'd promised her up and down when I checked out of the hospital that this time, all of the sneaking around and lies were really over.

"Not everything. But enough that she feels horrible that her actions hurt so many people," Trey said. "Although I don't know if she really believes that there was a curse, or evil. I mean . . . it's probably hard for anyone who hasn't seen what we have to believe any of it."

Trey's grandparents' house wasn't the only abandoned house around Willow. Like the others, the old Svensson house had quickly become the kind of place where college kids partied when they were home on breaks, and occasional transients passing through town made it their temporary home. Its front windows had been smashed and then haphazardly covered from the inside with cardboard boxes. The front door hung loosely on its hinges, unlocked and water-damaged, slightly ajar to welcome curious creatures of all species.

The house in front of which we stood could not have been more different from the Simmons mansion. Even when it had been in great shape, it was still miniscule in comparison. Humble in its design. It wasn't so different from the one-story ranch-style houses on Martha Road, like the ones in which Trey and I had grown up.

"I guess we should both start cutting, and then dig after we clear the branches?" I suggested. Trey agreed, and we each pulled on a pair of gloves to begin.

As I carefully cut, twisted, and pulled off the tenacious branches of the rosebush, I was reminded of the words of the spell that I'd found in Trey's mother's old journal.

As the plant grows, so will your revenge
Nourished by bitterness
With each cycle of the moon, year by year
As your plant blooms, your enemies will suffer.

Destroying the rosebush took us the better part of the morning. The sun was beating down on us by early afternoon, when Trey had started digging up the bush's roots so that we could destroy them, too. Watching Trey handle the shovel made my heart swell with love because it reminded me of when he'd helped me bury my dog Moxie in our yard. Although our project probably would have seemed ridiculous to anyone else, working alongside Trey outdoors reminded me fondly of all of our adventures as kids, when we'd race up and down our street on bikes and build forts every summer break.

I'd been listening for Jennie constantly on my radio app, scanning the AM and FM dials for her voice. But so far, I hadn't been able to connect directly with her again. Instead, she seemed to be reaching me without the radio, placing abstract words and phrases in my head in a familiar chorus of voices. *Tree, tree, tree,* I heard the voices in my mind chanting. Yes, when we were kids, Jennie and I had loved climbing trees with Trey. I wasn't surprised that she remembered that. I could only hope that in time, I'd get better at hearing her, and would be able to communicate with her inside my head just as easily as I'd been able to with the radio.

When Trey and I had cut down the entire bush, branch by branch, and had done our best to dig up its long, sinewy, dry roots, a pretty large hole remained in the ground where the bush had stood for the last nearly eighteen years. I wrapped my arms around Trey and kissed him tenderly.

"Geez. I didn't know shoveling turned you on so much," he teased.

We were both out of breath and overheated enough to abandon our winter coats, but our work wasn't done. Together, we made several trips from the front yard through the empty house to build a bonfire out back, taking care to contain the fire within a ring of large rocks.

I felt like I was trespassing each time I stepped through the house's front door and walked through its rooms to reach the back door in the kitchen, but reminded myself that this house was technically Trey's *real* inheritance. The house was in a pitiable state of decrepitude, with stained, sagging ceilings, trash and bottles littering the floor, and mouse droppings everywhere. Carrying my last armload of dirt and roots, I followed a sunlit hallway farther into the house toward the bright kitchen, passing family portraits that remained framed on the wall despite all of the other destruction that the house had endured. There was a studio portrait of Trey's mom and her sister as little girls, both holding parasols and smiling for the camera. That hung next to a picture of Trey's mom on the day of her high school graduation from Willow High School. In it, she wore a cap and gown, and beamed proudly with her arms around her parents' shoulders. She was different then, when she was our age, before she'd learned the hard way about greed and lust. It was easy to see from these pictures how Michael Simmons had been taken with her.

In the backyard, Trey and I held hands and silently watched the roots, branches, leaves, and thorns of the rosebush smolder. Smoke curled up toward the azure sky, and I let myself imagine that the smoke was pure evil, drifting out of our lives. We'd done it. We'd broken the curse. I tightened my grip on Trey's hand and felt certain that this was the beginning of the rest of our lives. I'd agreed to finish the rest of the school year in Florida to make things easier for my mom while she and Glenn resettled, but there was nothing standing in the way of Trey moving down there to be with me now. And the idea of the two of us, moving on from this nightmare together, over a thousand miles away from this town, made me more excited than I'd been in a long time.

Hours later, when we arrived back at the Emorys' house, my mom was waiting for me in her idling car. The sun was setting, and the warmth of the spring day had subsided to a wintry chill once again. Not wanting to say good-bye to Trey—but hoping it would only be a few weeks before we'd see each other again—I reminded him, "Just come down to Florida as quickly as you can. Get an apartment or something. You don't have to wait until July anymore."

"Oh, I'm coming to Florida," Trey teased me. "Nothing's ever going to keep me away from you again." Not caring if my mom was watching, he kissed me. He kissed me like it was the end of the world, and he'd been saving up love for me his whole life for this moment. When we finally parted, he said softly, "It may take a few weeks to sort everything out up here, though. Wait for me."

"I will," I promised.

10 YEARS LATER

E VERY ONCE IN A WHILE, I'D READ A STORY IN THE newspaper about a family that lost a child in an accident, or of someone suffering unbearable grief after losing a spouse, and I'd take the time to find their e-mail address. I'd introduce myself and offer my services, and usually a few days would pass before I'd receive a reply. Everyone to whom I reached out accepted my offer in the end, even though sometimes a year would pass before they'd reply. Henry didn't think it was the healthiest of hobbies, but he'd still often accompany me when I'd drive out to meet them, and I'd pass along messages from the recently departed. Usually, the spirits of the deceased would just want me to convey the abundant love they hadn't had the chance to express before their death. One woman's recently deceased husband provided her with information about a secret bank account he'd opened in Switzerland that she could access. In another instance, the spirit of a woman's dead son told me where he'd hidden her Mother's Day gift in the garage, and she was beside herself with emotion when she found it exactly where I'd assured her she would.

I never charged money for my services as a medium. In working with a psychic I'd met through Kirsten to try to reestablish a method of directly communicating with Jennie, I got better at understanding when spirits were trying to communicate with me. I experienced an indescribable sense of joy through bringing closure to people who were grieving. Often, I wished that I could bring the same kind of closure to my mom, but I kept my services a secret from both of my parents.

My hobby was something I didn't discuss with friends, but both Violet and Cheryl were aware of it. Cheryl had surprised everyone in Willow by joining the police force after high school, and she called upon me from time to time for help in solving cases involving missing kids across Shawano County. Although in high school I'd always figured that Cheryl would end up studying some advanced science at an Ivy League school, she was a great cop. Cheryl had a persistent compulsion to make everything in the world right.

Violet and I became very close friends in college. She and I had both been accepted at the University of Wisconsin–Madison, and although her mother really wanted her to go to Stanford, she chose to stay close to home. Not surprisingly, she and Pete had broken up during senior year, and she'd spiraled into partying in college, probably as a way of coping with the horrors to which she'd been subjected in high school. It wasn't uncommon for her to knock on the door of the apartment I shared with Henry at odd hours of the night or early morning, drunk and emotional, and crash out on our couch. Gone was the prim and smug Violet who'd arrived at Willow our junior year of high school with her cashmere sweaters and rosy cheeks. That girl had been replaced—at least temporarily—by a young woman with an appetite for every destructive habit life had to offer.

As much as I suspected it secretly upset Henry that Violet was around so often, especially since he could never forgive her for what she'd done to Olivia, he understood that she and I shared a bond that no one else understood. I was the only person who fully comprehended what she'd had to do to keep her mother safe, and she was the only person who fully appreciated the lengths to which I'd gone to relieve her from the burden of delivering a soul every month. Violet grieved the loss of Trey much more severely than I ever would have expected she would, and keeping her—as Trey's half sister—in my life was the only real connection to him I had. Sometimes she'd mutter something sarcastically under her breath, and she'd remind me so strongly of him that I'd break into tears.

Violet had been the one to call and tell me about Trey's death the day after I'd returned to Tampa. Michael Simmons had left a considerable portion of his estate to Trey, with no strings attached. Of course, Trey wasn't the one who told me this. Violet was. Mr. Simmons's team of attorneys had briefed Mrs. Simmons about Trey's paternity in advance of the reading, and Violet informed me that although her mother was aware by then that Trey was her late husband's biological son, she'd had no idea about the threats that her late husband and his attorneys had made to Trey's mom.

Violet had also told me shortly after Trey's death—without a hint of regret—that she'd destroyed every bit of evidence she found on her dad's laptop and in his home office about his request to his legal team to put pressure on Trey while at Northern to donate a kidney to Violet. Her father was already dead because of his selfishness and carelessness, Violet had reasoned. There was no need for her mother to also know that Michael Simmons had been a ruthless bully, willing to resort to murder under the right circumstances. The generous amount of money that he had designated for Trey made it clear that Michael Simmons had never had any real ill will toward his son; his motivation had always been to keep his paternity a secret from his wife. He must have decided when drafting his will that once he was dead, the secret wouldn't matter anymore.

The amount of money Trey had inherited would have been presented to him in enormous lump sums upon his eighteenth, twenty-fifth, and thirty-fifth birthdays. He would have received a generous living allowance, renewed via direct deposit on a monthly basis. And any educational expenses that he submitted to the law firm for approval would have been covered by the trust, so he could have gone on to earn as many degrees as he wanted, paid for by Michael Simmons. However, Trey hadn't stuck around to hear the details. He had politely thanked Lawrence Strohmann of Ekdahl, West & Strohmann for his time, and had walked out of the reading of the will before even reviewing the documentation that he was supposed to have signed to legally acknowledge that he was the recipient of the trust.

He didn't want the money, didn't want anything to do with the Simmons family name.

But Trey hadn't turned eighteen yet the day the will had been read. His mother and Walter Emory were still his legal guardians.

So he may not have even known that his mother remained behind in the law offices that day, and that she signed those documents on his behalf.

And as Violet told me all of this tearfully over the phone the day she called to tell me that he'd died—she said that he'd never even made it back home after learning of his inheritance. Within ten minutes of his mother signing the paperwork to accept the terms of the will, Trey had collapsed outside on the sidewalk. His autopsy had confirmed that he'd been suffering from internal bleeding for over a week, presumably since he'd been attacked at Northern.

Just as excruciating as it was for me to lose him, my heart ached with the knowledge that he must have been in unbearable physical pain the entire time he was in Willow with me the last week of his life. Instead of throwing in the towel on helping me break the curse to seek medical attention for himself, he'd followed my orders. Stayed hidden at Glenn's house. Accompanied me to Violet's. Participated in saving Mischa.

In the days following my hospitalization, I'd been deeply touched that Henry had taken a bullet for me. He hadn't even hesitated; he'd just leapt in front of me. But Trey had knowingly sacrificed his life for mine too. He'd known that if we didn't break the curse in time, I would have died before the new moon. If he'd gone to see a doctor, that stand-off with Mischa and Mr. Simmons could have had much more tragic results. One thing I was sure of was that if Trey hadn't been there that day, if he hadn't pulled the pins out of my voodoo doll at the right moment and trailed me and Mr. Simmons up to the roof, I would have died. And the curse would have remained in play, quite possibly following Mischa into adulthood.

Of course, what I didn't realize for many weeks after Trey's death was that we all should have seen it coming. When I'd predicted Violet's death, it was far off in the future, after she'd lived a long and healthy life. That should have made it clear to us that she wasn't going to die of complications from Alport syndrome, whether Trey gave her a kidney or not. Kirsten had warned us all about the rule of three, and while we were destroying the rosebush that his mother had planted, Trey had told me about his mother's parents dying in a car crash. Their obituary was easy enough to find in the *Willow Gazzette*. They'd been hit head-on by a driver who fell asleep and crossed over into their lane, and they had both died instantly.

They'd died in November of the year Trey was born, less than a month after Mary Jane had cast her spell to do harm unto Michael and Vanessa Simmons. Their deaths counted as two out of three terrible things happening to punish Mary Jane for her selfish spell-casting. I didn't have to reconnect with Trey's mother to ask if that was the reason why she'd left the house abandoned soon after. A little Google research revealed that her sister had gone to college in Ohio and had never returned to Willow, probably because Mary Jane had urged her to stay as far away as possible.

She knew.

She'd known all along that there was still a third terrible thing hanging in the ether for her, but her desire to provide Trey with the life that she believed he deserved outweighed her fear. And ultimately, he paid the price for her hope that he'd one day be welcomed into the Simmons family. As soon as he officially was, the rule of three claimed him.

On some level, I'd known too. Maybe I'd just been in denial because I wanted so desperately for it to not happen the way I dreaded it would. But in hindsight, I realized the chanting that I'd heard the day we dug up the rosebush and burned its roots had not been *tree, tree, tree*.

It had been *three, three, three*. Jennie had been warning me as best she could, and I'd refused to believe that I might ever lose Trey.

Many weeks after I'd returned to school in Tampa, when I was still dazing off in classes and wandering the hallways bleary-eyed with grief, Ernesto approached me after calculus and handed me a small envelope with my first name written on it in looping, curly cursive. It was dime-store stationery with little red cardinals on it, and I knew immediately that it was a note from his grandmother.

"My mom and I were cleaning out my grandmother's room and found this," he said.

I'd been formally fired from my job at Oscawana Pavilion for taking time off so close to the Easter weekend, and then not returning when I'd promised I would. The last few times I'd called Mrs. Robinson's room, Ernesto's mom had answered the phone and hadn't let me speak with her. I had feared that she'd been on her way to the next world. But having my suspicion confirmed by Ernesto felt like a punch in the gut.

"Thank you," I said. I wasn't aware how close I was to tears until I heard my voice crack.

Ernesto nodded. "She liked you a lot. She said you two had important business."

"We did."

I waited until I was on the bus home to open the letter.

> *Dear McK,*
> *Your sister's still in that dark place, but now she's not*
> *alone. She's working hard to keep whatever's there*
> *with her from escaping. You'll hear from her again.*
> *Let your bright light shine for others.*
> *Your friend,*
> *Cherie*

Although I hadn't been able to communicate with Jennie directly since the day at the Simmons house, she'd found other ways to reach me. Every month, a few days before the new moon, I'd come home to find something—a pencil, a tissue—levitating in my bedroom, and I would know what I'd have to do. Online, I'd find a recent obituary from someone nearby in Florida, and leave that web page open on my phone for Jennie to observe. Then I'd burn some sage in my bedroom, call Mischa, and tell us both the story of how I died by falling off the roof at Violet's house in April.

Wherever she was in the fabric of space and time, Jennie would offer up the soul of the person described in the obituary in a way that matched my story. Mischa and I would chant the chorus, since I always needed the energy of a second person to "play the game." And then we'd be done until the next cycle of the moon.

We hadn't broken the curse the day that Mr. Simmons fell off the roof. But Jennie *had* successfully led the spirits to an area of the dark place where she'd been able to imprison them. I never dared to find out what would happen if I didn't transfer a soul in time. This was simply a condition of my life, and I believed wholeheartedly that when I did die, the curse would die with me.

It took me a while in college to figure out what I really wanted to do with my life, flipping between majors almost every semester. My father scolded me about wasting time and money, especially because I could have gone to school in Florida at the university where he taught for free, but I didn't feel like I was wasting either. I'd been accepted to the University of Wisconsin with a generous scholarship after winning an essay contest on the topic of perseverance.

I'd been inconsolable with grief over losing Trey throughout my senior year of high school. The only person with whom I communicated regularly was Henry after we resumed our morning FaceTime chats. He'd convinced me to come back to Wisconsin to be closer to him. When I did, it felt so normal and right to be back in Wisconsin and around him that I was in no hurry to graduate and move on with my life.

Ultimately, I settled on veterinary studies because through my work with Brian, my psychic mentor, I realized that I had sympathetic communication abilities with animals in addition to dead people. I couldn't very well tell my dad how gratifying it was for me to hear from someone's sick pet what was wrong with them, or to provide dogs and cats with comfort on their way to the spirit world. Being ever mindful of Mrs. Robinson's request that I be a bright light for those who needed my abilities, I considered it an obligation to help people whenever I could. Dad never came right out and said it, but I knew he considered my decision to go to veterinary school as a form of betrayal because he saw it as my following in Glenn's footsteps—and in a way, it kind of was.

Mom and Glenn relocated to a modern condominium in Ortonville that looked kind of like a gingerbread house. While I knew it was hard for my mom to close the chapter of her life that had unfolded on Martha Road, she knew there was no turning back after the second fire. She and Glenn never married, but they seemed very happy together whenever I visited. Glenn was delighted to help me with homework and even let me spend weekends when I drove up to Ortonville working as an aide to gain experience.

Dad and Rhonda's son, Stevie, named after Rhonda's father, shared a birthday with Olivia, but after I'd survived the new moon on which I'd half expected to die, I made every effort to stop placing significance on days of the month. Because of our enormous age gap, I mostly got to know my half brother over video chat after I left Tampa for college. I often wondered what Dad and Rhonda had told him about me and Jennie, or if they'd mentioned Jennie at all, but I figured Jennie was keeping an eye on him no matter what.

Henry and I remained in Madison after we'd both graduated. The bullet that Violet had shot at Henry had left fragments in his shoulder, effectively ending whatever might have become of his tennis career. On rainy days, he wound his left arm around in circles, bent at the elbow, as if he thought he could ease the stiffness in the shoulder joint if he could just reposition his arm the right way. I wasn't a believer in silver linings, but his injury made him focus more intensely on his interest in political science. By the time we were newlyweds, he had earned his law degree and landed a job with a firm specializing in civil and social justice. Henry, always the peacekeeper, had dedicated himself professionally to defending people who had been victims of crimes.

Mischa and I kept in close contact after high school, although once she and Matt married and she had their daughter, Lindsay, our phone calls became less frequent. Eventually, Henry took over the role as the listener for Mischa in my monthly routine, since her parenting schedule was so erratic. Not long after she'd had Lindsay, she had confessed to me over coffee that ever since the evil spirits had kicked her soul out of her body and we'd transferred it back in, she'd never felt completely "back." That strange feeling of disconnectedness had ended her gymnastics career, and she never had a chance to become Willow's first Olympian. Amanda, her older sister, had miraculously regained the use of her arms through advanced stem cell treatments, and ended up winning a silver medal for rowing in the Paralympics three years after the tornado touched down in Willow.

Mischa was fond of nagging me about when Henry and I would start a family. I didn't dare tell her that we'd been working on that for a while, but for whatever reason, it just didn't seem to be in the stars for us. Violet knew better than to nag. After she earned a master's degree, she moved to Europe. Whenever she called to tell me that she'd broken up with yet another boyfriend and was afraid that she'd never meet anyone special and have a family of her own, I reminded her of what I'd predicted for her on the mountainside in Michigan: a long life, a healthy family.

Henry and I kept visits with his parents to a minimum, often insisting that they come to our home in Madison instead of having us over to theirs in Willow because returning to our hometown took an emotional toll on both of us. When we had no choice but to go there, we drove miles out of our way to enter town from the south to avoid driving past Martha Road.

However, I often returned to Willow in my sleep. When I woke up from vivid dreams about the freshly mowed front lawns of Martha Road, about fires consuming one-story ranch houses and the silhouettes of little girls in front windows, about beautiful boys in moonlit backyards, and of dangerously pretty girls wearing lockets, I calmed myself down and reminded myself that I was in the present, in Madison, with Henry. I was safe.

Autumn was almost unbearably nostalgic for me. The smell of fires in fireplaces, the rich orange and red shades of leaves, and the laughter of teenage girls I'd sometimes overhear when walking around town always brought my thoughts back to Willow. After all, it was the town where I'd escaped from death, the town where the bones of my twin sister, my true love, and the friends I couldn't save were buried and would remain forever.

Although I often scanned the radio dial hoping to hear Jennie's voice, I was never able to find it again. But I often sensed her presence, and knew that she was the reason why I was able to both feel the sentiments of animals and receive messages from souls on the other side with such ease.

And I never stopped listening for her.

ACKNOWLEDGMENTS

My heartfelt thanks go to my editor, Jessi Smith, for her guidance in taking the characters in this trilogy to the end of their respective journeys. Thank you so much for helping me refine my vision for this story so that the stakes were always being raised for McKenna in her efforts to save her friends. Because of your encouragement and ability to identify areas where my characters needed further development, Willow, Wisconsin, will always be a cherished destination in my memories of these last few years.

For everyone at Simon Pulse, thank you so much for investing your time and talents in this story. And very special thanks to the art direction team at Simon Pulse and illustrator Avery Muether for creating book covers more perfect than I ever could have imagined.

For the team at Wattpad, my deep gratitude for helping me establish a readership and for recruiting the original fans of McKenna, Trey, Henry, and Mischa.

Thank you to all my friends who have been supportive of the creation of these books since the very beginning: Chiraag Bhakta, Kelly Anne Blount, Pen Densham, Elizabeth Bales Frank, Greg Greenberg, Kerry Hallihan, Eugene Hwang, Julie Noiman, Sherry Park, Lauren Puglia, Julie Trelstad, and so very many more.

For my friend—the brilliant YA author Robin Epstein—thank you so much for the brainstorms and the pep talks!

I wrote the first page of the first book quite a long time ago, never imagining back then how drastically my life would change by the time I wrote the epilogue for the third book. I wish I could personally thank every reader who has taken the literary journey to Willow and played Light as a Feather along with the guests at Olivia's birthday party. It has been quite an adventure, and I am so glad you could all join me.